BLOOD HEMLOCK

Part 3 of the White Lotus Trilogy

LIBBIE HAWKER

Running Rabbit Editions

I

WHISPERER

❦　I　❦

CAPTIVITY

Rhodopis held herself rigid and silent in the litter, all the long ride from the northern quay back to Charaxus' small riverside estate. She had refused to speak to the man who had once been her patron and lover, even as Charaxus had tormented her with barbed comments or slung outright insults at his fuming captive. Rhodopis refused to be moved by his deplorable efforts. She stared straight ahead as if she could see through the litter's thick curtains—through night's darkness itself—to the streets of Memphis beyond. Even when Charaxus lapsed into a half-hearted explanation of his actions, almost pleading for her understanding, she remained with arms crossed tightly over her middle, never so much as blinking in the man's direction. She could still feel a line of cold fire where his sword's edge had pressed through her shawl and the plain servant's smock to the flesh beneath. It was a wonder and a mercy she wasn't bleeding.

"I had to do it," Charaxus whined in the darkness. "I had to take you that way—don't you see? I can't allow you to leave in that manner, Rhodopis. And with a man of Polycrates' reputation!"

Oh, he was plaintive enough—all but whimpering like a spurned pup on his silk cushions, and loud enough for the litter-bearers to hear. But not one word could soften Rhodopis' anger. It had sunk deep into her bones.

He hasn't apologized yet. Nor will he, unless I miss my guess. But that's just as well. I'm no fool; I'll never forgive him, not even if he were to fall on his face and weep with regret.

Before the litter reached his estate, Charaxus had yielded to Rhodopis' stubborn silence and ceased his useless talk. But when the litter lowered to the ground and one of the bearers pulled a curtain aside, he turned to Rhodopis with a brusque air.

"Get up. You're going inside now, and you'll stay there. I prefer not to make one of my men drag you in, but I'll do it, if you won't go of your own accord."

Rhodopis turned to him at last. She could feel the fire flashing in her eyes, and indeed, when Charaxus saw her hard, hateful expression, he flinched in the pale-blue starlight.

"What a fool you are," she spat.

"I—a fool? It wasn't I who lied, Rhodopis. Nor was I the one who attempted to take up with a pirate. You could have had the best of everything with me—"

"The best? I would have been your slave, just as I was to Xanthes and Iadmon!"

He seized her wrist, twisting the tender skin. Rhodopis bit her lip to stop herself from crying out.

"A wife is not a slave," Charaxus hissed.

Rhodopis jerked free of his grip. "In all but name! I never loved Polycrates, you simpleton. It was his ship I wanted—a way out of Memphis."

"I'll take you out of Memphis when I return to Lesvos."

"And before I go with you, I'll die by my own hand."

Charaxus grunted in disgust. "Typical hetaera; you've such a flair for drama. You could have made a name for yourself by acting in the *symposia*. Unfortunately, you've shown a greater predilection for whoring than for the honest arts a hetaera may pursue. I'm afraid you've been better suited to a common porna's life all along, my sweet."

"I am not your sweet," Rhodopis said icily. "I never was, Charaxus."

He rose from the litter and stood silently for a moment, the starlight hanging a halo of silver around his deep-golden curls. At last, he said, "No, I suppose you never were. Get up now, and come inside, or I'll order one of these men haul you in. You wouldn't like that, I presume."

"I wouldn't like to go into that prison you call a home, either."

"But one way or another, you shall." He waited, hands on hips, face coldly neutral.

Rhodopis sighed and rose from the litter. To enter the house under her own power was the best of her few bleak options. If she ran, he would only send his men after her, and Rhodopis had no doubt that Charaxus' guards could run faster than she. If she resisted, Charaxus would have her dragged in, just as he'd promised, and she could see little point in getting bruised.

Rhodopis followed Charaxus across his small courtyard. The paving stones below her feet were dappled by stars and the ink-black shadows of sycamore leaves. Behind her, she could hear the litter-bearers shuffle and murmur, relieved that none of them had been commanded to drag an unwilling woman to Charaxus' lair.

As she passed beneath the pillared portico, her mouth twisted in an ironic smile. It seemed a thousand years had passed since she had stood there last, welcoming Charaxus' guests as a good wife would have done. He had been a doting fool, then. There was no trace of affection in him now; every step he took was clipped with anger, and the very air around him seemed to crackle with a sharp disapproval bordering on hatred.

Charaxus opened his door and stood back, making way for Rhodopis to pass. She hesitated only a moment, wondering whether she had any hope of outrunning Charaxus. If she turned now and sprinted for the gate, she might be fast enough to evade him. But what lay beyond his estate? The city—Memphis, with its thousand eyes, with its uncountable throats ready to whisper. Yes, she might hope to fight her way free of Charaxus, but once she lost him in the streets, where could she go? What safety could Memphis offer—especially once Amasis heard Rhodopis had returned? No one would oppose the Pharaoh if he came looking for her. No one. She had no real choice but to follow Charaxus inside.

His house-slave had left several lamps burning. The amber glow and scent of hot perfumed oil would have seemed cheerful, even welcoming, under any other circumstances. As soon as he'd shut the door behind Rhodopis, Charaxus reached for her. She flinched back, baring her teeth in an animalistic snarl.

"Don't flatter yourself," Charaxus said. "I don't want to lie with you." He seized the knife sheathed at her waist, slipped it from its casing before she could stop him. "I'll keep this safe, where you can't find it. You won't be allowed any weapons, Rhodopis, so don't think to spill my blood. Despite what you seem to think, I am no fool."

Charaxus stepped closer and pulled the scarf away from her hair. His expression changed suddenly, melting from cold anger to something soft and regretful. He lifted a black-dyed lock and ran his fingers down its length. "You've ruined your hair." He sounded as if he recited a lamentation. "Your best feature. I don't suppose this color will ever fade entirely, nor wash away. You must wait for it to grow out."

Rhodopis was not one to miss an opportunity. She seized upon the change in Charaxus' mood with all the swift professionalism of a hetaera. She had no love for Charaxus, but if she could convince him that she had thought better of her refusal, and would marry him with a willing heart, she might hope to lull him into carelessness. Then she could make her escape.

Banishing the rage from her face, Rhodopis smiled, twisting her hair around her fingers. "The color might fade. We don't know yet. And in any case, it won't take long for my hair to grow out. I hear Lesvian girls have the loveliest hair in the world. It must be Lesvos itself that makes them so beautiful—something special in the air or water. Why, once we're in Lesvos, my hair will—"

Charaxus laughed bleakly. "Suddenly you're willing to come along when I leave Memphis."

"'Course I am, Rax. We had a row, but it's over and finished. Don't husbands and wives quarrel all the time? That's what I hear."

"You must be mad."

"Mad? How can you say such a thing? I only want to be your good, obedient wife."

Charaxus dropped the little knife in his belt pouch, then cinched the strings tightly. "The time for that is long past."

"Time for what?"

"For you to deceive me with your charms. I've learned my lesson, Rhodopis. I won't put my hand on a hot iron more than once. Now—I believe you know where the maid's chamber is. You'll sleep there."

Rhodopis clenched her fists. She did not move from her place beside the door.

"You heard me," Charaxus said.

"You're going to shut me up in that tiny room? It's no way to treat your future bride."

Charaxus pointed toward the maid's chamber, but still, Rhodopis refused to move.

"You will not be my bride," he said quietly. "It's clear to me now that I can never wed you. You're... unsuitable for a man of my status, a man with my connections."

Your status, yes, Rhodopis thought with bitter amusement. She knew how the great men of Memphis enjoyed mocking Charaxus when they thought he couldn't hear—or when they were certain he *could* hear. She said only, "If you don't intend to marry me, then what do you plan to do with me?"

"You will still accompany me to Lesvos. Your treacherous nature makes you unfit for the honorable role of wife, but there's no reason why I shouldn't keep you as a concubine."

She gasped. "After having been a hetaera? Do you honestly think I'll accept such a thing? Living like a mouse, scampering to avoid the mistress of the house—and with even less freedom than your wife! You really are a fool, Charaxus, and no mistake."

"If you keep up that sort of talk, you'll only make me angry again. I don't advise it."

"There must be a hundred girls back in Lesvos who would willingly live as your concubine. Why trouble yourself with me? If you don't want to marry me, then why don't you let me go?"

Charaxus lurched toward her, fists raised. For one frightened heartbeat, Rhodopis thought he would strike her. But he only shook his clenched hands in a gesture of helpless fury—and thwarted passion. "Because I love you!" he wailed. "Damn it, Rhodopis, can't you understand that? I love you and I want you, even if you aren't the sort of woman who will ever be a proper wife. Even though you crush my heart every chance you get. I was always good to you, always generous and loving. And how have you repaid my kindness? By deceiving me, and wounding me—by trying to run off with that black-souled beast Polycrates. You've made a mockery of my devotion. A mockery! How am I ever to forgive you? And yet I can't help loving you still. I would walk over burning coals for you, Rhodopis—not that you would care if I did."

Rhodopis shook her head helplessly. "Charaxus... I was only ever doing what needs must. What I had to do, in order to survive. Surely you understand that. I was a slave. I had no choice—not about you, nor anything else. I never intended to make you love me."

"But you knew I would fall in love—you must have known. What man could avoid loving you? Only a man with a heart of stone." He took her by the shoulders. She felt pinioned in his grip, trapped between his arms. "You knew I would surrender my heart to you, and you took it—coldly—without any thought for me. Like a child plucking flowers in a meadow, idly taking whatever pretty thing piqued your fancy."

"No, Charaxus, I—"

"You knew I couldn't help but love you, and you never had any intention of loving me in return. You used me for my patronage—all the gifts I gave you, all the money."

"But that's the way it is between hetaerae and their patrons. Surely you knew that, long before you ever chose me."

He clutched Rhodopis against his chest. She fought the urge to stiffen with disgust; it would do her no good now, to go rigid and tense in his grip.

"It was different between us," he cried. "We weren't like the others. I thought you knew it—I thought you could see it, too. But now I know the truth. You never loved me; you only encouraged me for your own amusement, so you could play your little games and feel gratified by the wealth I brought you."

Rhodopis could stand his touch no longer. She pushed away, breaking his grip on her shoulders. "You're talking madness, Charaxus, and I won't hear it. I never made you love me—not on purpose, at any rate. And I never knew you felt that way until it was too late to change things. I'm not responsible for your broken heart—you are! You did this to yourself! What kind of simpleton falls in love with a hetaera and dreams of making her his wife?"

"A kind and good man... that's what kind of simpleton."

Disgust welled up in Rhodopis' gut—disgust at his refusal to listen, his refusal to accept the gods' honest truth. She stamped her foot as she rounded on Charaxus, aware the gesture made her look like a petulant child, but unable to stop herself. It was the only outlet she could find for her thwarted, boiling rage. "You were *never* a good man, Charaxus—never, never! You never loved me then, and you don't love me now. You only want to own me! That's been the way of it, right from the moment you first saw me. Admit it—you know it's true! As a hetaera indebted to your favors, or as a wife—either way, you would have possessed me, if you'd had your way. And that's all you care for: whether you can control me and keep me on a fine leash, ready to do your bidding. But I'm not a slave any longer. No man owns me, and none will again, so long as I live and breathe. I swear it by all the gods. May Strymon drown me if I lie. May Isis appear before me and tear out my tongue with her own hands if I don't speak the truth!"

Coldly, Charaxus smiled. Her outburst seemed to have calmed him, as if he'd been waiting for her to reveal just how hotly her emotions could flare. "If you aren't mine to do with as I please," he said, "then how have I managed to bring you here? And you won't go anywhere without my permission, Rhodopis —make no mistake about that. You wouldn't want the Pharaoh to learn your secret, would you? You will do as I say."

He advanced—one step, then another, slow and looming. Rhodopis' heart lurched. He was too much like Psamtik when he moved that way, when his face went hard and emotionless. Would Charaxus do to her what Psamtik had done? Terror of that dreadful violence broke over her, eclipsing even her fear of Amasis. She spun on her heel, reaching for the door—but

Charaxus moved with the same unexpected speed he had shown in his duel with Polycrates. He seized her arm before she could flee.

"Let me go! Don't touch me, you beast!"

He shook her gently. "Calm yourself. I'm not going to hurt you. But you will do as I say—and that means you will go to the maid's chamber and remain there until I permit you to leave."

"I won't!" Rhodopis shouted, even as he dragged her toward that very room.

Charaxus thrust her inside; she stumbled across the threshold and caught herself on the small, narrow bed, then whirled to face him, tears of fury and humiliation streaming down her cheeks.

"You'll be comfortable here," he said. "I'll see to that. I'm not a brute, whatever you think of me. But I've told my door guards to keep you here, at all costs—so don't try to escape, Rhodopis. You'll only make yourself a nuisance to my staff, and then I shall be angry with you."

"I don't care if you're angry, you worthless fool!"

"Don't you?" Charaxus smiled, but it carried no hint of his former, lovestruck doting. "Perhaps you should care. You should care very much, my darling. When we reach Lesvos, you won't have any company but me. A wise concubine keeps her master happy."

Before Rhodopis could think of a reply, he shut the door and was gone.

❧

As the days unfolded, Charaxus' anger continued unabated. His household staff brought meals to the small chamber that had become Rhodopis' prison and carried away the cloth-covered pot that was her only privy. They spoke to her little, though, and Rhodopis was left to stew alone in a broth of fear.

Through her chamber's narrow window, hardly more than a slit, she watched the sun move across the small garden, watched birds dart in pursuit of flies by day and moths in the evening. The birds and her thoughts were her only company, her only solace. As she paced, restless as the penned antelopes in the Pharaoh's menagerie, she asked herself again and again who this strange man was. Who now wore the guise of Charaxus? What could account for this change in his demeanor? Had her former patron been possessed by an evil spirit—or had he always been this man, vengeful and possessive, carefully hidden behind the mask of an adoring lover?

On her second day of fruitless pacing, as she gazed enviously at the free birds outside, Rhodopis decided that it didn't matter whether Charaxus had changed or whether he had finally revealed his true nature. *Won't change the situation I'm in now, one way or the other. All that's left is to find some way out of this room—and out of Charaxus' hands forever.*

She left off her pacing and sat on the hard, thin mattress. Her ankles and hips ached from hours of walking, though she hadn't left the chamber since Charaxus had shoved her inside.

How long would it take Polycrates to reach Babylon? She thought back to her own journey. The pirate's fleet was faster than the Pharaoh's ship had been, but how much faster? And what might conceivably delay him—storms, tariffs, pauses at this port or that to replenish supplies? She thought Polycrates would reach Gebal in half a month's time, give or take a few days—and then he must embark on the overland trek across the desert.

Give it a month for Polycrates to arrive in Babylon, Rhodopis decided. *If Cambyses believes him and acts quickly, it will surely take twice as long for Persian forces to reach Memphis.* Rhodopis was no general. As a hetaera, she had never even entertained a general, but still, she assumed an invading army would take some time to mobilize.

Surely, by the time Cambyses fell upon Egypt, Amasis would be too preoccupied to trouble himself with Rhodopis. She would be safe, then—as safe as a woman can be in the midst of war. *But three months is a terribly long time to wait.* Only the gods could say what Amasis might hear—or do—in the meantime.

Charaxus could spirit her off to Lesvos in short order, and remove her far beyond Amasis' reach. But on a ship bound for Lesvos, what hope could Rhodopis have of breaking free from Charaxus? She certainly would never live as his concubine, any more than she would accept servitude as his wife. No; her only hope for freedom lay in escaping from Charaxus now, while he was still in Memphis. Memphis presented a host of dangers to Rhodopis, of course, but if she could leave the city on her own terms—perhaps disguised as a merchant's servant or a fisherman's daughter—she could flee to the Egyptian countryside and take up an ordinary life. She only needed to win her way out of this chamber, and away from Charaxus' estate.

"Think," she muttered aloud. "You're clever enough to find a way out of this mess."

Her mind wandered beyond the walls of her chamber to the house itself. She had spent countless hours in Charaxus' home, not only lying in his bed, but playing hostess to his guests. She could picture each room, every doorway and passage, with perfect clarity. If she could contrive a way to reach the kitchen, perhaps she could take the side door, the one Charaxus' cook used to access the clay ovens outside—but no. That door was too near the courtyard. His guard would certainly see. The upstairs balcony overlooked both garden and river. The grapevine growing up to its railing might be strong enough to support her weight... no. She couldn't get to the balcony without passing the door to Charaxus' bedchamber. Suppose he came out of his chamber at the wrong time and caught her sneaking away?

The house was too small for creeping about unseen. In a large estate—Xanthes' palatial home, for example—Rhodopis could hope to slip from corner to corner unseen. But here, there would be no escaping the notice of the household staff, or of Charaxus himself.

I must find someone to come and take me away, Rhodopis realized, *for there's no hope of slipping off on my own. Not without a friend to help me, to distract Charaxus and his men, or hide me from their view entirely.*

It was Aesop she needed. Who else could bring her aid—who was clever enough to devise such a plan? She must get a letter into Aesop's hands—something she had failed to do again and again. She mustn't fail now.

As she sat, darkly musing, the chamber door creaked. Rhodopis stood. This wasn't the hour when Charaxus' staff brought her mid-day meal—and anyhow, his servants always knocked before they entered. It could only be Charaxus himself who had come. When the door opened wide enough to reveal her, Rhodopis made certain she was wearing a soft and complacent smile.

Charaxus blinked at her expression. He had been expecting another defiant scowl. Rhodopis stepped toward him before he could speak.

"Oh, Rax, I'm so glad you've come. I've been terribly lonely these past two days. It's rather cruel, to keep me away from you so long."

"I've come to see whether this confinement has brought you to your senses."

"Of course it has. You're right, Rax: I could never be your wife. I'm too—well, rough and unrefined, as you say. But isn't that what you like about me best? I've been foolish, to think I couldn't be happy as your concubine. Why, there's nothing I'd like better! I see that now."

"It would be a good life." Charaxus still sounded a trifle

uncertain. He hadn't yet come to trust this turn in Rhodopis' mood; she could see as much in his narrowed eyes, in the way he toyed with the door handle, distracted and hesitant.

Rhodopis clutched his hand. "It would be the very best life. I know you'd keep me in comfort and style. I'd have everything I could want—you, most especially. And yes, I know you'll marry someday, when you find a proper woman, the sort of wife a man like you deserves. But I don't care! I'd have come first, wouldn't I? And that means I'll always be first in your heart."

"Yes," Charaxus said, with the slow-blinking air of a man waking from a daze. "Yes, that's the way of it."

"Oh, when do we leave for Lesvos? Tell me! I'm so eager to see it, and to start our life together properly."

A happy flush colored his cheeks. "We can't leave straight away, of course. I've too much business to tie up here. But I've already begun; I've hired a ship, too. We leave in five days' time —six, at the most."

Rhodopis fought the instinct to bite her lip. She fixed a grin to her face instead. She must give Charaxus no cause to doubt her sincerity.

But only five days... how will I ever get away? How can I reach Aesop in time?

"I must admit," Charaxus laughed, "I had expected you'd still resist me. I was prepared to tie you up, if need be, and carry you to the ship in a sack. How glad I am that won't be necessary!"

You could have tried it, you worthless bastard, Rhodopis fumed. *I'd have torn your bollocks off with my bare hands.*

She giggled and tapped Charaxus on the shoulder. "Darling! You ought to know me better than that. Let's never argue again. I can't stand it! You'll let me out of this room now, won't you?"

His smile was unbearably foolish. "Of course I will. But you can't leave the house, Rhodopis. You understand that, don't you?"

Coyly, she lowered her eyes. "Yes, I understand. I suppose I have been dreadfully wicked. I'll stay in the house as long as you please, if it means we can be together forever."

Charaxus swept her into his arms, burying his face in her black-dyed hair. "We shall—of course we shall. It has all worked out for the best, in the end. The gods are good. Now come up to my bedchamber, you sweet honey-cake. We have amends to make."

EVERY HOUR that passed was a torment to Rhodopis. The house seemed more confining than the small chamber had been, for wherever she went, she could feel Charaxus' eyes upon her—or the eyes of his servants. The necessity of simpering and smiling at everyone she encountered soon wore upon her spirit. By the end of her third day of captivity, Rhodopis was trembling with exhaustion and craved sleep the way a man in the desert longs for water. But whenever she crept to Charaxus' bed, he soon joined her there, and Rhodopis found neither rest nor respite from her fears.

At meals, she served Charaxus before taking her own bowl of food into the tiny, curtain-walled gynaeceum, where his female servants ate. *Just like a good concubine*, she thought bitterly, *or a good wife. S'pose there's little difference to a man like Charaxus.*

At night, she joined him in his bed and yielded the use of her body to his harsh, demanding hands. As she stumbled through her days, numb within but sunny and smiling on the outside, she kept a sharp eye open for whatever minute opportunity the gods might cast before her. Her fourth day as

Charaxus' prisoner slid darkly past, and still, Rhodopis had found no way out of his trap.

The ship will sail for Lesvos in three days, she thought dully as she watched the sunset from the vine-covered balcony. *Four days at the most. And I'll be aboard it, whether I go willingly or tied up in a sack, slung over Charaxus' shoulder. Oh, if only there were some way to tell Aesop where I am!*

"Rhodopis, darling," Charaxus called from inside the house. "Come here a moment, won't you?"

She sighed and went back inside. It was for the better; she had no desire to watch the birds dart over the garden now, anyway. They only mocked her with their freedom. She found Charaxus at his writing desk, an ornately carved, red-lacquered beauty he had brought with him from Lesvos. It was the pride of his estate; he had often taken pains to show it off to visitors when Rhodopis had stood beside him as his chosen hetaera. How he was bent over the desk, adding a few last lines to a bit of papyrus in his neat, elegant hand. A stack of similar letters, folded and sealed along their edges with hardening beeswax, lay to one side of the desk.

"Yes, my love?" Rhodopis said. "What is it?"

"I'm writing up instructions for my associates here in Memphis."

"Instructions?"

"Yes—what to do about my interests here in the city, once we've left for Lesvos. How to order things, whom to contact on my behalf... everything of that sort."

"I see." *It's almost come, then. We'll soon be gone. My time has all but run out.*

"I've just written up orders for a fellow to come here after we've cleared out, and pack the things I intend to keep in crates. The crates will follow us on a slower ship—one that's sched-uled to leave a few days after ours. I'll have this desk shipped to Lesvos, of course—I wouldn't part with it for a thousand hedj—

but I've added a few other items to the list; objects I've grown fond of while living here in Memphis."

"Are you sure you can trust this man? What if he makes off with all your best things?"

Charaxus chuckled indulgently. "It must have been your time among the hetaerae that made you so wary. Of course I can trust him, my sweet. We've been associates for many years, and he has close ties to my family. He's quite beholden to my sister Sappho, for example."

Rhodopis waited. She had no care for whether Charaxus' red desk made it to Lesvos, nor any other object he coveted. *And that's all I am to him, at any rate—a* thing *to be packed up in a crate and loaded on a ship.*

Charaxus heated a small stick of beeswax over the flame of his lamp. "I wanted to know whether you wish to bring anything to Lesvos. It will be your home, after all—you should be as comfortable there as possible."

She made herself smile yet again, hating the way it felt, the tension of her cheeks and the prickle at the corners of her mouth. She had done it too often, these past few days—forced a smile. "That's very kind of you, darling, but I can't think of anything I need."

Rhodopis caught the flash of suspicion in Charaxus' eyes as he fidgeted with his writing brush. "Nothing? Nothing at all?"

I had better play along, she thought wearily, *or he'll know I plan to evade him.* Not that she still retained sufficient hope of evasion.

"Well, since you're so pressing," Rhodopis said brightly, "I do like that green vase that stands near the entry door. I've always thought it's lovely."

"I have it already on my list, but I'll see to it that it's placed in the concubine's quarters when we reach my family's estate."

"And that carved stool with the ivory inlay. And—let me

think—you've so many nice things, Rax, I can hardly choose! We can't take it all, I suppose."

"No, not all. But I shall give you whatever you please; I promise you that. If we can't ship it out of Egypt, I'll buy you something new in Lesvos to replace it—whatever your heart desires."

"Then the best I can think of is good Egyptian linen. As many bolts as we can bring, and some of it embroidered after the Egyptian style. I can have lovely dresses made with it, once we're home—but I don't suppose they have such fine linen in Lesvos."

"No," Charaxus admitted. "It's mostly wool, there—though it is very fine, the way they spin and weave it—almost as fine as silk."

"Wool's all well and good, but I've grown accustomed to wearing fine linen. Oh, I should have some silk, too, for when the weather's cold. And you know I love jewelry, but I want you to choose it, Rax. Surprise me."

He added Rhodopis' requests to his letter, then folded the sheet of papyrus carefully and ran the melting wax along its edges. Then he stood and kissed her brow. "You shall wear the finest Egyptian linen Lesvos has ever seen, if that's what your heart desires, my love—and the best, brightest jewels money can buy."

"Oh, Rax, you're so good to me." She glanced at the letters stacked neatly on his desk. "Will you have a messenger come for all those notes, then? Or will one of your servants carry them all?"

"Gods, no—my staff will be too busy packing our things and shutting up the estate. A messenger will come for them early tomorrow morning. He'll see that they're delivered before mid-day."

Rhodopis passed the remainder of the day on the balcony above the garden, watching fishermen's boats and pleasure barges pass along the silver strip of Nile that showed between Charaxus' walls. Before, their unhindered movement would have seemed a mockery. But now a tenuous new hope had flowered in her breast, and she smiled dreamily as the vessels as they sailed by.

That night, when Charaxus finally slid deep into sleep, Rhodopis eased carefully from his bed. Pale starlight filtered through the window shutters, dappling the floor; she paused and listened to the hum of night insects and the distant whisper of the river, clinging to the fragile new hope that had flowered in her heart. Then she stole across the bedchamber and slipped through the partially open door.

The lamp on Charaxus' writing desk had long since been extinguished, but the balcony shutters stood halfway open, blown askew by a stray river breeze. There was just enough starlight to illuminate the red-lacquered desk, albeit faintly.

Rhodopis found a blank piece of papyrus and pulled the stopper from the ink pot with assiduous care, fearful of making the smallest noise. Charaxus' writing brush was large and unwieldy in her hand—though in truth, Rhodopis had had precious little experience holding a brush. During her time with Iadmon and Xanthes, she had learned to read passably well, but she could scarcely write her own name.

It can't be so difficult to write, she told herself stoutly. *You know what the words ought to look like; just make the proper shapes. No mystery in that.*

She dipped the trembling brush in the ink pot and began.

I am being held against my will by Charaxus at his house on the north end of the city. Three days hence he will take me away on a ship to Lesvos and I will never return nor be free of him. You must come to this place at night by boat and I will meet you in the garden when it is dark. You can't come any other way because Charaxus has guards watching over me at all times. I am in grave danger and need a friend's help.

Rhodopis paused, considering the words she had written. Her hand left much to be desired; the letters were slanted and over-large, and she blushed when she realized she had scrawled a few of them backward. A child could have made neater work of it, but surely Aesop would understand the message. That was all that mattered now.

She dipped the brush again and signed her name—the old name, the one Aesop was certain to remember.

Doricha.

Rhodopis blew on the papyrus to dry the ink, and looked around desperately for some way to seal the letter. She couldn't light the lamp and melt beeswax; the glow might wake Charaxus. She tried scrubbing the stick of wax along the letter's edges and pressing them together, but the papyrus unfolded in her hands like a wilting flower. She breathed on the wax to warm it, then clamped it beneath her armpit and counted to a hundred, but still the papyrus refused to stay closed.

The letter would have to go unsealed. The best she could do was to fold it carefully, tucking its unsealed edges under and creasing them sharply against the side of the writing desk. When she was finished, the folded edges of her note looked almost as smooth as if they had been sealed in wax. With any luck, neither Charaxus nor the messenger would notice.

Finally, Rhodopis dipped the brush again and addressed her message. She wrote slowly, praying the gods would guide her hand and disguise her childish scrawl.

Good Man Aesop
  To be found at the estate of Good Man Iadmon, Trader.

She slid the note into the middle of Charaxus' stack of letters, then crept back to his bed. But although Charaxus slept soundly through the night, Rhodopis remained awake and fretful. The hours seemed to pass as slowly as cold honey dripping from a spoon. When morning filtered through the bedchamber shutters, tinting the room with a gentle, rosy hue, Rhodopis' eyes were painfully dry and her stomach felt weak and sickly.

"Darling," Charaxus said when he saw her face, "are you well? You look ill."

"I'm well enough. Only, I couldn't sleep all night long. I'm... too excited about our journey, I suppose, and the new life we'll make together."

He took her hand. "The gods have given us much to look forward to. But I've many duties to see to before we leave Memphis." He rose and dressed in a fresh tunic of red bordered with emerald green. "I'm afraid I must attend a party tonight. I'd prefer to skip it, for I expect the most tedious men in the city to be there, but alas, I must keep a few contacts open here in Memphis."

"A party?" Rhodopis sat up, her weariness dissipating.

Charaxus mistook the reason for her interest and chuckled fondly. "Yes, my love—but you mustn't attend. I know how much you enjoy these events, but you look wrung out. You must stay in bed and catch up on lost sleep. It won't do for you to fall ill before a sea voyage. The gods know, sailing is hard enough on strong, healthy men—let alone a woman weakened by sickness."

Rhodopis sighed and sank back on the cushions. "You're right, of course. I'll remain here. You go and attend to your business. I'm not needed for that, I suppose."

Charaxus smiled at her as he fastened a matching red chlamys at his neck. He paused as the chlamys settled around his shoulders; the smile faded. "But you know, Rhodopis, I shall set an extra guard on the door."

"Oh, Rax! Are you still telling your men to keep an eye on me?" She pouted. "Haven't I convinced you that I'm serious this time, and I want to go away with you, and be yours—only yours?"

He brushed back her hair. "Let's say I haven't quite decided to trust that the gods would really be so kind to me. This all seems too good to be true, Rhodopis. I'll remain a wary man until I've got you safely aboard my ship."

Before Rhodopis could frame a suitable reply, one of Charaxus' servants called out from somewhere near the front door. "Master, your messenger has arrived."

"Ah." Charaxus turned away swiftly. He headed for his writing desk; Rhodopis' throat filled with the pounding of her own heart. Would he notice the extra letter with its clumsy folds thickening his stack of messages? Or would he glance through the notes one last time and see her poorly written address? But Charaxus was intent on his business; he left the upper hall and hurried down the steep staircase to the first floor.

Rhodopis scrambled from the bed and ran after Charaxus, tugging over her bare shoulders the tunic he had discarded on the floor the night before. What would she do—what could she do—if the messenger looked through the letters now? Surely he would notice her poor handwriting and the haphazard fold of her unsealed note. But she arrived on the first floor just as Charaxus passed the stack of messages to the newcomer.

The messenger was a young Greek man, hardly more than a boy. He tucked the notes at once beneath his arm and stretched out his hand to receive his pay.

Charaxus handed the silver hedj to the messenger, then added a few more as an afterthought. "Extra pay for extra speed," he said. "I'm afraid my business is urgent."

The young messenger's eyes widened at Charaxus' generosity. "Understood, Good Man. I'll be sure every letter is delivered swiftly."

"Before mid-day," Charaxus reminded him.

The messenger bowed, turned briskly, and vanished beneath the portico.

Charaxus brushed his hands together, grinning in his eagerness to be finished with Memphis and back in his homeland once more. He turned to find Rhodopis at the foot of the stairs.

"Back up to bed with you," he chided. "You need rest. I'll send one of the servants up with bread and broth and wine, but then you must sleep. Promise me you'll get plenty of rest, my darling. You're positively red; you haven't caught a fever already, I hope."

It was no fever, Rhodopis knew—only a flush of triumph. But she yawned and stretched for Charaxus' benefit. "I am awfully tired. It seems sleep has caught up to me at last. Don't worry, my love—I won't stir from bed until you're home from the party."

If the gods are merciful, I'll be long gone by then.

❧ 2 ❧

ESCAPE

Night came at last. Rhodopis feigned sleep in Charaxus' bed until his servants left her supper on a tray beside the door, withdrew quietly from the chamber, and returned to the first floor. Alone in the stillness, she sat for some time, listening to the advance of night—the rising chorus of frogs and insects, the sleepy calls of birds finding their roosts in the garden. When she was certain as she could be that the household servants had retired for the night, Rhodopis slipped from the bed and pulled on her tunic of simple, unbleached linen—the one she had worn to the quay. The pair of simple sandals she had hidden beneath Charaxus' bed earlier that morning still lay where she had left them; she laced them quickly and tied the straps around her ankles with hard, secure knots. Then she slowly pushed the chamber door open, mindful of its creaking hinges, and padded across the hall to the second-floor balcony.

The night air was cool, rich with the Nile's fresh, green scent. Grape leaves stirred along the railing, teased by a light wind. Rhodopis eyed the dark twists of the vine and swallowed hard. She had considered sneaking down the stairs to the first story, then out the rear doors into the garden, but she knew from long experience that those garden doors squealed violently when opened—a terrible, high-pitched shriek like an animal being slaughtered. Charaxus had never found a craftsman who could rid those hinges of the sound. If she were to try leaving by those doors, Rhodopis would surely wake the entire household and draw the attention of Charaxus' guards. The grapevine was her only egress from Charaxus' pretty prison.

But Rhodopis had no idea whether the vines would hold her. Indeed, she didn't know whether Aesop had received her note at all, let alone whether she could expect to find him waiting on the narrow strip of shore at the far end of the garden. There was too much left unknown—left to the capricious gods. But unless she tried her luck tonight, while Charaxus was away, she would remain his captive forever.

She glanced back into the darkness of the house one last time, then swung her leg over the balcony's rail. Groping blindly, scuffing at stone and vine with the sole of her shoe, she found a twist of crackling wood that might serve as a toe-hold, if the gods were good. She tested it slowly, lowering herself onto the vine by degrees. It sagged, and the grape leaves trembled, but it held her weight.

This is it, then.

Rhodopis reached lower with her other foot, found another wobbly perch among the shivering leaves. Inch by inch, she eased herself down from the balcony, hands chafed by the rough texture of the peeling vines, breath coming fast and shallow in her throat. Once, she misjudged her grip, and the grape plant hissed and lurched; she stifled a scream as she plunged toward the ground, but a heartbeat later, the vines tangled in a knot overhead, mercifully arresting her fall. For several moments after, Rhodopis couldn't convince herself to keep moving. She hung precariously in the darkness, too frightened to flinch, let alone to continue the treacherous climb. But as the muscles of her arms began to burn with the strain, she soon saw that there was little sense in hanging from the plant until the sun rose and Charaxus returned from his party. Heart pounding, she continued her timid descent until at last her sandals touched solid ground, and she expelled a long sigh of relief.

A white half-moon sailed high and small above the river. By its weak light, Rhodopis stared up at the balcony; it seemed to stretch to an impossible height, as imposing as the terraced gardens in Babylon. *There's no getting back up now. Reckon the vine won't hold me a second time. If Aesop doesn't come for me tonight, I must find some other way to escape Charaxus, for I can't go scratching on the garden door, begging to be let back in like a spoilt housecat.*

She set off down the garden's length. Moonlight showed the path clearly enough, but the dense, black shadows of nighttime seemed to turn every fern and lily into a crouching, sinister thing with sharp teeth and jagged claws. Rhodopis wrapped her arms around herself and shivered as she walked, fighting the urge to run. The last time she'd ventured into a garden alone and by night, Psamtik had found her. In Babylon, when she had strolled across moonlit terraces, Amtes had never been far away, and in Cambyses' harem she had felt safe, anyhow. But there was no one looking out for her in Egypt, and the only walls here were meant to entrap, not defend.

Charaxus' garden was not a large one, however, and she soon reached the bank of the Nile. The great expanse of water glittered in the path of the moon; far across the river's breadth, Rhodopis could see pinpoints of orange light, distant fires or torches burning against the blackness of the land. She hugged herself tighter and gazed downstream to the north, then upstream, to where the Nile seemed to merge with a starry horizon. A few boats made their slow way northward, carried gently on an easy current. Lamps flickered on their decks, and now and then, she could hear the soft splash and whisper of oars or the voices of men in conversation. But all the boats that passed were too large for one man to row, and too far away for her to signal. Aesop seemed not to have come.

I must wait, that's all. I've hours to go before the night's through. I mustn't panic, and while I'm waiting, I'll think of another plan. Whatever might come, she would not board that boat to Lesvos. Let Charaxus think what he would; she would throw herself to the crocodiles before she submitted to concubinage in that loathsome creature's household.

The garden walls extended out into the river, blocking all view of neighboring properties. Rhodopis had no idea how deep the water was. She might hope to wade along the wall, slip around its edge, and let herself into the next garden—but what if the river's bottom dropped off? Rhodopis had never tried to swim before. She had watched Egyptian women swimming in the garden pool nearly every day in the Pharaoh's harem. But she had never attempted to swim herself, and hadn't the first idea how it was done. No grapevines climbed the walls of Charaxus' garden, as far as she could see—and even if there had been, Rhodopis was not at all confident she dared to use such a treacherous ladder again.

If I can't wade around the wall, then there's no way out of this garden, she thought miserably. *And if I try to wade, but the water goes too deep...*

Overcome by despair, she sank down among the reeds, clutching her knees to her chest. The light rustle of her movement stirred another furtive sound from somewhere close at hand.

She sprang back to her feet. "Who's there? Show yourself." The memory of Psamtik flooded into her mind—into her body, jolting down her veins in a flash of hot fear. She could feel his grip again, hard and cruel, digging into the soft flesh of her upper arm—yet she knew no one touched her; there was no one to threaten her, no one to hurt her, no one to drag her into the trees.

There was no one, except whoever hid among the reeds. Could it be a crocodile? She stumbled back, away from the water's edge. The small garden behind her now seemed a vast and forbidding wilderness, its shadows hiding untold, uncountable terrors.

The reeds parted. The face peering up was familiar, even through the distortion of moonlight and hard shadow. The man was crouched in a tiny, low-sided skiff, which rested in the silty shallows of the bank.

"Aesop!"

Rhodopis ran to him, parting the reeds before her with outflung arms. She embraced him as he stood, wobbling with the motion of the boat.

"Steady." Aesop laughed softly, barely audible over the murmur of the insects.

"You came," she whispered. "Thank the gods. It was such a gamble—I was half certain you'd never get my letter—didn't know if you could be found at Iadmon's place, for one—and if you did get the letter, I thought you might never find this place."

"I nearly didn't find it. I had to ask around, to learn which of these fine estates belongs to Charaxus, and even then, it was all guessing and praying, once I was out on the water."

"His is nearly the only two-story house in this part of Memphis."

"Ah, but one can scarcely see the house at all from the river. Look."

Rhodopis turned, glancing back at Charaxus' home. What Aesop had said was true: by night, the building blended with the dark, featureless shapes of Memphis.

"If I was clever," Rhodopis said, "I would have thought to leave a lamp burning in the window, to guide you here."

Aesop's smile took a wry twist. "You've been an expensive hetaera, an ornament of the Pharaoh's harem, and a bride of the Persian king, yet you still speak like a back-country goatherd with mud up to her knees. I despair of ever curing you of the habit."

"What d'you mean?"

"'If I *were* clever,'" Aesop whispered, grinning to take the sting from his correction. "That's what you ought to have said."

"Get me out of here, and I'll speak any damned way you please. Charaxus is set to take me away to his blasted island, and keep me as his slave—or near enough as makes no difference."

She made as if to climb inside the boat, but Aesop stalled her with a hand on her shoulder. "I can take you away from Charaxus—that much, I can certainly manage tonight. But what am I to do with you afterward?"

"Anything! So long as Charaxus doesn't find me when he returns. He might come home at any time! He's only at a supper party, and he tires of them so easily—or the hosts tire of him. We must go at once, Aesop. Please!"

"If you knew what you headed into, you might not be so eager. You might wish to leave Memphis with Charaxus, after all."

"I never would," Rhodopis muttered. But she held back, folding her arms and waiting for Aesop to explain himself.

"Your messenger found me at Iadmon's because I still handle many of his affairs, as I told you once before," Aesop said. "Unfortunately for you, Doricha—and to the dismay of Xanthes—Iadmon has climbed rather high these past months."

A sinking sensation dragged at her stomach. "How high do you mean?"

"As high as the Pharaoh's court. Amasis has come to rely on Iadmon for certain tasks. I almost think he considers Iadmon a personal friend...if a Pharaoh can truly hold common men in such high regard. That means—"

"You work with Amasis on Iadmon's behalf."

"Yes. I find myself at the Pharaoh's court more often than not. It's not an unpleasant life for me, but I can well imagine it wouldn't be to your liking."

Rhodopis took Aesop's arm. "You don't have to bring me to the palace. I wouldn't go, anyway; I'm no fool. You only need to row me upriver, for I can't swim. Once I'm away from this estate, I can make my way."

"What—running loose in the streets?"

Rhodopis tilted her head, amused. "You make me sound no better than a stray dog!"

But there was no hint of humor in Aesop's level stare. "The streets are too dangerous for you, Doricha. Or should I call you Rhodopis—the brilliant dancing girl, the one who set the record at Iason's auction party? The one whom all Memphis is talking about, when all Memphis isn't busy rioting. Since you danced so beautifully at Iadmon's party, you've become a popular subject among the city's gossips. No, my friend—there is too great a chance that you'll be recognized, or suspected, at the very least. Even the common folk might recognize you, considering how well this city loves a good rumor. Amasis mustn't hear one word of your return, but every tongue that wags increases the risk that he *will* hear, sooner or later."

Rhodopis sighed. Was it better to remain Charaxus' captive forever, or to face Amasis? She may have been the Pharaoh's favorite, yet she was under no delusions that he would treat her gently if he realized the rumors were true, and she had returned to Memphis without his leave.

If only I could get away from this gods-blasted city and Charaxus, both!

"Can't you get me out of Memphis?" she whispered. "Seems to me I'll be safe, once I'm clear of the city."

Aesop tapped his chin, pondering her request. "With time, I'll find a way to spirit you off—a ship sailing north, perhaps, or a merchant's caravan headed south to Kush. Iadmon certainly has enough trading contacts that something can be arranged. But I have no immediate plan, Doricha; this is all too sudden. I need more time to consider our options, to think it through carefully."

"But Charaxus may be headed back from the party now. He won't allow me to leave the house, Aesop; I had to wait until nightfall and climb over the balcony! And in two or three days, he'll force me on that ship bound for Lesvos. There's no time to think it through; you must help me now. Please, Aesop. I'm fearfully desperate!"

"Be calm—be calm. I can't get you out of Memphis tonight, but I won't abandon you. You'll have to lie low until I puzzle out exactly how I can get you away safely."

"Then you'll truly get me out of here—now, this very hour? I won't have to fret over Charaxus any longer?" Glad tears sprang to her eyes and spilled down her cheeks before she could wipe them away.

"Yes, of course. Get in the boat. Carefully, now; it tips something awful."

Rhodopis scrambled into the little skiff. There was only one seat, made from a rough plank, and Aesop was obliged to take it while he worked the oars. Rhodopis huddled cross-legged on the flat, damp floor, staring up at her friend with wide-eyed gratitude as he pushed the boat out into the river. When he set the oars in their holders and began to row, Rhodopis shuddered with the force of her relief.

"I'll take you to my own home," Aesop said. They had put several lengths between themselves and Charaxus' garden; his voice rose above a whisper, though he still spoke with marked caution. "I'm afraid I don't live in any sort of luxury—certainly, my home can't rival Iadmon's estate. My life is nothing, if not humble. But I think you'll be safe there, as long as you remain inconspicuous."

"I will, I swear it. I'll do whatever you think is necessary."

"You may not like what is necessary."

Rhodopis grinned. "Reckon I'd like facing Amasis even less —nor staying with Charaxus a moment longer."

"For one thing," Aesop said sternly, "you *must* stop speaking like a Thracian waif. No more 'reckon' this and 'reckon' that. Too many people recall Iadmon's little dancing girl with her rustic speech and uncultured ways. We must give tongues no reason to wag."

"I understand," Rhodopis said soberly. "I *can* speak proper, when I put my mind to it. I meant to say, I can speak *properly*. I did it in Babylon, and when I went about as Lady Eulalia, too."

"Good. Be on guard, Doricha. Think before you speak— always. There's no room for error in this; not anymore, with rumors of your return flying through the streets of Memphis."

He rowed on in silence for a moment. Rhodopis turned back to watch the garden wall fade into darkness. She was free from Charaxus, at last.

"I can hide you under my roof," Aesop said at length, "but one way or another, your presence will be noted. The only way I can see to bring it off convincingly is to make you my slave."

Rhodopis sat up straight. "Your slave? Aesop, you wouldn't!"

"No, not in truth. But most slaves are quite invisible; hardly anyone pays them heed. It would be a feasible disguise."

"Will anyone believe it? As you said yourself, you don't live like Iadmon. Why would a fellow like you own a slave?"

"You'd never be convincing as my bed slave, if that's what you're asking. At any rate, I'm not wealthy enough to own a girl for pleasure. But a man of my position might own a single slave for more menial work—carrying things, running to the market, cooking meals when I'm too busy with my work to bother doing it myself. As that kind of slave, you might just pass for plausible."

"Cooking meals? I've never so much as baked bread before!"

"I won't require you to actually do a slave's work, Doricha—though you must play the part where others can see, if the disguise is to hold. That means you must look the part, too. You'll wear a slave's sash again. We might need to alter your appearance in other ways, as well. And you must keep your head bowed, your eyes lowered. You mustn't speak unless spoken to—in public, that is. Do you understand?"

"Yes. I'll do it, Aesop, and gladly. I'll do whatever is required, as long as I can get out of Memphis safely."

"You always were a sensible girl. And if truth be told, I'm glad to be in your company again—even if it will only be for a few short days."

As Aesop rowed on, the river bank slid by, smooth and dark as the richest wine. Memphis hid uncountable dangers in its alleys and market squares—in the halls of great men and the palace of its failing king. But Rhodopis would soon be free of all that, too. Knowing as much, she could almost take pleasure in the sight of the city at rest, peaceful and featureless in the night, softly slumbering.

A DECISION MADE

RHODOPIS HAD LOST TRACK OF THE HOURS AS SHE'D LAIN AWAKE in Charaxus' bed—and later, as she had cringed among the shadows of his garden. By the time Aesop rowed his boat to an aging stone pier and tied it to the broken stump of a pillar, the first blue-gray dusting of morning light paled the eastern horizon.

"Dawn has come," she said, surprised, as Aesop helped her clamber up from the floor of the skiff to the pier.

"Of course it has. No darkness lasts forever. Now follow me closely; my home isn't far." His voice lowered to the faintest whisper. "Keep your face turned down, Doricha, and speak to no one. If you're to play the part of my slave, you must do it from the start. Anyone may see us before we reach the safety of my house—and whenever you're beyond my walls, you must take care to maintain the illusion."

Rhodopis followed her friend through the streets of Memphis. Though morning had not yet fully broken, people lingered in nearly every doorway and alley they passed— women beating the sand from rugs with wooden bats, or returning from the nearest well with jugs of water balanced on their heads or hips; men arguing in unseen corners, their shouts and rough exclamations rolling out into the street like balls tossed carelessly by children. Rhodopis didn't know whether they were early risers, or whether they had remained awake all night. This was a part of Memphis she had never seen before. In its grimy, unrefined features—the stink of rot and human waste, the scampering of rats, the air of undefined yet undeniable danger—it reminded her more of Tanis than of Egypt's shining capital. Time and again, she longed to remark on the sights that unfolded as light crept over Memphis. But she recalled Aesop's admonition to play her part. She kept her face turned toward the hard-packed earth of the street, as a proper slave should.

By the time true sunrise had come, dazzling its fiery light along the flat rooftops of the unfamiliar district, Aesop had slowed outside a beer shop, turned down an alley, and ascended a set of steep stairs to the upper floor. There was no handrail bolted to the mudbrick; Rhodopis shrank against the wall as she climbed after Aesop, careful not to look down to the alley far below.

Aesop pushed open the door at the top of the steps and led Rhodopis inside. When he had safely closed the door behind them, he exhaled in relief. "You did well. I doubt anyone glanced your way. If they did, they saw what we meant them to see: a woman resigned to bondage, not the famous dancing girl of popular rumor."

Aesop's home was nothing, if not humble: a single room with two small windows, one looking out on the street, the other on the dry, yellow brick of a nearby building. Rhodopis didn't need to approach that window to know another reeking alley lay below. The interior walls were lined with banks of low shelves, each piled with little pyramids of tightly rolled scrolls. A writing desk stood beside the door—not as fine as Charaxus' red-lacquered desk, to be sure, but Rhodopis had no doubt that

Aesop made far better use of his. Aesop's bed was a narrow pallet, barely elevated on a set of plain wooden blocks and pushed snugly against one wall. The chest at the foot of the bed must hold his clothing, Rhodopis assumed, while a small, orderly collection of wine jars and sealed baskets on a simple table probably made do for Aesop's kitchen and larder.

As she stood gazing about, the general hum of noise outside turned abruptly to angry shouts. She and Aesop edged to the streetside window and peered cautiously through a crack in the wooden shutters. The pitted wooden floor creaked as they crossed the room. In the street below, two men shoved one another outside the beer-shop door; the larger of the two staggered backward into the street and nearly toppled over. A few more men jeered, and his smaller attacker redoubled his assault, flailing at the big fellow with fists and kicks quicker than a cobra's strike.

"It seems Memphis is as angry a place as it's ever been," Rhodopis said.

"Indeed. If anything, the violence has grown worse, these past few months. Amasis has done nothing substantial to calm the fears of his people—and he has done even less to restore harmony between Greek and Egyptian factions."

In the street below, the men watching the fight began to chant a coarse, taunting rhyme. Aesop winced at their language, then tugged the shutters more tightly closed. "I'm no longer a slave, yet I don't always feel as if I've come up in the world since leaving Iadmon's household."

"Surely even this is better than being any man's property."

"It is far better, to be sure. There are moments when I wish for the peace and dignity of Iadmon's estate. If I could have both dignity and freedom, I would be a happy man indeed. But barring access to both, I'll gladly take my freedom."

He turned away from the window. "This room is small, I know, but I've no doubt we can live here comfortably, the two of us. After all, you will only be here for a few days, until I find the safest way to get you clear of the city. There's another small mattress in the bottom of that trunk; it will make do for your bed. Or I'll use it, if you prefer. We can hang a blanket from the ceiling as a screen, so we each may have some privacy while we're bathing or using the waste pot. I know these accommodations are dreadfully rough when compared to Charaxus' house—"

"But I'll gladly take my freedom," Rhodopis said, grinning. "Really, Aesop, it's as marvelous as a palace to me. I don't mind a bit if it's humble. I came from much worse, after all."

Aesop patted her shoulder, grateful for her cherry cooperation. He gestured to one bank of shelves. "All of those papyri are yours to read, if you're so inclined. They're purely for entertainment: poetry, dramas, adventure tales—I will confess a weakness for a good story. You're welcome to share them, but you must leave the other scrolls alone. Those are important documents pertaining to my work, and they must be kept in order, or I'll have a terrible time finding the information I need."

"I understand."

He indicated a large, blue-dyed basket below the table and larder. "My most important documents of all are in that basket, so please be sure you leave it be. That small ebony box to the right contains my hedj—all the money I have. Yes, I'm afraid my entire fortune fits in a box hardly larger than your two feet put together. Ah, well—at least we both are free."

They shared a laugh, even as the fight carried on outside.

"I've hardly been happier in all my life," Rhodopis said. "There's such a weight off my back, to be free of Charaxus. I really thought I'd have no choice but to go with him to Lesvos, and then—oh, I'd be his prisoner for the rest of my life! And I despise him, Aesop. He's such a fool."

"He was kind to you, in the beginning."

"Yes, but only because he wanted to control me—to own me. You're the only man who has never wanted that. You've always been content to leave me as I am... to let me be myself, without expecting me to pretend I'm anyone else. Except for making me speak like a proper lady, of course, but I'll forgive you that. I'm glad I've found you, Aesop. Don't mistake me; I'd rather I never was a slave at all. But at least we've become friends as a result, and that's worth something to me."

Briefly, he took her hand, patting the back of it. "I'd say it's worth a good deal, indeed. Though you may come to curse my name, after I've kept you penned up here above the beer shop for days on end. I'm afraid this life will grow tedious in short order, Doricha—but I will do my best to get you out of Memphis as quickly as I can manage."

"Surely it won't be as bad as that. Why, there's the market to visit, and—"

Aesop shook his head. "No, my friend. You mustn't roam about. There will be occasions when we must venture into the streets together, now and then—it's unavoidable. We'll need food and other supplies, and you'll invite fewer remarks if you accompany me to the market as my slave than if merely allow you to lurk behind the shutters unseen. But we must do our best to keep you hidden away as much as possible. The danger that you'll be recognized is too great. Though—" he hesitated, his brow creasing as he studied her face. "We will, of course, take steps to disguise you."

"Amtes told me where to find the black hair dye—what sorts of merchants sell it, I mean. I can get more, if you'll give me the silver to pay for it."

"I don't think hair dye will be sufficient, now that you've danced at Iadmon's party. Anyone who hopes to find you and verify whether the rumors are true will be searching for a black-haired woman."

"I can tie a scarf around my head—hide my hair."

"What if you venture out into the streets, and are caught in a brawl like that one happening outside? What if your scarf is torn away? No, Doricha—I'm afraid we must take more extreme measures."

Rhodopis shrank from him, anxiety replacing eagerness. "What do you mean, exactly?"

"I'll tell you—but first, I must know whether you're truly ready to commit to this ruse."

Her temper flashed, but by the grace of the gods, she managed to avoid speaking like a Thracian sheep-herder. "It seems to me I have little choice."

"You *do* have a choice, now. You may pretend to be my slave, but you are no one's property anymore. If you wish to leave this room at all, we can disguise you. But if you won't accept a disguise as my slave—or can't accept it, after so long a captive of other men—then we must agree that you'll remain here in this room, and never leave, nor even linger near the windows until we can spirit you out of Memphis."

Rhodopis sighed, sinking down on the three-legged stool beside Aesop's writing desk. "You say I'm free, but am I—really? I don't call this freedom, to be under the threat of discovery. Anyone in Memphis might recognize me and go straight to Amasis with the news. Or perhaps Charaxus will hear where I've gone and come to find me. I'm not free if I'm still at the mercy of so many powerful, angry men."

Aesop laid a hand on her shoulder. "Even free women fare scarcely better than slaves."

"Women used to fare better," she muttered, staring at the old, uneven planks of the floor. "In old Egypt, generations past..."

As silence stretched between them, Rhodopis remembered the light of Phanes' lamp, swinging gently from its thin chain. She recalled how that light had moved across his face as he'd told her of the Egypt he had once known, the Egypt he believed could live again—if only a worthy Pharaoh held the Horus Throne. And she remembered, too, her determination to bring about Phanes' vision—not for her gratification, but for the sake of countless girls and women like her.

It's still within my power to do it, Rhodopis realized. *Charaxus kept me from returning to Persia, but that doesn't mean I'm cast out of the plan.*

Powerful men may still control her, but Rhodopis could sense true freedom somewhere just ahead, beyond the veil of shadows that had dimmed her life. The promise of real liberation—to say nothing of taking her revenge on Psamtik—tantalized her like the glint of sunlight on cool water.

Rhodopis lifted her gaze from the floor. She turned to Aesop with a peaceful yet determined smile. "I *am* committed. Entirely. I'll do whatever you think is necessary, so long as it brings me access."

"Access? I don't understand."

"Forget about taking me out of Memphis, Aesop. I want you to take me somewhere else."

He seemed to know what she meant, without her having to speak those terrible words. Aesop took a step back, recoiling from the mere thought. "I will not take you to the Pharaoh's court. It's far too dangerous."

"But it's where I ought to be. You remember what I told you about Babylon—the physician called Phanes, and King Cambyses, and the need for Polycrates' ships."

"Yes." Aesop's voice was tight with caution. "I remember, all too well."

"Who better to find the information Cambyses will need? If I'm inside the palace again, I can—"

"Are you mad?" He seemed sincerely worried; he laid a palm against her forehead, checking for fever.

"I'm not mad. Don't play that way; I'm serious, Aesop— deadly serious!"

"'Deadly' is an apt word. You know the Pharaoh will kill you if he finds you, and yet you propose to set yourself below his very nose? This is foolish talk, Doricha. I trained you better than that."

"If you can disguise me as your slave—and well enough that no one on the street will glance at me twice—then why wouldn't the same disguise hold just as well in the palace? I could be useful there. What if Polycrates doesn't make it to Babylon? What if none of the messages Amtes sent got through? Cambyses and Phanes need to know what to expect— where the Pharaoh's weaknesses lie, and how best to exploit them."

Aesop threw up his hands, a halfhearted surrender. "I thought you wanted me to get you out of Memphis, and sooner rather than later. But now—this wild plan!"

"I do want to leave Memphis," Rhodopis said, quiet and reflective. "Yes, very much. But I haven't left yet, and only the gods can say whether you'll find a way out. Perhaps you never will."

"Do give me more credit than that."

She clutched his hand, overcome by a sudden wave of passion—trembling fear and earnest courage. "I give you all the credit in the world, Aesop. But Memphis is a dreadfully tangled place, with danger around every turn. No one knows that better than I do. If I never get out, Aesop—if something happens to me, or to you, before you can find a way—then I want the satisfaction of having tried one last time to set Egypt to rights. Egypt can be what it was, long ago. Phanes believes that, and so do I."

Aesop sighed. He passed a hand over his face, as if trying to shed his doubts and fears like dust from his skin. Then he straightened—as much as he could, with his bent back and crooked shoulders. "Very well. It is your life to risk, Doricha— and you aren't mine to control. I can't force you to safety, if you insist on running into danger."

She smiled, but Aesop did not return it.

"Go over to the table," he told her, "and look in that small green basket. You'll find my razor there, and a jar of shaving oil."

"Going to have a shave, then?"

Now Aesop did smile, though his expression was distinctly grim. "Yes, but I won't shave my face. I'm going to shave your head—clear down to the scalp."

She flinched. "What?"

"You heard me. It's the best disguise I can think of—far better than dye or a head-scarf."

She seized the long, wavy locks that fell past her shoulders. Her hands tightened to white-knuckled fists. "But... but it's my *hair!*"

Aesop raised a single brow. "Hear me out, before you object too strongly. Sometimes disobedient slaves are punished in this way—especially women. The shaven head is a mark of shame. And it's startling, Doricha; a bald pate on a woman is so startling, a person can't see anything else about her—not even her face. We'll have no need to fear that your exotic red-gold hair will be recognized, and Lady Eulalia's black curls and erudite ways will vanish, too. This is the most powerful way I can think of to force those who will encounter you to see what we wish them to see: a silent, now-obedient slave, with her face turned down and her eyes dimmed by the severity of her punishment. If you insist on going with me to the Pharaoh's court, you must do it this way, or not at all. Any other way is too risky."

Rhodopis sniffed once, curbing the threat of tears. Slowly, she nodded. "Very well; I'll do it. I'll play the part so well, no one will see me at all. I'll be invisible to Amasis, even if he trips over me."

Or so I pray.

She fetched the basket and paused, holding the razor for a moment, testing its weight in her hand before she passed it to

Aesop. The bronze blade was slightly curved, so sharp it picked up a beam of morning light with a wicked flash. Rhodopis sank onto the stool once again and waited for Aesop to begin his work. When his first stroke of the razor tore through her hair, she bit her lip so she wouldn't cry, and thought of the ships sailing north for Babylon.

❧ 4 ❧

IN THE PHARAOH'S COURT

THE PALACE OF MEMPHIS STOOD ON A HILL ABOVE THE CITY, BUT Rhodopis had never considered that hill to be either high or daunting until she was made to climb it with a basket of scrolls on her back. The sun hung hours short of its peak, yet it beat down on the road with merciless intensity. Sweat dampened her simple tunic of unbleached linen and ran down her back to pool behind the tightly bound sash that marked Rhodopis for a slave. The straps of the basket bit into her shoulders with every step, and the light hood she wore—her only protection against the sun—kept slipping down to obscure her vision.

Rhodopis was already weary, and yet her day had scarcely begun. She had slept poorly the night before, constantly jarred from sleep by the sounds of carousal in the beer shop below Aesop's room. Each time she'd awoken to toss and turn on her hard pallet, she had been amazed to find Aesop snoring lightly in his bed. He had grown so used to the noise that he slept through until dawn's first light, but Rhodopis had felt sure she would never become accustomed to the din of the beer shop.

They had set out early for the palace, Rhodopis doing her best to stifle yawns as she followed Aesop through the streets.

She was careful to keep her eyes down, as Aesop had admonished, though she couldn't resist glancing up now and then, swiftly and surreptitiously, at the people she passed. No one paid her any heed. Aesop had been right: a common slave was all but invisible, no worthier of notice than a pebble lying in the road. She began to feel more confident as they wended through Memphis—there was nothing an invisible woman need fear inside the palace—but the trudge up the hill toward the Pharaoh's gate soured her mood again. By the time she and Aesop stopped for the guards to question them, Rhodopis was panting and scowling, with the first throb of a headache blooming behind one eye.

Three guards left the shadow of the high, flat-topped wall and approached across the sun-struck paving stones.

"Pull your hood back," Aesop whispered. "We'll soon be out of the sun. Remember to let everyone see your shaven head; they'll never look past it."

Rhodopis did as she was told. The guards were young and strong-bodied, Greek in appearance. Rhodopis was not surprised to find Greek men in Amasis' service. They wore the same uniform she remembered from her days in the harem—kilts striped in blue and white, a long-standing Egyptian tradition—yet each man had an amulet dedicated to a different Greek god slung around his neck. Their eyes slid over Rhodopis dismissively as they gathered around Aesop and his slave.

"State your name," one of the guards said.

"Aesop of Memphis, representing Iadmon."

"Iadmon, eh? Doesn't he peddle girls?"

"Boys sometimes, too, I'd wager," another guard added with a wry grin.

The third man said, "What business does a porna merchant have at the palace?"

"I have come to court many times in the past on Iadmon's

behalf," Aesop said smoothly. "The Pharaoh often finds it useful to provide companions for visiting dignitaries. Iadmon deals in hetaerae, not only in pornae—as I am sure you know, my good men."

"Has the Pharaoh summoned you?"

"Not today, yet he has summoned Antemion, a man with whom Iadmon has some urgent business. Antemion cannot leave the palace for several days—the Pharaoh needs him close at hand, it seems—and so Antemion requested that I come here to conduct Iadmon's business when he isn't attending to the king." Aesop added politely, "I have visited the court many times in the past on similar errands. If you check the rolls, my good men, you will find my name."

"I remember you," said the youngest guard. "I've seen you at the gate a handful of times, in fact. But you never had a slave before."

Aesop shrugged his slanted shoulders. "My back, you know. I have a twisted spine. I managed well enough for several years, but the older I get—well—I find a young slave with a strong back useful, these days."

"A girl, though? Wouldn't a nice, strapping boy be of more use to you?"

Aesop gave a small, self-deprecatory bow. "We make do with what we can afford. And this girl is stronger than she looks."

The first guard grunted in acquiescence, then gestured curtly toward Rhodopis. "We'll have a look through that basket."

"Of course," Aesop said. "Isa, put the basket down. Let these good men do their work."

Rhodopis responded at once to the false name; she and Aesop had chosen it the night before, as he'd shaved away the last of her hair. She wriggled out of the hateful straps and lowered the basket to the ground, rolling her shoulders to ease the pain. One of the guards untied the strings that secured its lid and pawed through Aesop's collection of scrolls. He straightened, still paying Rhodopis no mind, though he stood very near her. "Only documents. Nothing to trouble us."

"Very well," the first guard said to Aesop. "Go about your business. But remember: all petitioners and persons who have not been summoned to court by the Pharaoh must clear out before sunset. No lingering in the gardens, or anything of that sort. If you're caught trying to stay beyond the allotted time, you won't be allowed past the gate in the future."

Aesop bowed again. "I understand. Thank you, good men. Come along, Isa."

Rhodopis scrambled to tie the basket shut. She hoisted it onto her shoulders as Aesop strolled away; she was obliged to hustle along at a half-run to catch up with him, an awkward and graceless gait that made the basket's straps cut into her skin worse than they'd done before. But when the shadow of the gate closed overhead, Rhodopis sighed with relief. It was good to be out of the sun, even if she was now closer to Amasis than any sensible person would dare to go.

Aesop knew the route through the outer courtyards and gardens better than Rhodopis did—though, to be sure, when she had been ensconced in the Pharaoh's harem, she had seldom ventured beyond the women's quarters, the feast hall, or the corridors that led to Amasis' private chambers. The palace and its grounds were far more substantial than Rhodopis remembered. Courtyards stretched from one high, square-topped building to the next; gardens lay beyond the pillars of shady porticoes, fragrant with blossoms and filled with ambassadors, dignitaries, and members of noble Egyptian families, who strolled in groups of two and three, more engrossed by their conversations than by the brilliance of flower beds and trellised vines around them.

"How do you fare?" Aesop asked quietly when no one was close enough to hear.

"Well enough," Rhodopis answered, "though the straps on this basket are plain vicious. I'll be bruised before the day's out."

Aesop clicked his tongue in sympathy. "I should have thought of that and made some alteration. It can't be helped now, though."

"It's nothing to trouble over." She smiled, though she kept her face turned down. "I'm strong enough to bear it."

"I dare say you are. Ah—there's the fellow Iadmon has sent me to meet. Let's pray he'll be amenable to Iadmon's proposal, so we can finish our business quickly and leave before you're exposed to even more risk."

"I don't mind if we stay all day. The more I can see or hear, the likelier it is I'll find something worth reporting to our friends."

Aesop shook his head slowly. "I'd admire your tenacity more if it hadn't fallen to me to keep you safe."

"It hasn't fallen to you. You've been good to me, Aesop, but I don't expect you to charge into any worse danger. It's my task, and my burden to carry." She bounced on her toes, adjusting the weight of the basket to emphasize her point.

"You don't think I'd abandon a friend to folly. I'm not as cruel as that."

Aesop turned away abruptly, raising his hand and calling out to Iadmon's contact. "Good Man Antemion! A moment of your time, if you please."

Rhodopis followed Aesop across the courtyard, past a pair of stone benches to a large, low urn standing in the shade of a portico. A Greek man, curiously dressed in the wool robe and tasseled belt of the nation of Carthage, crossed the garden from the opposite direction. He nodded a greeting to Aesop. Antemion was quite tall, standing head and shoulders above

Aesop and most of the other people who wandered along the garden paths. His eyes were such a pale shade gray that they seemed almost colorless. Light-brown hair threaded with silver swept back from his deeply lined brow; creases around his eyes spoke of advancing age. He carried himself with the same arrogant poise that had so impressed Rhodopis on her first sight of Iadmon.

"Aesop. How good to see you again," Antemion said, sounding faintly annoyed. But he clasped Aesop's hand dutifully. "You've come on Iadmon's behalf, I suppose."

"Yes, Good Man Antemion. I had hoped we might discuss terms for an acquisition. Iadmon seeks to expand into the Delta region, and wants some excellent new girls, bright and trainable enough to make fine hetaerae."

"Hetaerae in the Delta? Will the cities there support such a thing? So far from Amasis, I mean—"

Satisfied that Antemion had turned his full attention to the conversation, Rhodopis eased the basket down and crouched on her heels beside it. She gave every impression of a slave taking advantage of her master's distraction to catch a few moments of rest, but she scanned the garden and courtyard, as keen for news to send to Babylon as a hawk searching for mice.

Men in the robes and tassels of foreign nations clustered in rare patches of shade, speaking to one another as earnestly as Aesop and Antemion. A few noble women of the city moved about the garden, clothed in Egyptian finery; the small papyrus scrolls clutched in their hands bore, no doubt, the petitions they would present to the king. Here and there, servants and slaves paused as Rhodopis now did, waiting on their masters' commands—but no one in the courtyard seemed notable to Rhodopis, none worth remarking on to Phanes or Cambyses.

Aesop's conversation broke into her thoughts.

"I still have my doubts that any city in the Delta region will take to such a trade," Antemion said. "In the north, they simply aren't Greek enough. Hetaerae do well here in Memphis, but we have the support of the Pharaoh; Greek culture is welcome. Though," he added gloomily, "one may be forgiven for wondering how much longer Greeks will be welcome in this place. The streets grow more dangerous with each passing day."

"Iadmon understands your hesitancy. But do consider this: everything that is shipped out of Memphis passes through the northern cities—Tanis in particular. Why shouldn't one of the finest luxuries in Memphis also become a popular export? There are plenty of wealthy men in Tanis and in some of the port towns along the seashore. Surely, any of those men would appreciate the attentions of a well-trained hetaera. I can't think of any reason why you and Iadmon shouldn't be the first traders to introduce such an exciting new commodity."

Antemion sighed heavily. "As you say... but it's a great risk, Aesop—investing so many resources into an acquisition, and then investing in the training of the girls. What if hetaerae shouldn't catch on after all?"

"Ah, but what if they should? Would you rather take the profits for yourself, or let them pass to more daring men—say, Xanthes' fellows?"

Across the courtyard, a man stepped from a shadow-darkened doorway. His clean-shaven head and red-hemmed kilt marked him as one of the Pharaoh's personal stewards. The man cupped his hands around his mouth and called in a melodious voice, "Guests of Pharaoh Amasis: the king's audience will begin shortly."

Antemion ducked his head politely. "You must excuse me, Aesop; I've business to take up with the Pharaoh. I should make my way to the audience hall."

"I understand. If I can secure your word now—"

"No, not now; I'm afraid I need more time to think it over, to evaluate the information you've given me."

"Certainly." Despite his effort to remain cool, there was no mistaking the tension in Aesop's voice. "But of course you realize it's imperative that you act on this offer as quickly as possible, if you hope to—"

"Gods," Antemion chuckled, "you are the most stubborn man I've ever encountered. Listen, Aesop: come with me to the king's audience, and we might work something out—*might*. I make no promises, here and now. I still have my reservations, but I know Iadmon's a sensible fellow. I'm willing to discuss it further, but there's no time just now... unless you're game to stand about in the Pharaoh's hall for a few hours while he hears the petitions of his subjects."

Aesop glanced at Rhodopis.

She swallowed hard. *Go into the audience chamber? With Amasis there on his throne?* She had felt prepared to wander the palace grounds, gleaning the conversations of nobles and stewards, if she chanced to overhear anything worth passing along to Cambyses. But Rhodopis hadn't thought to actually face the Pharaoh.

If Amasis recognizes me, I'm as good as dead.

"Well," Aesop began, stalling.

Antemion shrugged. "It's all one to me, my friend. You can convince me here and now, this very day, or find another trader to work with."

Antemion dipped his head again and started off toward the shadowed doorway, joining the other dignitaries and representatives who now streamed in from the gardens.

Rhodopis stood and sidled close to Aesop. "We must do it," she whispered. "I don't like it, but we must."

"We must *not*."

"Iadmon will be angry—or disappointed, at the very least—if you don't secure this fellow's cooperation."

"Iadmon is a reasonable man. While Antemion, quite

clearly, is not." But Aesop shifted uncomfortably as he watched Antemion walk away.

Rhodopis hugged her body tightly, stilling the shivers of dread that seemed to ripple just below the surface of her skin. "We may as well join him. You need his business, and I've found nothing worth noting out here in the courtyard. Why have I come to the palace at all, if not to discover something we can send to our friends?"

"By the gods, I wish I knew the answer to that question," Aesop muttered. "But you're right; we'll gain nothing if we go home now—not for my cause, and not for yours. But for the sake of all the gods, keep your face down and behave like a proper slave."

"Haven't I done as much already?"

Aesop lifted the basket and handed it to Rhodopis. "Come along; we'll catch up to Antemion now, and see if we can't lure him to the back of the audience hall. It will be better for us to whisper about our business there, anyhow—but the farther I can keep you from the Pharaoh's dais, the happier I'll be."

RHODOPIS HAD STOOD in the large audience chamber many times before, but now, its very familiarity jarred her senses and set her heart to pounding. The brightly painted pillars that ran down its length seemed to her like sentries, stationed row on row as they searched the crowd for traitors. The remembered scent of myrrh smoke hung in the air, still noticeable above the growing odor of so many bodies pressed close together, but the sweetness of the incense did nothing to soothe her anxiety. The dark, well-polished stone floor reflected her downturned face. She could see fear glittering in her own eyes.

There is no cause for worry, she told herself again and again. *Amasis will never see me at the back of the hall. And his stewards' eyes will pass over me, for they'll see nothing but my shaven head, and will know me for a meek slave.*

When Aesop and Antemion added their voices to the rising hum of conversation, Rhodopis gathered her courage and ventured a quick glance at the Pharaoh's dais. Amasis already sat upon the golden Horus Throne, waiting as the hall filled. Even that brief look across the great distance of the chamber stirred nausea in Rhodopis' stomach. The moment she caught sight of the king's familiar, stoop-shouldered posture, his embroidered white kilt and his boldly striped, cloth-winged Nemes crown, she dropped her eyes again, swallowing hard and gripping the straps of her basket in trembling fists.

Yet even as she stared at her pale face in the warped mirror of the floor, the image of Amasis remained emblazoned across her mind. The tingle of a new type of caution crept up her spine. Though she hadn't seen the Pharaoh for many months— and her glance at Amasis had been brief—still she detected something *wrong* in his appearance.

Rhodopis pressed her lips together and listened to the hum of conversation around her. Aesop and Antemion chatted on, discussing the terms of Iadmon's proposal, but gradually, she became aware of more voices. Throughout the audience hall, the ambassadors and merchants murmured over the Pharaoh's condition.

"Doesn't he look rather sickly?" a nearby man said quietly.

"Indeed," someone answered. "The Pharaoh is rather old. Perhaps it's only natural."

"No," replied another person, "he looks as if he's caught a fever... or the plague, gods forbid. I hope there's no contagion here in the palace."

From another direction, Rhodopis picked up more quiet words. "I knew the Pharaoh was aged, but I never thought he would look quite so poorly."

"I think the poor fellow's ailing."

"Do you think a sickness is spreading? Has it caught on in the streets of Memphis, I wonder?"

The lump of fear expanded in Rhodopis' throat. She swallowed again, but nothing could alleviate that pressure. Was it an illness—fever? Plague? She hadn't seen Khedeb-Netjer-Bona on the dais; the Great Wife's throne had been empty. That fact hadn't struck Rhodopis as unusual on first glance; Khedeb-Netjer-Bona hadn't always attended the Pharaoh's audiences. Now Rhodopis wondered whether the Great Wife lay abed, stricken with some terrible illness.

Disease in the palace is news worth sending to Cambyses, and no mistake.

A steward at the foot of the dais rapped the end of his staff sharply on the stone floor. Silence fell over the long hall as the man recited Amasis' royal titles and called the audience to session. Every face in the chamber turned toward the Pharaoh, slouched upon his throne.

Now's the time to look again, if you've got the courage to look at all, Rhodopis told herself. *With every face turned to him, Amasis will have no reason to look twice at any single person.*

Though her heart pounded and her skin turned to gooseflesh, she gazed at the Pharaoh directly.

Her first impression proved correct. Whatever ailed Amasis went far beyond mere age. The Pharaoh's cheeks were sunken; darkness ringed his eyes, evident even beyond the edges of the kohl that lined his sagging eyelids. His skin had a grayish cast. Sweat glistened on his brow, and he slumped on the throne as if exhausted by the trappings of kingship. Even from the rear of the audience hall, Rhodopis could sense a dullness in his stare. When the steward finished his recitation, Amasis leaned forward slowly on this throne and seemed to struggle for words— for thoughts—until the steward prompted him with a whisper.

"Let the first petitioner step forward," Amasis finally said. His voice hardly carried the full length of the chamber.

Rhodopis lowered her face again. Even with the Pharaoh in such a state, she dared not push her luck too far. But as the ritual of the audiences proceeded, her mind worked busily, searching for the right words to send to Phanes and Cambyses —trying to decipher the mystery of the Pharaoh's illness.

❧

WHEN THEY RETURNED to Aesop's simple apartment above the beer shop, Rhodopis dropped her basket to the floor and groaned in agony. She rolled her shoulders, wincing at the tension in her muscles.

"Blast that basket straight across the Styx," she said. "Oh, gods preserve me, I've got terrible cramps in both my shoulders. I'll act the part of your slave, Aesop, if there's no other way to get by, but we must find something for me to carry other than that damnable basket."

Aesop chuckled as he crossed to his table-larder. He folded the linen wrapping back from a great, round loaf of barley bread and cut two generous slices with a small knife.

"I've oil and honey for the bread—unless you'd prefer pickled onions."

Rhodopis grimaced. "Oil and honey, thank you." She reached for her supper as Aesop returned to her side, but her tense shoulders protested again and she hissed in pain.

Aesop pulled the stool away from his writing desk. "Sit—on the floor, if you please, right here in front of the stool. I'll work the knots from your shoulders while you eat."

"What about your supper?"

"It can wait. You did far more work than I, carrying all that weight. You must be famished."

"I am."

Rhodopis tore eagerly into her honeyed bread while Aesop squeezed and pressed her shoulders. The tension loosened almost at once; she sighed, rolling her eyes in delight.

Mouth full, she said, "All day I've been wondering what I ought to tell Cambyses and Phanes."

"About what?"

"The Pharaoh, of course." She swallowed her bread and licked honey from the corner of her mouth. "You noticed how ill he looked, didn't you, Aesop?"

"I did, but I don't know what to make of it." He massaged Rhodopis' shoulders for a few more moments, then took up his own dish of bread and pickled onions. "At first, I supposed old Amasis was just—well—*old*. The longer I looked at him—"

"There's something wrong. He's fallen dreadfully ill. And Khedeb-Netjer-Bona was nowhere to be seen. Could it be plague in the palace?"

"We've no way of knowing."

"But if we go back again tomorrow, we might learn more."

"Absolutely not. Put that foolish thought right out of your head."

"But, Aesop!" Rhodopis turned about to look up at him. "What am I to tell Cambyses? 'The Pharaoh looks unwell, but no one knows why'? 'It might be an illness severe enough that you can strike while he's weak—but perhaps not. Perhaps he'll be fit as a horse by the time you reach Egypt, and you'll come straight into danger'?"

"I think Cambyses will come straight into danger, no matter what ails the Pharaoh. And I believe Cambyses knows that all too well. Amasis may be weak at the best of times, but his army is strong."

Rhodopis left her dish of bread on the floor and scrambled to her feet. "That's the very trouble, though—that's what has gnawed at me all day, worse than the straps on the basket. The army will fight for Amasis, of course. He's the king; how could they not? But they'll be weakened if he dies. *When* he dies, for he surely will, sooner or later—whether this illness takes him to his tomb, or old age does it."

"Weakened? How so?"

"A good many of the Pharaoh's soldiers are Greeks—the present Pharaoh, that is. But once Amasis is gone, you know who will inherit the throne."

Rhodopis found she couldn't bring herself to speak Psamtik's name—not yet. Memories of all his outrages were still too fresh in her mind.

Aesop had no such reservations. "Psamtik, of course."

"And he loathes Greeks—hates us more than anything else the gods ever made."

Aesop took her meaning straight away. "So once Psamtik is Pharaoh, he'll dismiss all Greek soldiers from the king's army. Until he can find new men to flesh out the army once more, his forces will be depleted."

"Just so. That's why we must know, Aesop—what exactly has sickened Amasis? If we can guess when he's likely to die, then Cambyses can time his arrival to take advantage of Egypt's weakness."

Deep in thought, Aesop ran his fingers through this short, curly beard. He stared past Rhodopis, out through his half-open shutters to the city beyond. Sunset painted the sky above Memphis with the colors of fire and blood. From somewhere in the distance came the shouts of a disturbance—a riot, or merely a street fight?

"I see," Aesop said at length. "Yes, I do see your point, indeed. If Cambyses arrives in Memphis—or even at the Delta —at precisely the right moment, he'll encounter very little opposition. Psamtik may gnash his teeth, but without a proper army at his back, he'll be all roar and no bite."

"We must find a way to send the message to Babylon. With

Amtes gone, and her pigeons with her, I haven't the first idea where to turn."

"Memphis is a big city," Aesop said rather slyly. "Somewhere in the markets and alleyways, there's a fellow with the right contacts in Babylon. Perhaps I might even find such a man in the palace itself, among the ambassadors."

"We might find him."

"Oh, no—not you." Aesop returned to his bread and onions. "You've seen the court once; let that be the end of it. There's no good reason for you to go on risking your life, Doricha—not when I can do the work for you. And there's every reason for you to leave Memphis as quickly as possible. I haven't forgotten that; I'm still committed to getting you clear of this mess, one way or another."

She smiled tremulously. "It gives me such a funny pang when you call me that—my old name, I mean. Doricha."

"You don't call yourself Doricha anymore?" Aesop seemed truly surprised. "I remember how anxious you were in Iadmon's house, those first few days—afraid he'd take your name from you."

"I can't explain it." Rhodopis sighed lightly, turning away. She watched the sun sink lower behind the rooftops of Memphis, smoldering like a coal in a glowing brazier. "I'm not the girl I once was, am I? Memphis has changed me—Memphis, and everything I've seen here, everything I've done." *And everything that has been done to me.* "I'm Rhodopis now, for good or ill—and all thanks to this city. Memphis has got right under my skin. Transformed me."

"Like a caterpillar turning into a beautiful moth."

Rhodopis turned back to her friend—her only true friend. Her eyes stung with gratitude. "You're kind to say it. I'm as ordinary as I ever was, but... different, too, in ways I can't explain."

"I don't suppose any person can live the life you've lived and remain untouched by the gods. Perhaps, after everything you've gone through, it's only fitting that you should have a new name."

Rhodopis took a few steps toward him. She longed at that moment for a kind touch, the nearness of a friend, and she would have taken Aesop's hand. But she didn't know how he would react, so she wrung her own hands instead, gaze fixed on the floor. "I don't mind if you call me Doricha, Aesop. It's good to remember, sometimes, where I came from and who I used to be. I had a sister, you know, back when I was Doricha. I *have* a sister—if the gods are merciful, then she still lives, along with my mother and my twin brothers."

"I recall you speaking of your sister, once. Long ago, in Iadmon's house."

"Her name is Aella. She would be ten years old by now—gods, I can hardly believe it! Almost eleven." Rhodopis looked up at her friend, sober with sudden intensity. "I was twelve years old when Iadmon bought me from my mother."

"I know," Aesop said quietly. "I remember."

"That's why I have to do it, Aesop. For girls like Aella… and me."

He sat up straighter, staring at Rhodopis with a hint of alarm tensing the skin around his eyes. "Do what? I don't understand."

"Stay in Memphis. At least until I know what's wrong with the Pharaoh, and what I ought to tell Cambyses."

"Doricha—Rhodopis! Every day you remain, you expose yourself to ever greater danger. The gods were merciful today, and we escaped from under Amasis' nose without any harm. We won't be so lucky a second time. You must allow me to remove you from this city."

"I can't. Not yet." She took his hand, after all, clutching it tightly, staring desperately into his eyes. "Please, Aesop—please understand. I have to do my part to help Cambyses. I have to help Phanes—help him change Egypt back to the way it was, long ago."

"You've done more than enough already. The gods know—my sweet, young friend—you've done more than any one person ought to have done. You've earned your safety, Doricha. You've done your part."

"But still, I feel I can't stop until Egypt is restored, and girls like me are safe. Until Aella is safe."

He patted the back of her hand briskly. "Aella is back in Thrace. No Memphian slave-trader can reach her there. And anyway, this plot with Cambyses won't wipe slavery from Egypt." He sighed heavily, as if burdened by an unbearable weight. "You know I understand how you feel. After all, I was a slave, too... and I, too, lost everything—the life I once had, my family, the very culture of my birth. I've often wondered what my life would be like—who I would be—if I'd never been taken by slave traders. If I'd been left in peace to live among my family, my true people.

"And sometimes I wonder," Aesop went on morosely, "whether the gods will damn me for what I do now."

"What do you mean?"

"Assisting Iadmon—that's what I mean. I don't relish my role, believe me. I don't like to help him with his trading—help him acquire more 'goods', tear more lives and families apart. Yet how else may I support myself, now that I'm free?

"I would see this foulness undone entirely, if I could—every slave freed, and the word 'slave' itself scrubbed from the hearts and minds of all people. But what hope do we have of that?"

"None at all," Rhodopis said. "Still, we must try."

Aesop arose from his stool. He gathered Rhodopis in his arms, pulled her close until her head drooped to rest on his shoulder. The embrace of friendship brought peace to Rhodopis' heart, more serene and comforting than any sweet dream she had ever known.

"Then let me help you," he said. "I know we've no hope of eliminating the slave trade, but if we succeed in restoring the Egypt that was, we might give a few people hope who'd had none before."

"That's it exactly. That's all I want to do, Aesop—all I can hope to do."

"I'll go back to the palace for you. I'll do whatever work is too dangerous for you to undertake. I'll observe Amasis and report back to you—and you may decide what to do with the information, what message to send to Cambyses."

Rhodopis sniffed, drying grateful tears on Aesop's tunic.

"But once your message is sent," he said, more forcefully now, "I'm sending you out of Memphis. Let me hear no more arguments about that, Doricha."

She pulled back just long enough to grin at him. "You'll hear no arguments from me, I swear it." Then she kissed his cheek twirled away, dancing across the room, her feet moving to a glad rhythm only she could hear.

5

BRICK AND EMBERS

THE NEXT SEVERAL DAYS MOVED WITH AGONIZING SLOWNESS FOR
Rhodopis. She remained in the tiny apartment, hidden away
from the public as she'd promised Aesop she would do. But
every passing hour weighed heavier on her mind.

Each morning, she bid Aesop farewell and watched
through a crack in the shutters as he made his way toward the
palace, armed with excuses convincing enough to fool the gate-
guards, intent on learning more about the Pharaoh's illness. As
morning turned to afternoon and the heat of the day intensi-
fied, she threw open the shutters and lay on the floor just below
one window or another, where she could gain some relief from
passing breezes without being seen from the street below.

Rhodopis did her best to lose herself in the scrolls of poetry
and adventure tales from Aesop's collection. But now, matter
how beautiful the words she read, no matter how thrilling the
stories, her thoughts always strayed to the audience hall. The
memory of Amasis slouched upon his throne, dull-eyed and
sweating, replayed endlessly in Rhodopis' mind. The sound of
the Pharaoh's failing voice, weak as it had been, overrode the
hum and clatter from the beer shop below. Each evening, when

she heard Aesop climb the stairs to the little room, Rhodopis hurried to greet him, trembling with hope—but always, Aesop reported that he had learned nothing new.

On her fifth day of waiting, when she felt she would burst or scream or break down in furious tears from the maddening confinement, Aesop returned from the palace grinning.

"You've learned something," Rhodopis said, taking his light dust-cloak and hanging it on a peg beside the door.

"Don't let your hope run away with you," Aesop cautioned. "What I've learned is significant, yet it's still only a sliver of knowledge."

"Tell me; I can't wait any longer."

"Bring me a cup of beer first—from the blue jug, if you please. My throat is dry from the long walk. Thank you."

He drank deeply, then said with an air of triumph, "No one else in the palace is sick. No one except for a few children in the harem, but they have common symptoms—painful ears, runny noses—nothing out of the ordinary for little ones. The Pharaoh has remained in a declining state for weeks now, but the rest of his household remains in good health."

"And his servants? The people who tend to him every day?"

"To a man, all as fit as horses. By every account I could glean, the whole palace is perfectly hale. All, except Amasis."

"It's not likely to be disease, then."

"Not any sort of disease that's catching. There are illnesses which devastate the body as surely as the worst plagues but never spread beyond the sufferer. They're particularly likely to occur among the elderly—or so I've read."

"But is Amasis likely to recover? That's what we need to know."

"And that's what I've been unable to learn, as yet." Aesop sank wearily onto his bed and removed his sandals. He brushed the day's dust from his feet with a linen cloth. "It's slow going. Every day, I must first determine who's in a position to know what I'm seeking to learn. Then I must pry at him—ever so gently—teasing out whatever information he might have, without arousing suspicion. I find the work quite exhausting, I'm afraid. But of course, I'll go on as long as necessary. You needn't fear."

Rhodopis fixed Aesop a bowl of supper, taking dried fruit and meat from his stock of supplies, adding the last wedge from the bread loaf. She passed the dish to her friend.

"We'll need to venture out to the market soon. Our food supply is getting low."

"I'll go tomorrow."

"Let me do it—please, Aesop. I feel like a dog in a pen, shut in and tormented 'til I'm ready to bite!"

He looked at her soberly. "You know how I feel about your leaving this room."

"But if I don't get out soon, I'll go mad!"

"Then let me transport you out of Memphis for good."

"When we're so close to learning what's gone wrong with the Pharaoh?"

Aesop sighed. "You've made your reasons for wanting to remain clear to me; let's not hash it out again. If we do, I fear we might argue over it, and I want no hard feelings between us."

She settled on the floor cross-legged, her dish of supper balanced on one thigh. "Perhaps," she said, picking at a leathery bit of dried fruit, "we ought to ask a physician for his opinion. If we can find one we trust, he might know what's ailing Amasis—and whether he's likely to recover."

"I think a physician can tell us very little of value," Aesop said gloomily, "without examining the king himself. And I daren't approach Amasis' personal physician for information. If I attempted it, someone in the king's service would be sure to find me suspicious. But we can let it rest for one day. Let's go to the market tomorrow morning—both of us. We'll spend the whole day there, if you like. The exercise will do us both good —as will a change of scenery."

"Then I'm not going to worry about Amasis anymore," Rhodopis said comfortably. "Not tonight, anyhow. I'll just think lovely thoughts about the market square. Oh, it'll be perfectly delicious to leave this room for a while, even if I must do it as your slave, with my head hung low and my eyes downcast. And carrying that damned basket."

"Speaking of your head," Aesop said wryly, "we will need to shave it again before you go out. You've got a nice crop of stubble growing, and it's all as red-gold as those slippers you used to wear. Not many women in Memphis have hair of that color."

Rhodopis passed her hand over her scalp. New growth bristled there, velvety as a horse's muzzle. "Gods, you're right. And those slippers! I had them in my pack when I tried to leave with Polycrates. I only brought them along because I thought I might trade them somewhere downriver for traveling supplies. I left them on the deck of Polycrates' ship, along with everything else I'd brought. I wouldn't mind getting some of my nice things back, if the gods could ever arrange it—but if I never see those shoes again, I'll die happy. They would only serve to remind me of Charaxus, and the sooner he's forgot, the better."

Aesop raised his brows in silent disapproval.

Rhodopis blushed, recalling what she'd just said. "The sooner he's *forgotten*. I'm trying to speak properly, Aesop—honestly, I am!"

He returned to his supper. "I know you are; I can tell. You've made impressive progress, I must say. You rarely slip anymore."

"I can't afford to slip—not with all the city whispering about my return. But it's hard, whenever I think of Charaxus. He makes me so angry... simply furious!"

Aesop uttered a short, barking laugh. "Charaxus is all the reason we need to keep your head shaved down to the skin, and to keep you locked away in this room. He didn't leave for Lesvos, you know."

"Didn't he? More fool him."

"I overheard some interesting gossip about your former patron while I waited for the Pharaoh's audience to begin. It seems Charaxus has been haunting the north end, making himself unwelcome at supper parties he hasn't been invited to. You aren't the only one who's furious; Charaxus has been ranting at whoever will sit still long enough to listen."

"Ranting about what?" she said cautiously, knowing the answer already.

"Stolen property. Did you take anything when you fled his house? I know you had nothing in your arms or slung over your back, but I suppose a bit of jewelry would be easy enough to make off with—or a few silver hedj."

"Aesop, how could you?" Rhodopis answered playfully. "You know I'm not a thief. No, I've no doubt Charaxus is angry as a hornet over *me*. I'm his 'stolen property'. Though who he thinks made off with me, I can't begin to guess."

"I assumed as much. I've never put much stock in anything Charaxus has said. Why, one time, he told Iadmon—"

A rap at the door silenced Aesop. Rhodopis stared at him in shock, a half-chewed chunk of dried fruit pouching out her cheek.

"Aesop," a man's voice called from the other side of the door. "Are you in?"

"A moment," he replied in an untroubled voice, even as he leaped up from the bed. "Allow me to dress."

To Rhodopis, he whispered, "That's Ajax; I know his voice. He's one of Iadmon's messengers, and a friend—but even so, it would be better if no one found you here."

"But if I'm your slave—"

"Iadmon doesn't know anything about my owning a slave. And since I don't intend to ever own one in truth, let us keep it that way. It will make my dealings with Iadmon easier. Here—"

Aesop snatched the stool from beside the writing desk and whisked it behind the hanging blanket, their makeshift privacy curtain. Rhodopis needed no further instruction. She stepped up on the stool's seat, then sank to her heels, clutching her knees to her chest. Not for nothing had she been a dancer; her balance was excellent, and the moment she felt confident of her stability, she nodded to Aesop. He pulled the curtain shut across its dim corner, leaving her alone with the privy pot, a copper wash-basin, and a large, clay jar of tepid water. Rhodopis listened as her friend opened the door.

"Ajax," Aesop said smoothly. "How good to see you. Thank you for waiting; I was preparing for my evening bath when you knocked. Do come in."

Footsteps shuffled halfway across the floor. Rhodopis tensed. Balled up as she was on the seat of the stool, she knew the messenger would see nothing through the gap at the bottom of the curtain. Still, she couldn't help but feel as if Ajax knew she was there.

"I've come with an urgent message from Iadmon," Ajax said. His voice was gruff, yet through its gravelly hoarseness, Rhodopis detected a hint of youth.

"I'd supposed as much. What can I do for the good man?"

"He has heard back from Antemion regarding the Delta trade. He needs you to secure the final details on his behalf tomorrow, so that he may begin work straight away."

"I see. And where shall I find Antemion—did Iadmon have any sense of it?"

"He'll be at the palace again, working on some other business with one of the Pharaoh's ambassadors."

"Perhaps it would be better to wait, and speak to Antemion at a more convenient time."

Ajax chuckled. "Iadmon knew you'd suggest that very thing.

I'm to tell you that Antemion is leaving Memphis the day after tomorrow, at first light. There's nothing for it; Iadmon's business must be concluded in the king's palace. Of course, he'll pay you well for the extra trouble of going all that way."

"Of course he will. Iadmon has always dealt fairly with his associates. Please tell him I shall see to everything; he needn't worry." The footsteps moved toward the door again, and Rhodopis allowed herself to breathe more freely. "Good evening, Ajax. Until next time."

The door closed. Over the growing noise from the beer shop downstairs, Rhodopis could just make out the thump of Ajax's steps as he descended the stairs. When the sound lost itself among the beer shop's din, Aesop said, "He's gone, Doricha. You can come out now."

She unfolded herself from the stool and pulled back the curtain. Aesop stood beside the door, massaging the place between his eyebrows with two fingers. His eyes were closed, his mouth straight and pale in the blackness of his beard.

"You heard everything," he said.

"Of course."

"I'm sorry to disappoint you—I know how much you looked forward to a day at the market. But I need Iadmon's money; I can't refuse this work, I'm afraid."

Rhodopis sighed. "I understand, Aesop—really, I do." She attempted a smile. "Iadmon will pay you extra for going all that long distance—that's what the messenger said. Wouldn't it just about knock Iadmon to the ground if he knew you've been walking to the palace and back every day?"

Aesop's shoulders jumped once, a silent and humorless laugh. "Wouldn't it just? Well, this does give me another opportunity to observe the Pharaoh and learn whatever else may be learned about his condition. That's some consolation, at least. We'll go to the market the day after—and we won't let anything prevent us."

Rhodopis nodded, but her smile faded away. The prospect of another long, tedious day shut in that room was enough to make her weep. But she blinked away the tears before they could fall. She could bear one more day of confinement, if she set her mind to it. Hadn't she crossed the desert to Babylon in a camel litter? That had been far worse than her present predicament. The market would wait for her. She was a free woman now, after all, regardless of the disguise she wore.

THE NEXT MORNING, after seeing him off with a stoic nod, Rhodopis watched through the crack in the shutters as Aesop vanished at the end of the street. When he had gone, she sighed and took the cushions from her bed and Aesop's, dropping them in her usual place below the window. She sank down and unrolled a story scroll, determined to read through every long hour—to make the day pass as swiftly as the gods would allow.

But as the heat of afternoon came on, Rhodopis' eyelids grew heavy. She dozed on her cushions—and at length, her dozing turned to deeper sleep. The scroll she'd been reading coiled itself closed on the floor as her hand relaxed against the papyrus; she slid peacefully into the respite of dreams, where there was no Pharaoh to threaten her, no menace of Charaxus hunting her through the streets.

In her dream, there was a great, golden boat that carried her north on a river of sweet honey, smooth and slow. Beyond its bow, on a glowing island far in the distance, she could make out a tiny figure waving to her, beckoning her on—and somehow, she knew it was Aella.

Rhodopis raised her hand, gesturing to her sister—but as she did so, the image of the luminous island and the sunset-colored river burst. The dream shattered into splinters of darkness; her body jerked reflexively, and she woke on her pile of cushions, cramped and dazed with a sour taste in her throat.

What had roused her so cruelly from that pleasant state? She longed to return to the dream, yet even in her grogginess, she knew it had been something in the waking world—something real—that had jolted her from sleep. Something harsh and very near.

Something dangerous.

Slowly, Rhodopis pushed herself up to hands and knees, tense with the strain of listening. At first, all she heard—aside from the constant noise of the beer shop—was the pounding of her heartbeat and the straw-stuffed cushions crackling with her movement. Had someone knocked on Aesop's door? Perhaps the messenger Ajax had returned.

What will I do if he has? It won't do me a bit of good to hide behind the curtain again—not in this tiny room.

She waited for another boom at the door, but none came. Gradually, Rhodopis grew more aware of the noise from the beer shop—the din of argument and song, of workers' movements and drinkers' shouts that filled the space below Aesop's humble home almost every hour of the day and night. The nature of that sound had changed. It had grown from its usual volume, and men's shouts peaked above the thud and scrape of tables being moved abruptly. A woman screamed—one of the servers, Rhodopis assumed—and half a moment later, the shouts erupted into one wild roar. The beer shop was positively boiling with anger; Rhodopis could feel the vibration of it through the floorboards, tingling in her palms and racing up her arms to quicken her heart.

She reached up and pulled the window shutters more tightly closed, then crouched beside the window, peering out through the narrow gap between.

The beer shop disgorged a writhing knot of men into the street. They stumbled as they poured from the doorway, swinging fists at faces, tearing at each other's clothes. In the open space of the street, the crowd formed into two rough factions, and Rhodopis was not surprised to see Greeks and Egyptians facing one another, baring their teeth and snarling like dogs in a fighting pit. It was the same story Memphis had told for months—for years, while Amasis sat idle on his throne. The fight was as familiar as the sight of the Pharaoh's palace rising above the city, but its nearness terrified her. She remembered the night she had cowered with the rest of Xanthes' girls in the Stable, listening to the muffled sounds of the riot beyond their master's wall. This fight was much closer, and there was nothing between Rhodopis and all this searing hate, save for the mudbrick of this humble building and the wooden shutters screening her from view.

"Get out!" someone shouted in Egyptian. And half the street took up that cry in a rhythmic chant. *Get out! Get out! Get out!*

A Greek man, big and broad as an ox—and evidently no cleverer—swaggered into the center of that terrible gathering. He grabbed an Egyptian as the man darted past—apparently choosing his victim at random—and lifted the man into the air, then slammed him down against the hard-packed, sunbaked dirt of the road. The Egyptian landed on his side and lay as if stunned, eyes closed, barely moving, while his fellows roared in outrage. They surged toward the Greek faction; Rhodopis saw three Egyptians pile into the big, bullish man, tackling him to the ground; another wave of Egyptians surged past them, clawing for Greek flesh like hawks set loose among a farmer's fowl. A line of Greeks pushed back, smashing the faces of their Egyptian foes with bloody fists. Rhodopis stifled a scream as a Greek jerked an Egyptian's arm across his body, wrenching the man's shoulder from its socket. The crunching pop of his injury carried above the noise of the crowd, all the way up to Rhodopis' window. She shuddered in fear and disgust, choking back the nausea that rose in her throat.

Then the crowd staggered back, clearing a sudden space in the street. In that opening, there stood two young men—boys, really—with hard, narrow eyes and faces glowing with triumph. One of them held a clay lamp in his hands, lit—Rhodopis couldn't imagine from where he'd produced it. The other held a brick or a stone, some heavy object wrapped in a length of linen. The knot ended in a ragged, grayish tail of cloth. A heartbeat before the boys set the cloth ablaze, Rhodopis realized the fabric must have been soaked in oil.

The cloth blazed at once, bright as a bolt of lightning, and the boy who held the brick hurled it toward the beer shop. It arced through the air, streaming acrid black smoke while the crowd redoubled its terrible roar.

The boy's aim was true. Rhodopis couldn't hear the brick strike its target over the noise of the crowd, but moments later, the serving women bolted from the beer shop, dodging in a panic through the crowd.

Gods almighty! Rhodopis reeled back from the window. There were wooden tables and benches in the shop below, and dry woven baskets full of food—plenty of fuel for a fire. But worse than the tables and reed baskets, the shop contained jugs of wine—only the gods could say how many. If just one of those jugs cracked from the heat and spilled its contents, the blaze could turn deadly.

Threads of dark smoke rose from the floor, working up through cracks between rough planks. The smell stung Rhodopis' throat, choked her until she began to cough and her eyes filled with water. Heat crept up into the soles of her feet. She ran toward the door.

But Rhodopis stopped herself before she could throw the door open and flee the room. The fire below was already burning steadily, and this was a poor district of Memphis. No one would come to put out the blaze; the building would be left to burn until everything inside was consumed, and only the mudbrick shell remained. Aesop's work would be lost unless Rhodopis saved what she could now.

The basket with its hateful straps lay beside the door. She tore off its lid and scurried to the larder-table, then hauled out the basket containing Aesop's most important documents—the one he had told her never to touch. Rhodopis upended the whole collection into the carrying-basket; there was no time to pay heed to order. Next, she dropped the box containing Aesop's money into the basket. The heavy box crushed several scrolls, but with luck, they would still be legible.

Rhodopis turned toward the shelves, stabbed by an agony of regret. There wasn't room in the carrying-basket to take all of Aesop's work, let alone any of his wonderful collection. The poetry and stories would have to be left behind, where they would burn to ashes.

No time to weep over stories, Rhodopis told herself sharply. She reached for the scrolls on the nearest shelf—Aesop's lists and tallies, the work of a free man—and crammed as many into as her basket as would fit. Then she knotted the lid back in place, slipped her feet into her sandals, and hefted the basket to her shoulders with a grunt.

It was heavier than she could have imagined, thanks to Aesop's money box. The straps cut into her shoulders worse than ever before, sending twin stabs of pain down her back. Rhodopis threw open the door and coughed in the fresher air of the alley—grateful, for once, to breathe in the stench of refuse and stale piss.

The narrow stairway seemed to spin and lurch beneath her as she made her way down. She pressed herself close to the building's wall so the basket couldn't over-balance her, plunging her to the alley below. She could already feel the heat of the fire through the bricks; it sent rivulets of sweat running down her back and dripping down her temples, barely missing the corners of her eyes.

When her feet found the alley floor, Rhodopis paused, swallowing hard and trembling. The alley opened on the fight —a dizzying tangle of thrashing bodies, hoarse voices, and bright spots of blood. Brick walls loomed to either side. Behind a pile of stones, broken baskets, and heaped-up ash, she could see that the narrow lane ended in another smooth, impassable wall of brown brick. There was no way out, except through that terrible crowd.

Gods give me strength, she silently prayed as she hiked the basket higher on her shoulders. Then she marched toward the riot, leaving Aesop's home to burn behind her.

Rhodopis didn't hesitate at the edge of the crowd. She knew if she did, she would lose her nerve, and remain shivering in the alley until some villain, drunk on the madness of the fight, noticed her—or until the burning building collapsed in a roar of brick and embers. She must hope the fury of the fight itself would distract the men from her presence and shield her from too much harm.

She stepped out into the fray, only to be knocked aside immediately by a staggering man. She stumbled under the weight of her burden, but she didn't fall; Rhodopis pushed on, dodging as best she could between men, trying to shut her ears to the sounds of hate and rage all around her. A Greek man, bleeding from a cut across his forehead, pounded an Egyptian in the gut; Rhodopis ducked and spun away, leaving them to their brutality. An Egyptian kicked the feet out from beneath a Greek, sending him sprawling with a groan; Rhodopis danced aside, narrowly clearing his flailing limbs as he struggled to right himself and take revenge on his attackers. The crowd buffeted her this way and that, as men fell against her carrying-basket and pushed off again, or lurched in front of her, howling like jackals on the hunt. Rhodopis breathed steadily and pushed on—ever on, never stopping—until at last she broke free of the crowd and found herself on a more open street.

People hurried down the road—women hitching up their skirts to run faster, children shouting for their mothers, men calling for soldiers to come and give aid, though surely, they must know the Pharaoh's men would do nothing. Rhodopis pressed on past a few more shops, then leaned against a baker's doorframe, breath rasping in her throat. Her legs shook so violently, she wondered dimly how she still managed to stand.

"All right, girl?" a woman said.

Rhodopis started, peering into the shadows of the bakery. A white-haired woman crept from behind a heavy table, its surface pale with flour. She held something in her hands —a cup.

"Water," the woman said. When she drew close, she smelled of warm bread and sea salt—a comforting odor. "Here, child; drink."

Rhodopis couldn't forget Aesop's warning that even the commoners of the city might recognize her. But her throat was on fire; water was more than she could resist.

"Thank you." Rhodopis took the cup and drained it in one long draft. The water was cool and sweet, soothing the rasp of smoke and fear from her parched throat.

"A narrow escape," the woman said. She pulled a square of linen from her belt and dabbed gently at Rhodopis' lip. "Though it seems you didn't get away unscathed."

Rhodopis winced at the woman's touch. Now she felt the heat and pain of a split lip—though she never recalled a blow to her face. Perhaps she had caught some man's flailing fist or elbow as she pushed through the crowd. She held still while the baker cleaned the blood from her chin, then nodded her thanks.

"Server at the beer shop, are you? *Were* you, I should say."

"Yes," Rhodopis said at once.

The baker's eyes darted up to her shaven head, and doubt

deepened the wrinkles in her face. "Your story's good enough for me. I don't ask questions; I'm only glad you got away safely."

"As am I, Mother."

"You'll be looking for new work, unless I'm mistaken. That smoke says your beer shop won't be needing any more servers for some time yet. Come and see me if you want a job. You look like a good, strong girl—one I could use." She looked again at Rhodopis' stubble of red-gold hair, the mark of a reprimanded slave. "If you're free to look for work, that is."

Rhodopis nodded. "I must be going now. Thank you for your kindness."

"Take this." The woman pressed the kerchief into Rhodopis' hand. "It's ruined with your blood now, anyway. Keep pressure on that lip until the bleeding stops."

"I will. Thank you again."

The baker tilted her gray head, eyeing Rhodopis' over-stuffed basket. "Where are you going, anyway?"

"To the..." Rhodopis pressed her lips together and cringed at the pain. In her fear and exhaustion, she had nearly said, "To the palace." She covered her hesitation with a cough, then said, "To the south side. I've someone there waiting for me."

The baker patted Rhodopis' arm. "Be brave, then, girl—and thank the gods you got away safely. These riots are getting worse every day."

With a few more words of gratitude, Rhodopis set off again, stumbling as the basket sank its teeth into her shoulders, pressing the red-stained kerchief against her mouth. Behind her, the sounds of the riot seemed to go on and on, inexhaustible, eternal, like the river that was Egypt's very blood.

❧ 6 ❧

A DANGEROUS REFUGE

BY THE TIME SHE REACHED THE PALACE GATE, RHODOPIS COULD no longer hold back her tears. Her body was one hot streak of pain, from her eyes stinging with sweat to her cramping back, from her split lip to the soles of her weary, stumbling feet. She sniffed miserably as she approached, choking back desperate sobs.

Guilt gnawed at her, too—if only she could have saved more scrolls!—and fear shook her to the very core. It was one thing to come to the palace with Aesop as a guide. But it was another matter entirely to stand before the gate alone, vulnerable and exhausted, with her tell-tale hair exposed. What would she do —what could she hope to do—if the guards recognized the fugitive harem girl? She hadn't thought to bring her headscarf when she fled Aesop's room. There had been no time to consider a disguise. She must hope the demeanor of a slave would divert the guards' attention.

Rhodopis blinked the tears from her eyes and stood with lowered head as a guard approached.

"Here, now," the man said. Rhodopis didn't look up, but she

could hear the concern in his voice. "You look a proper fright. What's happened to you, girl?"

"Please, good man," Rhodopis said tremulously, "I must find Aesop, Good Man Iadmon's free servant. Do you know him?"

"Short fellow, with crooked shoulders and a funny way of walking. Is that your man?"

"Yes. I'm his slave; my name is Isa. Please, I must find Aesop. I wouldn't trouble you if it weren't an emergency."

Another guard called from the shadow of the gate. "What's that, then, Karpos?"

"Slave come looking for her master."

"Send her away! We've more important things to do."

Rhodopis glanced up quickly, catching Karpos' eye. "Please," she whispered. "I must find my master. Something terrible has happened—something he must hear about, right away."

Karpos squinted back at his fellow guard. He hunched his shoulders in distaste and muttered, "More important things to do? Holding up the wall is what it amounts to. Lazy Thales... wouldn't do a day's work if his life depended on it."

Rhodopis couldn't have said whether her pleas moved the guardsman's heart, or whether he simply wished to irritate Thales. But he made up his mind quickly, scrubbing his hands together in a businesslike way. "Right. Your master'll be in the audience hall now, and the audience is nearly over. I can find him, easy enough. You wait here in the shade, girl. You'll have to keep company with Thales, I'm afraid, but he won't pay you any mind. He's not interested in anything but dicing and keeping out of the sun."

Karpos spoke a few quick and quiet words to Thales, who grunted peevishly as the former passed through the palace gate. Karpos was soon lost to sight among the pillars and fountains of the first courtyard.

Thales, leaning against the soaring brick edifice of the

Pharaoh's grand gateway, turned his sour frown on Rhodopis. "Set that basket down, girl, and let me have a look."

Rhodopis took a step back.

"Don't be a fool," Thales grumbled. "Even if that bastard Karpos can find your master, you won't step beyond this gate with an unsearched load on your back. You might have anything at all hidden in there."

"Nothing but my master's scrolls."

But Rhodopis knew better than to argue with a royal guard. She eased the pack from her shoulders and let it slide to the ground, then rubbed at the bruised areas where the straps had left their vicious marks. Thales gestured impatiently; she untied the basket's lid and stepped away, praying the man wouldn't find Aesop's money box. It seemed unlikely that this guard would deal fairly with a woman left alone—especially a slave woman.

Thales pawed through the basket. The scrolls had been crammed in so tightly that several burst from the rim and scattered on the ground. Rhodopis moved to retrieve them, but Thales warned her back with a sharp jerk of his head. He chose a scroll at random and unrolled it, frowning over its contents, then rolled it again and tossed it in the dust. He inspected several more and likewise discarded them, but then he located the money box and the dull, angry expression fled from his face, replaced on the instant by keen interest.

"Hello, little friend," Thales muttered, grinning. He lifted the money box from Rhodopis' basket.

At that moment, Aesop appeared beneath the gate, clutching a few scraps of papyrus to his chest as he all but ran toward Rhodopis. "Isa! Gods have mercy, what has happened to you?"

The frown returned to Thales' face. He opened the money box, gave its silver contents a cursory glance, then returned it to the basket and stepped away. "You're cleared to enter, I suppose."

Rhodopis stooped to gather the spilled scrolls, but Aesop reached her first. He held her by the shoulders, taking in the sight of her. His wide-eyed alarm grew with each passing heartbeat. "Speak, Isa! Tell me what has happened."

"A... a fire," Rhodopis stammered. "There was a riot, and they set fire to the place. I saved what I could, but I couldn't take everything."

"You're safe; that's most important."

"But your work, Aesop—"

A new voice called from the shadow of the gate. "Is everything all right, my friend?" It was Antemion, Iadmon's trading partner. He came forward briskly, the hem of his chlamys hitched over one arm. "You left in the middle of our conversation."

"I am sorry," Aesop said smoothly. "That guardsman told me an urgent messenger had come to the gate, seeking me—and the matter is urgent, indeed. But Isa is a quick thinker. She made the best of a bad situation."

Rhodopis scooped the scrolls into her basket and tied the lid shut. She kept her face turned down so no one could see her blushing at Aesop's praise.

Antemion looked directly at Rhodopis—for the first time, perhaps. Such was the invisibility of a common slave. "Hera have mercy; you're covered in soot. Was there a fire, girl?"

Rhodopis darted a swift glance at Aesop. He nodded, encouraging her to speak.

"Yes, Good Man. I fear my master's home has been destroyed."

Aesop sighed wearily.

"An ill turn of events," Antemion said. "I'm sorry to hear it, Aesop. Where will you go now?"

"I haven't asked myself that question yet." Aesop massaged

the place between his brows. It was the most he ever allowed to show of his private turmoil. "I suppose Iadmon might find a place for me in his estate until I can secure new lodging. I pray whatever I find will be in a safer district."

Rhodopis stiffened at the mention of Iadmon's estate, but she kept her face turned resolutely downward.

"You know," Antemion said, "Ambassador Kurunta is departing with me tomorrow morning for his native Carthage— you now I've had many occasions to deal with the Carthaginians, and Kurunta and I are on good terms. The Pharaoh has been hosting him here at the palace for several months now, in the diplomats' wing. But his quarters will be quite empty— already are, in fact. He had his belongings loaded onto our ship this afternoon while we were at the king's audience."

"I couldn't stay in the palace," Aesop said. "I'm not an ambassador."

"But there is still work to be done here on behalf of Carthage. Kurunta had thought to employ a scribe—someone who can observe the audiences and send along word of any decrees or actions that might be of interest to the Carthaginian king. There is no one I would recommend more highly for the work than you, Aesop. And it would qualify you to remain in the ambassador's quarters."

Aesop shook his head. "I would only be pushed out again when a real ambassador came along—someone who could make better and more official use of the space. Better to find more suitable quarters from the outset."

Antemion took Aesop by the arm. Soberly, he said, "You know there are no more suitable accommodations in the city just now. Memphis is in a sorry state. You'll be safer here than anywhere else."

Rhodopis swallowed hard, fighting the urge to laugh with wild hysteria.

Antemion glanced down at the basket—the sorry, soot-darkened thing that now held the remains of Aesop's shattered world. "Within the palace walls, you might hope to put your life back in some semblance of order. Out there, in the wilderness of Memphis... who can say? Take the work, Aesop. You need it now."

Rhodopis looked up in time to catch Aesop's eye. The glance they shared was fleeting, yet still, Rhodopis could read her friend's reluctance. Antemion was right, and well did they both know it. There was nowhere else for them to go—not where they could be safe from riots or rumor.

"Very well," Aesop said, forcing a smile. "I will take you up on the offer—you and Ambassador Kurunta. You have my thanks, friend."

THE DIPLOMATS' wing was mercifully distant from the king's chambers—and from the halls and offices that made up the functional heart of the palace. It was far removed from the harem, too—as far as one could go without leaving the royal grounds. That put Rhodopis' mind somewhat at ease as a servant led her and Aesop to their new temporary lodging.

Ambassador Kurunta's former quarters were impressive, even emptied of his belongings. A fine woolen rug stretched from wall to wall, patterned in blood-red and deep indigo-blue; the bed at the chamber's far end stood on ebony legs, piled with colorful cushions. A sturdy couch waited beside a low meal table; both couch and table were draped in bright-green silk. And two wide windows opened on the private garden shared by every resident of the diplomats' wing.

A narrow door led to a private bath, complete with a tile-lined tub sunk into the floor. A wooden screen hid the privy pot from view. Beside the bath, another door led to a small side chamber, plain but airy.

"This room will do for your servant's quarters, Ambassador," the palace worker said, bowing as he addressed Aesop. "Unless, of course, you prefer to house her elsewhere."

"No; this room will suffice. Please bring a mat and bedding for her to sleep on—the most comfortable mat you can find. We will also require fresh clothing for both of us. My... er... the baggage from my journey has not yet arrived, and I would like to change into a clean robe."

"At once, Ambassador." The servant cast a curious glance at Rhodopis, clearly mystified by her grime, the soot darkening her skin. "May I bring you anything else?"

"Bath water," Aesop said, "and oil. And food—something fortifying. That will be all; thank you."

When they were alone, Aesop and Rhodopis stared at one another for a long moment. The room was silent, save for the splashing of a fountain and the long, lazy calls of a small bird out in the garden. Rhodopis sucked in a ragged, shuddering breath, then laughed in sheer disbelief. Aesop lurched forward, throwing his arms around her in a long embrace.

"Gods have mercy." He sounded half choked by his emotions. "You look a proper mess. It's a shame Kurunta didn't leave a mirror behind; you'd never believe your own reflection."

"I've been terrified someone will recognize me, with my hair uncovered."

"No danger of that. I can't tell what color your hair is under all that ash and grime."

They broke apart.

"I'm worn out," Rhodopis said weakly. "I never thought a load of scrolls could be so heavy. Though I suppose most of the weight comes from your money box, not the scrolls. They're only papyrus, after all."

"I meant what I said to Antemion. Your quick thinking

means the world to me." He nudged the basket with the toe of his sandal. "All my work as a free man… it would have been lost without you. Gone in mere moments—in an actual puff of smoke."

"But I couldn't save it all, Aesop!"

He laid his hand affectionately on her head, chuckling at the feel of her sooty stubble. "What you saved will be enough for me to go on with my work. I'll make it so."

He turned away, wandered to the garden window and stood with his hands locked behind his back, staring pensively out into the late-afternoon sunlight. "For now, I needn't worry about putting my work back in order. My most pressing concern is to get you safely away. Gods, it was proving difficult enough merely to spirit you out of Memphis unseen. Now here we are, stuck in the palace itself. This is a fine net of fish and no mistake."

"No, Aesop—don't you see?" Rhodopis hurried to his side. "The gods have brought me here—they've brought us here. Now we're better placed than ever before, to learn what has happened to Amasis."

Aesop groaned. "Doricha, live up to the praise I just gave you and think more clearly than that, for Zeus' sake."

"I know it's dangerous," she began.

Aesop cut her off ruthlessly. "'Dangerous' is too soft a word. Try 'foolish'—'mad'—even 'deadly.'"

"I'll stay here in this room the whole while."

"You nearly lost your mind from the strain of confinement, once already. It's an experience neither of us needs to repeat."

"This place is much nicer than your old room above the beer shop." She threw her arms wide, taking in the spacious chamber and the pleasant garden outside.

"And I've no doubt these quarters are crawling with palace servants—any of whom might recognize you from your days in the harem. Besides, if I keep you here in my own chamber, the palace staff will assume you're more than just my slave. They'll think you're my lover."

Rhodopis giggled. "What if they do? I can't see how that would make a bit of difference. Plenty of men keep lovers, don't they?"

"Not me. I've a reputation for being dedicated to my work. I'm so well known for my solitary ways that my colleagues would take note of any change in my habits. They would remark on it at once. Aesop's lover would be far too conspicuous; you'd have even less hope of remaining hidden than you have already. No—you must maintain the illusion that you are my carrying-girl, and nothing more."

"Then I am staying here in the palace." She clasped her hands together.

"For now—for a day or two. And only because our backs are against a wall. We have no other choice. I don't like it, Doricha—not one bit. You shouldn't like it any better."

"But here in the diplomats' wing, we're more likely to find a fellow who can get a message to Babylon. Consider that."

"Yes," Aesop said thoughtfully, returning to his study of the garden. "That is true."

Someone knocked at the door. Rhodopis and Aesop both spun about to face the sound.

"Who's there?" Aesop called.

"I'm a servant of the palace, Master," a young man's voice replied, small and muffled through the door. "I've brought the bath water you requested."

Aesop sighed with relief. "You may enter."

A boy of some fourteen years let himself in, pulling a small, two-wheeled cart behind him. A great clay jug with a tight-fitted lid sat atop the cart. It sloshed and wobbled as the boy dragged it across the chamber.

"The water isn't hot, Master," the servant said as he worked. "But I suppose that's best on a day like today. Maids from linen storage are coming just behind me, if it please you, with the clean clothes you sent for, and bath oil, too."

The boy hauled his heavy burden into the small bathroom. Rhodopis could hear the splash and gurgle of water as he filled the sunken bathing tub.

"We'll never find a place with such fine service out there in the city," she whispered to Aesop.

He murmured in reply, "I'll take safety over fine service, thank you very much."

Two women, dressed in the simple tunics of palace staff, arrived with fresh linen and oil for the bath.

"We brought your servant the same clothing we wear, Ambassador," one of them said to Aesop. "We didn't know what else we ought to provide for her."

"That will do nicely; I thank you kindly for your service."

When all the servants had withdrawn, Rhodopis shut herself in the bathroom and undressed. She gasped at the sight of her old tunic, discarded on the floor. It had been the creamy shade of unbleached linen when she'd donned it that morning. Now it was brown with dirt, streaked with the ugly black stains of the fire.

It's a wonder they let me through the gate at all. I must look a proper fright.

When she reached for a jar of bath oil, Rhodopis found a small hand mirror on the floor beside it; the maids must have left it for her use, or Aesop's. She picked up the disc of polished bronze and looked at her reflection with timid apprehension.

A proper fright didn't begin to do justice to Rhodopis' state. Patches of red-gold showed here and there through the grit and soot masking her hair, but on the whole, she was unrecognizable. Tears and sweat had cut tracks through the grime darkening her face.

The sooner I'm into that water and clean, the better off I'll be.

She returned the mirror to its place and stepped down into

the warm water. The water clouded with dirt the moment her skin touched it, but Rhodopis trickled bath oil into her hands and rubbed herself vigorously, delighting in the precious scent of myrrh and roses, and in the soothing sensation of warm water. Some of the tension eased from her tight shoulders and aching back.

She sank into the bath with a contented sigh. Perhaps what she had told Aesop had been true, after all. Perhaps the gods had brought Rhodopis here, to this very time and place, so she might fulfill her role in the Persian plot all the sooner—and with greater success.

Could it be so? She wondered. *Even if it's not the truth exactly, I'll make it so by my own will. With the gods as my witness.*

7

THE PHARAOH'S FALL

RHODOPIS AND AESOP DWELT AS UNOBTRUSIVELY AS THEY COULD
in the diplomats' wing of the great palace, avoiding all but the
most necessary contact with the Pharaoh's servants. They
passed two days in the seclusion of the ambassador's chamber,
venturing into the small adjoining garden—and no farther—
when confinement became too much to bear. The sights and
sounds of palace life struck Rhodopis with strangely
comforting familiarity. The quiet, efficient bustle of the staff,
their simple yet finely made garments, even the scent of lotus
lilies and sun-warmed pond water impressed her with a sense
of having come... not home, exactly. Neither the harem nor the
palace had ever felt welcoming enough to count as a home. But
this was a place that was known to her, and her understanding
of the rhythms of palace life imbued her with a pleasant
confidence.

On their third morning in the diplomats' wing, a knock
sounded at their chamber door. Aesop found a steward there,
bowing and asking forgiveness for his intrusion.

"Your pardon, Ambassador," the steward said. "I've been
sent to request your presence in the Chamber of Letters in two

hours' time. The Pharaoh has reason to request certain goods from Carthage, and naturally, your assistance with the communication would be most useful. Egypt has no wish to give inadvertent offense to your king."

Rhodopis, who had been enjoying a scroll of poetry from the comfort of a feather-stuffed cushion, stood and watched the exchange with cautious interest.

"Of course," Aesop said, blinking in surprise. Evidently, this steward had no idea that Aesop was not truly an ambassador from the Carthaginian kingdom. "Will the Pharaoh himself grace us in the Chamber of Letters? If so, I must dress more suitably, but I'm afraid I have nothing finer to wear. There was a fire, you see, and—"

"No." The steward waved his hand dismissively as he broke in. Rhodopis could detect a certain strained impatience in the man's face, an uncomfortable pressure. "The Pharaoh is... occupied. He will send a competent representative in his place."

Aesop nodded. "In two hours' time, then. I shall be ready."

When the steward had gone, Aesop turned to Rhodopis and let out a long, slow breath.

"You've been raised up to ambassador."

"I've little experience with royal stewards, but it seems to me they ought to know who is an ambassador and who is not."

"Ah, but he was distracted—upset. Surely you noticed. What do you think it signifies?" Rhodopis tucked her scroll into a nearby shelf. The summons was already more interesting than the poetry she had been reading.

"Perhaps nothing. Perhaps everything. Amasis is too ill to dictate the letter himself. He must be sending a closer, more trusted steward in his place. It's possible that the king's best stewards find it necessary to perform tasks they don't usually handle and have sent more junior men with less experience to handle the menial work."

"Like fetching ambassadors?"

"Precisely. Or..." Aesop trailed off, pensive and troubled.

"What is it, Aesop?"

He shook his head. "I thought perhaps that inexperienced steward might signify a transition in royal power. An entirely new staff brought in, quietly displacing the old. But that seems unlikely; if anything had befallen Amasis over the past two days, we surely would have heard of it, even here in this relatively quiet, secluded wing. Pharaohs don't die without shaking the world; Amasis couldn't sink into the underworld without rattling his own household."

Rhodopis stretched her arms above her head. "You're fretting too much. It's like I told you already: the gods brought us here to the palace so that we might serve their purpose. We're exactly where they mean us to be. If that steward didn't know you from the real ambassador, then it's all for the best. We're meant to go and take that letter from the Pharaoh's steward; it's an opportunity to find the last missing bits of information and send them off to our friends in the north."

Aesop chuckled drily. "I haven't your faith, my friend. The gods have always been too unpredictable for me to trust so completely in their designs. And what do you mean, 'we' are meant to take the letter?"

Rhodopis drooped where she stood. "You aren't going to make me stay here, are you? You heard that fellow; Amasis won't be present."

He raised a single brow. "Let us not have this tired old argument again."

"Aesop, be sensible! You've a role to play now—acting the ambassador to Carthage. How are you to stay sharp for our purpose if you're concentrating on the writing? Let me come along and carry your things. While you play the part, I'll sit quiet as a shadow in some corner—watching and listening. If I'm right, and the gods intended us to be here in the palace, then we mustn't waste any opportunity to learn more about the Pharaoh's affliction. Aren't two sets of eyes better than one?"

Aesop relented with another long sigh. "All right. But let me shave your head again before we venture out. One never knows who else might be sitting in the corner, quiet as a shadow, and I'm in no mood for taking unnecessary risks."

❧

AT THE APPOINTED TIME, Rhodopis and Aesop followed the new steward through the palace grounds to the Chamber of Letters, silent and wary in the man's wake. The chamber lay much nearer the king's private quarters than Rhodopis had intended to go; as she recognized more familiar features from her days spent entertaining Amasis, her stomach grew ever sourer with anxiety. But she said nothing of her misgivings, tending only to the small basket she carried in her arms—thankfully not the beastly contraption she had packed through the streets of Memphis like some beleaguered donkey. This basket held Aesop's writing implements, along with a few fresh sheets of papyrus for taking the dictation.

Everything will be well, Rhodopis told herself as they crossed the final courtyard before the king's quarters. *No one can see me, in this guise as Aesop's slave. No one expects to find Rhodopis here in the palace again, and so I'll be invisible to them all.*

The steadiness she'd found in the bath returned to her. She breathed deeply now, calmly, but kept her face turned sensibly down to the floor as the steward rapped his staff outside the Chamber of Letters.

"Come."

That gruff answering voice snuffed Rhodopis' confidence in an instant, replacing it with a well of dread that rose so swiftly from her gut, it was more instinct than rational reaction. But she had no time to think, no time to prepare herself for what she sensed would come next. The steward opened the door, filling her mind with lurching terror.

Psamtik stood at the far end of the modest, practical chamber. His back was to the door as he gazed through an unshuttered window to the courtyard beyond, but Rhodopis recognized him at once, without seeing his hateful face. His broad, imposing shape—even the air of casual confidence with which he held himself—were stamped, deep and indelible, on her mind. Aesop entered the chamber, murmuring a greeting to the man he thought was a steward, but Rhodopis balked at the threshold. Her heart pounded in her ears and her tense, tight throat; every nerve in her body tingled with the urge to run.

The young steward who had led them to the chamber cleared his throat and said quietly, "Is there something you require?"

She took hold of her senses once more, stilled her trembling, and turned to the man with an apologetic bend of her knees. She shook her head—silent, as a slave ought to be in the presence of powerful men—and followed Aesop into the chamber.

Psamtik raised his hand without turning from the window, gesturing vaguely. "You may be seated, Ambassador."

Aesop settled on one of the stools at the long table. Rhodopis took a few lengths of papyrus from the basket and slid them across the polished wood to Aesop, then passed him his writing brush and a vial of dark ink. She retreated to the chamber door and stood with her head bowed, praying Psamtik's cruel eye would pass over her, cursing herself for the foolish confidence that had led her into this mire. But though her face was downturned, she couldn't help watching the King's Son through the veil of her lashes. To take her eyes off Psamtik was a hazard even she wouldn't risk.

Psamtik turned from the window. The urge to shudder—to

shiver like a hare beneath the hawk's shadow—wracked Rhodopis, body and spirit, but she mastered herself with an effort that brought sweat to her brow and dampened her tunic beneath her arms. She noted Aesop's surprise in the shifting of his weight. His stool creaked sharply.

"My apologies, King's Son." Aesop rose, then bowed deeply to Psamtik. "I did not expect your royal presence."

From the corner of her downcast eye, Rhodopis saw Psamtik wave, a dismissal of Aesop's apology. "The throne's business with Carthage is too important to leave in the hands of any steward. You will take this letter on papyrus, but when the final version is sent to the Carthaginian king, it must be inscribed in clay and fired. Five copies will be made and sent to Carthage by way of my swiftest messengers. I will not risk this letter going astray or being damaged; papyrus is far too fragile for my purpose."

"I understand, King's Son. I am ready to begin whenever you please."

Rhodopis listened as Psamtik began to dictate his message to the king of Carthage. At first, the low rasp of his voice was all she could hear—the sound of it, its harsh and fearsome quality. She seemed to hear the words with which Psamtik had taunted her that terrible night in the harem garden—*I'll spill your blood without a second thought, you Greek bitch.*

The memory curdled her stomach and sent a bitter taste rising to the back of her throat, but she forced it away and made herself ignore the words Psamtik had spoken long ago. Instead, she concentrated on the words he spoke now. Although she had gone quite cold with fear, Rhodopis knew her shaven head and unmoving posture made her all but invisible, even under Psamtik's eye. So long as she remained unobtrusive, she was unlikely to attract his attention. He was too intent on his message to pay any heed to the ambassador's slave who waited, still and obedient, beside the door.

"To the mighty King Hasdrubal," Psamtik said, "strength of the gods in the land of Carthage:

"I come to you as a brother-king, seeking the aid of my brother. My kingdom is under attack; I must have more soldiers to repel those who would take what the gods have given me. In the name of the alliance that binds us, and in our unity against the Greek menace which we both despise, I ask that you send me five thousand men. They will be treated with all consideration and held in reserve, only brought into battle should the need arise.

"As compensation, I offer you a quarter of Egypt's acquisitions of gold, derived from our subjects in Kush and beyond, from this day until ten years from this date. In addition, I shall send you two hundred talents of silver upon the arrival of your soldiers in Memphis.

"Send me word of your acceptance with all haste. Together, let us give neither triumph nor succor to this Greek plague upon the earth."

Aesop's brush whispered across the papyrus for a few moments more. Then he read the message back while Psamtik returned to his contemplation of the courtyard beyond the window.

"Is there anything you care to add, King's Son?"

"Nothing. You may sign it with my usual titles."

Aesop's stool creaked again as he sat up straighter, surprised. "*Your* titles, King's Son? Not the Pharaoh's?"

Psamtik wheeled with the speed of a cobra's strike; Rhodopis couldn't stop herself from starting and cringing in fear. "You heard my command," he said to Aesop. "I won't be questioned."

"Of course not, King's Son. I intended no offense." Aesop was smooth and unflappable, as ever. "I shall make five copies in clay, in accordance with your wishes. I'll see to it that they are fired this evening and ready to send by the next sunrise."

Hot fury drained from Psamtik. He relaxed where he stood and waved in dismissal. "Good. You may leave me now, Ambassador. Send in my steward when you've gone."

Aesop rose, glancing around for Rhodopis. It was only with a monumental effort that she forced herself to cross the chamber again, drawing nearer to the beast who had plagued her nightmares for far too long. She gathered Aesop's brush and ink, stowed them in her small basket, and laid the letter to Carthage carefully between unmarked sheets of papyrus so Aesop's careful writing would not be smeared. When Aesop turned to exit the chamber, her legs quivered with the need to flee Psamtik's presence. She bit her lip hard to keep from shrieking with fear, and the cut she had received in the street riot reopened, filling her mouth with a hot, metallic tang.

In the hall outside the chamber, Aesop spoke a few words to the steward, then headed back toward the diplomats' wing with an air so casual it nearly infuriated Rhodopis. They remained silent all the long way back to their quarters. Only when Aesop had shut their door, then checked the bath and Rhodopis' tiny chamber for working servants, did he finally speak.

"The King's Son is raising a mercenary army," he said grimly. "You know what this means."

She was still trembling so forcefully that her voice shook as she answered. "He's certain Amasis will die soon. And he sees what we see: the moment of weakness between their two reigns. His only vulnerability."

Rhodopis sank back against the closed door. She covered her face with her hands, unwilling to allow Aesop to see her own weakness—it was bad enough that he could hear it in her voice. But her shoulders soon began to lurch with the force of her silent sobs.

"Doricha, what's the matter? You were so bright and happy this morning, so sure of... *everything*."

"Oh, Aesop. I would still feel just as confident if it had been a steward in that chamber. Not him."

"Psamtik?"

She flinched at the hated name.

Aesop came to her, lowering her hands gently. He searched her face, then frowned at sight of her lip. He dabbed at the blood with the edge of his chlamys.

"There, now. Tell me what troubles you."

"I don't like to talk about it. I don't like to think of it, either, but it seems I can't help that now."

Aesop took her hand in wordless commiseration.

Rhodopis drew a deep breath, forcing herself to speak. "You remember, I told you how Psamtik hurt me."

"Yes—I remember." Aesop's words held an unexpected sharpness. Rhodopis had never heard him speak that way before, darkly angry. After a moment, he said more gently, "You poor thing. It must have been terrible, to be so near him again —as if the palace weren't already treacherous enough for you. If I'd known it would be Psamtik, not a steward—"

Rhodopis shook her head, wiping her lip with the back of her hand. "It makes no difference now. He gave me a fright, but I've recovered."

Aesop's half-smile spoke eloquently of his doubt, but he didn't argue.

"What's important," she went on, "is what we learned today. And didn't I tell you we would find something worth telling Cambyses?"

"You did, at that," Aesop reluctantly agreed. "There's no doubting what that letter means. Psamtik expects the Pharaoh to die soon, and he intends to have a stable army when death comes for old Amasis."

Rhodopis gasped, stepping away from the door. "Oh, gods. Why didn't I see it before? Why didn't I think—? Aesop, it's

Psamtik who's doing this to the Pharaoh. He's poisoning Amasis. He must be!"

"Are you sure?"

"Sure as I can be. He told me once... that night, when he caught me alone... he said he would kill his father someday, and never care one bit what the gods thought of it. That explains everything, doesn't it—the sickness that has touched no one but Amasis."

"It does make a tidy explanation. But it could just as easily be some ailment that affects only one person, and never spreads."

"If it were only an illness, Psamtik wouldn't be so sure of his succession to the throne. Nor would he feel this urgency to buy mercenary soldiers. He must realize that he'll be suspected of killing the king. He's preparing to defend his right to the throne."

Aesop nodded thoughtfully. "Yes, I see. He's preparing to refute any accusations of wrongdoing with the point of a sword. You must be correct, Doricha."

She edged farther from the door and lowered her voice to the faintest whisper. "How long do you suppose Cambyses has to act?"

"We can't possibly know. I don't suppose we'll ever find out how long Psamtik has been playing this game—nor what kind of poison he has used."

"We can't delay any longer. We must send what little we know to Babylon, and urge Cambyses to act. Now."

"I've managed to sniff out one potential messenger, a man with strong ties to the palace in Babylon. That's one benefit of finding ourselves in the diplomats' wing, just as you predicted. If anyone in Egypt can get word to Cambyses, it's this fellow."

"Then we must send the message tonight."

"I doubt we can make the message ready by tonight. We must think up some clever way to disguise the information—

riddles, codes, that sort of thing—yet we must be certain Cambyses will understand. It's too risky to tell what we know in plain language. Imagine what would happen if one of Psamtik's men were to intercept our letter."

At that thought, Rhodopis went cold all over again.

Aesop saw the color drain from her face; instant guilt flashed in his eyes, and he took her by the shoulders. "I'm sorry, Doricha. I shouldn't have said that. But you needn't fear—not anymore. You're stronger than Psamtik, stronger than the evil things he did to you. I know it's true."

"I hope you're right," she said faintly. "It gave me a bad turn, seeing him today. Being so near him. I barely kept myself from falling to pieces."

"But you did it. You managed well enough."

She smiled shakily, grateful for the praise—but fresh tears threatened, burning in the corners of her eyes. "I managed well enough, but I'd rather not be so close to him again. If the gods wanted me here in the palace, then surely I've done what they needed me to do."

"Does that mean you've finally seen sense?"

Rhodopis nodded, clutching Aesop's hand. "I won't try to stop you getting me out of the palace now—or out of Memphis. Once our letter is sent, I want to go away and never see this place again."

THE NEXT MORNING, as Aesop prepared to attend the king's daily audience, Rhodopis considered remaining in the diplomats' wing. The shock of seeing Psamtik again still quivered within, as a bell's vibration hums beneath the hand long after the sound has died away. But the difficulty remained, and gnawed at her thoughts: how could she and Aesop safely convey knowledge of Psamtik's maneuvers to Babylon?

"I'm going with you to court," she said to Aesop—suddenly, surprising even herself.

"You should remain here. You know it isn't safe for you in the throne room—or anywhere else in the palace."

"It may not be safe," Rhodopis conceded, shaking out a fresh tunic, "but I'll feel far more frightened if I stay here alone. And in that crowd of people, neither Amasis nor Psamtik is likely to notice me—especially if we hide at the back of the room."

Aesop looked over Psamtik's letter to Carthage again, reading it for what must have been the hundredth time since their meeting with the King's Son. "If you stay here with this letter, perhaps you can think of a creative way to tell Cambyses—"

"You never sent his letter off to be written in clay and fired," Rhodopis said. She giggled nervously. "He won't like that."

"Assuming he ever finds out."

"He will. The Carthaginians may be his only hope for a successful coup. He'll inquire, Aesop—surely you must see that."

"By the time Psamtik thinks to send a pigeon to Carthage, asking whether his clay tablets arrived, you and I will be long gone from Memphis."

"So we both pray," Rhodopis said rather ominously. "If we can't get out—"

"We will. I'll find a way."

"If we can't," she insisted, "I shouldn't like to feel Psamtik's anger. He is very unpleasant when his will has been denied."

Aesop returned the letter to his writing desk. He said quietly, "I suppose no one knows that better than you. But what should I do, Doricha? What if I make the tablets and send them off to Carthage, and they agree to give Psamtik his soldiers?"

"Polycrates' fleet is fast enough to bring Cambyses and his forces to Egypt long before a Carthaginian army can mobilize."

She had no idea whether it was true, but she fervently hoped it was so. "We can get word off to Persia first, then the tablets. That way, we'll be safe from Psamtik's wrath."

"All the more reason for you to stay here and work out a cipher. You're clever enough to do it; I've no doubt about that."

It was high praise, coming from Aesop. Rhodopis blushed with pleasure, but she stood firm. "If all goes as we hope, then this will be our final day of watching—one last audience to glean whatever information we can about Amasis' condition. Then, this very evening, our message will go winging off to Babylon. Our final opportunity, Aesop! You know two pairs of eyes are sharper than one."

"You'll look wherever I happen not to look," he said wearily. "And you'll listen for whatever I fail to hear. Is that the way of it?" He passed a hand over his face, and Rhodopis knew she had claimed her victory. "We're nearly through with this madness, and I thank the gods for that. I shall be glad when that message is out of our hands, too. Then we can finally get ourselves away from Memphis, once and for all."

Satisfied, she teased him comfortably. "What about Carthage? You can't leave the Carthaginian king without an ambassador in Egypt."

"The king of the Carthaginians already owes me for the work I've done on his behalf," Aesop answered wryly. "It's none of my business who he finds to replace me. Let Ambassador Kurunta or Antemion sort it out with their king in their letters. It's all one to me; as soon as we've made our escape from this city, I'll be glad never to think of Memphis or the palace again."

"So will I."

"Hand me my chlamys," Aesop said. "I had better finish preparing for court."

That was how Rhodopis came to be waiting in the great courtyard outside the Pharaoh's audience hall, pressed into the shade of a pillar, watching the ambassadors and Egyptian noblemen mill about the courtyard. She caught bits of conversation as groups of men passed, talking easily among themselves. So long as they kept moving, they seemed voluble enough—secure in the knowledge that no one could overhear their conversations. Yet Rhodopis gleaned much from the few sentences she picked up in broken fragments. Tariffs in Mitanni, a slaves' revolt in Etruria, an outbreak of plague in Kush. It was remarkable, how little attention these great men paid to the slaves and servants who moved among them. No one took the least notice of Rhodopis, so long as she cast her eyes low and remained on the periphery of their bustling world—and because no one took notice, no one feared to speak plainly as they passed by.

Foolish old Amasis had it all wrong when he sent me off to Babylon. Her private smile was more than a touch bitter. *A Pharaoh's daughter is too conspicuous to learn anything of importance. If he'd been wiser, he would have sent me as a servant in Cambyses' palace.*

Rhodopis rested her back against the pillar. The painted stone still retained some warmth from the morning sun, though it now stood in crisp blue shadow. She allowed the pleasant contrast of coolness and heat to wash over her, heightening all her senses. She closed her eyes, giving every impression of an overworked slave catching a moment of welcome rest, but she focused on the murmur of many conversations rippling around her, listening for whatever stray bit of information might enhance or clarify the message she and Aesop intended to compose later that afternoon.

"Did you see how poorly the Pharaoh looked yesterday?" one man asked.

"Indeed, I did," his companion replied. "And he attended none of his scheduled meetings or offices after the public audience. I had expected to speak with him about those gold mines in Kush, but he sent a steward in his place."

Rhodopis turned her attention to another voice, coming from a point behind her left shoulder. "They say it's a fever, and the Pharaoh isn't likely to survive."

"It's never a fever," a man answered shortly. "If it were, half the court would be ill by now."

"Do you suppose the Pharaoh will see to the audience today? He looked half dead yesterday. The man can't keep on, or it'll be the death of him in truth."

"I wouldn't be surprised to see his chief wife sitting in his place. If the king has any sense, he'll take to his bed and stay there until he's recovered."

Rhodopis' stomach lurched, but she remained as she was, lounging with her eyes closed, giving no outward sign of her sudden anxiety. She hadn't thought of Khedeb-Netjer-Bona in some time. The chief wife had spent considerably more time with Rhodopis than Psamtik ever had. Might Khedeb-Netjer-Bona recognize her, even though the King's Son had not?

There was no time to worry about the possibility, for at that moment the steward called for the audience to begin.

Aesop returned from across the courtyard as the crowd began to file toward the great double doors, carved with scarabs and set with lines of polished lapis and carnelian. "Are you ready?"

Rhodopis nodded once but didn't speak. She was determined to be perfect in her role as Aesop's slave, quiet and biddable—so invisible, she could drift like a breeze through the Pharaoh's court, seeing and hearing everything with no one the wiser.

They made their slow way into the audience hall, shuffling with the crowd, and took up Aesop's favorite place, well to the rear of the long, echoing room. The chamber filled with the din of conversation. Thanks to the way sound bounced from the pillars and thick walls—even from the smooth stone tiles of the floor—Rhodopis could no longer sort the threads of individual conversation unless the speakers stood very close by. If she was to be of any use, she must use her eyes instead of her ears. Tentatively, she lifted her gaze from the floor and glanced around. The nearest men wore the colors and styles of Kush; beyond them stood a cluster of Greek merchants, milling and gesturing urgently over a scroll held by one of their number. The left side of the hall seemed dominated by an Egyptian presence; the native petitioners had separated themselves from the rest of the crowd, presenting a subtle show of force. With a tingle of fear, Rhodopis recalled the riot outside the beer shop. She hoped no violence would erupt today between Egyptians and Greeks. The audience hall had only one exit, so far as she knew, and she had no desire to repeat her trek from the alley through the roiling beer-shop fight. Her lip still smarted from that experience.

Beyond the Egyptians stood a rank of stewards with their tall staffs of office, alert for any signs of disorder among the petitioners. In a tidy row, they waited for the king's signal to begin. And beyond the stewards, the royal dais stood above the crowd on its pale stone steps.

Rhodopis dared a glance at the king's high seat. Like some ancient statue, Amasis occupied the throne. He was still and weathered, practically crumbling under the weight of his crown and the jeweled falcon pectoral that hung lopsided across his chest. Even from the rear of the hall, Rhodopis could see that his lips were moving, yet no steward paid any heed to the Pharaoh's words.

He's muttering, she realized. *Delirious, and his staff knows it. They all can see he's in a bad way. Why hasn't someone taken over his audience—Khedeb-Netjer-Bona, or even Psamtik? Why wasn't it canceled altogether? Amasis is in no fit state to continue.*

A slight movement near the corner of the dais drew her eye. She clenched her jaw when she recognized Psamtik—his slow, lazy confidence, the arrogant set of his shoulders. Her teeth soon ached from the pressure, but Rhodopis didn't look away.

He's arranged for all of this. He wants the court to see Amasis muttering like a weak, witless old fool.

Had Psamtik already consolidated so much power within the palace? How many of the stewards now answered to the King's Son? Surely, Khedeb-Netjer-Bona would never approve of the Pharaoh being displayed in this way; his failing health paraded before every faction of Memphian society and the ambassadors of nations. Where was the chief wife, and why had she not exercised her influence over the court?

Amasis winced suddenly, clutching at his side, his face crumpling with pain. The collective voice of the audience swelled; Rhodopis could read a distinct note of concern in the sound. After the way Amasis had so cruelly disposed of her, shipping her off to Babylon for his own purpose with no regard for her preference or safety, Rhodopis held no more affection for the old king. Yet he was plainly suffering now, and she couldn't help but pity him, as she would pity any creature in distress. The pain must have been great.

It's poison, surely. I know I'm right. Didn't Psamtik tell me once that he would kill Amasis someday?

And now the King's Son felt certain enough of his victory to parade his terrible deed before the court. Now Psamtik stood gloating at the foot of his dying father's throne.

Rhodopis turned to Aesop, nudging him with a surreptitious elbow. He leaned closer.

"Psamtik wants us all to see," she whispered. "He wants us as witnesses. He must have half the stewards on his side, at least. Otherwise, they never would have allowed Amasis to show himself to his subjects, looking as he does."

Aesop nodded. He seemed about to speak, but the same steward who had ushered the crowd into the hall ascended the first step of the dais, faced the crowd, and rapped the metal-capped end of his staff hard against the stone. The sharp knocks brought silence to the hall.

"He Who Embraces the Heart of the Sun, Ahmose called Amasis, King of Upper and Lower Kmet, calls this audience to session. Let the first petitioners come forward."

A few men edged from the crowd toward the rank of waiting stewards, but their reluctance was apparent. Even a blind man could have perceived that Amasis was in no fit condition to tend to his subjects. As a new murmur of uncertainty made its way down the great hall, Aesop tipped his head, directionally, indicating a man in a humble gray cloak who stood some two or three spans away.

"That's our fellow—our messenger. I've verified everything, sounded him out with the greatest care, and I know he's willing to help."

"You're sure he's safe?"

"Safe as anyone can be in this place. He's the one who will send our letter off to our friends in the north. As soon as we've finished our business here, we'll discuss how to—"

The crowd's murmur changed suddenly, rising in pitch, climbing with a frightening urgency to ring among the vaults of the high, cedar ceiling. Rhodopis gasped at the sound, and her gaze flew instinctively to the throne. Amasis had sagged forward, leaning precariously over his knees. As she and Aesop watched—as the whole court stared—the Pharaoh seemed to shrink, balling himself around his pain. The noise of the chamber rose to a collective shout of surprise and despair. Amasis drooped yet more, his head sagged toward his chest— and he fell from his throne. The Nemes crown slipped from his head as he toppled; the blue-and-gold striped cloth of the sacred Egyptian head-dress crumpled in a heap at the foot of the Horus Throne.

"Gods have mercy!" shouted someone close by.

Another man cried, "The Pharaoh is dead!"

Rhodopis clutched Aesop's hand. The audience hall seemed to toss and heave with unrest, like the terrible ocean waves that had tormented her on the journey to Babylon. Would the riot she had feared erupt after all? She knew she ought to make for the scarab doors, dragging Aesop along behind her—yet she was transfixed by the scene at the far end of the chamber, unable to tear herself from the sight of old Amasis sprawled like an antelope struck by a hunter's spear.

While shouts thundered among the pillars, Psamtik calmly climbed the steps of the dais. He paid no heed to his father, who moved feebly at his feet, but he bent and retrieved the Nemes crown, then stood holding the circlet with a small but self-congratulatory smile. The crown's striped lappets fell over Psamtik's forearms as he locked eyes with the golden cobra that reared from the circlet.

Rhodopis felt sure he would place the crown on his head. But after a moment, Psamtik lifted his hard face to stare thoughtfully down the length of the chamber. His smile was gone now, but even at a distance, Rhodopis could have sworn she saw the light of a stark, terrible joy in his eyes.

❧ 8 ❧

RISE OF THE LION

EVEN WHILE THE PALACE SHUDDERED WITH THE TURBULENCE OF the Pharaoh's fall, the small garden that graced the diplomats' wing remained quiet and serene. The windows of the many ambassadors' quarters looked out on that bright array of flower beds and vine-wrapped arbors, stone benches and fountains splashing softly in the afternoon sun, but every window was shuttered as the ambassadors of Egypt's allied nations worked frantically with their scribes inside their chambers. Rhodopis and Aesop took advantage of the relative seclusion. The garden with its open space was preferable to their chamber; one never knew who might lurk on the other side of a closed door, and only the gods and Psamtik could guess where any given servant's or soldier's loyalty might lie.

Amasis, as it happened, was not dead—not yet. Psamtik had been followed up the dais steps by a handful of stewards, who had lifted the Pharaoh and helped him from the room. Amasis had walked under his own power—though he had leaned heavily on his servants and his progress from the hall had been painfully slow. It was only a matter of time—hours, perhaps— before the gods called him to the underworld.

Rhodopis and Aesop sat side by side on a shady bench, their backs to the palace wall, facing the emptiness of the diplomats' courtyard. Aesop held a small, portable writing desk across his lap, and a piece of papyrus lay open on its surface, weighted at the edges by small stones so the garden breeze couldn't steal it away. But the papyrus remained blank while the ink dried on Aesop's brush.

"There must be some way to tell Cambyses exactly what has happened today." Rhodopis' voice never rose above a whisper, though she felt like wailing.

Aesop rubbed his eyes with an ink-spotted knuckle. "We've been sitting here for the better part of an hour, trying to puzzle out a suitable cipher. But I can't see that we're any closer to a solution. I blame myself entirely; I should have foreseen this difficulty. We should have begun working on this problem before today."

"How were we to know, though, that Amasis would collapse? Or that so many stewards and guards would already be under Psamtik's control?"

"That, too, we should have foreseen." Aesop rolled the stem of his brush between his fingers. "There is enough unrest among native Egyptians that we should have expected it to have seeped into the palace itself. We were careless to assume otherwise. Still, there must be a few soldiers who remain tied to Amasis. Servants, too."

"The Greeks, no doubt." Rhodopis paused, listening to a distant murmur that drifted from the palace's larger and more populated courtyards. Were the factions among the palace guard clashing now, Greek against Egyptian? Or was it merely the sound of rumor she heard? If the fighting had already begun, which side would prevail in the grim struggle?

"If we knew how much of the guard is made up of Greeks, and how many are Egyptian, we might hope to guess at how long Amasis can hold out against Psamtik—and when Cambyses should time his strike."

"It won't matter much, I suppose—not now. It will take Cambyses weeks to travel from Babylon to Memphis, and Amasis is as good as dead already."

"So we return to where we started—the same ground we've been treading for an hour. How do we tell Cambyses that he must move now, without further delay—and how do we do it without drawing attention to ourselves?"

"I don't think there is a way to tell Cambyses what he needs to know—not secretly," Rhodopis said. "We should come right out and say what we mean... leave no chance that our message can be misunderstood."

Aesop paused, tapping the end of his writing brush against his chin. "Perhaps you're right. I suppose the time has come to—"

A man's shout, harsh and commanding, sounded from somewhere near the entrance to the diplomats' wing. "Ambassadors! To me! By order of the royal house, to me!"

Aesop and Rhodopis exchanged a wary look.

"That's a guard," Rhodopis said. "It can only be."

"'By order of the royal house.' Not by order of the Pharaoh."

"One of Psamtik's men, then. What should we do?"

A new murmur of voices came to them, gathered near the wing's entry arch. The foreign dignitaries had abandoned their scribes and letters—for the time being, at least—and were now assembling to the guard's call.

"We had best see what this is all about." Aesop rose and set his lap-desk aside.

They passed quickly through their chamber and into the open-air corridor beyond. Three palace guards stood beneath the square arch—native Egyptians, all—backlit by the rosy glow of late afternoon. Men in the traditional garb of Egypt's allies milled around them. Aesop quickened his pace as one of the guards began to speak; Rhodopis had no choice but to lower her eyes and hurry after him.

"You are all to proceed to the throne room," the guard said. "At once, by royal decree."

One of the dignitaries said, "Might we wash first, and dress more appropriately? I—"

"No time," the guard answered shortly.

Aesop spoke next. "The throne room? Not the audience hall?"

"You heard me," the guard said. "Don't delay."

He spun on his heel and strode away, flanked on either side by his companions.

"Of all the strange orders," one of the ambassadors muttered.

"I don't like it," another said. "These events are moving far too quickly. That hot-headed son of Amasis—"

Aesop threaded his way through the group of ambassadors, gesturing for Rhodopis to follow. "There's nothing to be learned or gained by standing here," he barked so every ambassador could hear. "We must go now, if we're to make full reports to the kings we serve."

The ambassadors crossed the palace grounds together, whispering behind their hands, pausing at every courtyard and portico to search for signs of unrest. Now and then, they encountered knots of soldiers locked in conflict—shouting, shoving, slinging insults at one another through the halls. None of the soldiers' brawls seemed to have escalated yet to outright battle within the ranks, but the sight of such uncontrolled discord made Rhodopis' skin tingle with anxiety.

When they reached the doors to the throne room, only a handful of guards stood in their way. One stepped forward—a towering man, with chest and shoulders broad as the beam of a ship.

"State your business here."

"We've been expressly summoned," Aesop told him, calm and self-possessed despite the man's superior height and strength. "We were told to come at once, by royal command."

The hulking guard eyed the flock of ambassadors for a moment, scowling and suspicious. But finally, he jerked his head toward the double doors. "Let them in," he barked to his fellows.

The other guards were quick to obey. They pushed the heavy doors open, revealing the luxurious expanse of the throne room. Unlike the audience chamber, which served for the daily administration of Memphis—indeed, the whole of Egypt—the throne room was set apart for occasions of great ceremonial import. Its high purpose was reflected in its opulence. The pillars that flanked the hall were slenderer, more graceful than those found elsewhere in the palace. Deeds of the countless kings who had lived before Amasis circled the pillars from floor to ceiling, depicted in vibrant colors. The gods were there, too, looming over the conquerors in their chariots or lurking behind the numberless images of Pharaohs upon the Horus Throne. Tripods lined the hall, oil lamps burning at their pointed pinnacles; the flames illuminated the brilliance and richness of the throne room, lighting the space almost as brightly as midday. But where most tripods were made of dark wood or sturdy bronze, these were of lush, glittering gold. Some burned incense instead of lamps; a haze of blue myrrh smoke hung in the air, so sweet it was almost cloying.

The throne room was large enough to hold a crowd of hundreds, but only a few dozen people were gathered at its far end, milling uncertainly near the foot of the golden dais. As she and Aesop drew nearer, Rhodopis recognized some of those men from her days as a hetaera. Everyone, whether Greek or Egyptian, was clothed in the expensive garb of nobility, and even in their anxious state, each man bore himself with the unmistakable poise and restraint of privilege. Psamtik had summoned only the most influential men of Memphis to witness his ascendance.

The King's Son already occupied the Horus Throne, the great, gilded seat that had belonged to Egypt's Pharaohs for thousands of years. He lounged, poised and arrogant, on the seat of power that was still his father's by right—unless Amasis had succumbed in the past hour, while Rhodopis and Aesop had fretted over their letter. Light from the gilded lamps sparkled over the ornate chair, and over Psamtik himself—for he was dressed already in a Pharaoh's regalia. His kilt, folded and pressed into countless linen pleats, fell all the way to his ankles—an old-fashioned mode of dress that recalled Egypt's ancient, traditional days. A pectoral, made in the shape of a fierce-eyed falcon, spread its wings across his bare chest. Its talons were outstretched as if to strike an enemy—or seize its weak and frightened prey. Rather than the soft cloth Nemes headdress Amasis had preferred, Psamtik wore the Khepresh crown, a high blue dome imitative of a soldier's war helm. And though his hands rested on the arms of the Horus Throne, he held in his fists the crook and flail, the gilded sigils of Egyptian royalty. The braided lashes of the flail fell all the way to Psamtik's feet, their lapis-beaded ends pooling carelessly beside his golden sandals.

"Ah," Psamtik said as the dignitaries entered. "The ambassadors have arrived. Good. You are here as witnesses to the succession. You are to tell the kings you serve what has happened here today. Tell them at once."

The ambassador from Etruria stepped forward, bowing rather timidly and clearing his throat. "Your pardon, er... Majesty. What exactly are we to tell the lords we serve? Has Pharaoh Amasis died?"

Psamtik's smile was like spoiled wine, sharp and unappealing. "Not yet."

Murmurs of disapproval rose at once from the crowd, and

Rhodopis was sure they hadn't all come from the Greek faction. Young though she was, her training as a Memphian hetaera had given her ample knowledge of Egyptian ways. What Psamtik did now—donning the trappings of a Pharaoh while the king still lived, taking his place on the Horus Throne—flew in the face of the very tradition Psamtik claimed to uphold. Until Amasis died, and Psamtik had performed the proper rites over the old king's body, the successor had no right to the throne.

Psamtik seemed unmoved by his future subjects' displeasure. He gave the flail a casual shake; its beads rattled on the dais tiles. "There is nothing to fret over," he said lazily. "Amasis is as good as dead; he won't recover. It's better this way, with a strong young man on the throne—a true Kmetu. No doubt that's why the gods have arranged—"

The sound of a scuffle outside the throne-room doors interrupted Psamtik's speech. The crowd of nobles and dignitaries turned as one, staring at the two great doors as the shouts and thuds grew louder. Then the doors squealed open on their hinges, and Rhodopis wasn't the only person who gasped in shock.

Khedeb-Netjer-Bona swept into the throne room, even as the score of guards behind her continued to grapple with Psamtik's men. She was dressed as divinely as a goddess in a red gown shot through with golden threads, which picked up the glow of the lamps; she sparkled like sunlight on the edge of a well-honed knife. Her dark hair was covered by the gilded wings of the vulture crown, traditional symbol of the great power wielded by the Pharaoh's chief wife. Khedeb-Netjer-Bona looked at no one as she crossed the long, pillared hall— no one save Psamtik, and her black eyes seemed to pin him to the carved back of the Horus Throne.

With Psamtik's guards subdued, the chief wife's soldiers

hurried to catch up to her, flanking the woman with a protective half-circle of hard muscle and bristling weapons.

Psamtik recovered quickly from the surprise. He leaned over the edge of the chair and growled, "I didn't summon you."

"You have neither the right nor the power to summon anyone to this room," Khedeb-Netjer-Bona replied coolly. "The king still lives, which means you are not the Pharaoh. So long as Amasis still draws breath, the Horus Throne is mine—mine to rule in his stead, as his regent."

She stopped at the foot of the dais. Her soldiers' hands tightened on the hilts of their swords.

"Now—get off my throne, Psamtik, before I have you thrown off."

Psamtik's insolent grin spread slowly across his face. "The gods have already made their will known. Amasis will not recover."

"Perhaps that is so," Khedeb-Netjer-Bona said, betraying no sadness as she spoke. "But until the proper rites have been completed, and Amasis rests in his tomb, the Horus Throne is mine. Vacate it at once, or I shall have you dragged down like a hare savaged by hounds."

Rhodopis heard the thunder of many soldier's feet at the throne-room door. She and Aesop turned to stare as a pack of guards flooded into the hall, drawing their swords as they came. Psamtik's triumphant laughter rose above the din as Khedeb-Netjer-Bona's smaller force unsheathed their weapons.

The crowd of nobles and ambassadors cried out in alarm, scattering to the left and right of the dais. There was no hope of fleeing the throne room; Psamtik's men blocked the door.

"Blast!" Aesop grabbed Rhodopis by the hand and hauled her toward the nearest pillar. They cowered behind it, watching cautiously around its bole as the two factions clashed before the dais.

Khedeb-Netjer-Bona remained among her men, shouting and gesturing until her largest guard turned her forcibly about and thrust her aside. She staggered, face blanching with surprise, but sense seemed to find her at last, and she hitched up the skirt of her gown and dodged toward the relative safety of the pillars.

Her quick retreat carried her directly toward Rhodopis.

"Gods have mercy," Rhodopis exclaimed, huddling down beside Aesop. She turned her face to the floor just as the chief wife crouched to her right.

Khedeb-Netjer-Bona's hands trembled faintly as she pressed them against the pillar and leaned to peer out into the throne room. Through a heavy perfume of rose oil, Rhodopis could smell the woman's sweat, acrid with fear and rage.

"That thrice-damned fool Psamtik," she hissed. "The gods will destroy him for this presumption if I don't get to him first."

But the next moment, Khedeb-Netjer-Bona gasped. A shiver wracked her body. A glance at the fight showed Rhodopis why: the tide of the battle seemed set now. Psamtik's men were beating back Khedeb-Netjer-Bona's guards, driving them toward the double doors and out of the hall. Someone was shouting, "My lady! chief wife!"—the captain of her guard, Rhodopis assumed. But the chief wife's forces were pushed out, and a moment later the throne-room doors slammed shut. A few of Psamtik's men dropped heavy cedar bars into their holders—a barricade to Khedeb-Netjer-Bona's men.

"No," the chief wife whispered.

Rhodopis couldn't help but pity the woman—and fear for her. Surely Khedeb-Netjer-Bona's fate was sealed now, and Psamtik would not be gentle with her.

"My lady," Rhodopis said softly, throat tight with sympathy.

Khedeb-Netjer-Bona turned to look at her. For a heartbeat, she only stared into Rhodopis' face, an expression of mild confusion mingling with her fear. She saw nothing but a common slave. But then recognition struck. Khedeb-Netjer-Bona's eyes widened in shocked disbelief.

Rhodopis swallowed hard. *What have you done, you fool?*

Rough hands seized Khedeb-Netjer-Bona by her shoulders, hauling her to her feet. Psamtik's guards dragged the chief wife to the foot of the dais. She struggled to free herself, jerking this way and that in her captors' grip, but to no avail.

Psamtik had won.

"Khedeb-Netjer-Bona." The name was almost a purr in Psamtik's throat. The sound of his voice soured Rhodopis' stomach. "I had expected you might visit me this afternoon, but I never thought it would be quite so... exciting. But I'm glad you've come, all the same. It amuses me that you suddenly defend the old traditions—you, who have sat by and done nothing while my father has turned Kmet into a Grecian wreck. Nevertheless, I'm sure you and I agree on the importance of upholding some of the old ways."

As he spoke, the crowd Psamtik had assembled crept out from behind their sheltering pillars. Rhodopis hung well back, pressing close to Aesop, uncertain whether Khedeb-Netjer-Bona would call her out. Surely the chief wife had greater concerns now—or so Rhodopis prayed.

Psamtik gestured curtly with the crook sigil. One of his guardsmen strode around the dais, making for the curtained anteroom behind the Horus Throne. There was a muffled sound of frightened weeping, the scuff of reluctant sandals against the stone floor—and then the guard re-emerged, leading four more of his fellows. Each pair of guards held a young woman between them—girls, really, their youth and inexperience evident in their wide eyes and tear-streaked faces. Rhodopis recognized them at once from her time in Amasis' harem. They were Khedeb-Netjer-Bona's daughters.

When the chief wife saw her children, caught as she was between two of Psamtik's men, she ceased her struggles.

Outwardly calm, showing nothing of the turmoil that must have wracked her spirit, she stared up at Psamtik on the Horus Throne.

"What do you mean by this, King's Son?"

Psamtik shrugged, a languid and haughty movement. "The old ways. You know of what I speak. In generations past, when Kmet was its true self, the heir to the throne was strengthened in his righteousness by marriage to the King's Daughter."

Khedeb-Netjer-Bona darted a glance at her eldest daughter. The girl was near Rhodopis' own age—sixteen, perhaps seventeen, but no more. She quailed in the grip of her guards, chin shaking and eyes welling with fresh tears as Psamtik gazed down at her, unblinking.

"You can't have Tjenmutetj," Khedeb-Netjer-Bona declared.

The older girl whimpered and cast a desperate look at her younger sister.

"You won't have Ta-Sheren-Iset, either," the chief wife said. "They are not for you."

"They are for whoever holds the Horus Throne. That has been the Kmetu way for thousands of years."

"It has never been the Kmetu way to usurp the Horus Throne from a still-living Pharaoh," Khedeb-Netjer-Bona retorted. "If you can justify this outrage, then you have always been a pretender to the old traditions."

"I have ever been loyal to old traditions," Psamtik flared. "It's you and my father who have neglected the proper order, the righteousness of ma'at. Kmet has paid the price for too long. I have come to set our nation to rights. And I will begin by marrying the last king's daughters—both of them—as is our people's royal custom."

Both girls broke into unrestrained sobs. "Help us, Mother, please," the elder girl wailed, while Ta-Sheren-Iset, the younger, looked as if she might crumple to the floor if the guards weren't holding her up. Rhodopis' heart beat painfully in her chest as she watched the girls weep, struggling weakly against their terrible fate. Ta-Sheren-Iset was thirteen at most —not much older than Aella would be now, and the same age Rhodopis had been was when she was carelessly wagered away by Iadmon.

I can't allow him to hurt those poor girls.

The King's Daughters had never been particularly kind to Rhodopis when she had lived alongside them in the harem. Nevertheless, the thought of Psamtik doing to any other woman what he'd done already to Rhodopis burned her to the core of her heart.

What have I stayed in Memphis for, if not to help girls like Aella —girls like these?

But what could she do against Psamtik and all his power?

Psamtik raised his voice over the sobbing of the trapped King's Daughters. "The rest of the women in the harem are mine now, too. I claim them; I possess them. You will tell them as much, Khedeb-Netjer-Bona, as is your duty. Make my will known."

"I will do no such thing," she said coolly. "They are still the wives and concubines of Amasis, for as long as he lives. And when he dies, they will be free to leave the harem and return to their families, if that is what they wish. That is the *old way*, Psamtik. That is ma'at."

"They will choose to stay." Psamtik's cruel smile chilled Rhodopis' blood. What means did he have of manipulating the harem women, she wondered. Would he threaten their children, as he did now to Khedeb-Netjer-Bona? Would he menace their mothers and sisters, who lived beyond the palace walls in the elegant districts of Memphis?

"Amasis still lives." Khedeb-Nether-Bona's voice broke subtly, betraying her rising desperation.

"For now. He won't last much longer."

"How can you know that?" As understanding dawned on

her, the chief wife jerked again in her guards' grip. "Unless this is all your own doing! You've poisoned Amasis. You've attacked the Pharaoh!"

Rhodopis and Aesop exchanged a silent look, laden with meaning. It filled Rhodopis with a terrible thrill of triumph—and sickening certainty—to hear her own suspicions spoken aloud by another. She was more convinced than ever before: Amasis truly had been poisoned.

And by his own son, too, gods help us all.

"I will not be insulted by your foul accusations," Psamtik said, coldly amused. "Guards, remove this offensive woman from my presence."

"Where are we to take her, my king?"

Psamtik paused for a moment, considering—toying with Khedeb-Netjer-Bona in her fear and desperation. "Take her to the Temple of Horus. It's there she'll be tried by the priests when the time comes—when the old Pharaoh goes down to the Duat, and there are none left to question my right to the throne. Let the priests keep her confined until I am ready to deal with her myself."

Khedeb-Netjer-Bona tried in vain to break free from the soldiers as they dragged her down the length of the throne room. The long hall filled with Psamtik's laughter and the hopeless cries of the King's Daughters. When Psamtik dismissed his audience to spread the word of his rise, the haunting sound of the girls' weeping seemed to follow Rhodopis all the way back to her chamber in the diplomats' wing.

9

SMOKE AND TWILIGHT

THE MOMENT THE DOOR TO THEIR QUARTERS CLOSED, AESOP turned to Rhodopis with a strained and urgent expression. "Right. I'm going to write out our message to Babylon—no time to be clever and disguise our meaning—and then I'll carry it directly to our messenger. There's no more time to delay, not even another hour; that much is plain."

Rhodopis pulled the stopper from his vial of ink and handed him a writing brush. "And after the letter is sent?"

"Then I'll take you straight to Iadmon's estate. You can shelter with him until I've arranged safe passage out of Memphis for both of us. And," he added sternly, "I'll hear no arguments about it."

"You'll get no argument from me—not anymore. Khedeb-Netjer-Bona recognized me."

Aesop froze over his papyrus. "Are you sure?"

"Dead certain. She would have done more—called me out in front of Psamtik, and the gods know what else besides—if her men had won that fight."

"Then there's no telling what she might say at the Temple of Horus—or to whom she might speak."

"Back to Iadmon's, then," Rhodopis agreed briskly.

She headed for the little side chamber where her sleeping mat and clean servant's tunics waited. Those simple garments were the only possessions left to her—those, and the blood-stained kerchief she had received from the baker.

"Am I to go to Iadmon as your slave, or as Doricha?" she asked as she pressed her clothing into a compact bundle.

"Iadmon will take you in as Doricha, provided I explain everything to him." Aesop never looked up from his letter as he spoke. "He trusts me. He'll keep you hidden and safe until we can both get out of this mess."

The diplomats' wing lay far from the bustle of the palace, yet the sounds of unrest still carried into their chamber. The hoarse shouts of men seemed to split the air from all sides, and the ring of clashing blades shivered all too often across the grounds. Now and then, Rhodopis could hear women screaming or weeping. Were they palace servants or girls she had known in the harem? Either way, the cries reminded her of Khedeb-Netjer-Bona's daughters struggling hopelessly against the guards who had held them. She closed the shutters on the garden window, but that did little to stifle the noise, and nothing to loosen the knot of fear inside her chest. Rhodopis had never known Memphis at peace—it had been a cauldron of boiling conflict from the moment she had first set foot on Iadmon's stone quay. But now, with Psamtik on the Horus Throne, the city seemed on the verge of eruption into madness. She could feel the tension building, pressing at the city's seams, threatening to rip through.

It took only minutes for Rhodopis to wrap up her tunics and adjust the ties of her sandals. "Let me pack your scrolls while you go on writing," she said to Aesop. "I'll do it more neatly this time than I did the day of the fire."

By the time Rhodopis had secured Aesop's things inside the

basket, he was waving his hand above the small piece of papyrus, drying its ink.

The papyrus wasn't even as long as a girl's hand, and no more than two fingers wide. "It seems such a small thing," Rhodopis said.

"It must be small. Any larger, and it would tire the pigeon. Let us hope the bird flies fast and evades all the falcons between here and Babylon. I don't have time to make more copies, though I suppose we can send more from Iadmon's estate, once we've arrived. He used to have some birds trained for Babylon. I don't know whether he still keeps them—Iadmon never communicated with any merchants in Babylon, all the years I served in his household—but if he's gotten rid of the pigeons, he'll know someone who still keeps Babylonian birds."

Aesop rolled the letter tightly and tucked it into the basket. Then he shouldered the load himself.

"Merciful gods," he said, wincing. "Why didn't you tell me this thing is so uncomfortable to carry?"

Rhodopis gave him a shaky smile. "A slave can't talk back to her master. Come on; the sooner we've left this place, the better."

The corridor of the diplomats' wing was empty, save for an unsettling drift of smoke. Rhodopis couldn't discern where it had come from—perhaps it was only from the outdoor fires of a nearby kitchen—but its presence brought memories of the beer-shop riot forcibly to mind. She hugged her bundle of clothing tighter against her chest and followed Aesop swiftly from the corridor.

As they made their halting way through the palace grounds, they attempted to avoid the more populous areas—the porticoes and gardens where servants gathered, consulting one another in urgent voices, and the long halls that rattled with the sound of bronze on bronze and the coarse shouts of soldiers. Aesop dodged and turned without notice, threading the most secretive route he could find from the diplomats' wing to the scribes' quarters where their Babylonian messenger waited. Now and then they paused, half hidden by vine-veiled arbors or covered by the shadow of a soaring gateway, and watched as a tangle of men fought their way across their path. Aesop surged forward as soon as the way was clear, and Rhodopis scuttled on his heels, hunching her shoulders reflexively, braced for an attack.

Starting and stopping, running and hiding, they straggled across the palace grounds into territory Rhodopis began to recognize. The angry shouts of dozens of women filled the air; above a line of dwarf sycamore trees, she could see the distinct, red-painted roofline of the harem quarters.

Aesop ducked into the shelter of a bed of tall white lilies, and Rhodopis followed. A handful of soldiers jogged across the path, intent on a skirmish Rhodopis couldn't see, but could certainly hear—the clang of bronze swords and the curses of men shivered through the evening air.

"The scribes' chambers are just across this courtyard," Aesop said when the pack of soldiers had passed. "Around that bend. Let's go—quickly, now."

They rounded the curve in the path, and a low, plain building appeared before them. It was humble; the painted bands on its entry pillars were simple, and even in the twilight, Rhodopis could see that the pigments had long since faded. But she could hear many men inside; the palace scribes were frantically coordinating their work, arranging their letters and sending for runners who could carry word of the day's events down into the city.

"Our man is in there." Aesop nodded toward the scribes' quarters. "Or he should be, gods willing. Let's go in quickly, and—"

A handful of men burst from cover, roaring as they charged

toward the scribes' building. Rhodopis and Aesop leaped back together, cringing once more in the cover of a garden bed. They watched from their hiding place as another faction of guards emerged from around the corner of the building.

A tall, blocky man led the newcomers. He had a distinctive scar on his left cheek; Rhodopis recognized him at once. She had seen him often enough in Khedeb-Netjer-Bona's company. He was Si-Amun, leader of the chief wife's personal guard. Now that Khedeb-Netjer-Bona was imprisoned, Si-Amun seemed bent on wreaking vengeance in the chief wife's name. His sword dripped blood along the garden path, and his face was contorted by a snarl, made all the more terrible by the pale scar that puckered the flesh of his cheek.

"Drive back the usurper's dogs!" he shouted to his men. They surged forward as one, hacking wildly at Psamtik's men.

The faction of the King's Son retreated almost at once, several of them clutching new wounds. Si-Amun paused for a moment at the mouth of the scribes' quarters, surrounded by his men, who jeered after their quickly defeated foes.

"They're driving Psamtik's soldiers back." Rhodopis couldn't keep the thrill of hope from her voice.

Aesop shot her a quick, grave look. "Don't be too sure about that. We can't say what may be happening elsewhere in the palace. Come along; we must hope these men will allow us through to the scribes."

As they approached the pack of soldiers, Aesop raised his hand in greeting. "Well done, loyal men. We serve the true Pharaoh, Amasis, may the gods preserve him. If you please, we must step inside. Only for a moment; I have need of a certain scribe—"

As Aesop spoke, Si-Amun glanced at them dismissively and looked away, returning his attention to Psamtik's retreating men. But then he snapped back to stare at Rhodopis, narrowing his eyes suspiciously.

"I know you."

Rhodopis swallowed, edging backward.

"I know you," Si-Amun insisted again. "You were in the harem—"

She shook her head.

"My slave, Isa," Aesop said smoothly. "If you saw her in the harem, she went there at my command, working on my behalf."

"No," Si-Amun said slowly. His brow fell into a thoughtful frown. "You were one of the Pharaoh's girls. Red-gold hair... I remember."

Some swift instinct whispered in Rhodopis' ear, and she obeyed it without question. Recalling the distinct sound of the Persian tongue, she spoke in a feigned accent—but the quiver in her voice as all too real. "I am sorry, Good Man. You are mistaken." She dropped her eyes and turned her face to the ground so that the guard could see little more than the stubble-covered crown of her head. "I am only a slave."

"Isa has been with me for several years," Aesop said. "She must bear a resemblance to some other woman."

Si-Amun took one step toward Rhodopis, then another. His sandals, dulled by dust and spattered with blood, edged into her line of sight. "I could swear—"

"Ah!" Aesop exclaimed suddenly, turning away. "There's the scribe I intended to meet. He's not in his quarters, after all. Heading for the gate, it seems. I must hurry along now, and catch him before he leaves the grounds. This message is far too urgent to wait for his return. Gods protect you, loyal soldiers!" Aesop bowed hastily and took Rhodopis by the arm. "Come along, now, Isa—and quickly, too."

They hurried away from the scribes' building before Si-Amun could speak again, or reach out to stop them.

"May this whole palace be damned," Aesop grumbled as they headed toward the high, square-topped gate.

"I'm sorry," Rhodopis said. "I only saw him a time or two

when I was in the harem. I would never have thought he'd be the one to recognize me, of all the people in this palace. But still, I'm sorry."

"It wasn't your fault. Neither would I have suspected that ox of a man could have such a sharp memory—and at a time like this, when the world is about to catch fire."

"Do you truly see our messenger?" Rhodopis asked, craning her neck, stretching to see over Aesop's shoulder.

"No; that was only a fabrication so we could get away from that brute with our skins intact. I've changed the plan."

"Again?"

Aesop hitched the basket higher on his shoulders. "One does what one must. We're leaving the palace right now. It's far too dangerous to remain another minute. We'll sort out the question of who's to send our message to Babylon when we're under Iadmon's roof, and safe."

Rhodopis and Aesop pressed on toward the palace gate, but the skirmishes between soldiers only grew more numerous—and more vicious—the closer they came. Little by little, one reluctant step at a time, they were pushed eastward, toward the grounds of the harem.

They paused beside a statue of some long-forgotten Pharaoh, crowding between the carven stone and a thorn-bristled shrub growing alongside.

Rhodopis despaired as she panted for her breath. "The gate seems farther away now than ever before."

"We can wait here and hope the fighting dies back... or we can hope it moves to some other sector of the palace."

She was about to reply when the general din surrounding the harem rose in pitch and intensity. The women were screaming now—not in fear or pain. Their anger—their searing, flame-hot rage—was plain to be heard.

"Something is happening in the harem," Rhodopis said, turning toward the sound.

Aesop laid a hand on her shoulder. "We can't help them."

"But listen to them, Aesop! Psamtik's men must be—"

"Whatever Psamtik's men are doing, we can be of no aid. Look at us: we are only two, and unarmed." He paused, listening to the furious screeches of the Pharaoh's women. "But that caterwauling might be distraction enough to allow us to slip past all these soldiers unnoticed. The gate isn't far."

There was no time to argue. Rhodopis followed Aesop as he trotted across the courtyard and rounded the edge of a portico. The wall of the harem quarters stood before them. A pack of Psamtik's men waited there, laughing and shouting at the women who had arrayed themselves shoulder-to-shoulder across the mouth of the gateless entry. More women clustered along the wall's upper edge, slinging stones and even pieces of fruit down into the crowd of soldiers. The men raised buckler shields above their heads, deflecting the women's missiles with casual unconcern.

"Bring back the chief wife!" one of the women cried.

Another shouted, "Down with Psamtik!"

"We will never submit to the usurper!"

"We will never be his!"

One of the women in the mouth of the entry hurled a fist-sized stone into the crowd of soldiers. A man's pained shout rose above the cacophony; in retaliation, two soldiers leaped forward and seized one of the harem girls from the gateway. Rhodopis gasped as Aesop led her past the distracted troops. She knew the woman whom the soldiers had caught: it was Nebetiah.

"We'll bring you shiftless whores to heel!" a soldier bellowed. He drew his sword while his mates turned Nebetiah about and held her before him. The man lifted his blade.

"No!" Rhodopis cried, but her voice was lost in the roar of the crowd.

The soldier struck, but only with the flat of his blade. Still, the smack of bronze against Nebetiah's back was loud and sharp. She screamed, twisting to free herself from the men who held her. The next moment, Aesop and Rhodopis had passed the jeering pack of soldiers and the gateway to the women's quarters. The dreadful sight was behind her, but Rhodopis could still see Nebetiah's face contorted in pain when she squeezed her eyes shut over tears.

"Look," Aesop said breathlessly.

Ahead, near the vine-covered corner of the harem wall, a few women had gathered, pressing themselves into evening shadows. Children milled around the women's legs, clinging to their mothers, hiding their faces against pleated skirts.

"There's a small door in that corner of the wall," Rhodopis said. "I remember it. It was always guarded from above—a soldier patrolling the wall. But the guard must be elsewhere tonight."

"Fighting to keep Psamtik's men at bay, I presume. Come; let's join them. A group with children might pass through the gate more easily than two people alone."

There were perhaps ten women huddled in the shelter of the vines. Every one of them shepherded at least one child. The women's faces were tear-streaked, their eyes red-rimmed with terror. But they did not weep now. Each one was grim and quiet, determined to escort the children to safety.

"They're the mothers of the harem," Rhodopis said as she and Aesop approached. "And I'll wager they're trying to get the children out of the palace." She had never forgotten what Khedeb-Netjer-Bona had said about young male lions. Surely the mothers of the harem knew the threat Psamtik posed to their little ones.

As Aesop and Rhodopis approached, the women shrank back against the wall, gathering their children closer—but they relaxed subtly as Aesop spoke.

"We're no friends of the usurper. You're making for the gate, aren't you, my ladies?"

"Yes," one of the women said. Rhodopis recalled her—Mutnedjmet, a quiet woman who had always kept to herself, never joining in the other women's gossip. She held a girl of about three years on her hip. "We must wait a moment longer. One more mother is coming with her two sons. Our sisters at the gateway are a distraction—cover, so we might make it to the gate unnoticed. But I don't know how much longer they can keep the attention of Psamtik's men."

"We'll join you, if you'll allow it," Aesop said. "We, too, are trying to reach the gate."

"Let us pray we make it there safely."

As Mutnedjmet muttered those dark words, the last woman appeared. She was older than Rhodopis had expected—forty years or more. She slid through the corner door, then stood back, beckoning her sons to follow. When they emerged, red-faced and with downcast eyes, Rhodopis nearly gasped in surprise. They were practically men—fifteen years old, at least—and they were so much alike they could have been clay figures pressed from the same mold. What was more, their near-identical faces struck her with a bolt of familiarity. She must have seen them before, when she had lived in the harem... but surely she would have remembered meeting twin boys so close to her age.

Mutnedjmet turned to the newly arrived mother. "Thank the gods you got away safely, Muyet. You're the last, aren't you?"

"Yes. I couldn't get the boys to follow me, but there is no one left behind now. We've accounted for all the children."

Rhodopis blinked. *Muyet*. Where had she heard that name before?

"We aren't children," one of the twins said in a breaking voice. "We should be fighting with the other men."

"Yes," the other boy added. "We aren't Amasis' sons, in any case. We aren't in the same danger as the little ones."

"Keep quiet," Muyet snapped. "Do you think Psamtik will stop and ask who fathered whom before he strikes? Of course not. You'll do as I say, and I'll hear no more about it."

Rhodopis stared at the boys. *Of course.* It was Phanes' features she saw on the twin boys' faces—it was Phanes she had recognized. These could only be his sons, grown now almost to manhood—and Muyet was his lost, beloved wife, taken into the harem by the envious Amasis. She burned with longing to take Muyet by the hand and tell the woman that her rightful husband still lived—indeed, that he would return to Egypt soon, if all went according to plan. But before Rhodopis could move toward her, Mutnedjmet boosted her small daughter higher on her hip and gazed around the gathering with a stern, commanding air.

"Now's the time," Mutnedjmet said, silencing the murmurs among her troop of women and children. "Stay together, everyone—and under as much cover as you can manage. If you're separated from the rest, keep heading toward the gate, no matter what may come, no matter whom you encounter. We must reach the outer gate at all costs."

The women and children hurried away from the harem grounds with Aesop and Rhodopis hard on their heels. They encountered no more packs of soldiers—neither Psamtik's nor the Pharaoh's. But when they arrived at the palace gate, they found the massive, bronze-strapped doors barred shut. A line of the king's soldiers stood arrayed across the gate's breadth.

Grim and pale, Mutnedjmet handed her child to another woman and stepped forward. "You must let us out," she said to the soldiers.

A guard detached from the line and came forward to meet her. Rhodopis recalled him—Thales, the one who had searched her basket of scrolls. The one who had considered stealing Aesop's silver.

"My lady," Thales said, "no one is to pass through the gate in either direction. Pharaoh's orders."

"Be sensible," Mutnedjmet replied. "These are the king's children. If Psamtik overthrows you, these little ones will be doomed."

"Psamtik won't overthrow anyone," Thales said lazily. "Amasis is the Pharaoh; the gods are on his side."

Muyet raised her voice. "Talk sense, you great fool! We're only trying to protect our children."

"You've no need to leave the palace. The Pharaoh's guards will protect your children; that's our duty."

"Then do your duty!" Muyet cried. "Let us out!"

Mutnedjmet, thin-lipped and pale, gestured for Muyet to subside. "Surely you can see sense in letting the children go," she said to Thales. "I'm sure you're right, and Psamtik will not prevail, but... think of this as an extra precaution. It does no harm to see these innocents clear of the fighting."

"I will not open this gate," Thales said. "Not for you or anyone else—not unless I hear differently from Pharaoh Amasis. Now return to the harem and remain calm."

A few of the women began to sniffle—then to weep openly. Soon the youngest children were wailing, frightened by the flagging spirits of their mothers.

"Hush, hush," Mutnedjmet said desperately, struggling to hold her little group together. To the guard, she said, "Have you no heart—no sense of decency? These are defenseless children!"

As Mutnedjmet and Thales went on arguing, Rhodopis turned to Aesop, tears clouding her sight. "Can't we do something to help them—anything?"

"I'm afraid we cannot," Aesop said. "Unless Amasis gives the order to open the gate, this brick-headed creature won't let anyone through. There's no point in arguing. We should go back to the diplomats' wing."

"And leave them here, helpless? All these mothers and little ones?"

Aesop took her hand. "I don't like it any more than you do. But we can do nothing to convince this man to change his mind. Remember the role we must play—what we're trying to accomplish."

"I don't care about that now! I want to help them. There must be some way—"

Aesop pulled her away from the gate—away from the sobbing children and their weeping mothers, away from Muyet, who, beyond Mutnedjmet's control, now hurled insults at the line of guards.

"Let me go," Rhodopis cried wretchedly. "I can't just leave them." *To face Psamtik, the lion.*

"Please," Aesop said quietly. "We must think of our duty and nothing else. Don't make this harder for me than it already is."

Because she saw the tears shining in his eyes, Rhodopis relented and followed her friend back into the depths of the palace grounds. But every few steps, she turned to watch the knot of desperate mothers as they huddled around their children, until at last, they were out of sight behind a haze of smoke and twilight.

BY WILL OF THE GODS

THROUGHOUT THAT TERRIBLE NIGHT, THE DIPLOMATS' WING remained forgotten by the clashing factions of palace soldiers. Its garden and quarters remained eerily at peace, an island of stillness surrounded by shouts and desperate screams and the nerve-rattling clangor of blade against blade.

Rhodopis lay curled on her sleeping mat, blanket pulled up to her chin, but she didn't sleep. All her thoughts were for the women and children of the harem—the mothers, their innocent sons and daughters, all of whom would fall prey to Psamtik as soon as he had dealt with Amasis' loyal guards. Whenever the cries of fighting died away, the memory of Nebetiah's shrieks and sobs filled the silence. Rhodopis would have found no rest, even if she hadn't been heartsick over the plight of the harem's children.

Shivering in the cool of night, she scolded herself again and again for her folly. She had been so confident, so thrice-damned convinced the gods had brought her here for a reason. But with Psamtik all but certain to take the throne, and every route from the palace barred, the only design Rhodopis could read in the gods' caprice was her own destruction. Once, in the deepest and coldest part of night, she found herself tempted to rise from her bed, walk calmly out among the fighting, and confess who she truly was to the first guard she found—surrender herself to fate. At least then, this terrible anguish of uncertainty would finally end.

It was concern for Aesop that stayed Rhodopis. If she admitted any treachery, Aesop would be presumed just as guilty as she. He had only tried to help her—and save her from her own foolish actions. Death would surely come for her—soon—but she must do her best to keep Aesop clear of the disaster she had created. She couldn't go to the underworld knowing she had led her only friend to his death, too.

By the time dawn filled her tiny chamber with pale-gray light, Rhodopis was groggy from lack of sleep and sick to her stomach from hours of fretting. It was only very gradually that she realized she could hear nothing but birdsong from the garden. All sign of the battle had died away. The palace was silent, as if it, too, had surrendered to the inevitable.

Rhodopis dressed in a clean servant's tunic and entered the main chamber. She found Aesop already awake at his writing desk. He had pulled his chlamys up snugly against the morning chill, and he toyed aimlessly with his writing brush.

"Composing our letter?" Rhodopis asked dully. The long, harrowing night had stripped away all her usual energy. Her legs trembled and she wished for something to eat—anything, so long as she might take a little strength from it. But there was nothing with which to break her fast. No doubt, the palace staff was still in a frightful turmoil after the night's fighting.

"I had thought to write to Iadmon, but I don't know what to say. Nor can I imagine how I might get my note into his hands."

"Iadmon will be all right."

Rhodopis couldn't even convince herself it was true, but still, she felt compelled to say it. She hoped the city beyond the palace walls had not succumbed to last night's turmoil, but there was no way to know, no way to find out. For all she knew, Memphis could have burned to ashes while she lay sleepless in her bed.

"There's no telling yet how the coup played out," Aesop said quietly. "If Psamtik came out on top, then every upstanding Greek in the city could be in grave danger."

"I know."

Rhodopis was about to say more, but a horn called from a nearby courtyard, brazen and sharp. She jumped and turned toward the sound. A man shouted as the horn's note died away, but his voice didn't carry the rage and desperation of the night's long fight. There was a formality to it, a cadence, though the diplomats' wing was too far removed to make out his words.

Rhodopis and Aesop exchanged a wary look, then hurried together to their door. They edged into the corridor beyond as more ambassadors appeared, each looking as sleepless and harried as Rhodopis felt. More horns sounded, distant across the palace grounds.

"What is it?" the ambassador from Kush asked peevishly. "What now?"

"It sounds like a formal summons." Aesop turned to Rhodopis and added quietly, "I have a feeling we're about to find out who came out on top." His tone said that he expected no good news.

The ambassador from Etruria appeared suddenly around the farthest pillar of the wing's small portico. His face was as red as the tassels swinging from the ends of his tightly wrapped cape; he panted as he spoke, hurrying toward the muttering, milling crowd of diplomats. "I've just come from the central courtyard! I heard the command. Every man, woman, and child on the palace grounds is summoned to the throne room. Even servants and slaves. We are to proceed there at once!"

The ambassadors' muttering rose to a commotion of peevish conversation. Angry gestures flashed throughout the group; servants and scribes went scurrying back to their masters' rooms to scrawl new letters to the countries they represented.

Aesop took Rhodopis by her arm, pulling her back into the shelter of their chamber. "There's no reason for you to go. He may have summoned every person on the palace grounds, but he can't possibly know whether one individual is missing from the crowd. I doubt he even keeps a count of all the people within these palace walls."

There was no need to specify who Aesop meant.

"Someone surely keeps a count," Rhodopis said.

"Undoubtedly. But after last night's chaos, will any steward stand at the throne-room doors and mark a tally as we file in? It's an absurd thought. People were surely killed last night, and some too injured to leave their beds, even in the face of a royal decree. Whatever count may exist can't have been amended so quickly. You won't be missed if you stay here, and there's no good reason why you should stand in the presence of that contemptible beast again."

Rhodopis turned away, staring blindly out the garden window. She hugged herself tightly, but to her surprise, she neither shivered nor shuddered. Psamtik's coup had succeeded. She was utterly convinced of it, without knowing how she knew. He now controlled the palace, the gates... and the fate of every person unfortunate enough to be caught in his web.

Distantly, half surprised at the calmness of her own thoughts, she recalled the reckless impulse from her sleepless night—the driving desire to turn herself in, to surrender to the gods' cruel and erratic whims. She still felt compelled to surrender to divine imperative, to go wherever forces far greater than she directed. Why should those dark impulses bring such serenity to her mind? To play the gods' game—to move without resistance along any path that opened before her, regardless of what lay at its end—felt as natural to her now as breathing, as good as cool, clear water. She drew a deep breath, feeling anxiety give way to the same clear-headed poise and confident readiness she'd so often felt just before the music began, and she took up the first steps of a dance. Her head still swam with disbelief and exhaustion, but she nodded to herself—to the gods—in acceptance of her fate.

Rhodopis turned back to her friend. "I'll go. I can't explain it, Aesop, but something inside me wants to see what will happen next. Something in me *needs* to see. There's nothing for me to fear in the throne room—nothing all of Egypt shouldn't fear. The crowd will be so large, and he'll be focused on whatever show of power he intends to make. He won't so much as notice me; I feel certain of that."

Aesop's brow creased with his worried frown, but he nodded in silent agreement. Rhodopis was no man's slave; she was as free now as Aesop himself. The choice was hers to make.

"We had better go," she said. "The other ambassadors are leaving."

Rhodopis and Aesop took up with the herd of diplomats as they made their way toward the throne room, hanging at the rear of the crowd. All across the palace grounds, scribes and officials, nobles and servants flowed toward the grand, ornate hall like tributaries running inevitably toward the great river. Their lives, like Rhodopis', were now Psamtik's to control.

But with every step she took, a mysterious conviction bloomed in Rhodopis' heart. She wasn't only Psamtik's, now. She belonged to the gods. She was theirs, above all others— theirs, to do with as they willed.

THE VERY AIR in the throne room seemed to crackle with tension. The ambassadors were directed to a point far closer to the empty dais than Rhodopis would have preferred. A relentless hum of frightened talk pressed on her from the rear of the room, and nearer to the dais, the acrid smell of sweat hung thick as incense smoke.

The unoccupied Horus Throne stood flanked by two gilded chairs inlaid with lapis and ivory. The chairs, intricately carved with images of winged scarabs and leaping antelopes, were humbler than the great seat of Egypt, which glowed in the lamplight, a halo of polished stone and the finest yellow gold. Yet the two accessory chairs were finer than anything Rhodopis had encountered in the wealthiest homes of Memphis. She didn't like the presence of the additional thrones. Her stomach soured with pity for Khedeb-Netjer-Bona's daughters.

When the throne room was nearly full, a steward climbed to the first step and rapped his staff against the stone. No answering hush settled over the crowd; if anything, the murmuring only rose in volume.

"By the will of the gods," the steward shouted, "I present Ankh-Ka-en-Ra, Psamtik, Lord of the Two Lands, Pharaoh of Upper and Lower Egypt!"

Shouts of disbelief—perhaps of outright denial—echoed among the chamber's pillars. Rhodopis watched the heavily embroidered curtain behind the dais ripple and stir; a moment later, Psamtik appeared, back stiffly upright, his broad shoulders covered in gold dust that glittered with his every stately step. His eyes, outlined in heavy black kohl, were narrowed with amusement above a small, triumphant smile. On his brow, he carried the tall, red-and-white double crown of Egypt. That traditional symbol of unity and peace only seemed to raise fresh protests from the assembly. Psamtik climbed to the Horus Throne and fanned out the pleats of his long kilt as he sat. Then, gazing stonily down the length of the hall, he accepted the crook and flail from the hands of a steward.

A moment later, Khedeb-Netjer-Bona's two young daughters appeared from behind the curtain. They huddled close together, cringing and wide-eyed. Their faces were freshly painted, but Rhodopis could plainly see the puffiness of their eyes. The girls' reddened cheeks spoke of the countless tears they had shed throughout the long, terrible night. They had dressed in matching gowns of red linen shot through with golden threads, their necks and arms encircled with a wealth of jewels. Each wore a cobra circlet, too—the chief wife's crown. The weight of their trappings only seemed to slow them, or to freeze them in place like rabbits frightened by a hawk's shadow. They shivered before the vast crowd, and the younger began to sniffle again.

Another steward appeared behind their backs, prodding them both toward the dais, but neither moved. Psamtik's head snapped toward them; his eyes narrowed. The elder girl gave a visible shudder and, dropping her eyes from Psamtik's, she sprang forward, pulling her sister along behind. They climbed the steps on shaky legs and settled, cringing, on their thrones.

Psamtik flicked the lapis-beaded flail casually toward the hall. "You are summoned this day to bear witness to the will of the gods. The deities of the true and ancient Kmet have made the way clear for their most loyal son. I am Pharaoh now, by the will of Lord Horus and every god of earth, water, and sky."

From deep within the hall, a man shouted, "This is not the Kmetu way!"

Psamtik smiled coolly. "Little has gone according to Kmetu tradition, for far too many years. I have been sent to right the wrongs perpetrated by my father—"

Another man cried, "Where is the chief wife?"

"Yes—Khedeb-Netjer-Bona!" a woman shouted. "Give us the chief wife, the rightful regent!"

Again Psamtik waved the staff of the Pharaoh's office, a lazy gesture. "Khedeb-Netjer-Bona is being held securely at the Temple of Horus. She is safe; you needn't fear on her account.

But she is not your rightful ruler. I am. Kmet is mine, by blood and by right of my strength."

"What has become of Pharaoh Amasis?" a man called out.

Psamtik scowled. "This shouting is unseemly, and an insult to the dignity of the throne. Silence! I will entertain no more of this insolence."

Still the crowd muttered. Now and then, shouts for Amasis peaked above the general commotion.

"Where is our true Pharaoh?"

"Give us Amasis!"

From somewhere disconcertingly close to Rhodopis, a man bellowed, "Tell us what's become of our king! Have you poisoned him?"

Psamtik lurched up from his throne. He pointed the gilded crook into the crowd, staring down from the height of the dais with a deadly glint in his eyes. Rhodopis shrank behind Aesop, wishing he were tall enough to hide her from Psamtik's view.

"I did not poison Amasis," Psamtik thundered.

The crowd came as close to jeering as anyone would dare in the presence of royalty. Shouts of opposition—even derision—crested like waves on a storm-tossed sea.

"Silence!" Psamtik cried again. His stewards brandished their staffs, a clear threat; the crowd surged backward, jostling and pressing. Panicked screams split the air as people lost their feet. But a moment later, the crowd settled, and those who had fallen were pulled upright.

A few rows in front of Rhodopis, the women of the harem stood arrayed like some terrible offering before the dais. Someone had instructed them to dress in their most expensive garb, but despite the beauty of their display, every woman's face was hard and bitter with resistance. They seemed to glare up at Psamtik as one united body, firm in their shared resolve. Rhodopis was relieved to see Nebetiah among the women, her fine jaw set and her eyes blazing with hatred. The beating the night before hadn't been serious enough to dampen her spirit.

When a semblance of quiet had returned to the hall, Muyet thrust her way to the forefront of the harem women. "Amasis still lives! No one has announced his death. Do you deny it?"

Psamtik settled on his throne again, smirking down at the harem. "If he still lives, it won't be for long. Last I saw him, his breath was rattling and the physicians had ceased trying to work their healing incantations. His sickbed has long since turned to his deathbed."

Again a man in the crowd called out, "Give us Amasis! Give us our true king!"

Muyet persisted. "If Amasis lives but is too ill to rule, then the Horus Throne belongs to the chief wife by right." She thrust a fist into the air. "This man is a usurper! He has no claim to the throne!"

Mutnedjmet stepped forward and took hold of Muyet's arm. "I apologize," she said hastily to Psamtik. "It has been a long night for all of us. Muyet isn't thinking clearly."

Psamtik chuckled deep in his chest. "Muyet—yes. I've had little to do with you over the years, but I heard about your... *insistence*... at the gate last night. You and your friends tried to escape, didn't you?"

Muyet and Mutnedjmet both fell silent, stilling under Psamtik's stare.

He went on: "I heard you attacked a guard, Muyet. Scratched his face when he wouldn't let you out. Is that true?"

"It is," she said levelly. "I would do it again. My reasons were just."

"Your reasons. Indeed." Psamtik gestured to one of his stewards; the man leaped to obey, disappearing around the dais and behind the embroidered curtain.

The crowd rippled, murmuring, wondering what was to

come. Rhodopis watched as Khedeb-Netjer-Bona's daughters paled; the younger covered her face with trembling hands.

The steward re-emerged, leading two guards as large and strong as bulls. They dragged a pair of prisoners behind them —a pair so perfectly matched, each could have been a mirror's reflection for the other. Muyet gasped, clasping her hands in front of her throat as her twin sons came stumbling to the foot of the dais. The guards kicked their feet from beneath them, and both boys fell to their knees before Psamtik, stifling cries of pain.

Rhodopis' breath froze in her throat. Though the crowd rippled with the sounds of anxious protest, she could hear nothing but Muyet's pleas for mercy and Psamtik's low, lazy chuckle of pleasure.

The creature on the Horus Throne nodded to his guards. Each drew a lash from his belt, and Muyet's words turned to a high wail of despair.

"There will be no more scratching," Psamtik said.

The lashes cut through the air, faster than the blink of an eye; the sound of knotted leather against flesh seemed to split the atmosphere of the throne room in two.

Muyet heaved a strangled sob.

"No more attempts to escape."

Again, the lashes rose and fell, drawing grunts of pain from the boys.

"No more thwarting of my will."

Crack. A cry of pain came from one boy, then the other.

"No one will challenge me."

Crack.

"No one will deny me."

Crack.

"I am your king now!"

Crack. This time, when the lash whistled through the air, red-dark drops like garnets flew from its cruel, hard knots.

Muyet sank to her knees, begging Psamtik's forgiveness, his pardon—pleading with him to take pity on a mother's heart and release her sons.

The lashes rose and fell again, tearing cries of agony from the boys' throats.

The crowd had gone silent as death, save for Muyet's weeping and the stifled sobs of Psamtik's new young wives on their thrones. The silence stretched as Psamtik gave the order for his guards to cease.

Rhodopis could all but hear the thoughts that raced through every mind in the hall. *It's bad enough, for a King's Son to claim the throne before his father has even died. That is not the Egyptian way. But this... torturing young men to obtain obedience— terrorizing mothers... this is something darker still. There is no ma'at left in the world.*

The crowd's shock at such a brutal display was evident. But Rhodopis, of all people, was not surprised. She knew what darkness clouded Psamtik's heart. She knew what agonies he was capable of inflicting, and how he gloried in the suffering of others.

The guards began to drag the twins away, and Mutnedjmet pulled Muyet to her feet, wrapping her arms around the broken woman to quiet her weeping.

Psamtik, gloating on his stolen throne, gazed after the bleeding twins for a moment, then turned to face the stunned and subdued crowd. He opened his mouth—his lion's maw— on the verge of speaking, but in that moment, the double doors at the rear of the vast chamber squealed open.

Rhodopis turned to stare, as did most other people in the throne room. Through the jostling bodies, she could just make out a single man standing on the threshold. He was simply dressed in a plain white kilt, with a green cloak pleated neatly across his shoulders. Gray had lightened the hair at his temples, and though she wasn't near enough to make out his features, Rhodopis could tell by the way he carried himself that he was a man of dignity, used to deference and respect.

The newcomer bowed toward the throne. "I apologize for interrupting your royal assembly, my lord."

"Ankhnefer," Psamtik said with some surprise. "Royal physician to the old king. Do not apologize; speak, if you have news."

Rhodopis pressed her lips together, disliking the note of gleeful anticipation in Psamtik's voice.

"The Pharaoh Amasis has gone down to the Duat," Ankhnefer said. "The old king is dead."

A sound like a sigh of despair moved down the length of the hall. It seemed to wrack every person in the room, scouring them with a wind of terrible change, leaving their minds and hearts barren.

Psamtik rose from the Horus Throne. He crossed the crook and flail before his golden chest. "The gods have spoken. Let their will be done."

II

A STARLESS SKY

ONCE THE DAZED CROWD HAD EXITED THE THRONE ROOM, AESOP turned down a small garden path that snaked away from the large central courtyard, delving into a secluded corner of the palace's perimeter garden. Rhodopis hurried after him, barely aware of the overgrown branches that reached out from hedges and rose bushes, snagging her tunic and scratching her arms. Aesop glanced around now and then, leaning this way and that to peer through dense thickets of flowers, trying to discern whether they had found enough privacy to speak.

"Our messenger is still in the palace," he said quietly as they forged on through the garden. "I caught sight of him in the crowd."

"'Course he's still here," Rhodopis replied, forgetting for a moment the imperative to speak like a refined Memphis lady. "No one got out last night, near as I can tell."

"I can take our letter to him today, I think—within the hour, provided he has gone back to the scribes' quarters. But the older the day grows, the less chance we'll have. It won't be long before desperate people begin bribing the guards to let them out: mark my words."

"There's no reason for Psamtik to keep us penned up now, is there? Amasis is dead."

"But everyone knows where Khedeb-Netjer-Bona is being held, and Psamtik is well aware that he has scarcely any support among the nobles and ambassadors. Without the ambassadors' cooperation, he will get little aid from foreign countries, should the need arise to reinforce his claim to the throne. No—until Egypt settles and learns to accept this new regime, he won't like the thought of anyone making for the Temple of Horus and convincing the priests to free the chief wife from captivity. The gates will remain officially closed... but there are side gates, smaller ports, lightly guarded. And there are guards who owe more allegiance to their coin purses than to the Pharaoh. That's always the way."

"We must write a new letter," Rhodopis said, struck by a sudden, hot bolt of conviction.

"Why? Can we spare the time? Every moment is precious now."

"Those boys—the ones Psamtik had beaten. They're the sons of Phanes."

Aesop stopped abruptly on the narrow path. He turned to stare at Rhodopis, brow creased by a perplexed frown. "Are you certain?"

"Sure as I can be. The boys look just like Phanes, at any rate."

Aesop resumed his trek through the garden, pushing ever closer to the diplomats' wing. "It will cost us time—and we can't spare a moment, just now. I can't see that it will change anything if we tell Phanes what happened here today."

"It would be a kindness," Rhodopis insisted.

"Would it be? As far as I can tell, it would only cause Phanes pain—or worry, at the very least."

"Phanes doesn't know whether his wife and sons still live, Aesop. It will do him good, to know they're well. As well as they can be, under the circumstances. Psamtik is a beast, a demon. Everything about him is inhuman, and he'll turn us all to wreckage if he can—terrify the goodness out of our spirits, beat us and torment us and *hurt* us, until we're ready to turn on one another rather than risk his wrath. If we're to fight back against him—truly fight back—we must be good to one another. We must care for as many other people as we can." She nearly choked on her words. Fear had wrapped its fist around her throat—fear for Khedeb-Netjer-Bona's daughters, for the women of the harem, for the children they hoped to protect.

Aesop paused again, watching Rhodopis soberly as she struggled to swallow her tears. "Very well," he said at last. "I believe you're right, anyhow. Faced with a creature like Psamtik, it's more important now than ever before that we remember our humanity. Come; our chamber isn't too far now. You can tell me what to write when we get there."

As they pressed on, Rhodopis composed the letter in her mind. She took no pleasure in the words she chose. Indeed, she had seldom faced tasks more distasteful. How did one describe the brutal beating of a man's sons without inflicting unnecessary pain? But as she ordered her thoughts and selected her words, she grew aware of a curious thrill deep in her chest. It was her desire to take revenge on Psamtik—the same fierce resolve she'd found in the gardens of Cambyses' palace.

If the gods did intend me to be here, after all, Rhodopis thought, cautious of her fragile optimism, *then perhaps it's to do this work. Perhaps they have made me their instrument. Perhaps I am a knife in their hands.*

She recalled with an uncomfortable flash the stab of Archidike's nail pressed against her flesh. Knives could be false —weak and breakable as human bones.

But if I don't try—if I don't do what I can, for Khedeb-Netjer-Bona's girls, and the children of the harem, and for girls like Aella, girls everywhere... yes, and boys, too...

Her thoughts drifted away there, as if her mind and heart were unwilling to confront the consequences of trying—and failing. Rhodopis understood all too well how dangerous Psamtik was. Even if she succeeded—if she proved to be a knife in truth, and not some bluff by the gods—she still might not survive.

The path to the diplomats' wing opened before them, and Aesop led the way, walking so briskly he all but ran. Rhodopis followed, the message to Phanes complete and ready in her mind. Every step seemed to solidify her resolve; each stride over the flagstones straightened her back and strengthened her will, until, by the time they returned to the chamber and Aesop took up his brush and ink, Rhodopis felt as hard and cold as iron.

The gods had brought her here—to Egypt, to the palace, into the confidence of Cambyses, King of Persia—testing her, honing her, shaping her to their purpose. She was more than a dancer, more than a hetaera, more than the many identities she had worn like masks over the course of her strange life. She had played many roles since her coming to Memphis: the slave girl, the ambitious young hetaera on the make, Charaxus' lover, Eulalia, and Lady Nitetis, the Pharaoh's Daughter. Now, though, her greatest act lay ahead. She was ready to take up the work.

Let the gods do with her whatever they would. Psamtik's days on the throne were numbered. Rhodopis would count every one.

&

SHE WOKE in the still of night, listening to a chorus of insects from the garden. No other sound disturbed the peace, though something she could not identify filled her with a vague, half-formed anxiety. The crickets and beetles sang as they did every night; now and then, from some distant part of the palace grounds, she caught the faint tones of men speaking, but there was no strain of battle in their voices.

It's only Psamtik, she told herself. *He has you on the edge of fear.*

That wasn't so, and Rhodopis knew it. She was committed to her plan, comfortable in the gods' hands, resigned entirely to her fate—whatever turns it may yet take. Something else haunted her tonight, stirring a twinge of superstition in her breast.

A light breeze moved in the garden; when it drifted in through the narrow chamber window, it smelled muddy and cool as the river bank, though leagues of city streets lay between the palace and the Nile. Rhodopis breathed deeply, considering the damp breeze, its thick touch upon her cheek. She blinked in the darkness—then her eyes widened, though there was nothing to see.

The room was darker than the best wine, blacker than kohl. Neither moon nor stars shone in the sky; there was no faint silver luminescence on the sill of her window, no touch of pale light to reveal the walls and corners of her room.

Slowly, Rhodopis pushed back her linen coverlet and rose from the sleeping mat. The strange new chill in the air raised goose flesh along her limbs; she stretched a cramp from her upper back, then located her tunic by feel, shook it hard to frighten away any spiders or scorpions that might have crept inside, and pulled it quickly over her head. She knotted the sash around her waist, then removed the little linen kerchief— the one given to her by the baker—from beneath the corner of her mattress. She tucked the square of cloth into her sash. It served no real purpose, but it was her only possession. Somehow, it seemed unjust to leave behind the only thing in the world she could call her own.

Rhodopis returned to the corner of the mattress and found the scrap of papyrus she had folded and hidden earlier that evening. She had written out the note in Aesop's absence when he'd left to find the Babylonian messenger. Her handwriting had not improved since the plea for help she had sent to Aesop from Charaxus' home; she was glad the night was too dark to read her childlike scrawl. Besides, she could still see the words of her message tumbling through her mind—could all but hear the words, as if they whispered in her ear.

Aesop,

I've gone to do the gods' bidding. I will be in the palace still, but don't try to find me. It would be too dangerous for you if you were to interfere. I will be safe, at least until the gods are satisfied. That's all that matters now.

You have been good to me. I will always think of you with love, however long I live.

I am not afraid.

Rhodopis

(your Doricha)

By feel, she found her way from the tiny servant's chamber into the ambassador's quarters. The windows were larger here, and Aesop had left the shutters open. Framed in one window was a smear of light, a patch of ill-defined silver glowing weakly in the sky. Rhodopis stared for a long moment before she realized what it was: the moon, bright and full, but hidden behind veils of heavy cloud. It struggled to send its light down to the world, and every star in the sky had been blotted out.

As a young girl in Thrace, Rhodopis had seen more cloudy skies than she could count. But years had passed since then; day or night, summer or winter, the skies of Egypt had always been clear, except for the occasional high, white daytime haze caused by a dust storm far out in the desert. No wonder this night had filled her with an eerie sense of unease.

At least her body was rested now, even if her mind was not.

Once Aesop had returned with the news that their message had been sent, Rhodopis had settled on her mat and surrendered to sleep. Soon Cambyses would know of Psamtik's coup—and Phanes would know his family still lived. She had made her decision and written her note to Aesop; the day's work was done, and all was in the gods' hands. Her sleep had been deep and healing; now, standing in a pool of weakened moonlight, Rhodopis felt stronger and more secure than she had since coming to the palace.

Against the far wall, Aesop slept soundly on the ambassador's bed. The soft, gray light brushed him, revealing his dark curls and the steady rise and fall of his chest. Rhodopis crept a few steps closer—she didn't dare go nearer. If Aesop heard her now and woke, it would be the end of her plan. He would talk her out of it, steer her onto some other course. He had been willing to give Rhodopis her way in most things these past few days, but this—this would surely be the end of Aesop's indulgence.

"Good-bye," Rhodopis whispered. "And thank you."

She watched him a moment longer, wracked by a curious pang of longing and regret. Then she turned away, blinking back tears, and left her folded note on the writing desk.

Rhodopis eased open the chamber door, slowly and carefully, fearful the sound of the hinges might be enough to wake Aesop. When there was just enough space for her slim body to slip over the threshold, she squeezed through, shut the door softly behind her, and hurried down the diplomats' corridor.

The night's unnatural darkness filled the corridor with ink-black shadows. Rhodopis felt her way from one pillar to the next, seeing little, save for a faint brush of muted moonlight along the tops of those high, stately columns. When at last she passed beneath the portico and out into the nearest courtyard, she heaved a sigh of relief. That dense darkness had pricked her with tiny knives of dread; instinct had shivered up her spine, shouting about all the dangers of the night in a voice only she could hear. Might a lion not be lurking somewhere behind her, crouched in the shadows, ready to spring? Might spirits of the vengeful dead not pursue her—or worse, a demon? Pale and stifled as the moon was, it lit the courtyard enough to make out the planes of the paving stones, the granite benches, mounds of flowering herbs in their orderly beds.

The light was sufficient to reveal a group of men and women clustered in the center of the courtyard, too. There were perhaps a dozen of them, pressed close together, murmuring fearfully as they stared up at the sky. And every last one wore the same simple tunic and sash as Rhodopis. They were palace servants.

She smiled. *It couldn't have worked out better if I'd arranged for it.* Surely this was yet another a sign that she was on the gods' path now—and they would sustain and defend her, at least until her work was done.

Rhodopis slipped to the edge of the crowd. There, she hugged her body tightly and looked up, just as the others were doing. Now that she took the time to examine the sky, she had to admit the lack of stars was shocking. A ring of feeble, bluish light surrounded the misty spot where the moon hid its face, but beyond that circle was a black void, seemingly endless.

"What do you suppose it means?" one of the women asked softly.

"The gods are displeased," a man replied. "What else could it mean?"

Another said, "Is it any wonder? No one wants that unpredictable creature on the throne."

"Be careful." This woman's voice was low and cracked with age. "There are many who do want Psamtik on the throne. It's dangerous to cross Psamtik—or any of his allies."

"Are you one of them, Neni?" the first man asked sharply. "One who wants *him* on the throne?"

"You know I'm not," the old woman replied patiently. "But I've seen more of palace life than you have, Si-Hor. You'd be wise to take my advice. Until the dust settles, keep your head down and your eyes on the floor, and do nothing to anger Psamtik or any of his supporters."

"But we can't just let him have the throne," Si-Hor said. "King's Son or no, the way he went about it was not ma'at."

One of the younger women jeered at Si-Hor. "Are you going to pull him from the throne yourself? Or do you intend to raise an army of servants to do it?"

Si-Hor pointed to the kohl-black sky. "Someone must do something. The gods have taken the very stars from the heavens!"

There was nothing to fear in a cloudy sky, even here in Egypt—Rhodopis knew that. But she couldn't deny what effect the strange phenomenon had over the native servants. She wondered whether Psamtik had noticed the surreal darkness. Had his supporters looked up and noted the eerie darkness? If they had, did they feel the same thrill of fear, the same misgivings?

"We won't be the ones to do anything about it," the old woman Neni said. "At least, none of my washer-girls. We've work enough in the laundry; we don't need to add 'Pull the usurping Pharaoh from the Horus Throne' to our list of chores. And it's time all you girls were abed. Not that any of you will sleep tonight, I dare say, now that Si-Hor and his friends have set you to wondering what this sign from the gods might mean."

"You aren't going to send us back to the wash-house now, are you?" one of the young women protested.

"Do you truly want to stand about gawping at the gods'

displeasure? Any sensible woman—or man—would go back to their bedside and pray. And that's just what you'll do now if you work for me."

Neni clapped her hands lightly; the women muttered, but began to wander away from the courtyard in groups of two or three.

Rhodopis fell in with the last of the washer-women. Neni, thick and stout in her old age, eyed Rhodopis sharply as they followed the other women.

"You aren't one of mine," Neni said. "I know all my girls."

Rhodopis thought quickly. "No, Mistress—not yet. I was told to come to the wash-house two days ago, but with the trouble and danger, I thought it better to wait."

Neni narrowed her eyes at Rhodopis. "Coming from where?"

"The harem, Mistress. I cared for the linens of the Pharaoh's wives and concubines." It was the likeliest story Rhodopis could invent, with so little time to prepare. She knew more about the harem than any other part of the palace; with a bit of luck, she thought she could give a convincing account of a harem servant's life and daily routine.

"I'd heard I might receive a few girls from the women's quarters, but when none of you showed, I assumed your mistress had changed her mind. Here you are after all. I could have done with more than one of you, to tell the truth. Well, there's nothing to be done about that now, and I shall be glad to have you, even if one girl is all I'll get. There will be plenty of work for us in the weeks ahead. With so many people forbidden from leaving the palace grounds, the wash-house will be almost as hectic as the kitchens."

Rhodopis hadn't known the wash-house had expected new servants. Surely this was another sign that the gods had arranged everything for Rhodopis—paved her path.

She said demurely, "I shall do my best and work hard, Mistress."

Again, Neni eyed Rhodopis sharply. "You're Greek."

"Yes, Mistress."

"But you speak Kmetu well. Your accent isn't terribly thick."

"I've lived in Memphis most of my life, Mistress, and have worked in the palace for three years now."

"What's your name, girl?"

"Isa, Mistress."

Neni waved her hand abruptly as if chasing away a particularly annoying fly. "Enough with this 'Mistress' nonsense. I am your mistress—you'd be wise not to forget it—but I don't require my girls to bow and scrape to me. You may call me Neni; everyone else does. But when I say jump, you're to ask how high. And then I expect you to jump exactly as high as I've specified. Do I make myself clear?"

"Yes, of course." Rhodopis nodded eagerly.

As yet, she had no idea whether the wash-house would bring her any closer to Psamtik. She had merely taken the first opportunity that had presented itself, moving as the gods directed. She must trust they would guide her straight and true. If that meant toiling with the laundry maids, she would do the work gladly. The work couldn't be more taxing than what she had done in the Stable.

"We're almost at the wash-house now," Neni said, "though I can scarcely see it without the stars to light the way. Gods, what a strange night! When we're inside, I'll light a lamp and show you to your sleeping mat. Get all the rest you can; it's 'up early' for the washing-girls, every morning. Laundry waits for no one, even in the midst of a coup."

The wash-house proved to be crowded—Rhodopis could see that much by the light of Neni's small clay lamp. Young women rolled out their mats across the floor, arranging themselves in neat rows, as Rhodopis followed Neni to the back of the room. Neni took a heavy, tightly rolled mat from a shelf and stacked a thick, folded blanket atop it.

"You'll be there, in that corner. The girl who sleeps beside you is called Teti. Wake her if you need anything in the middle of the night; she's sweet-tempered, and will show you where the chamber pots are, or anything else you require. I'm afraid that corner is the draftiest place in the house, but it's no trouble on most nights—only tonight, when it's so damnably cold and damp."

Rhodopis thanked the laundry mistress and hurried to her place. She untied the mat, rolled it out quickly, and spread the blanket over its surface. The mat was not as soft as the one she had used in the diplomats' wing, but it was scented with lavender and cedar to keep insects at bay. As she wriggled beneath the cover, Neni vanished with her lamp. The room settled into silence, broken only by the occasional rustle of women turning over on their straw-stuffed mats.

Rhodopis stared up into the perfect darkness, eyes wide with disbelief. *I've done it. I'm among the palace servants, and no one is the wiser.* Whatever would come next, only the gods could say—but Rhodopis felt certain that if she remained alert for an opportunity, by and by it would come.

It was not the light of that woke her several hours later. When she opened her eyes, she could see that morning had come, but the day was scarcely brighter than the night had been. Only the palest light filtered into the wash-house, warmly tinted but weak as a new-hatched bird. A strange sound had pulled her from sleep: a loud, sustained hissing as if the palace —as if the whole world—were surrounded by a nest of cobras.

Rhodopis sat up on her sleeping mat. She wasn't the only one; across the room, women threw off their blankets and rose to haunches or knees, shaking their heads with disorientation or muttering in sudden fear. For a moment, Rhodopis too allowed fear to shake her. What was that unusual noise—had the gods of Egypt descended upon the palace, shaking their holy iron rattles to sound their displeasure?

But in the next heartbeat, she recognized the sound. She hadn't heard it since her childhood in Thrace.

Rhodopis leaped to her feet and picked her way across the room, threading between sleeping mats, dodging blankets as the other maids tossed them aside. She was the first to reach the door, and when she pulled it open, the fresh, clean scent of rain entered like a breath of salvation.

"Mother Iset, have mercy," one of the women said.

Another asked fearfully, "What is it? What's happening?"

Rhodopis didn't answer. She stepped out into the deluge, raising her arms to the heavy sky in gratitude and acceptance.

"You, new girl," one of the others called. "Come back! Get out of that... that water."

"It might be dangerous," someone added.

Rhodopis grinned at them. Drops ran over her shaven head, down her cheeks, and into her mouth. The taste was like honey, wholesome and sweet.

"It's not dangerous," she said. "It's only rain."

"I've heard of rain," one of the girls muttered, watching the downpour with more than a little trepidation. She bit her lip for a moment, then said, "Nothing like this has happened for years—not since my mother was a little girl. It has to be a sign. The gods are angry."

"We must get out of the palace," another girl said darkly. "None of this is ma'at. We're fools if we stay."

Rhodopis turned away again. She strode out into laundry's wide, barren courtyard, arms thrown out, twirling among the fire pits where the laundry kettles would boil. The rain saturated her tunic, ran beneath her collar, trickled down her chest and spine. Dust stirred by the pounding droplets covered her bare ankles with an iron-dark grit; but as she spun and leaped among the gathering puddles, rain rinsed the dust away again.

Rhodopis laughed as she danced to the music of falling water, laughed as it washed her clean.

Let the Egyptians cower in fear. Let them murmur about the gods' displeasure. Rhodopis was no stranger to rain; she knew it for a friend, a blessing. This was a sign, indeed—and the gods had meant it just for her.

❧ II ❧

ASSASSIN

AN ADDER IN THE GARDEN

THE UNEXPECTED RAIN—A RARITY IN EGYPT, SO FAR FROM THE Delta coast—left the young women of the wash-house subdued and occasionally tearful with superstitious dread, so that Rhodopis' first day in the laundry yard was quiet and confusing. Neni was nowhere to be found, having been called off to some distant corner of the palace on business of her own. Rhodopis was left to tease out the washing process from the girls around her, who spoke little as the rain dissipated and cringed every time a drop struck their skin. But as the morning passed, she learned how to stoke the fires beneath the large, smoke-blackened kettles, and soon she and Teti, the girl who had slept beside her, were stirring their kettle with cedarwood paddles, sending plumes of steam rising into the unnaturally cool air.

Teti proved to be every bit as sensible as Neni had claimed. The girl was younger than Rhodopis, by the look of her round cheeks and large eyes—yet she alone had remained unfazed by the rain, blinking out with curiosity from the wash-house door. Teti had been the first to venture out and join Rhodopis in the yard, once the deluge lost its force and the rain had slackened to a gray drizzle. The fact that the gods never bothered to strike Teti dead seemed to encourage the other young women, who trickled out to the yard to begin the day's work, wiping tears from their faces.

Though Teti had a sensible demeanor, she seemed little inclined to conversation. It was only by watching her and the other laundry maids that Rhodopis learned the rudiments of her new duty. She quickly came to appreciate the soothing rhythm of stirring the kettle, even if her paddle was heavy and cumbersome. The warmth from the fires was welcome, too. On a normal day—warm and dry even in the midst of winter—the fires would surely prove tedious, prickling one's legs with heat and sending sweat running down the back. But now, with the unseasonable coolness of the rain, Rhodopis felt positively cozy as she worked beside the fire pit.

Teti showed Rhodopis how to gather stems from the white-flowered plants that grew in profusion around the yard. When crushed, the plants exuded a slippery, frothy sap, which bubbled in the kettles and coaxed the most stubborn stains from the linens simmering within. There was something distinctly satisfying about watching the capes and gowns release their grime into the water, to be drawn from the kettles as spotless as they day they had first been made.

But as the days passed, laundry duty lost some of its charm. Hot water chapped Rhodopis' hands almost as badly as the sap of the soapwort plants. Worse, she couldn't remove the sharp smell of sap from her skin, no matter how many times she dunked her arms in the buckets of fresh water and scrubbed with a rough cloth. Teti seemed untroubled by heat and sap alike—but then, she was a girl well experienced in the laundry yard, with calluses to protect her hands from the worst of the work. The hands of a former hetaera were soft and smooth; Rhodopis had no such luck where her skin was concerned. Her back and shoulders ached now, too—every hour, waking and sleeping. Teti assured Rhodopis that her body would soon grow used to the work; soon she would feel no pain. But when every movement brought a twinge from her overworked muscles, Rhodopis had a hard time believing what her companion said.

At least the girls of the wash-house were friendly. When the day of the rains passed without further incident, most of them forgot their fear. Another day of normal Memphian weather—clear blue sky, forceful sun—brought the rest of the girls around. They soon took an interest in "Isa," the newcomer among their ranks, and asked Rhodopis all manner of questions about the harem while they worked.

"Why were you sent away?" Teti asked in one of her rare talkative moments.

Rhodopis pushed back the edge of her light linen sun-hood so she could give her companion a sober look. "I displeased one of the highest concubines. It was a small thing if you ask me—I was clumsy, and knocked her favorite vase off a table while I was changing the linens on her bed—but that was enough for her. She had my head shaved to punish me, as if I were a slave instead of a servant, and insisted I be sent out of the harem forever."

The girls at a nearby kettle gasped with sympathy—and no small amount of delight, Rhodopis knew. She had already discerned that the life of a laundress could be tedious. Such a dramatic tale brought much-needed color to the wash yard, where everything seemed to be the same unappealing brown-gray shade of ash and dirty water.

"Did she hate you?" Neferubity asked. "Was she jealous of your beauty?"

Rhodopis blushed and stirred her kettle more vigorously. "I'm flattered if you think I'm beautiful."

"Of course you are," Neferubity said, squeezing a bundle of soapwort into her kettle. "I'm not one of those sorts who think all Greeks are bad. You're kind and funny, and pretty to look at. I like working with you, Isa."

Rhodopis let her hood fall lower, obscuring her face so the other girls wouldn't see her bashful smile.

"Tell us more stories from the harem," Neferubity said. "Give us all the best gossip you know."

Several more girls raised their voices, urging Rhodopis on. Even Teti grinned her encouragement. Rhodopis obliged, weaving stories of harem life. She found it easy to satisfy her audience's craving for adventure and romance, providing she embellished her true experiences of harem life with twists and exciting details she had gleaned from Aesop's collection of story-scrolls.

The stories even distracted Rhodopis herself—not only from the hard work in the washing yard, but from the concerns she carried in the back of her mind. At night, however, when she would fall exhausted onto her sleeping mat, all the worries she deflected by day would come crowding to the forefront of her thoughts. Life in the washing yard was pleasant enough, except for the physical toil. But the life of a laundress would bring her no closer to Psamtik: that much was clear to her now. Her world had shrunk to the wash-house and its flat, colorless yards. The laundry women seldom left their small domain, except when Neni announced their meal hours and they walked to the servants' kitchen, which was not far away. Now and then, Neni allowed the girls to explore the gardens at night, so long as they remained quiet. But Rhodopis was so weary from her work that she couldn't bring herself to go strolling with her new friends.

Yet she knew she must find some way to reach the usurper. And she must trust that the gods would make her path clear— and make their will known—once she had placed herself within Psamtik's reach. Rhodopis certainly had no plan of her own; she hadn't the faintest idea how she might carry out her work, and the puzzle grew no easier to solve, no matter how many hours of sleep she wasted tossing and turning and fretting in the darkness of the wash-house. She asked herself how far away Cambyses might be now—whether he had received her letter at all, whether he still planned to fall upon Egypt. She asked herself, but she had no answers, and the gods deigned to send neither signs nor comfort. Night after night, the last thought she had before stumbling into fitful sleep was this: *I must simply get close to Psamtik... find some way to reach him, to stand before him again. Then I reckon the gods will show me what to do.*

By her seventh day in the wash-house, Rhodopis had grown quite restless. She was not so quick anymore to tell stories of harem life, and whenever the distant sounds of a skirmish reached the washing yard—the occasional clash still flared now and then between Psamtik's men and holdovers from the old Pharaoh's court—Rhodopis would pause in her work and listen, frowning with impatience.

She stood gazing across the laundry yard, stretching a cramp from her back and listening to the far-off shouts of angry men. A line of sturdy young fellows made its way through the garden, each balancing a large basket on his shoulder. The baskets were piled high with linen goods in need of washing. By now, this strange procession was nothing new to Rhodopis. These were "Neni's soldiers," as the washing-girls called them —a troop of strapping youths who went throughout the palace, fetching dirty linen in their labeled baskets and toting their loads to the yard for cleaning. But as Neni's soldiers came nearer, Rhodopis felt her heart quicken. Their baskets had been tied with red-and-white ribbons, indicating that they boys had just come from the harem.

Rhodopis waited beside her kettle, slowly stirring the water with downcast eyes until the boldest and most amusing of Neni's soldiers approached. Djedu had a wink and a smile for every young woman in the wash-house; Rhodopis knew better than to read any special favor into his flirtations, and most days, she brushed off Djedu's advances with a shrug and a light-hearted laugh. Today, though, she resolved to draw Djedu into a conversation. Willing as Djedu always was to idle away time with a pretty girl, perhaps Rhodopis might learn where Psamtik could be found—and how a laundress might cross paths with the usurper-king.

"There's our Greek acquisition," Djedu said, swaggering to her kettle with his basket. "Our little alabaster goddess, the mysterious Isa."

Rhodopis pulled back her linen hood, giving the young man full view of her face. She allowed her lashes to flutter. "Djedu, you're a tease, and nothing more. I'm never a goddess."

"You might be. Everyone knows the gods and goddesses have golden skin. Your hair is just about the right color. I can tell, now that it's grown in some."

"You'd find a reason to compare every girl to a goddess if you thought you might get a kiss in the bargain."

"Every girl is a goddess, as far as I'm concerned." Djedu poured the contents of his basket into Rhodopis' kettle while the other laundry maids tittered and whispered.

"But you've just come from the harem," Rhodopis said. "That's what the white-and-red ribbons on your basket mean unless I'm mistaken. The real beauties are in the harem, aren't they?"

"That's so," Djedu said. "*All* the beauties are still there, too."

Rhodopis looked up quickly. "What do you mean?"

"The new Pharaoh has opened the gates again. Well," Djedu amended quickly, "some lucky souls have been able to come and go freely, providing they've made pledges of loyalty to the king... and providing he believes they are truly devoted. But I'm afraid he hasn't let any of the harem women leave the palace. I don't think they're permitted outside the harem wall, in fact. It seems he doesn't trust them."

Rhodopis swallowed a sudden lump in her throat. She said casually, "Is that so? I thought he might send that Muyet away, after the show she put on in the throne room. We all saw it... or heard, at least. I was too far in the rear of the hall to see much, but I heard Muyet shouting."

"Muyet—she's the one whose twin sons were beaten?"

"Yes, that's right." Rhodopis worked her paddle through the kettle, trying not to seem too eager for news. "If he hasn't sent her away, then what has become of her and her sons?"

"She's well enough. I saw her in the harem just today—and her sons." Djedu spoke so lightly that Rhodopis felt sure he would have leaned one arm on the rim of the kettle if it hadn't been so hot. When she caught his eye, Djedu winked and grinned at her. "Tell me, little Isa: will you walk with me in the garden tonight when all the laundry is finished?"

Giggles filled the washing yard. None of the other girls would look at Rhodopis, but their smiles, half-concealed behind their hands, reassured her that no one was envious. Djedu was like one of the tiny, strutting cockerels some priests kept as pets: all show and crow, with little else of substance.

"I might walk with you," Rhodopis said, "if you give me more news of the harem. I used to work there, and I'm all knotted up to know how the women and the other servants have fared since Psamtik's takeover."

"Ask me anything. I'll give you any honest answer I can, O goddess of the laundry kettles."

"Very well." Rhodopis stirred in silence for a moment. "Muyet's sons—were they badly hurt?"

Djedu shrugged. "They seem no worse for wear. Recovered nicely, from what little I saw of them, but they seemed as grim as everyone else in that place. No one likes being shut away, after all—especially not now that Psamtik has opened the gates again."

"And what about the little children? Are they still safe?" She offered a weak smile, though she dreaded Djedu's answer. "I used to see the little ones often when I came to tidy their chambers. I've been ever so worried about them."

"Every precious babe in the harem is snug as a kitten on a cushion," Djedu said airily. "Why, when I went to gather the linens, all the little mites were outside playing with their mothers and nurses. There's no reason to fear on their behalf."

This time, Rhodopis' smile was genuine. Contrary to Djedu's opinion, she had every reason to fear for the harem children.

If Psamtik has kept them alive, it can only be for his cruel purposes.

He must intend to use the little ones as leverage against Amasis' wives and concubines. Why else had the lion not yet savaged the cubs? The mere thought of what Psamtik might do —how he might use those innocent lives to extract the loyalty he craved from their mothers—sickened her stomach and made her legs shake with terrible urgency.

In the wake of his coup, Psamtik surely had other matters on his mind. But sooner or later, he would remember the harem. He would turn his gaze on the women and children, and none would be safe any longer.

"And what of the new king?" she asked. "Does he visit the harem often?"

"Often? I couldn't swear to it," Djedu said. "But he is expected there this evening, to visit the two new chief wives. That's why we were summoned: to haul away everything in need of washing, so the grounds and the chambers look as clean and lovely as possible. Everything must be perfect for the Pharaoh's arrival—I'm sure you know the way."

Rhodopis nodded, smiling, but would say little more. Djedu

picked up his basket and headed back across the washing-yard with an expression of faint dismay, as if he weren't quite certain whether the little Greek washer-girl had rebuffed him—and if so, what he'd done wrong.

Rhodopis wasted no time worrying about Djedu's feelings. She had learned everything she needed to know. The gods had proved themselves worthy of her trust; they had opened a way for Rhodopis, and lit the path. She could see already what she must do next.

If Djedu came to call for her that evening, he wouldn't find Isa in the wash-house. No one would find her there again.

SHORTLY AFTER MIDDAY, Neni appeared in the yard, cupped her hands around her mouth, and shouted, "Paddles down, my girls! It's time to eat."

A murmur of relief and expectation flowed through the crowd of laundresses. The midday meal was the best and largest the servants had, and though the fare was never lavish, at least it was filling. Rhodopis fell in eagerly with the others; now that she had come to a decision, a good portion of her anxiety had fled. She was ravenous, and her mood was buoyant; she chatted happily with the other girls as they trekked across gardens and courtyards to the long, low brick building that housed the servants' kitchen.

The washing-girls and Neni's soldiers took their meals together, sitting cross-legged in the shade of a great sycamore tree with their dishes of fish stew and bread balanced on their knees. Djedu seemed to avoid Rhodopis, though now and then he cast her surprisingly timid glances. She realized with some surprise that perhaps his sweet words hadn't been silly flirtation after all. Perhaps he truly had set his heart on Isa. But Rhodopis had neither the time nor the inclination to fret over

Djedu's bruised feelings. Much more important business lay ahead of her now.

When half an hour had passed, one of the girls began collecting dishes and carrying them back to the kitchen. The laundry maids stood, reluctant to abandon their rest. But as Neni had said, there was more washing to be done—always more, in a palace as full as Psamtik's still was.

Rhodopis arose with the others and brushed the dust from her tunic's hem. She lingered while the other girls headed back toward the wash-house, then joined the final few laundresses—but before she'd gone more than a few steps, she turned to her companions with a pained, embarrassed expression. She clutched her lower belly with both hands.

"I've come over bad," she muttered. "I need a chamber pot."

"It's not far to the wash-house," one of the other girls said.

Rhodopis shook her head, flushing with a show of panic. "I won't make it. I'll dash into the kitchen—they're sure to have privy pots somewhere! I'll meet you back at the yard."

"Suit yourself." Her companions giggled as they walked away.

Rhodopis turned and entered the servants' kitchen, still clutching her belly.

The cook looked up as she darkened the doorway. "What's all this, then?"

"I need a privy, Mistress. Quick!"

The cook recoiled with a grimace, then jerked her head, indicating a small, humble portico behind her. "Out in the garden, behind the jasmine trellis. Mind you cover the pot with one of those cloths when you're done! I won't have flies plaguing my kitchen. Go on; be quick about your business!"

Rhodopis darted past the cook, who tutted in annoyance. The kitchen garden was quite small, no bigger than the ambassador's quarters Rhodopis had shared with Aesop—and unwalled, except by an informal, knee-high barrier of mudbricks. Herbs grew in profusion from pots and dark-earthed beds sunk into the ground, filling the afternoon air with a heady, bracing scent. Bees hummed lazily among the small pink blossoms of rosemary and thyme.

Rhodopis found the jasmine trellis and a small collection of pots behind that sheltering screen. Soon the gardeners would come to take the pots away, spreading their contents over newly planted flower beds or burying the muck at the roots of trees—but a few unused and uncovered pots remained. Rhodopis picked one up, took a covering-cloth from a nearby stack, and draped it over the empty pot's mouth. Then she braced it on one hip, stepped over the garden's barrier, and strode briskly away from the kitchen, making for the heart of the palace grounds.

She had pulled her linen hood up to shelter from the sun; with her face turned down to the garden path, she was inconspicuous—or so she hoped. With a privy pot balanced on her hip, few would care to stop her and question her. It wasn't the cleverest disguise, but it was the best she could do on short notice, and if luck was on her side, it would have the desired effect. She only needed to reach the harem wall without Neni catching her and sending her back to her laundry kettle.

Rhodopis encountered few other people as she made her way across the palace grounds. Most were servants, going about their business without a glance to spare for the girl with the covered pot. Now and then, she approached small groups of nobles who murmured among themselves, too absorbed in their clandestine talk to notice her presence. Every time, Rhodopis stepped off the path, offering ample room for the men to pass. When they finally took note of the nearby servant, they scowled at the burden she carried and hurried by, as if fearful she might drop the pot and splatter its contents on their robes.

Luck was on her side: she encountered no one who might

know her, and soon she spotted the red-painted roof of the women's quarters. Rhodopis slowed her pace. She examined the harem wall carefully long before she reached it. Though there were no doors across the gateway, a handful of Psamtik's men paced the wall's upper edge, while at ground level, three more guards lounged in the shade of the pylons. Did their presence mean Psamtik had already arrived to terrorize his poor young brides? Or were these guards a regular feature of harem life since Psamtik's takeover?

The answer hardly mattered. Whether Psamtik was in the harem now or had yet to appear, Rhodopis knew she would find him on the path to the harem gate—coming or going. She found a young sycamore with a sturdy gray trunk, set her pot beside it, and sank down in the tree's welcome shade, watching the footpath through a tangled screen of shrubbery.

Many men and women passed, tense in the wake of Psamtik's coup or strutting with renewed confidence, depending on where their loyalty lay—but none noticed Rhodopis behind the curtain of glossy leaves. An hour slipped by—then another. She soon caught herself nodding in the afternoon warmth, eyelids heavy and thoughts muffled. Seven days in the wash-house hadn't been enough to acclimate to the strenuous work; she was still weary to her bones. It was a measure of her strength—and her faith—that she felt no fear over what must come next. The certainty that she would confront Psamtik openly troubled Rhodopis less than her aching muscles. But she couldn't allow herself to sleep, no matter how exhausted she was. Psamtik might slip by if she closed her eyes even for a moment... and then this golden opportunity would be lost forever.

The sun was sinking toward the west, mellow and slow, by the time Psamtik appeared. Rhodopis heard the footsteps of several men first—brisker than any who had passed before, with a rhythm of formality and alertness that jerked her from a drowsy reverie. She moved carefully on her knees, parting the leaves delicately with a single finger so she could obtain the clearest possible view. There was Psamtik, surrounded by four of his guards, moving with the same arrogant, powerful stride Rhodopis sometimes saw in her worst and most haunting dreams. Her heart began to pound; the skin between her shoulder blades prickled as the sweat of fear sprang up like a Thracian storm, sudden and unnerving. But she breathed deeply, clenching a fist to steady herself. The gods had brought her here—to this time and place, through all she had survived —so that she could carry out their most important work: justice. Vengeance. The restoration of ma'at. She had nothing to fear—not anymore. She was hard as iron, a blade in the gods' steady hands.

It's already going your way, she realized, flushing with a strange emotion, half excitement, half dread. *He's coming from the Pharaoh's quarters, not the harem. He hasn't been inside yet, hasn't put his hands on Khedeb-Netjer-Bona's daughters.*

Rhodopis did not doubt that Psamtik had already inflicted his foulness and violence on those poor girls at least once, but at least now she might spare them more torment.

She scuttled around the sycamore tree, rose to her feet, and took the time to stretch the cramps and stiffness from her limbs. It wouldn't do to hobble like an old crone when she approached the man. Then she stood for a moment, eyes closed, breathing in the calm air of early evening as she listened to Psamtik and his entourage draw closer.

Just as the usurper drew level with her hiding place, Rhodopis stepped from her cover onto the pathway—directly in front of Psamtik and his men. The guards' hands flew to their weapons; two were even quick enough to draw their blades before they saw Rhodopis' empty hands, held out in front of her, palms up. For a long moment, they stood frozen in that strange tableau—the girl in the servant's tunic, the guards bristling with suspicion and bronze knives, and Psamtik, the usurper-king, frowning at Rhodopis with startlement—and recognition.

"Put your blades away," Psamtik said.

Daggers slid back into sheaths. Subtly, the guards relaxed as Psamtik stepped forward.

"What in the name of Hathor's teats is this?" he growled.

Rhodopis pulled back her linen hood, exposing her short-cropped hair, its telltale golden-red hue. "Do you remember me, my king?"

"Of course I do. The little Greek slattern from my father's harem. *My* harem, now." His eyes narrowed with suspicion. "But you're back from your journey. Why?"

Rhodopis forced herself to smile up at him. "I never left—not truly. Oh, I got on the ship, just as the old king made me do. But by the time the boat stopped in Tanis for supplies, my mind was made up. I left there—the captain couldn't stop me—and made my way back to Memphis."

Psamtik waited. His frown grew deeper with each passing moment, his eyes harder.

"I had to come back... to you," Rhodopis said quietly. Gripped by an urge to swallow hard, to dispel nausea rising in her gut, she took a step toward him instead, as if she couldn't help herself—as if she was drawn to him, a bee to a flower's sweet nectar.

Psamtik's grin was slow, but Rhodopis could see the smug pride in his face, the glint of self-congratulation in his dark eyes. He believed her.

Psamtik gestured for his men to withdraw. They did, pulling back some distance along the path, so their master was left virtually alone with the young woman in the servant's smock.

"You told me," Rhodopis said, feigning breathy anticipation, "you would show me what a real man is like. A real Kmetu man. And you did. I haven't been able to stop thinking of you, my king." At least the latter part was true, even if Rhodopis' thoughts were all of revenge.

Psamtik chuckled deep in his throat. His falcon pectoral winked slyly in the declining sun.

"It's true," Rhodopis insisted, moving toward him again. So close to her attacker now, every hot pulse of instinct screamed at her to run, to put as much distance between herself and Psamtik as she could manage. But her training as a hetaera served her well. She gazed at him with wide, yearning eyes, and if she trembled, she knew Psamtik would read the desire she wished him to see, not her fear. "I knew I couldn't return to the harem. Amasis would have killed me. But I had to be near you; no other man can satisfy me. So I took up work as a servant and cut off all my hair so no one would recognize me. But you knew me, didn't you, my king?"

"Yes, I know you. I know just what you are, hot between the legs and yowling for it like a cat in heat. Whores are all the same."

With those last words, Rhodopis thought for one terrible, ice-cold moment that Psamtik would turn her away. But his hand flashed out; he seized her by the upper arm, and his grip was hard, possessive. Now her heart raced with true terror; memories of the assault crowded in, threatening to make her weep or beg for mercy. She mustn't drop the ruse now. Not when she had come so close.

It's no worse than dancing before a crowd, Rhodopis told herself. *No worse than lying with Xanthes, or any other man who repulsed me. It's all a show—only that.*

She had performed in this way dozens of times; the gods knew as much. With their strength behind her, she would battle her fears until they were exhausted, until they lay in the dust behind her. And she would give Psamtik the greatest and most convincing show any hetaera had ever performed.

Rhodopis giggled as Psamtik pulled her back along the path

—away from the harem, toward his private chamber. The two young chief wives were forgotten now; Rhodopis promised greater delights, and it seemed Psamtik was eager to partake of whatever she had to offer. His baffled guards fell into step as he headed toward the royal apartments.

Despite the fear quivering deep inside her chest, Rhodopis felt her face burn with triumph. Whatever came next was sure to be unpleasant. But she had survived this before. She was strong enough to survive Psamtik, more powerful than he or any man knew.

And now, by the grace of the gods—by dint of her quick wits—she had worked her way inside. She was in Psamtik's grip. But like a deadly adder, it was only a matter of time before she sank her fangs into his flesh.

❦ 13 ❦

COUNTING BRUISES

MIDDAY CAME, BRINGING THE RELIEF AND SOLITUDE RHODOPIS craved—the precious hours of rest she had learned to live for since she had made herself Psamtik's plaything ten days ago. She sat still on the eating couch as Psamtik left the grand apartments of the Pharaoh. Outside the door, his guards saluted; she could hear the coordinated stamp of their feet as they snapped to attention. Then, moments later, the rustle of their slow relaxation carried into the silent chamber. Psamtik was gone now, sweeping off toward the audience chamber with his small contingent of personal soldiers, ready to see to the day's business.

Reassured that he honestly was gone, Rhodopis sagged back against the cushions, sighing in relief. She pressed a hand to her forehead, struggling to control her racing thoughts, and was disconcerted to feel her fingers trembling.

Ten days. Ten days in Psamtik's chamber—in his bed, in the very jaws of the lion—and still there was no word of Cambyses. Perhaps the Persian king had thought better of invasion, after all.

If so, then it's all left to me. No one else will destroy the usurper. No one can.

Hastily, she gathered a few items from the remains of the breakfast she had shared with Psamtik: a crust of bread, a slice of melon with sweet, orange flesh. Psamtik kept no incense in his apartments, as far as Rhodopis knew. If he had any, he likely would have made Rhodopis suffer if she had presumed to use it without his permission. The only offerings she could make to the gods were these bits of food gleaned from breakfast trays. It was a poor substitute for sweet smoke and the chants of priests, Rhodopis knew. But she had to believe the gods heard her prayers, all the same.

Rhodopis hastened out into the Pharaoh's garden, a magnificent spread of shade trees and climbing vines, fountains and reflecting pools carpeted in sweet lotus blooms. She found her way to a little patch of ground she had adopted as her own, a grass-carpeted sward of pond-side shadow, hardly wider than the length of her body. The tiny glade was screened on one side by a trellis of climbing roses that blocked the palace entirely from her view. There—and only there—she could convince herself for a few blissful minutes that she was not in the palace, that Psamtik had vanished from the world like morning mist. There, she could tell herself all was well, and she was safe.

Every day, when Psamtik left to see to the business of the throne, Rhodopis visited her private glade, hugging her knees to her chest as she watched insects with shimmering wings dance above the pond's surface. Sometimes she would sleep, when Psamtik's demands the night before had left her tired and aching—and then, she would wake only to the gentle calls of birds in the nearby trees, or to the feel of rose petals drifting down from the trellis to caress her face and shoulders. Beside the quiet pond, she could quell her fears, banish her anxiety, and rule once again as mistress of her own heart and mind.

But ten days had passed. Ten long, agonizing days and

nights; Psamtik had used her however he pleased on each and every one. Even when her monthly flux had come, he had taken her to his bed to play his games of pain and humiliation. Rhodopis had no relief, but every moment she was awake—save for these few quiet hours in her hidden glade—she remained alert for her next opportunity. Surely, she thought, the gods must open a door for her soon.

Rhodopis sank to her heels and crumbled the bread, then cast it down at the pond's edge. She placed the slice of melon at arm's length, and waited, silent and perfectly still. Within moments, the birds arrived to peck her meager offering. She had no smoke, no copal or sweet myrrh to send up to the heavens. But birds could fly. They could come and go from the palace grounds as they pleased, carrying her prayers to the sky. Bitterly, she remembered watching the birds from the confinement of Charaxus' estate. Not even a month had passed since she had slipped from Charaxus' hands, and yet those days seemed clouded by a distant past.

"Please," she whispered as the tiny creatures hopped and fluttered among her offering. "Please keep me strong. Let me endure. I don't know how much longer I can last."

When her prayer had finished, and the melon rind had been picked clean, Rhodopis stretched out on her back, watching the midday sun dazzle through the leaves and blossoms of the rose trellis. The grass tickled her neck, but she made no move to scratch. She only watched the sun make its slow progress through the roses. Flares of golden light stabbed her eyes until tears welled up and ran.

Not for the first time, Rhodopis asked herself whether she could still claim sanity. This idea must have been borne of madness; it had undoubtedly been ill thought out. When she had decided to find her way to Psamtik, Rhodopis had known she was likely to end up in his bed. But she had thought herself better prepared for the work, had presumed she would be able to call upon a hetaera's professional detachment and go about her business as she had done countless times before. But Psamtik was different from the clients she had entertained. He was the beast of nightmares, looming in the waking world again. Though Rhodopis hadn't broken—not where Psamtik could see; indeed, the smile had never slipped from her face— every time he touched her or pushed her down across his bed, she felt her spirit crack a little more, felt a scream of desperation building in her chest. She didn't know how much longer she could force herself to silence.

Far across the garden, Rhodopis caught the distant sound of children's laughter. A poignant throb shuddered through her body, wracking all her limbs at once. The children were still in the harem, still living—as were their mothers. As for Khedeb-Netjer-Bona's daughters, Psamtik had left them entirely alone, as far as Rhodopis could tell. For the time being, the new Pharaoh seemed interested in Rhodopis alone—as if by abusing and insulting her spirit and flesh, he was enacting some gleeful vengeance on Greece itself, on every Greek who still dared to inhabit his country. The sick pleasure he took in using Rhodopis had kept him distracted from other delights.

At least I've accomplished that much, Rhodopis thought. *I've kept him away from those more vulnerable than I.*

But for how much longer could she hold Psamtik's attention? Sooner or later, he would tire of Rhodopis. She knew as much; any fool could see it. When he decided to be rid of her, casting her away like a child's broken toy, he would turn his cold stare on the harem once more.

"Show me the way, gods," she whispered to the sun. "Make my pathway clear, before it's too late to save the innocent."

Despite the day's warmth, a chill stole across her flesh. She hugged herself where she lay, but as her hands pressed tight against her upper arms, she winced in pain, then lifted one arm to examine it. Blue-and-purple bruises had appeared, spotting her pale skin. Last night, when Psamtik had handled her more roughly than ever before—except for that first night, in the sapling grove—she had known the bruises would come. Their presence seemed a grim confirmation of her worst and most nagging fears.

The birds scattered, leaving the glade empty, save for Rhodopis. With her arm held high above her head, she rotated her wrist this way and that, counting the ugly splotches on her skin. Ten on her right arm—she noted the number with dark amusement. One for every day she had spent trying to serve the gods. One for every day she had sent up her prayers and what little else she could offer; one bruise for every day of hope that had faded behind her.

She pressed one blue-black circle hard with a forefinger; pain tensed the muscles of her arm, but she pressed harder still until the pain seemed to sing along every nerve, a chorus calling out from every secret, outraged part of her body.

I didn't come here to fail, she told herself or the gods—if the gods cared to listen. *I knew in Persia that I'd make Psamtik pay for what he did to me. I knew I would bring him low.*

Nothing had changed. The monster of her darkest, most persistent terrors was real—as real as her marred flesh. But she was stronger and cleverer than Psamtik ever could have known.

She pressed another bruise, jabbing it hard. Her face flushed at the leap of pain. She recalled the beer shop below Aesop's humble little home—how it had burst into an unquenchable blaze all at once, fueled by the barrels of wine within. Every bruise, every violation was another barrel of wine stacked within Rhodopis' heart—laden with fuel, waiting for the spark that would ignite her and burn Psamtik to ashes.

Rhodopis lowered her arms and relaxed in the grass, watching the sun's progress more calmly now. The tears had dried on her cheeks; the scent of roses was sweet and comforting. She breathed deeply, drinking in the perfume, and watched as the small, dark garden birds rose to a clear blue sky.

AS THE SUN began to decline, casting a warm hue across the garden and lengthening the shadows of the trees, Rhodopis reluctantly abandoned her refuge. Psamtik would return to his quarters soon, having finished the day's work; at the end of duties, his moods were often as sharp as his hunger. Soon Rhodopis would wear new bruises on her skin, livid and fresh among the older marks, which were already aging to an ugly violet-brown. She shuddered as she walked back toward the Pharaoh's chambers, but she knew that every evening Psamtik spent with her—instead of the poor women trapped in the harem—was a secret victory. She could endure a while longer —however long was required. She was stronger than Psamtik, stronger than even the gods knew. If now and then her fear rose too fast for her to quell it, and if she sometimes cried at night while Psamtik slept contentedly beside her, what of it? Her strength would rise again like a bird on the wing.

Forget that there are falcons in the sky. Forget that they strike small birds from the air and rip their flesh with their talons.

She entered the Pharaoh's apartments just as Psamtik arrived. Across the central room, already draped with the violet shadows of evening, he saw her coming in from the garden and smiled, lazy and satisfied. The sight raised a chill on Rhodopis' skin, as his smile always had. But again, her hetaera's training served her well. She gave no sign of discomfiture but simpered at Psamtik with a flirtatious air.

"Back from the audience halls so soon?"

Psamtik grunted as he entered his bedchamber. She could hear him opening one of the cedar chests that held his many garments. Whispers of silk and linen came to her as he rummaged through his belongings.

"I've no time for your insatiability, you cheap whore," Psamtik said. "Not just now. There's a whole group of fools who wish to swear their loyalty to me within the next hour. But this heavy kilt has become unbearable, and the evening shows no sign of cooling off. I need a change of clothes before I can stand to listen to their mewling."

"Shall I send for your body servants? They can dress you, and—"

"No. There's no time. You'll have to do it; get in her at once and make yourself useful."

Rhodopis hurried into the chamber, averting her eyes from the bed—the place where so many outrages had been inflicted upon her flesh. Psamtik held up a length of red silk, embroidered along one edge with a motif of bees and sedge flowers. Rhodopis took it from his hands, folding and aligning it while he loosed the knot on his long, formal kilt of linen. It fell in a heap to the floor.

Rhodopis refused to see his nakedness, too, even while she dressed him. Psamtik held out his arms and allowed her to walk around his body, draping the silk about his hips and fussing with the arrangement of the fabric. He spoke as Rhodopis worked, pleasure at his cleverness evident in the thickness of his voice, the suppressed laughter bubbling just below his words.

"This crowd of sycophants—mindless as dogs. They think it will be as simple as bowing before my throne and saying a few words. Just like that, I'll let them pass through the gate—so they think. But I have ways of ensuring they keep their word. Those who have sons will send one son each to me, to serve in my guard. Those with daughters will pledge at least one girl to my harem. That will keep the old creatures tied to their oaths, and no mistake."

"Clever," Rhodopis said, stepping back to check the drape of his new kilt.

Psamtik's hand flashed out; before Rhodopis could flinch, his fist tightened in her hair. The red locks had barely grown long enough to grasp; after one brief flare of pain, her short hair slid naturally from his clenched fingers. Rhodopis looked at him steadily then, neither smiling nor making any move to evade him. One could never tell just what he sought when these violent moods came upon him: resistance or cooperation.

"You were prettier with more hair," Psamtik said. "Pity I won't see it long again. But now that I've found a way to build my own harem, I won't need you much longer. I won't need those worn-out harlots my father kept, either. I can be rid of them when the time is right." He lifted her chin forcefully, fingers digging into the soft flesh just above her throat. "I'll be rid of you, then, too."

Psamtik said nothing more. Neither did Rhodopis. She only bent to retrieve his discarded kilt, shaking out the wrinkles and draping it over the cedar chest for his cleaning staff to find. Psamtik chuckled as he swept out of the bedchamber and through his apartments. A moment later, the outer door opened and shut with an echoing boom.

As soon as she was satisfied Psamtik had gone, Rhodopis pressed her hands over her face, breathing deeply to slow her racing heart. It had been no surprise to hear him speak that way. Indeed, his words had only confirmed what Rhodopis had known all along: her time was growing short. She must find some way to strike at Psamtik, and soon, before he claimed the final victory.

Peace, she reminded herself, repeating the word until it sank into her bones, until her trembling stilled. The gods would not abandon her. Not when she had been so faithful to them, so obedient to their will, going of her own free choice into

Psamtik's hands. *Peace, peace.* All would be well. The way would open for her—soon.

At least she had a few more hours of silence this evening, more time to think and plan. She returned to the garden, pausing to revel in the honey-hued glow that preceded sunset, allowing the pure, gentle music of birdsong and the rising hum of the night's insects to wash over her. For a moment she was relieved of all thought, all anxiety, wrapped in the protective armor of solitude. But all too soon, her obligation called again with a voice she couldn't deny. Whatever path the gods made for her, Rhodopis knew she would never find it by lingering in the garden with her eyes closed. She must search—think—work, or the way would remain barred forever.

She set off along the garden path, following its gentle curves with automatic steps while she asked herself again and again what she had learned about Psamtik today, and whether he had shown her any small chink in his armor—any crack into which she might slip a dagger, however small. As the sun sank ever lower and the sky flushed a brilliant flame-red, she looked up from the path to find the two stone urns ahead.

Rhodopis stopped, staring. In the ten days since she had willingly come to Psamtik's bed, she had avoided this end of the garden. She had never wanted to see those dark vessels again, for they seemed to hold every terrible, vivid memory of Psamtik's first attack. What was more, they marked the boundary between the Pharaoh's garden and the harem's. With Amasis dead, there was no threat to her life if any of the harem women recognized her—but even so, she had felt no desire to make herself known. The palace was still entangled in the aftermath of Psamtik's coup, and the harem women were more frightened than anyone else who remained within the great mudbrick walls. Their children were under threat—and if Psamtik's cold promise in his bedchamber proved more than mere words, the women's lives would soon be at risk, too. There was no telling what a group of people might do, how they might react to an unpleasant surprise when their backs were against a wall.

Yet now, there Rhodopis stood, confronted by the two dark urns and the gap between them, staring out from her captor's garden into the lush, open greenery of the women's domain. Ought she to reveal herself, after all? Who in the harem could she go to for help—or to spread warning of Psamtik's plan?

No—Rhodopis could say nothing to the women. She realized that at once. They had no way out, no recourse if Psamtik struck. If she were to tell them what Psamtik had said, it would only spread panic and make them even more miserable.

As she stood gazing across the open space, two figures appeared in the women's garden, strolling from the cool shadows beneath a stand of trees toward a glinting, mirror-smooth pond, which reflected the sky's molten gold. Rhodopis' first instinct was to shy back against the nearest urn, hiding from view. But then she recognized one of the figures: dark of skin and unmistakably male, even if he was rather short, with a distinctive slant to his shoulders. He carried a small, portable writing desk under one arm.

Aesop.

What was he doing in the harem garden?

Rhodopis gasped, pressing her palm against the rough stone of the urn, trying to remain upright on legs that suddenly shook like reeds in the wind. Desperately, she willed Aesop to turn, to glance over his shoulder as he walked, to *see* her. She needed only a moment to catch his eye, a mere heartbeat. Dizzy with shock, she wondered whether she ought to call out his name. But that would draw the attention of the woman who walked beside him, too, and then Rhodopis would be forced to explain herself to the harem.

Aesop and his companion moved on, turning along the pond's edge, then heading for the main path that cut across the garden to the women's quarters. Rhodopis' heart dropped into her stomach, raising bitterness to the back of her throat and bringing a flood of tears to her eyes. How could the gods be so cruel—how could they taunt her so? She wrestled with grief and anger, struggling to stifle the cry of protest that built moment by moment in her chest.

But just before Aesop disappeared from view, he slowed until his companion moved ahead by a few steps. He paused, suddenly rigid and still, as if listening to a distant voice only he could hear. And then, to Rhodopis' surging relief, he turned and glanced back toward the stone urns.

Rhodopis didn't hesitate. She stepped to the center of the path, filling the gap between the urns, and raised her hand, beckoning. She could feel a shaft of low sun strike her, spilling its warmth over her face and shoulders. It must have lit her like a torch in the darkness, making her distinctive hair glow—for even across the distance that separated them, she could see Aesop's body jerk with the shock of recognition.

Confident that he had seen her, and almost giddy with gratitude, Rhodopis ducked behind the urn again, whispering prayers of thanks. Her heart pounded in her ears as she waited; her breath came fast and sharp, and she was obliged to take each one with exaggerated care, lest she make herself dizzy. By the time she heard Aesop's step on the garden path, she was calm again, composed.

"Doricha—is that you?" Aesop called softly.

Rhodopis stepped around the urn again, grinning. Aesop, dressed in the garb of a court scribe—unpleated white kilt with a hem of darkest indigo—tossed his small lap-desk onto the grass and they rushed together, wrapping one another in a long embrace.

"By the gods' mercy," he said, "I thought you were gone— dead! I'd convinced myself that once Psamtik found you, he would—"

"He will." Rhodopis sounded far calmer than she felt. "He'll get rid of me, soon enough. He said as much earlier this evening, when I saw him last."

Aesop drew back, eyeing the depths of the Pharaoh's garden anxiously.

"He's not here now," Rhodopis said. "Gone back to the throne room to toy with some of his subjects. But I don't know when he'll return; we shouldn't talk long."

"No, of course not. But gods, you're alive! I've never been happier. When I found your note, I cursed you for a fool and felt sure you would meet some terrible end. I suppose I should have given you more credit than that."

"I am a fool," she said with a rueful half-smile. "I'm in danger, and I know it now—there's no pretending, no denying it's true. But Psamtik is worse off than me... or at least, I mean to see to it that he lands in danger. If the gods are willing. But why are you here, Aesop? How did you get into the harem, of all places?"

Aesop shrugged, then chuckled uncomfortably. "I can scarcely believe I'm in the harem, myself. An ordinary man walking among the Pharaoh's favorite women—normally, it's only a few select stewards who are permitted such access."

"And scribes," Rhodopis said, glancing down at his uniform.

"Rarely, yes. I've been lucky; since Psamtik's rise, there have been so few real scribes available for the women's use. Yet they are all clamoring to send word to their families, as you can imagine. The poor creatures only want to reassure their loved ones that they're alive and well, but they've had little opportunity. The court scribes are all occupied, sending out Psamtik's proclamations and composing letters to foreign kings, alerting them to the news. I'd heard there were no scribes to take the women's letters, so I stepped in."

Rhodopis tilted her head. "Why? Psamtik has allowed some

people to leave the palace grounds. Why didn't you leave when you could?"

Aesop waved a hand dismissively. "You didn't think I would leave you here to face Psamtik alone, did you? Of course not. I had to learn what had happened to you... and whether I could still save you."

Blushing with gratitude, Rhodopis lowered her eyes. "That was good of you, Aesop, but you shouldn't stay here. I'll do what I must, and then... whatever the gods will."

"Nonsense. I've lost track of all the times I've promised to get you away from the palace—away from Memphis—to some-place safe. I still mean to do that. Nothing has changed, Doricha—not for me. Now tell me..." He hesitated as if he feared what she might say. "How have you fared since you left the diplomats' wing?"

"Well enough."

Aesop reached out, brushed a bruise on her arm with a touch so gentle she barely felt it. "These marks tell a different story."

Rhodopis shrugged, turning away from him. The sun had set; a few streaks of amber light still hung in the western sky, but dusky blue was rapidly overtaking garden and palace alike. The first stars hung low, just visible over the palace wall.

"I can take this," she said at length, gesturing to her bruises. "The pain is nothing to me. And the other things he does to me —they're nothing beside what I mean to do to him."

She met Aesop's eye now, and her conviction must have shone on her face like a full moon, for he stepped back, lifting his dark brows in surprise.

"What exactly do you mean to do?" Aesop asked.

"You know."

"You can't, Doricha. The risk is too great. Cambyses is coming—"

She clasped her hands, hopeful. "Is he? You've had word?"

Aesop sighed, then shook his head reluctantly. "No, I've heard nothing. But that's to be expected. We must trust that he is on his way to Egypt with—"

"We can't simply trust," she cried, filled with sudden passion. "Anything at all may have gone wrong. The bird may have died, or our letter may have been intercepted. Cambyses might have decided Egypt isn't worth taking, after all."

Aesop chuckled. "I doubt any king would come to that conclusion."

"But what if the Persian forces never come? What then, Aesop?"

"Then I suppose," he said grimly, "Psamtik will be king."

"I can't let that happen. I *can't*. I won't." Her hands clenched into fists, nails biting palms. She had sworn to herself in Persia that she would bring Psamtik down, would strip him of his power and his throne. She would leave him with nothing, not even his life. Rhodopis still meant to see the usurper fall—her enemy, the only man in all the world she truly hated—even if it cost her final breath. "If Cambyses never comes, then we must bring Psamtik down. I must. Too much depends on it now, Aesop—too many people are in danger. Every woman in the harem, and their children, too—"

"Surely he wouldn't harm the women. What purpose would that serve?"

"He will, Aesop! He told me as much, this very evening!" Rhodopis breathed deeply again, struggling in vain to calm herself. "As for what purpose their deaths would serve—or their suffering—Psamtik needs no excuse. Pain and terror serve their own ends, as far as he's concerned. I won't let him do it to another girl, another woman. I won't allow his evil to spread."

Aesop seemed to see the fire of her determination flare against the approaching darkness. He nodded soberly. "Very well; I understand. But how? Have you decided on a means, a method? Perhaps I can help you. I could bring a knife, a dagger—"

"No. It can't be a blade. As much as I would like to watch his blood spill, a blade will never do. He always checks me for weapons—every day and every night, before he… has his way with me." She folded her arms and drew herself up, suddenly business-like. "I've thought about it plenty; I've nothing else to do, most hours, but think about how I'll bring him down. It must be poison. That's the only weapon I can hope to sneak past him, the only way I can hope to cause him harm."

"That would be most fitting," Aesop said, scratching his short beard thoughtfully. "After the way he destroyed Amasis, poison would be justice fit for the ages."

"Look at us." Rhodopis swept out her arms, taking in both of the vast gardens with a single, bitter gesture. "Here we stand, surrounded by plants of every kind, and ignorant as children. I have no doubt these gardens contain what we need—some herb or flower that would do the trick, neat and clean—but I know nothing about herbs. Nothing. If Phanes were here, he could tell me which plants to use. But he's not here. We're on our own."

"On our own," Aesop agreed, "but not hopeless. I believe, if I put on an ambassador's garb once more, I can secure privileges to come and go from the palace. And, of course, I must make a good show of fealty to Psamtik. Once out in the city, I can move more freely, speak openly to anyone I please."

Eagerly, Rhodopis took his hand. "Can you find a poisoner? Or someone who knows which plants to use, at the very least?"

"Of a certainty," he said, patting her hand. "It may take time, of course—"

"I don't know how much time I have left, Aesop." Tears sprang to her eyes. She wiped them away with a quick, furious motion. Weeping would do nothing for her—not now, not ever.

"I know." Aesop's voice was soft and sad. Then he said more

briskly, "Once I'm out of the palace, I'll go straight to Iadmon. He keeps several pigeons trained to fly straight to the Pharaoh's quarters."

Rhodopis blinked at him through the dusk. "The king's quarters?"

"Yes. There's a cote on the roof of those very apartments. In that way, the Pharaoh can receive messages quickly and directly, if need be. Didn't you know?"

She shook her head. "I've never been up to the roof. Never seen it."

"I don't know how Iadmon got those specially trained birds, and I doubt he has ever used them before, but he always said they would be useful someday. I recall them well; the birds trained for the king's quarters are all white as linen, and unmarked. I'll send one flying straight to you the moment I have information—any least bit of information that may help. Do you think you can get up to the rooftop?"

"I don't see why not," she said. Just enough of her tension eased to bring a smile to her face. "There's no guard on the roof or the stair, since the Pharaoh's quarters stand apart. Only the garden walls are protected."

"It's settled, then. I'll find what you need—poison, or how to make it—and you will wait on the rooftop for my bird." Aesop retrieved his lap desk from the grass, then gave Rhodopis a lingering look. He smiled, but his brows were drawn together in worry. "And until we meet again, may the gods keep you—blessed, brave girl."

❧ 14 ❧

A DESPERATE GAMBLE

THE NEXT DAY, AS SOON AS PSAMTIK LEFT HIS APARTMENTS TO SEE to his duties, Rhodopis hurried out into the garden. On this morning, however, she shunned the private sanctuary tucked behind the rose trellis. Instead, she climbed the stone staircase to the roof of the Pharaoh's quarters.

As she had predicted, no one attempted to stop her. Indeed, there were no guards close at hand, though Psamtik's usual contingent of soldiers paced slowly along the top of his garden wall, watching the ground below for any sign of intrusion. But on the broad, flat rooftop, which smelled of sunbaked dust and the herbal breezes of the garden, Rhodopis found herself as comfortably alone as she had been in her hidden corner near the pond.

For long moments, sheltered only by her linen sun-hood, Rhodopis leaned out over the hip-high wall at the roof's edge, taking in the vast sweep of Memphis and the deep, green-blue spread of the river. She had always known Memphis was large —indeed, she had been told by many men that it was the biggest city in the world. Having seen Babylon with her own eyes, she doubted Memphis was larger, but she had never known until that moment just how grand and imposing the city was. If it couldn't best Babylon in size and population, then surely it came close. Her vantage was impressive: one of the highest elevations on the palace grounds, and the palace was perched atop the dusty, yellow hill that rose above the city like the slope of a bull's shoulder. It seemed she could see everything from the Pharaoh's rooftop—every house below her, every street and narrow alley. Rhodopis even fancied she could see every person who called Memphis home if she squinted her eyes and stared hard enough into the shadowed grid of its roadways.

No wonder Egypt's Pharaoh holds such power. He sits atop the whole world, here in his palace.

For a while, Rhodopis amused herself by picking out the districts and great estates she had known in the hetaera days, though now they looked like children's toys, small and insignificant, utterly disposable. There was the great, green garden of Iason the horse breeder, and there were the docks where she had accompanied Archidike to her tryst with the white-haired old merchant. The limestone estate in the northern city with its high wall could only be Xanthes' place, and the long wing attached to its western side must be the Stable. She couldn't find Iadmon's estate in the jumble of riverside houses, but she thought she could make out a small, pale sliver of rooftop that must have been Charaxus' home, snug between two larger and more elegant properties. To the south, she recognized the crooked streets and narrower buildings of the district where Aesop had lived as a free man. There was even a gap among charred, smoke-stained rooftops where the beer shop had once stood.

But when she tired of searching for landmarks she recognized, Rhodopis looked beyond the city to the land—Egypt itself. Where the fringes of Memphis gave way to farmland, she made out slashes of brightness glittering among the green flush of growing things. The annual flood had almost entirely receded now, leaving behind a coating of rich, black mud; the farmers had worked quickly, planting the first of their crops. After so long living in cities, the open country fairly took her breath away, charming her with its countless shades of green—malachite and tourmaline, grayish greens and brown tints of olive, pale blue-greens like the winter sky just after sunset. Beyond the farms, hills sloped gently to the west, shedding their coats of color by degrees as cultivated fields gave way to the dull red and ochre of dry, barren wilderness.

The river and its dark, flourishing bank seemed to stretch on forever, beyond even the blue-white haze of the southern horizon into the gods' own eternity. Across the massive river, the dark band of farms and fields seemed no wider than a finger's breadth, and the endless stretch of desert was purple with distance. She had known Egypt was vast, but never had she appreciated its size and scope before—not even when she had sailed to Memphis with Iadmon, nor when she had gone north on Amasis' ship.

She turned to face north, and her heart lurched, for the view stretched so far, she felt as if she could see all the way to Thrace. Her family was there, somewhere—Mother, the boys, little Aella. A desperate longing to see them again, to feel herself wrapped in their arms, seized her with such sudden force that she lost her breath, and had to gasp and pant until the dizziness of her grief subsided. She squeezed her eyes shut, trying to distance herself from that yearning, but with her eyes closed, the image of Polycrates' fleet rose up before her mind's eye like a haunting spirit.

When I open my eyes, I'll see his ships like specks of peppercorn in the distance. I'll watch as they come closer, and closer still, bringing Psamtik's downfall in their wakes.

But even before she looked again, she knew it was a lie. She did not see Polycrates coming, nor Cambyses. The dark dots of ships and smaller vessels covered the river's surface, from Memphis clear to the northern horizon. But there was no fleet to be found, no swift pack of pirate's vessels bearing down on the city.

Despite that disappointment, the rooftop was so pleasant and the view so entrancing that Rhodopis climbed the staircase every day, whiling away the hours until Psamtik's return in the shade of the potted palms. Now and then she approached the pigeon cote and spoke softly to the birds inside, listening to their answers, a sigh of rustles and coos. She had discovered that a servant came late every morning to bring the birds water and grain and to sweep out their droppings, collecting the pungent white material for use in the garden. The servant was an older woman whose hair had just begun to turn as gray as her feathered charges. She smiled at Rhodopis whenever they met—though Rhodopis saw more than a touch of pity in the woman's eyes. No doubt, she saw the bruises on Rhodopis' arms and guessed from where they had come.

But the pigeon tender always greeted her happily, and within a few days, Rhodopis had convinced the woman to show her how to handle the birds. Their feathers were soft as drifting ash, and when Rhodopis lifted a pigeon in a single hand, the way the tender had instructed—wings gently restrained between her thumb and smallest finger, bobbing head protruding between her first two digits—the birds felt weightless as mist.

The pigeons made for a welcome distraction, but as the days wore on and still no fleet appeared on the northern horizon, Rhodopis sank back toward despair. Her will to continue lying with Psamtik—to bear his abuse and the sheer terror of his presence—flagged more every day. Night after night, more bruises blossomed on her body like poisonous flowers unfurling their dark petals. Psamtik's talk grew ever more oppressive, too. He taunted her with suggestions that her death was coming soon, promised her that the age of Greek prominence in Egypt was all but over now—assured her flatly, with cold, emotionless eyes, he would rid the city of every last Greek quite soon; any day, in fact. Each and every one.

Rhodopis was careful never to allow too much fear to show in her eyes or in the tension of her body. A little anxiety gratified Psamtik and kept his cruelty sated. Too much, and she worried that he would overindulge, beating her more than she could take or reverting to the same cruelties he had inflicted upon her that first time in the sapling grove. It was a delicate dance, with steps more intricate than any she had attempted before. Day by day, she felt her mind and body straining under the pressure. She couldn't say how much more she could bear. Sooner or later, Rhodopis knew she would break—shattering along the countless cracks Psamtik had inflicted upon her spirit.

One afternoon, she heard the scrape of sandals on the staircase and turned from the rooftop wall, expecting the pigeon tender or another servant. When she saw Psamtik standing there, she couldn't rein in her surprise. Her body gave an involuntary jerk of fear, a flinch as if from a vicious dog or a crocodile in a pool. But before Psamtik had crossed half the rooftop, Rhodopis was calm and poised again. She pulled back her sunhood and offered him a meek smile.

"I'd heard you had taken to lurking about on the rooftop," he said.

Rhodopis cast a quick glance over the garden to the soldiers patrolling the wall. Who but they would have reported her movements to the usurper king?

To Psamtik, she said only, "I like watching the river."

He braced fists on hips and gazed rather dully over his kingdom—his father's kingdom, stolen in an act of murder. The magnificent view seemed not to move Psamtik in the slightest. Perhaps, Rhodopis thought, he had looked upon it so many times that it no longer impressed him. Or perhaps he was a man who couldn't be moved by any beauty. Only power affected him—power, pain, and terror.

"You can see everything from up here," Psamtik said. "Did you see what I did at noontime? My great act, out there in the central square of the city?"

A sudden, inexplicable thrill of dread crawled along her limbs. "No." It took an effort to give that single word life, to be sure it didn't come from her throat as a strangled whisper.

Psamtik remained as he was, frozen in his stance of might, staring down at his city. He was waiting, Rhodopis realized… waiting for her to speak more. She mustn't disappoint him. The night would go more poorly for her than usual if she disappointed Psamtik.

She asked briskly, "What did you do, my king? I didn't even know you left the palace today."

Psamtik gestured; she stepped to his side obediently, though she tingled with fear. The rooftop wall only reached to her hips, and the ground lay far below. Would he choose this moment to rid Memphis of one Greek in particular?

He nodded, indicating the wide-open square at the foot of the hill, just below the palace gates. The view was mostly obscured by the corners of rooftops, but Rhodopis could make out some of the space, a flatness of wide pavers glaring yellow in the afternoon sun. At first, she saw nothing unusual. But then she noted the utter emptiness of the square—a space that was usually teeming with citizens, full of the bustle and movement of city life.

Something was making the people of Memphis avoid that place. Something terrible had happened there at midday— something dark and frightening.

She looked up at Psamtik, expectant, braced for his story

The usurper-king smirked. The pits of his eyes seemed to drink the brightness of daylight, leaving only shadows above his self-satisfied grin. "There, in that very spot," he said, "I made my first move against the Greek pestilence. My first move, but not my last. I had my soldiers apprehend a few troublesome personalities, those with meaningful connections outside of Kmet and little to offer my kingdom—no commerce, no tariffs to collect. I made an example of them for all to see—those useless hangers-on who bring nothing to Kmet, who would be better off back in their homelands. Their families and friends will soon learn what came to pass. They will think twice before they disperse more of their rats to my kingdom, to gnaw at Kmetu goods without offering anything of use in return."

"You... made an example?"

Psamtik chuckled, then drew his finger across his throat in a quick, slashing motion. "Five fewer Greeks to trouble me. It's a start, but my work is far from done."

Rhodopis pressed a hand to her mouth. Innocent men killed, for no better reason than the land of their birth. How long until Psamtik struck against Greeks who did contribute to Egypt's well-being? Iadmon? Xanthes... and the girls in his Stable? She bit her lip but said nothing.

Psamtik continued his hoarse laughter. "One of the men my soldiers caught had been looking for you, so I hear."

Rhodopis' heart ceased beating for one black, panicked moment. Then it lurched painfully, and her face flushed hot. "Charaxus of Lesvos."

"Yes, that's the one." Psamtik sighed, as if in appreciation of a particularly good joke. "I didn't know it at the time, when he dropped to his knees before me and wept, pleading for his life. It was only after I'd relieved him of his head that one of my guards mentioned that rumor had connected you to that yellow-haired fool."

He turned to her with sudden gravity, mouth tight with suspicion, eyes glittering.

"A long time ago," Rhodopis said quickly. She swallowed

hard, fighting back the nausea of guilt. "I knew him when I was a—"

"Whore." Psamtik's smile was slow to come, but he seemed mollified. He turned to gaze upon his city once more.

Rhodopis fought for every breath, struggling against the fog of shame and fear that encroached upon her thoughts. She must maintain a clear head, she told herself—must think carefully. This was no time to fall to pieces.

When she felt she was in better control—in no more danger, at least, of dropping to her knees and weeping, as Charaxus had done—she said lightly, "Tell me, my king: why don't you cleanse Kmet of the Greek pestilence now? All at once, I mean."

Psamtik glanced at her, huffing in surprise. "What, are you a hater of Greeks now? Think yourself better than your own kind, just because I've taken you to my bed? Don't fool yourself. I know what you are, even if you don't. You aren't Kmetu. You never will be."

"That's not what I meant, my king." She had to speak carefully now. She must rouse neither his temper nor his suspicion. "I was only curious. You're such a strong and decisive ruler, and all the world knows how you feel about Greeks. Why do you delay? What prevents you from ridding Kmet of my kind?"

His answering laugh was cruel; the sound put Rhodopis in mind of a cat purring over the mouse that squeaked and shivered beneath its paw. "You think to find some way out, is that it, Greek whore? You think you might discover in my designs a means of saving your skin, of staving off your fate. You shan't, but never mind. It does no harm to speak of my reasons, since you asked. I would rid Kmet of all Greeks in a single blow if I could. But the truth is, the functions of my country are too tied up now with Greek interests—the flow of silver and other wealth, you see. But that doesn't mean you pale invaders, you sucking leeches, will be spared in the end. I must go about this business more slowly than I like, but make no mistake, Rhodopis, I will do it. I am strong enough to carry out the work —my great work—and no one dares oppose me. Do you doubt that?"

Mutely, Rhodopis shook her head, then lowered her face to stare at her sandals. The lion, the beast, the usurper would do just as he had promised. Who had the strength to oppose him, now that his coup had succeeded?

Polycrates—Phanes—Cambyses! If only you would come. Don't the gods see what terrible danger we face?

If the gods saw, it seemed they weren't troubled by Psamtik's outrages. But Rhodopis cared. She alone, it seemed, had the will to strike against Psamtik. If only she could learn how it might be done. She had never hunted any creature before, never mind a lion.

Psamtik turned his back on the city, stretching his arms contentedly above his head. "I'm famished after such good and strenuous work. My appetites have certainly been piqued. I shall call for a feast tonight. Ahh, yes—a feast will be the very thing."

Below the sound of Psamtik's contented sigh, Rhodopis heard a quick whisper and shuffle, then the minute scrape of claws against dry brick. She glanced up—and nearly gasped aloud. A bird had landed on the rooftop wall, just behind Psamtik's back. A pigeon, white as linen, without a speck of gray to mark its feathers.

Iadmon's bird.

Word from Aesop had arrived. She could see a scrap of papyrus tied to the pigeon's leg with a bit of red thread. If Psamtik turned around, he would notice the pigeon. He would catch it, read the message. He would know everything.

Rhodopis tore her astonished eyes from the pigeon and stepped casually to Psamtik's side. She drifted a few feet toward the staircase—away from the white bird. "A feast sounds delightful, my king," she said airily. "But will the kitchen staff have time to prepare? Evening isn't far off now."

"They had better do as I bid, or they'll find themselves in the same place as your friend from Lesvos, pleading on their knees for their worthless lives." He began to turn as if he craved one more sight of the square where he had carried out the day's atrocity.

Rhodopis' mind flashed with desperate speed. She shrugged one shoulder just so, and the neckline of her tunic slipped, exposing her breast all the way to her nipple. Psamtik froze, eyes locked on her body like a falcon sighting its prey.

Her face was already red—she could feel the heat of fear and surprise burning her cheeks. Rhodopis cast her eyes down quickly, as if in embarrassment, and tugged at her tunic, covering her flesh. She moved again toward the staircase, and to her relief, Psamtik followed.

"Might we have music at the feast, my king?" Rhodopis asked. "It's been so long since I've heard musicians play."

"I never said you would attend my victory feast. What use have I for a common whore? Should I parade you before my court? I think not. I'm not like my father was, weak and easily influenced by women. No—I shall bring Tjenmutetj and Ta-Sheren-Iset out to display in all their finery. They are beautiful girls; I'll say that much for them, even if they are pathetic with their endless sniveling. But you're right about one thing: if I wish to enjoy a feast tonight, I had best give my orders now. Otherwise, the kitchen staff will be quite hopeless."

"Will I see you tonight, my king—after the celebration?"

Psamtik leered down at her as they walked side by side. "Eager for it, aren't you? You're a strange one, I must admit. Made wet between the legs by the death of your kind." He gripped her face suddenly, forcing Rhodopis to look up at him. She swallowed hard against the pain, his nails biting into her cheeks. "But I like it. And I'll avail myself of the pleasure for as long as it still amuses me to keep you."

Psamtik tossed her aside so that Rhodopis found herself staggering across the rooftop, clutching her aching cheek with one hand. With the other, she caught herself against one of the potted palm trees. By the time she had righted herself and turned, Psamtik had vanished from the roof. She was left alone, with only the sound of his receding footsteps and the pigeons cooing excitedly in their cote, calling to their newly arrived companion.

Rhodopis hurried back to the wall. Iadmon's white bird was still there, thank the gods, strutting impatiently along the bricks. Rhodopis slowed as she came nearer, moving with care, just the way the pigeon tender had shown her. She reached out one trembling hand and caught the bird gently in her palm, then slipped the message from its fragile pink leg.

When she had delivered the bird to the cote, Rhodopis unrolled the papyrus, as hungry for the message as Psamtik was for his feast. The sight of Aesop's small, neat hand nearly dropped her to the rooftop with relief. When she read her friend's words, renewed hope surged so high and hard in her chest that she almost cried out with the force of it.

Our friends in the north have received our letter. I have confirmed it. They will reach the Delta before the moon's next turn.

She turned again to the north, half expecting to see the low, dark mass of the fleet approaching. The Persian fleet was not there, of course—but through a warm haze of relief, Rhodopis could imagine she saw them, strong prows towering above the water and bright pennants flapping in the Nile breeze over fat, rounded sails.

Aesop has heard from Cambyses—or from Phanes. *They're coming. They're honestly coming.*

Psamtik's reign was nearly over... and yet, Rhodopis knew, the worst trials both she and Egypt would face hadn't begun. Even as the tears of relief welled in her eyes, reducing the magnificent view to a blur of green and ochre, a cold hand seemed to clutch at her heart. Anything could happen to the fleet: storms, raiders, a crew in mutiny. What if Cambyses hadn't brought enough men? Rhodopis knew that several garrisons were spread throughout the northern Delta region; might they be enough to stop Cambyses long before he reached Memphis? She shuddered to think of it. Even in this moment of joy, Rhodopis knew she couldn't allow herself to feel triumph. Psamtik was too dangerous a man. She couldn't count on hope alone. She couldn't even count on Cambyses. He was a man like any other, fallible and mortal.

She read Aesop's message again. There was no mention of poison. No doubt, Aesop had been content with the knowledge that the Persian fleet was headed toward Egypt. He saw no reason now to forge ahead with Rhodopis' plan.

But the gods brought me here for a reason. I have come to serve their purpose, to be the tool in their divine hands.

Perhaps the gods knew what no one else could imagine. What if Cambyses was fated to die in the coming war? What if Psamtik faced the Persian king in battle and prevailed? The thought was almost too much to bear. It sent such a wave of anxiety coursing through her that she felt her bowels clench. No, Rhodopis decided—she couldn't afford to wait until the fleet came, until the outcome of the battle had been determined. With or without Cambyses, she must find a way to bring Psamtik down.

Rhodopis crumpled the scrap of papyrus in her fist, turning slowly on the rooftop, noting the position of every guard along the garden wall. None seemed to be watching her; she took advantage of their inattention and popped the ball of papyrus into her mouth. She couldn't leave it where anyone may find it, here on the roof or tucked into some hidden fold of clothing. The papyrus sucked the moisture from her mouth and made her lips pucker with its curious, tannic flavor. She chewed and found that it was tough and fibrous between her teeth. Her saliva loosened the ink, which flooded her mouth with a bitter taste that nearly made her gag, but she went on chewing, working the stuff into a ball soft enough to swallow.

To distract herself from the unpleasant taste and texture, Rhodopis mulled over her options. There was nothing in the wash-house that might be of use; she was all but sure of that. If she could find some way to return to the servants' quarters, Neni might not let her go again. She doubted whether anyone remained in the diplomats' wing—Aesop had said most of the ambassadors had been freed from the palace grounds. But in any case, was unlikely that Psamtik would allow Rhodopis to wander about the palace by herself.

The doves in the cote erupted in a sudden clatter of wings and unsettled cooing. Rhodopis turned quickly, half expecting to see Psamtik on the rooftop again, but she remained alone. The birds were merely engaged in a squabble over grain. But the violent sound of their wings brought a memory to the surface of her mind. She recalled the day when Psamtik had first sat upon the Horus Throne—the sound of Khedeb-Netjer-Bona's men clashing with the usurper's loyal guards. Rhodopis could all but see the chief wife's face again, so close to her own —the expression of surprise, the startled arch of her brows.

Khedeb-Netjer-Bona was always the clever one, even if she was dangerous. It's a pity she's not here now; she would have no qualms about poisoning Psamtik. That much I can say.

Rhodopis paused in her chewing as a new idea came to her. Saliva flooded her mouth; she swallowed hard, and the papyrus slid down her throat.

That's it. If Khedeb-Netjer-Bona can't come to me, I shall go to her.

The chief wife could tell Rhodopis which plants in the garden would serve—or could tell her where to find a poisoner, and how to obtain their deadly wares. Rhodopis knew the chief wife was being held in the Temple of Horus, after all; it would be easier to locate Khedeb-Netjer-Bona than to track down a poisoner on her own. No doubt, Khedeb-Netjer-Bona would not be pleased to see Rhodopis again. But as a captive of the Horus priesthood, she would be unlikely to harm Rhodopis in any way.

And when she learned what Rhodopis intended to do, Khedeb-Netjer-Bona might choose to make herself an ally rather than an enemy.

It's worth trying, Rhodopis decided as she headed for the staircase and the garden below.

She only needed an excuse to visit the temple... one Psamtik was likely to believe.

RHODOPIS FOUND Psamtik in his bedchamber, studying the fine silken robes his servants had laid out across his bed. The two young men whose duty it was to see to Psamtik's appearance stood meekly against one wall, their hands folded behind their backs and their heads bowed. Psamtik muttered under his breath as he picked up the hem of one robe, dyed a brilliant turquoise shade and embellished with beads of gold and carnelian. It was a lovely garment, rich-looking and smooth. But his scowl spoke plainly of displeasure. He let the silk drop, shaking his head at the other options—linens of pure white and orange-red.

"These will never do," he barked at his serving men. "They're entirely too modest. This is to be a celebratory feast, you fools. I must look triumphant—resplendent!"

One of the men bowed low before he spoke. "As you say, my

king—but we will bring out your very best jewelry for the occasion. The wide gold cuffs with the lapis inlay will pair nicely with the turquoise silk. And we have acquired a new sash for you, my king. It is linen, but wait until you see it! Such embroidery—every inch is covered in gold and silver threads."

"And crimson," the other fellow added, voice shaking. "Don't forget the crimson, Ranefer."

"Yes, crimson threads, too, my king," Ranefer said, "to match the carnelian at the hem. And if we place your widest collar over your shoulders—"

Psamtik threw up his hands in disgust. "Very well! If that's the best you can do, I suppose I must be content with it. Go and fetch that collar of which you speak. I believe it's kept in my falcon-carved chest. The one near the bath."

His body servants scurried toward the door, starting in surprise when they saw Rhodopis. Psamtik noticed her for the first time, too. He smiled, but there was no warmth in it.

"Tell me the truth," he said. "What do you think of this turquoise robe?"

"It's very fine, my king. It will suit you well."

"But is it attractive enough for the night's celebration?" He looked at the garments spread across his bed once more, rubbing his sharp chin thoughtfully. "I want to leave no one in doubt of my splendor or my power. What I began today is only the first stroke of a craftsman's hammer, the first brick laid in a vast foundation. I intend to build upon this great work—create a new and glorious Kmet."

"You will, my king. Even if you were to be dressed in rags, no one who looks upon you could see anything other than a powerful Pharaoh."

He gave a dismissive grunt, pawed at the silk a moment longer, then glanced up sharply at Rhodopis. "I suppose you came to beg me to allow you to attend the feast. Is that why you're here?"

Psamtik sounded as if he looked forward to her begging—as if nothing would please him better at that moment.

Rhodopis lowered her eyes in a careful show of timidity. "I would delight in attending, if it is your will, my king. But in truth, I came to ask a different favor."

He looked at her more keenly now, eyes narrowing to a suspicious squint. "What favor?"

Rhodopis clasped her hands. "I wondered, my king, whether you would be so good as to grant me permission to visit the Temple of Horus."

For a heartbeat, silence hung over the bedchamber. Then Psamtik shattered it with loud snort of amusement. "You must think me a fool."

Rhodopis looked up at him, face heating with fear. Her eyes were wide and troubled; she made no effort to disguise her anxiety. It might work in her favor, after all. "No, my king—no! I would never think you foolish. I know better."

Psamtik advanced on her, crossing the room in a few swift strides, and grabbed her by the upper arm. She couldn't keep a strangled cry in check as his hand closed hard on her bruised flesh.

"Looking for a way to flee, are you?" Psamtik hissed close to her ear. "Thinking you can escape your fate?"

"Never! I don't want to leave you, my king. I know I never could, anyhow—you're too powerful, too clever."

He shook her roughly; Rhodopis' teeth clacked together and her neck tightened with pain. "Then what do you want with the Tempe of Horus? Why would you wish to go beyond the palace walls?"

Through her rising terror, Rhodopis clutched at the excuse she had prepared. She clung to her story like a spider to its fragile web. "I need the blessing of the Priests of Horus, my king. I need the favor of Kmet's greatest god."

Psamtik bellowed a laugh as he shoved Rhodopis away. Her

back struck the wall behind her; she winced at the pain, but remained there, leaning against the cool, painted brick, grateful for the space between Psamtik and herself.

"What would you need with any god of Kmet—you, a Greek?"

"I misspoke; forgive me. It's not that I need a priest's blessing. You do, my king." She placed both hands on her belly—low, in the place where a baby would grow. Then she waited, counting her ragged breaths as Psamtik stared at her hands—at her body, the flesh he had tried so hard to dominate.

Rhodopis' heart pounded, blood racing like liquid fire through her veins. Did Psamtik know the rhythms of a woman's body? He knew Rhodopis had bled only days before. Did this man understand that she couldn't possibly have fallen pregnant so soon after her monthly flux—did any man know? Rhodopis couldn't be sure. She had staked everything on this desperate gamble—even her very life, for if Psamtik knew she had lied to him, he would surely kill Rhodopis with his own hands.

But when he raised his eyes to meet her own, something had softened in Psamtik's expression. There was no love in his eyes, nor even appreciation—but satisfaction had smoothed away some of his hardness.

Rhodopis risked a tiny smile. "I have heard that the Horus priests know the right spells—the ones that will protect a boychild in the womb, and make him strong."

"You can't know that it's a boy," Psamtik said, but not gruffly. "Not so soon."

"I can't know, my king—but how can your child not be a boy? I can feel already that he is mighty and strong, just like his father. But I don't want to risk anything; this child is too important. Your firstborn son. I beg of you, my king: let me visit the Temple of Horus so the god can bless Kmet's heir."

Psamtik returned to the garments on his bed. Rhodopis

relaxed a little as he walked away from her, but she still had no answer. She watched as he lifted the turquoise robe again, this time with no air of disappointment. Rhodopis' news seemed to have put him in a better frame of mind. She was about to repeat the request when Psamtik spoke first.

"You won't go to the temple," he said. "I don't trust you—I trust no Greek, as you well know—and now more than ever, I won't have you running off and hiding among those worms you call your kinsfolk. But for the sake of the child you carry, I will bring a priest of Horus to the palace, to bless you and tend you here."

It was not what Rhodopis had hoped for, but it was a path forward, another way made clear by the gods. She resolved once again to keep her eyes open and make the most of whatever opportunity this turn of events brought her way.

She said heartily, "Thank you, my king. You are most generous."

"I'll see to it that the priest arrives tomorrow."

He paused, watching her with his cold, expressionless eyes. Rhodopis stroked her belly again, absently, the way she had often seen her mother do when Melaina had been pregnant with Aella and the twins.

"Perhaps," Psamtik said at length, "I ought to bring you to the feast, after all. You are carrying my child." But he shook his head, chuckling dryly. "No. My loyal men wouldn't like to know that my son is half Greek."

"But you will keep the child, won't you, my king? You won't... be rid of him because he's half Greek?"

"Of course I will keep the child. If it's a boy. Ta-Sheren-Iset and Tjenmutetj might never give me any children—they have been less cooperative than you, so far, and I haven't yet had the time to break them in and teach them their proper place. But those two useless cows could be barren, for all I know. Besides, they remind me of their mother, a most unappealing woman. I want them more for tradition's sake than for what's between their legs."

So the girls had been spared rape... so far. Rhodopis could be grateful for one small blessing, at least.

"Your child, if he is a boy, will be raised as Kmetu. He will never know of the Greek stain in his heritage. And if the gods should give me more sons—true Kmetu, by birth and blood—yours will not be my heir. But I do need an heir, and sooner rather than later. We here in Memphis have seen how fickle fate can be."

"You honor me and my child," Rhodopis said.

Psamtik's smile was slow and mocking. "I will keep a boy, Rhodopis. I won't keep you. Don't think this saves you, my little pet. This changes nothing about your fate, and nothing about my great work. I will still rid Kmet of every Greek that has plagued it, field and shoreline. You've bought yourself a little more time. That, and nothing more."

The body servants returned, carrying between them a heavy jeweled collar, a fan of bright stones set into brilliant gold. Psamtik nodded in approval, then waved at Rhodopis, a curt and silent dismissal.

She turned at once and left the chamber, trembling—but whether she shook with fear or triumph, Rhodopis couldn't have said. She would await the arrival of the Horus priest. Until then, she would try not to wonder how much time, exactly, her lie had bought.

THE PRIESTESS OF HORUS

THE NEXT DAY, AFTER PSAMTIK HAD SATED HIS HUNGER FOR cruelty and humiliation and left to see to his duties, Rhodopis sent for bath oil and fresh water, scrubbed the lingering feel of Psamtik from her skin, and dressed in a clean linen tunic, tucking the old, stained kerchief behind the sash as was her habit. The kerchief served little purpose, except to remind her that she was a free woman. A slave wouldn't have been permitted to own anything—not even such a tawdry thing as that blood-spotted square of linen.

Although he had taken her into his chamber as a constant bedwarmer, Psamtik had never bothered to provide Rhodopis with anything more beautiful than the servant's garb she had worn since coming to the palace as Aesop's slave. It was all one to Rhodopis; the simple tunics and unadorned sashes were comfortable and cool, even in the brutal heat of midday.

Psamtik, who had returned late from his triumphal feast, staggering and stinking of wine, hadn't bothered to tell Rhodopis when to expect the Priest of Horus. She thought it well enough to spend the day on the rooftop—when the priest arrived and asked for her, surely the guards would know to send the visitor up the staircase to the Pharaoh's roof. If the guards had taken note of her presence on the rooftop the day before, they would do so again.

Shielded by her light woven sun-hood, Rhodopis whiled away the late morning beside the pigeon cote, gazing north along the river, praying for a sign of Cambyses and his fleet. But neither ships nor Horus priest appeared, and by the time the sun had passed its zenith, her belly ached with hunger. She had just made up her mind to return to the garden level, track down a palace servant, and send for food when she heard low voices at the foot of the staircase. She crept closer to the stairs and strained to hear over the sighing of Nile breeze among the palm fronds.

"You will find the Pharaoh's… er… the Pharaoh's companion on the rooftop, Blessed One."

Rhodopis recognized that voice. It was Ranefer, one of Psamtik's body servants—the one who had convinced him to don the turquoise robe for his celebration. The Priest of Horus had arrived, then.

"I thank you, good servant of the gods. If I require anything else, I shall send for you."

When she heard the response, Rhodopis started in surprise. She had expected a male priest, but the newcomer's voice had been distinctly feminine—albeit with a rich, low quality. The sound sent a chill of recognition coursing through Rhodopis' blood, yet she couldn't say exactly where she had heard that voice before. She had no time to ponder it; the sound of sandaled feet on the staircase carried up to the rooftop. Rhodopis retreated to the shadow of the pigeon cote, waiting, tense with the sudden pressure of combined dread and expectation.

The priestess appeared at the top of the stone steps: head

and shoulders rising into view, covered as Rhodopis was by a linen sun-hood and capelet. Shadow pooled beneath the hood, obscuring the priestess's face—yet there was something distinctly familiar in her unusual height and obvious poise. The woman's bare arms showed below the hem of her short cape, and her skin was the soft mahogany brown of most native Egyptians. Why, then, did she wear a sun-hood? It could only be to hide her face. Anxiety gnawed at Rhodopis' stomach as the priestess came closer.

"Are you... are you from the Temple of Horus?" Rhodopis asked rather shakily. "The king has sent for—"

With a swift flash of her hand, the priestess threw back her hood and stood grinning at Rhodopis, but several ragged heartbeats thundered past before recognition struck.

Then, at last, Rhodopis let her mouth fall open in shock. "Amtes? Can it really be you?"

She didn't wait for a reply. Rhodopis threw herself across the space between them; Amtes hurried forward to meet her, wrapping Rhodopis in a long, comforting embrace. Face pressed against Amtes' shoulder, Rhodopis heard a strange sound bubble from her chest. She didn't know whether she was laughing or sobbing.

The guards, she reminded herself through the sudden, turbulent rush of emotion. *They may not be on the rooftop, but they can still see. They'll report everything I do to Psamtik.*

With an effort, Rhodopis quieted herself and pulled back from the embrace. But she couldn't stop herself from staring up at her friend in unrestrained awe.

"I never thought to see you again," Rhodopis said, struggling to keep her voice low. "What are you doing back in Memphis? And how did you come to be here, in the palace—in the king's private quarters?"

"I ought to ask you the same. When Polycrates sailed away that night, and we left you there on the quay with that horrible sod's sword pressed against your gut, I felt certain you'd be killed, my lady."

Rhodopis shook her head, laughing. "I'm no lady. You shouldn't call me that. But I wasn't killed—I got away from Charaxus. Poor old Charaxus... he's dead now. Psamtik took off his head. The fool should have gone to Lesvos when he had the chance."

Amtes lifted a brow. "That sounds like a story I'd enjoy hearing."

"We don't have the time for it." Rhodopis glanced around, eyeing each soldier on the garden wall. They were pacing out their rounds and seemed to pay no heed to the two women on the Pharaoh's roof. But one could never be too certain—or too cautious. "Tell me your story, Amtes. Why are you here, instead of the Horus priest I'd expected?"

Amtes lifted the edge of her sun cape, revealing at least half a dozen amulets and charms, all hung from her neck on braided linen cords or thin strips of leather. "I may not be a priest, but I am a priestess of Horus. Just as good, wouldn't you say?"

"Better. But I never knew you were a priestess. Have you always been?"

"I've been in service to Lord Horus for many years. My family committed me to the temple here in Memphis when I was twelve years old; where do you think that wily old cat Khedeb-Netjer-Bona found me? When she wanted a scribe to accompany you to Babylon, she chose me from the temple. Amasis wasn't especially loyal to the gods of Kmet, but the chief wife always was."

"Was? You make it sound as if Khedeb-Netjer-Bona is dead." Anxiety flared up anew in Rhodopis' stomach. "Psamtik said he would imprison her at the Horus Temple, but—"

Amtes shook her head. "We heard in the temple that Psamtik had taken the chief wife prisoner—we even heard he gave it out that she would be held by the Horus priests. But I doubt whether he'd ever intended such a thing. Khedeb-Netjer-Bona is not at the temple, my friend. I think it unlikely that she still lives."

Rhodopis exhaled—a long, drawn-out sigh of regret. "Khedeb-Netjer-Bona was my enemy, from the time she sent me to Babylon. Before then, too, I suppose. But there was still something about her I couldn't help admiring—a strength few other women have. She deserved a better end than the one she got. And her poor daughters—I wonder if they know."

"Perhaps it's for the best if they don't know—not just yet. Psamtik has claimed them as wives, hasn't he? We heard that, too."

"He has," Rhodopis said darkly. "I pity those girls. You're right; it would be a mercy if they didn't know about their mother's fate. I can imagine if I were in either of their places, the hope that I would see my mother again might be all that kept me from going mad." She wiped a tear from the corner of her eye, then said briskly, "I had hoped to speak with Khedeb-Netjer-Bona—to ask her advice on my predicament. There's no hope of that now, but the gods have sent you to me. Before I tell you what I need, though, I want to hear what has happened to you. This all seems so improbable, so strange! Tell me everything that's happened since I saw you last."

"I find myself rather in shock," Amtes agreed.

She spotted a low stone bench between two of the potted palms and led Rhodopis to it. They sank down together in the cool shade, side by side.

"This morning, when Psamtik's messenger came to the temple, it was only by chance that I overheard. The man said, 'The Pharaoh's woman is with child. Send someone who knows the proper spells to protect Lady Rhodopis and the baby, at once.' As soon as I heard your name, I felt as if a fire had been kindled in my chest. I knew I had to be the one who would go to the palace. It wasn't enough merely to know that you still lived; the god himself drove me toward you with such an overwhelming force. I went straight to the High Priest and fell on my knees, and begged him to give me the honor... even though I had only just returned to the temple after a long absence. I think he was inclined to tell me no, but he stammered over the word—he couldn't seem to force it out. So he finally said yes, and threw up his hands in disgust. Horus himself wouldn't allow the High Priest to refuse my request."

Rhodopis took her hand, squeezing gratefully. "How long were you away? Did you make it all the way back to Babylon?"

"Oh, yes—and I was not pleased to cross the desert again. Twice. But I've gotten ahead of the story. Let me tell you everything, from the moment we parted.

"Polycrates' fleet is faster than I'd imagined. The same night we left you in Memphis, we made it to the place where the river forks and the delta region begins. Polycrates' men were waiting for us there—his entire fleet of ten ships, and every one as fast as his own. It took just one day to reach Tanis, where we filled the boats with supplies for the journey. Then we were out to sea.

"Sea passage was closer to bearable on a Greek ship, but not by much. The one great mercy was that we arrived in Gebal just three days later. The speed of that pirate's ships can't be overstated. I wish the same could be said for the desert crossing, but it took every bit as long as it had taken before. If I hadn't kept a tally of the days, I would swear it took longer, and every hour tried my patience. I had to travel in Archidike's company the whole way; she didn't enjoy desert life, and seemed determined to make everyone else suffer along with her."

"Archidike went as far as the desert? I'd thought Polycrates would put her ashore in Tanis, or in some other Egyptian town."

Amtes laughed. "Polycrates would never part with

Archidike—not willingly. He's besotted with that woman. At first, I couldn't understand why. Archidike is worse than a stonemason's rasp; she's so abrasive. But the more time we spent in one another's company, the more I came to see her better sides."

"You're a better person than I, if you could find any good in Archidike's spirit," Rhodopis muttered.

"She's not so bad—not when you get to know her. Life hasn't treated her kindly, and so she lashes out. But if you can work your way in past her defenses, Archidike is a kind and generous woman."

Rhodopis barely restrained herself from rolling her eyes. The last thing she wanted now was to offend Amtes. "So you went all the way back to Babylon—and Archidike went, too."

"Oh, yes. It was just as you'd said: I stood in your place, vouching for Polycrates. Cambyses didn't remember me. I've never trembled so much in my life as I did at that moment, kneeling before him as he sat upon his throne, begging for him to believe my implausible story. But Phanes was there, and he recalled me—he stepped to my side and said, 'My king, this is the loyal servant of Lady Nitetis, who came to you as the Pharaoh's daughter. Let us hear what message this woman's mistress has sent from Egypt.'

"I told the king everything, then—how you wore your disguise as Lady Eulalia, how you worked tirelessly to find just the right ally for the Persian cause. When I'd convinced him you had remained utterly loyal to his interests, the king seemed most pleased to meet Polycrates and thrilled to hear how quickly his fleet had traveled from Memphis to Gebal.

"At that point, Cambyses put us all up in great style. We had rooms in the palace among his ambassadors, and he and his women feasted us every night.

"We'd been there only a few days when your message arrived by pigeon. I never read your letter, of course, but whatever news you sent whipped Cambyses into action, at twice the speed he'd been moving before. Phanes, too. Only a few more days passed before Cambyses declared himself ready. He had assembled a fat army—faster than I'd thought possible—and paid Polycrates well for the use of his fleet. And just like that, we were on our way back to Gebal."

"It's a wonder you didn't stay in Babylon," Rhodopis said. "I would have, if I'd had the choice."

"Babylon is beautiful. I was tempted to stay—don't think I wasn't. But I belong here, in service to my gods—the gods of Kmet."

Rhodopis looked warily around the rooftop again, but of course it was empty, save for the pigeons in their cote. Still, she lowered her voice even more when she spoke, as if she feared the guards on the garden wall might hear. "I'm surprised you still want Cambyses to come, now that Amasis is dead. Psamtik is a traditionalist—"

"No, he's not." Amtes scowled. "He can natter about the old ways until his face turns blue, but it's what a man does that tells the truth of his heart—not what a man says. A real, proper Kmetu King's Son would have observed the religious rites before taking the throne. He would have given the dead Pharaoh seventy days of embalming, and then performed the Opening of the Mouth ceremony at the king's tomb. Nothing else could qualify an heir to take the Horus Throne. What Psamtik has done is an abomination, an affront to all our gods. He doesn't deserve to rule Kmet; he has less right to the throne than Amasis had. So I say, let Cambyses do his worst. Let Persia cleanse the disease from Kmet, if that's the will of our gods. I trust Lord Horus; he would never direct me to wrongdoing. And my god has made clear to me what must be done if Kmet is to be restored."

"You and I are both on the gods' path," Rhodopis said.

"Doing whatever the Divine Ones direct, and nothing

more." Amtes grinned again. "I'm sure you pray as often as I do that they give you some way out, in the end... some slim hope of survival. This is a dangerous game we play; I've always known that."

"So you came back to Memphis," Rhodopis prompted.

Amtes picked up the dropped thread of her tale. "I knew I wanted to be in my homeland to see how this all would end, so I joined Cambyses and Phanes on Polycrates' fastest ship. But their plan was—and is still—to remain stationed just south of Gebal, clinging to the coast until the omens are favorable for an invasion. Then they will fall upon the Delta and sweep south to Memphis before Psamtik has time to react.

"The fleet is there now, waiting for a sign from Ishtar, with the Persian army camped on the shore. The king permitted me to press on alone to Memphis, for I reasoned I would be safest in the temple once the fighting began. Certainly, it would have been foolish to remain with the fleet. Psamtik will throw every scrap of power he can muster at those ships; I have no desire to stand on deck and open my arms wide, making myself a target for Kmetu arrows. The coming war will be one to cleanse the present disease from the Horus Throne and restore Kmet to its old ways—eventually, once Cambyses is assured of maintaining order. There can be no place safer than Horus' temple in a battle to make Kmet Kmetu again.

"Polycrates seemed to see the sense in my reasoning. He asked me to take Archidike along, with the hope that she could shelter in the temple, too. He didn't like to part with her, but Archidike seemed glad to leave the fleet behind. I believe she has some fondness for Polycrates, but not nearly as much as he has for her."

"Archidike is with you? At the Temple of Horus?"

"No; she would never fit into temple life. I can't imagine her passing for a priestess. But I found her a room above a weaver's shop not far from the temple. When fighting comes to the city

—as it must, sooner or later—she'll be close enough to the temple to seek refuge inside. That's the best I can do for her, I'm afraid."

"How long have you been in the city?"

"Four days."

"And the fleet is there, just beyond the Delta, waiting for a sign from the gods?"

Salvation—or at least an end to Psamtik's outrages—was so close. Yet somehow, Cambyses and his army seemed farther away than ever before. There was no telling when Ishtar might deign to deliver the omen for which Cambyses waited. He could linger just north of the Delta for days yet—for weeks— while Psamtik pressed on with his brutal reign. Every sunrise brought Rhodopis closer to the point of the usurper's sword, and every sunset drew his snare tighter around the Greeks of Memphis.

She took Amtes by the hand. "Listen, Amtes: I'm in need of some herbs, or something of the sort—"

"You're with child, aren't you? You want to be rid of it—is that it?"

Rhodopis shook her head. "That was only a story I told Psamtik. I had to get help from someone outside—someone who knows herbs better than I do. But I do need something deadly. For Psamtik."

Amtes' crooked smile was appreciative, but she shrugged in dismissal. "There's no need for that now. I've told you how close the fleet is. You need only wait; let Cambyses do the work."

"How long must I wait?"

"Until Ishtar speaks, I suppose."

"And how long will that be?" Rhodopis' voice dropped lower still, a rushed and urgent whisper. "Psamtik has already begun slaying Greeks in the streets. Surely you've heard about it. How many more will he kill?"

"He hasn't the resources to sweep all of Memphis,

massacring as he goes. He has enemies here in the palace—you know he must—and even in the temples, among the priesthood. If he stretches himself too thin, someone will be brave enough to strike, and pull the Horus Throne out from underneath him."

"I can't count on that—and neither should you. I can't count on Cambyses, either. What if he doesn't receive his sign for another moon's turn? What if he only finds a bad omen, and turns back for Persia with Psamtik none the wiser? I need certainty now. I have to be certain Psamtik can be defeated, absolutely assured he can never do to another person what he has done to me."

"It's not surety you want. It's revenge."

"What if it is?" She squeezed Amtes' hand again, gazing earnestly into her eyes. "The gods have brought me here, Amtes—to this place, this time. I don't know whether it's the Thracian gods I speak of, or the Persian gods, or the gods of old Kmet. All I know is this: I've gone where they have moved me without complaint. I've taken every path they open to my feet, without the least question. I've submitted to their will and made myself a tool in their hands. Why would they have put me here, in Psamtik's very bed, if they didn't intend me to be close to him? And why should they require me to be close to Psamtik, unless it's for this?"

Amtes made no response. She stared across the river, eyes distant and searching.

"The gods brought you here, too," Rhodopis persisted. "Lord Horus, whom you have always served so well. He stopped the High Priest's tongue, so he couldn't deny your request, and made the path clear for you to be here now with me. Horus intended you to hear my words, Amtes. He wants you to hear my plea."

Still, Amtes said nothing. Her gaze never wavered, fixed to

the low purple hills far across the river. But after a long pause, she nodded, then patted Rhodopis' knee.

Rhodopis smiled.

"It's risky," Amtes said.

"I know."

"I may not be able to come to the palace again. I don't know when Cambyses will strike, and I have many other things to see to before he does—family and friends in the city, whom I must convince to leave before the battle begins. And," she added wryly, "the High Priest may find his tongue unrestricted when I ask his permission next. But I'll do what I can. I will send what you require, even if I can't come myself."

"Use this as your excuse." Rhodopis patted her lower abdomen. "If we do our work well, you and I, Psamtik will never learn that I'm not with child. He won't be among the living long enough to realize it."

Amtes nodded and rose from the bench. "I'll send someone I trust if I can't come again." She paused, looking down at her sandals for a moment. When she met Rhodopis' eye again, tears beaded her lower lashes. "I missed you. I can't tell you how glad I am to know you're safe."

Rhodopis ran her hands reflexively up her arms, brushing away the chill of the river breeze—and wishing she could wipe away the bruises that marred her skin.

Safe—not yet.

She harbored little hope that the gods would preserve her much longer. They didn't require her to live, Rhodopis knew—only to carry out her work. But she wouldn't speak of that now.

She embraced Amtes. "If we don't see each other again, then know that I considered you a friend."

"And I you."

Amtes left a kiss on Rhodopis' cheek, then turned away, sweeping her linen sun-hood up to cover her face. A moment later, she had disappeared down the staircase, leaving

Rhodopis alone on the rooftop, with only the birds in their cote for company.

Rhodopis stood in silence for a long while, listening as the pigeons settled on their roosts. Then she stepped to the rooftop's low wall and turned her face to the north, watching... waiting.

❧ 16 ❧

ENEMIES AND FRIENDS

That night, despite Psamtik's proximity, Rhodopis slept more deeply than ever before in the Pharaoh's great lion-footed bed. Her dreams were half-formed things, a scattering of disjointed images and words only partially heard. But a pleasant sense of warmth came to her from the spirit-world of sleep; the gods blessed and comforted her with memories of Amtes combing gently through her hair, with the feel of sunlight in Iadmon's garden, with the soft, distant laughter of her sister Aella, unburdened and free. Everything she saw, everything she touched was colored a brilliant blue—lapis and turquoise, sky-blue and river-blue, and the deep, dark indigo of a starless sky. She remembered the Ishtar Gate in Babylon, tiled in every conceivable shade of that miraculous color, and for a moment she felt a stray wind against her cheek, dry as the endless desert, scented by the flowers of Cambyses' terraced gardens.

She woke with the first pink flush of dawn, watching through the window as the light's strength gathered slowly, warming the spaces between sycamore leaves and edging the fronds of palms with a honey-golden sweetness. Birds roused in the garden outside the Pharaoh's chamber. The first tentative notes of their morning song seemed to reinforce the pleasant calm of her dreams. She lay still, listening as the chorus grew, bird by bird. Soon their tiny voices drowned the rhythm of Psamtik's sleeping breath, and the pains in Rhodopis' ill-used body ebbed until they all but disappeared.

What had wakened her so early? She felt instinctively that it must have been something more than her piecemeal dreams, more than the birds in the trees. Below that subtle glow of contentment, she sensed an upwelling of readiness. Had the time come, then? Would she act soon, take the final path the gods would open before her, and strike with her whole being—the unbreakable blade in the divine hand?

Or had it only been the light of dawn that had pulled her from those pleasant dreams?

Beyond the Pharaoh's bedchamber, across the rooms that comprised his quarters, Rhodopis detected the faintest of sounds, a scraping and scuffling of feet, the low murmur of voices near the outer door. It was only the guards in their rotation, the soldiers assigned to morning watch taking the place of those who had stood beside Psamtik's door all night through. The sound was ordinary, part of the palace routine. But all the same, Rhodopis felt compelled—commanded—to slip from the bed and creep nearer the outer door.

Carefully, so as not to wake Psamtik, she moved the linen coverlet aside and eased herself from the mattress. She was naked, and the new day had not yet warmed; her skin tightened with gooseflesh as she went silently through the Pharaoh's bedchamber, moving on the balls of her feet with a dancer's easy grace. In the sitting room, she pulled a woven silk throw from a couch as she passed, wrapping it around her body to ward away the chill, but she didn't slow. The closer she came to the outer door, the more urgent her errand seemed until she had to fight the urge to run through the dim room with her bare feet slapping against the tiles.

Rhodopis pressed her ear against the crack between the two tall scarab doors. She could hear the soldiers clearly now, their uneasy shuffle and tense voices.

"Are you sure?" one man asked.

"Of course I am. D'you think I'd come to the king's chamber at this hour if I had any doubt? I tell you, the Delta is overrun. You have to alert the Pharaoh, man—now."

"Be calm, Sabu. There's no sense in losing your head. Better tell me everything you know, and leave out nothing. I'll make a full report to the Pharaoh." The soldier's tone said he didn't look forward to the task.

"Greek ships at the northern end of the Delta," Sabu said impatiently. "Somewhere between nine and twelve of them. We've had three messages already, and none agree on how many ships, but more birds were flying in when my commander sent me to tell you. They're fast ships, by all accounts—much faster than our own."

"Greek? But you said Persian—"

"Persian banners flying from their masts," Sabu insisted. "The ships are Greek in design, but the army they carry is not. This is an invasion, I tell you—and it's an alliance between Greece and Persia! If even the most conservative estimate from the Delta is to can be trusted, then the invading fleet will arrive here in Memphis in just a few days. That's assuming these Persian bastards don't stop to loot and burn every city and town along the way. We've got to act now, and keep them sequestered at the edge of the Delta." Sabu added with an ominous air, "If we can."

"Very well," the first guard said. "I'll wake the Pharaoh, if you're sure these reports are credible."

Rhodopis jerked away from the door and scuttled across the chamber, dodging around half-seen couches and huge ornamental vases. She reached the door to the privy and shut herself inside just as the door guard rapped his staff hard against the floor, sending a high, loud knock reverberating through the king's apartments.

Rhodopis waited in the darkness. The soldier rapped again, and when the echoes of his alarm died away, she heard Psamtik muttering in his bedchamber. A moment later, his curses drew nearer. Rhodopis pushed the privy door open and stepped out into the sitting room, feigning wide-eyed surprise.

"What is this?" Psamtik spat, glaring at Rhodopis through the half-light of dawn as if she had caused the disruption herself. He had tied a kilt hastily around his hips, the same wrinkled garment he'd discarded on the floor the previous night. It hung from his body like a beggar's rags. "When I command you to sleep in my bed, I expect to find you when I wake."

"I'm sorry, my king," she said hastily, pulling the silken wrap tighter around her shoulders. "I had a need, that's all. Of course I meant to return to your bed. What's that knocking?"

Psamtik turned away from Rhodopis, grunting with annoyance. "Come," he shouted to his guards.

One of the paired doors squealed open on its bronze hinges, spilling lamplight from the corridor into the king's quarters. The guard stood silhouetted against that light, but though she couldn't read his face, Rhodopis could see how the man trembled. One look at Psamtik's hard expression, and he dropped to his knees on the threshold.

"I beg your pardon and your mercy, my king. I would not have disrupted your sleep if I hadn't good reason to believe—"

"Get up, you fool," Psamtik said. "Tell me what you mean by this... knocking like a stonecutter while I'm still asleep."

The guard lurched back to his feet but kept his face lowered to the floor as he spilled out the news Sabu had brought. As he spoke, Rhodopis could feel the rage building in Psamtik, word by word—even from across the sitting room. Before the man had finished, Psamtik's breath rasped in a throat constricted by his fury.

"Go and fetch every general and commander on the palace grounds," he grated at the soldier. "Bring them all to the large audience chamber at once. You have a quarter of an hour. Do you understand?"

"Yes, my king!" The man saluted with a fist to his chest, then spun on his heel and vanished into the corridor. The remaining door guards closed the chamber, cowering when they moved into Psamtik's line of sight.

He rounded on Rhodopis, anger lighting his eyes with such heat and intensity that she shrank back as if from a metalsmith's white-hot forge.

"Persians!" Psamtik hissed through clenched teeth. "And Greeks. Gods-blasted, thrice-damned *Greeks*."

She shuddered inside the thin silk wrap, feeling smaller and more breakable than ever before. She was convinced Psamtik would enact his vengeance against all Greeks then and there, thrashing her, kicking her, cutting her with any blade that came to hand until her treacherous Greek blood ran out like a river and puddled around his feet. For one bleak, dark heartbeat, Rhodopis felt sure the gods would deny her the revenge she sought, after all. The knowledge of it burned her throat with an acrid, nauseous taste, and she railed helplessly against divine injustice.

But then Psamtik beat his palms against his wrinkled kilt. "Go and find my body servants," he shouted. "Now! There's no time to waste. I must be properly dressed and in the audience hall by the time my commanders arrive."

Rhodopis needed no further instructions. She ran for the chamber door, shoved it open, and sprinted past the startled guards toward the quarters of the Pharaoh's body servants, relief lending wings to her feet even as blind fear gnashed its teeth against her heels.

***

By the time Rhodopis returned to the king's quarters a few minutes later with his two panting, anxious servants in tow, Psamtik was too distracted by the grim news to pay any heed to his bed-warmer. She let the silk wrap fall in his bedchamber and dressed in her old tunic as quickly and unobtrusively as she could manage. When she tied the sash around her waist, the old kerchief fell to the floor. She grabbed it and stuffed it back in its place behind the knot of her belt, then stood tensely beside the chamber door, watching as Psamtik's servants draped him in his best long, pleated kilt and slid layers of golden cuffs onto his arms.

When Psamtik's back was turned to the door, Rhodopis took her chance. She dodged out of the bedchamber and rushed out into the garden, the only place where she might hope to find peace—the only place where she could hide from Psamtik's anger. In the golden glow of morning, she took the path toward the rose trellis, her hidden sanctuary beside the pond. Her thoughts raced, clamoring together until she could hardly sort one from the other.

So Cambyses had finally made his move. Ishtar had given her omen, made her will clear to the king of Persia. Rhodopis did not doubt that whatever garrisons existed in the Delta region would fight back with all force, utilizing every resource the Delta possessed to repel Cambyses—every ship, every man. Would their efforts be enough? The Egyptian fleet was more numerous by far than Polycrates' collection of pirating vessels. But the pirate's ships could sail far faster than any Egyptian boat. Polycrates could outmaneuver the Egyptians, too.

Yet Rhodopis couldn't rid herself of a terrible, sinking feeling, a heavy stone of fear dragging at the very center of her spirit. What if Cambyses were killed long before he reached Memphis? What if some lucky strike by a lumbering Egyptian boat were to stave in the hull of his ship and sink the king of Persia to the bottom of the Nile? Psamtik would win easily, then. Egypt would be forever in his hands—and so would Rhodopis.

If only I knew how the fighting fared. If only I could find out! Then I wouldn't need to fear.

She paused on the garden path before she reached her sanctuary. Then she turned and looked up at the rooftop of Psamtik's quarters. The building glowed in the morning sun, bright and steady, like the beacon of a torch shining through stifling night.

That guard said more birds were flying in all the time—more news from the north.

With Psamtik and all his commanders gathered in the audience hall, perhaps there would be no one left to intercept the messenger pigeons... for an hour or two, at least. Perhaps she could learn more about the action in the Delta, after all.

Rhodopis turned her back on the rose trellis and made for the rooftop instead. She sprang up the staircase two steps at a time. When she reached the flat terrace at its top, she hunched with hands braced against knees, catching her breath in the warmth of the morning sun.

The Nile sparkled below her, glittering in shades of soft turquoise and pale purple as the sun climbed higher in the east. Thin banners of smoke rose from cooking ovens across the city, hanging white and still in the morning air. The people of Memphis were already engaged in their morning routines, unaware of the turmoil within the palace—and blind to the danger that had descended upon the north.

As Rhodopis stood panting, two fat, gray birds winged

toward the rooftop and landed on the brick wall. There they strutted and cooed with an impatient air. She could see the small rolls of papyrus tied to their stiff little legs.

"Easy, friends," she said to the birds, approaching slowly with one hand outstretched, just as the pigeon tender had shown her. Perhaps these messages would teach her nothing new, but perhaps she might learn which way the fighting had gone, if any decisive action had yet been taken. Either way, she was determined to know what fateful news those scraps of papyrus bore.

One of the pigeons stilled beside her wrist, ducking its head and blinking its onyx-black eyes, ready to accept her touch. But just as Rhodopis was about to close her hand gently around its back, a commotion of voices at the foot of the stair startled both birds into flight. She cursed through clenched teeth, watching the birds circle the rooftop as those confined in the cote flapped in alarm, calling to their fellows in the sky.

"Where is the Pharaoh's companion?" a woman shouted roughly.

The sound of that voice—its timbre, its every inflection—sent a chill of recognition racing up Rhodopis' spine. She turned abruptly from the pigeons and stared in disbelief toward the staircase.

Ranefer, the king's body servant, answered. "A moment, please, my lady. You can't simply storm about the royal quarters at will! When the Pharaoh returns from his business and finds you here, he'll—"

"I've come from the Temple of Horus on an important errand. The Pharaoh won't impede the god's will."

"My lady, please! I—"

"Just tell me where to find the woman called Rhodopis. I've brought herbs for her condition. Once I've delivered them, I'll be gone again, and the Pharaoh will be none the wiser."

Oh, gods. Rhodopis' thoughts whirled about her head;

indeed, the whole rooftop and the garden beyond seemed to spin around her. She leaned one shoulder against the pigeon cote, fearful the sudden dizziness might cause her to fall. *Of course Amtes would send her, of all people. Of course.* The gods never left off toying with mortals, did they? This was a convergence of fate so toothsome, no deity could have resisted the temptation—even though Rhodopis had committed herself to their divine cause, submitted herself to their will. She was mortal, and therefore a plaything of fate.

Best to get this over with as quickly and painlessly as I can. If she has the poison I need, then I'll take it, and be glad for it. And if the gods have any shred of pity for their faithful servant, I'll never have to see her again.

Rhodopis called out, "I'm here, Ranefer, on the rooftop. Send that woman up to me."

She braced herself, but not hard enough. Nothing could prepare Rhodopis for the sight of *that woman*—the casually arrogant posture, the perpetual smirk on her full lips, the cold fire of those narrowed eyes, so shockingly blue against the deep-brown color of her skin. Rhodopis breathed in deeply, once, to steady her nerves. Then she folded her arms tightly below her breasts and waited for Archidike to speak first.

Archidike was dressed plainly for the first time since Rhodopis had known her. The unbleached linen tunic and tightly tied sash had more in common with the servant's garb Rhodopis wore than any expensive gown or robe she had donned as a hetaera. Amtes must have hidden Archidike in a humble place, indeed, for Rhodopis could scarcely countenance her former friend in such ordinary clothing.

It must grate on her terribly, Rhodopis thought (with no small portion of satisfied amusement), *to dress like the gutter trash she has always been.*

Archidike held a small basket slung over one shoulder; she

lowered it carefully to the rooftop, then stood with arms akimbo, fixing Rhodopis with a long, assessing gaze.

"Well," Archidike said at length. "Here we both are, in the Pharaoh's palace."

Rhodopis waited.

"Your hair. It's all shorn off. You didn't catch lice, did you? There are better ways to get rid of them. What a waste; your hair was your glory."

Rhodopis couldn't resist the urge to pass a hand across her scalp. Her red-gold hair had grown out just enough that it had begun to curl again.

"Never mind," Archidike said, and Rhodopis was startled to hear something very close to kindness the words. "It'll grow back, I daresay, and then it will be as beautiful as ever."

"Why have you come here? Where is Amtes?"

"Amtes sent me." Archidike nudged the basket with the toe of her sandal. "She couldn't come herself—had to see to some old grandmother or aunt in the city before things get out of hand. Things are about to get out of hand, aren't they? And soon, too, I'd guess."

Rhodopis glanced over her shoulder. The messenger pigeons had settled on the wall again. A third winged up from the city and joined them, bobbing its head in excitement. To Archidike, she said, "Don't know, exactly." *But I could find out, if you'd leave me alone with these birds.*

"Come, Rho; don't be cagey. You're in the Pharaoh's bed. Don't pretend you're not—I'm no fool. You must know some news. Surely you've heard something worth repeating."

"If I'd heard anything good, I wouldn't repeat it to you."

"I see." Archidike's hands slid from her hips; her arms hung limply. She seemed to diminish before Rhodopis' eyes, her very personality shrinking until she was as humble as the unbleached linen she wore. "You're still sore with me, aren't you?"

Rhodopis gaped at her, unable to countenance what she'd just heard. "'Sore' is too small a word. If I'd never seen you again, I would have counted it too soon."

She took a few steps toward Archidike, eager to take whatever herb or potion Amtes had sent, but reluctant to draw too close. Archidike may play at being modest, but Rhodopis was no fool. She would give the blue-eyed viper no chance to bite again.

"Give me whatever Amtes has sent—then it's best if you're gone. There's no telling when the Pharaoh will return, and Ranefer was right: Psamtik won't be pleased to find you here."

"Don't you want to ask me how I've fared since we saw each other last? Aren't you curious—even a bit?"

"No. Just give me—"

"I should thank you," Archidike broke in. Rhodopis could hear no sarcasm in her former friend's words, but she doubted their sincerity, all the same. "I was furious with you when you dragged me onto Polycrates' ship. I felt sure I'd never see Memphis again, just when I'd gotten free of Xanthes and made my way in the world. I could have killed you with my bare hands, just then—would have done it, if you'd been on that ship, too. I would have clawed out your heart with my nails. But when I got to Babylon—!"

Archidike paused, shaking her head in wonder. She stared out over the city to the great river and the violet hills beyond, but she seemed to see nothing but the Ishtar Gate and the grand spectacle of the Persian capital spread like a carpet at her feet. "I would never have gone there, never would have seen it, if it weren't for you. That city was like nothing I'd ever imagined. The art, the buildings, the music... even the colors, the robes the people wore in the streets. And that palace. By all the gods." She laughed, short and sharp, the way she used to. "I don't have to describe Babylon to you, I suppose. You were there. Amtes told me all about it, how you were wedded to the

Persian king and lived there in the palace. I spent only a few days in the palace and saw little more than the ambassadors' quarters, but I'll never forget those gardens, nor the view from the terraces. I once thought Memphis was the greatest city in all the world, but now it seems provincial by comparison."

Still Rhodopis waited in silence. As Archidike sighed, recalling Babylon's unparalleled glory, Rhodopis wondered whether she ought to take the basket herself and rummage in it for whatever slim salvation Amtes had sent.

"I must hand you this, Rho: I never expected you would send me all the way to Babylon. And back. What an adventure it's all been, though I could have done without Polycrates pawing at me the whole way."

Rhodopis shifted her weight from one foot to the other, biting her lip. Time was running short; Psamtik might return at any moment. Or his men might appear on the rooftop and pluck the messages from the pigeons' feet before Rhodopis had her chance.

The restless movement seemed to pull Archidike back from her reverie. She narrowed her eyes at Rhodopis—merely speculative, not in any threatening way. "You're afraid. Of what?"

"You know what. You don't think I'm foolish enough to say it aloud, do you? Here in the palace—in the Pharaoh's quarters?"

Archidike smiled. "You don't need to worry. I've seen..." She paused and glanced around, eyeing the guards on the garden wall. "Shall we say, I've seen what waits in the north, first-hand. It's a good army, well trained and fearless, and Polycrates' ships can fly like falcons on the wing."

"That's not what I'm afraid of."

Not exactly. Rhodopis didn't dare tell this creature more— that she feared Cambyses would fall in battle, that Psamtik would manage to cling somehow to Egypt. That even if Cambyses survived, and brought the fleet here to Memphis, Psamtik would spill out his hatred of the Greeks in one final act of violence, taking hundreds of innocent people with him to the afterlife. She would never admit what she had suffered at Psamtik's hands—why she knew him to be so dangerous. Not to Archidike, the betrayer.

"It's me you're afraid of, then, isn't it?" Archidike's brows fell into a regretful frown. She chewed on her thumbnail for a moment, a gesture of such startling insecurity that Rhodopis laughed aloud in shock.

"Please don't be afraid," Archidike said softly—almost begging. "I know you were with Cambyses, and yet here you are, in the Pharaoh's palace. Don't think I can't read what's written on this wall, Rho. I know what you are—what you're doing here. I won't betray you. I never could."

Outrage burst from Rhodopis' chest along with her words. "Never could betray me? You already have!"

Archidike hung her head. "And the truth is, I've always regretted it."

Silence hung heavy between them. Archidike hugged herself, watching her own feet as she fidgeted, nudging the strap of one sandal with the toe of the other. "Do you know how I became a hetaera?" she asked at length.

This shift in Archidike's demeanor sent a prickle of suspicion up Rhodopis' back. Her scalp tingled as if her short curls tried to stand on end. "No, and I don't care, neither." At that unwelcome slip of speech, Rhodopis' face burned hotter than a clay oven. Archidike affected her too much, made her forget all her careful composure, the rigid poise and firmness of purpose that had kept her alive in Psamtik's hands. Rhodopis had to send this viper on her way, and soon. It was too dangerous to remain in Archidike's proximity.

Archidike ignored her protest. "My mother sold me to a trader. Not Xanthes; a man even more boorish and tiresome, if you can believe it. And my mother didn't sell me the way your mother sold you—sadly, out of desperation. She did it to be rid of me. My mother had been a porna, you see—a common prostitute. I never knew my father's name—she didn't know, either. She had never intended to have a child, never wanted me—a useless mouth to feed, and always underfoot, always in the way. She had tried to be rid of me while I was still in her womb—she told me so, many times—but none of the herbs or poisons she took had any effect. I stuck fast and refused to leave her in peace.

"When I was old enough to sell, she counted it a blessing. She came back to the dirty little room that had been my home —our home—with money in her purse and a great jug of honeyed wine in her hands. She raised the jug to me, as if to salute me, and said, 'Today is the best day of my life because my bed will be my own again. You're going away, and I won't see you again. The deal has already been struck.' Then she drank the longest draft I've ever seen a woman take, and when she lowered the jug again, she was smiling and laughing. It was the first time I could remember seeing my mother happy."

Tears rose, unwelcome, to Rhodopis' eyes. She blinked them away, determined not to waste a single one on the friend who had betrayed her.

But one question gnawed at her mind. Rhodopis couldn't stop herself from asking, "How old were you?"

"Ten."

The word was a blow to Rhodopis' stomach. She flinched backward, sliding a foot along the rooftop floor; the sound barely masked her gasp of surprise. Ten years old. Aella's age. Rhodopis didn't bother to ask whether Archidike had landed in the care of a kindly master, one like Iadmon—one who would train her conscientiously, protecting her from harm until she was old enough to do the work properly. She could guess the answer already.

Archidike pressed on relentlessly. "I didn't begin as a hetaera, of course. I started as a porna, but as I worked the alleys and quays, I kept my eyes open and my wits about me. It wasn't long before I learned the difference between a hetaera and... what I was. What my mother had been. I was determined to rise above my lot in life—determined to rise higher than my mother. I had to cheat and steal so I could dress like a fine lady, but once I'd learned how to look the part of a hetaera, I ran away from the man who'd bought me and went straight to Xanthes. I'd heard he was the best, you see—that his girls were the finest in all of Memphis, and I was set on being the best. Nothing else would do.

"Well, when Xanthes saw my unusual eyes, he was dead gone. He said he had to have me for his Stable, and he wouldn't dream of my going back to the streets. He paid off my first owner and took me in, and my training began that very day. I've never forgotten the first thing he told me. He said, 'Despite the beauty, the luxury of this existence, it's a hard life, girl. You've got to be tough—far tougher than anyone else around you. For whichever girl is weak or soft, whichever girl fails to harden her heart, will find herself used up and discarded—utterly destroyed.'"

"I heard much the same, when I started," Rhodopis muttered.

Archidike sighed. "I suppose I took his advice too much to heart. I allowed myself to grow too hard, callused all over. Xanthes wasn't all wrong; it was a difficult life, and we never could let our guard down, could we? Not with the likes of Bastet lurking about, ready to claw out your eyes or steal your best jewels."

At the mention of stolen jewelry, Rhodopis pressed her lips together.

"But Xanthes wasn't entirely correct, either," Archidike said quickly. "You never hardened your heart. You never lost sight of who you truly are. You stayed good, Rho, right through to the middle of your spirit. And you weren't destroyed. Look where it brought you, in the end."

Look where it brought me, indeed. Trapped by Amasis, brutalized by Psamtik, caught between two powerful kings. Corralled into spying, with no real say in the matter, the way an untamed horse is corralled in a pen before it's broken to the harness—before its spirit is subdued forever.

But Rhodopis said nothing. She watched Archidike steadily, searching her face and posture for a hint of sincerity, for any sign that might confirm whether Archidike was manipulating her yet again—or finally telling the truth.

All at once, tears welled in Archidike's eyes. She made no move to wipe them away, nor to conceal her weeping. They spilled down her cheeks in twin runnels, dripping from her finely pointed chin. "I was hard—too hard—and it made me rotten to the core. But I really did care for you, Rho. I swear it's true. I cared for you as I've never cared for anyone else. I meant every word I said to you, back in our Stable days—about doing it all together, teaming up as a pair. Living together, too. I can't tell you how badly I wanted it—how I lived for that dream, the life I thought we could make together. But I was too rotten inside to see the goodness in you. I let my jealousy overcome me—the auction, you know." She shook her head, swallowing hard, but the strangled sound persisted in her voice. "Every night—every single night—I've lain awake and wondered what might have been, how good and happy our lives would be now —if only I'd been honest, and hadn't hurt you."

Rhodopis bit her lip. She could think of nothing to say. Against her better judgment, she believed Archidike. This torrent of emotion was so far removed from Archidike's cool, untouchable style; Rhodopis felt instinctively that it couldn't be a show. Against all odds, the she-viper had proved to be human.

Yet Rhodopis had not remained as unscathed as Archidike believed. She wouldn't trust this woman again. She couldn't trust Archidike, now that her life—indeed, the fate of Egypt itself—hung in a precarious balance.

"Can you ever forgive me?" Archidike asked quietly. She raised pleading eyes to Rhodopis, blinking through a blur of tears.

"No!" Rhodopis all but shouted. Her heart pounded horribly in her chest, tightening beat by beat in her throat, nearly strangling her voice away. "No, I can't forgive you! How can you even ask it? You've been terrible to me, Archi. I loved you, too, but not anymore. You ruined my life with your cruelty. The things you put me through, the turn my life took after the Stable... I won't waste the words on you. You don't deserve to hear it, don't deserve to know the least thing about me! And you dare to ask forgiveness, after all this—after all your cruelty and deception?"

"I deserve that," Archidike said. Her face crumbled with anguish; her shoulders slumped, and for a moment Rhodopis thought she would fall to her knees. She wondered what she would do if Archidike began to wail in grief.

But Archidike remained standing, albeit with her eyes squeezed tightly shut. It seemed she could bear to look at Rhodopis no longer. "I won't try to change your mind. It's more than I can hope for; I shouldn't have asked you to forgive me in the first place." She drew a ragged breath. "I only hope you'll be safe, Rhodopis, in the fighting to come. I do sincerely wish for that. I've prayed that the gods will protect you, every night and every day since I understood what must happen, what Cambyses meant to do."

Archidike opened her eyes, bent to her basket, and reached inside. She drew out a tiny glass bottle made of dark-green faience. Its narrow mouth was sealed by a band of dark wax. She held the vial out in a trembling hand.

Rhodopis stepped forward and took it, careful not to allow her fingers to brush Archidike's skin. She examined the bottle, running her thumb over the smooth glass, testing its weight in her palm. "What is it? Did Amtes tell you?"

"Hemlock. There isn't much there, but you don't need much to do the trick. A few drops in his wine ought to be enough."

Rhodopis pulled the kerchief from behind her sash. She wrapped the bottle in the linen, then held the bundle in her hands, staring in disbelief. She had never noticed before that the blood that had stained the linen—her blood—was red no longer. The spots had gone brown with time—as rich and dark a color as silt in the farmers' fields. Her blood had settled into the linen, too deeply embedded now ever to wash clean.

Archidike turned away.

"Where are you going?" Rhodopis asked reflexively before she could wonder why.

"Back to my hiding place. The little mouse-hole Amtes has found for me. I'll wait there—and hope I won't be noticed in the fighting to come—until all the dust has settled, and Polycrates comes to find me. I suppose Polycrates is my best hope now for a long and happy life, assuming the gods will give me a long, happy life. I'm not at all sure they will."

"Polycrates cares for you," Rhodopis said. "I can tell. After all, he sent you back to Memphis with Amtes so you would be safe."

Archidike glanced back at Rhodopis, smiling wryly. "Polycrates didn't send me to Memphis. I came along with Amtes of my own accord, and I'm sure Polycrates went wild with rage when he found out. I knew by then that you were here in the Pharaoh's palace, you see, and I wanted to find you—to be sure you were safe. And," she added with a catch in her voice, "I hoped to make amends for how miserably I treated you. But there's no safety for you here, Rho. Psamtik is dangerous; I realized that when you sent your letter to Phanes and told how he beat those twin boys before the whole court. A man who can do something like that has no control, no judgment. He'll hurt you if you're not careful."

"You have no idea how dangerous Psamtik is."

Archidike's glance slid to Rhodopis' bare arms—to the bruises that covered them. Her mouth tightened. "I've some idea, I think. May that little green bottle do its duty well, then."

Archidike took up the woven straps of her basket and made as if to leave, but when the basket bumped against her side, she stopped again. "I nearly forgot." Despite her sorrow, there was a hint of laughter in her voice. She reached into the basket and pulled out another object—a bundle far larger than the bottle of hemlock, wrapped in plain linen and tied with a green silk cord. She proffered the package to Rhodopis.

"What is it?" Rhodopis asked cautiously.

Archidike smiled. "You'll see. Go on; take it. It won't bite. I can promise that much."

Rhodopis tucked the small jar of hemlock behind her sash and took the bundle from Archidike. When she untied the green cord, the linen fell open, revealing the rose-gold slippers. Rhodopis felt her mouth fall open, too, but no words came. It seemed a hundred years since Charaxus had given her those slippers, a thousand years since she had lain in Archidike's arms in a quiet alcove of the Stable.

"You left these on Polycrates' boat," Archidike said, "along with Amtes and me."

Rhodopis shook her head, bewildered, but she couldn't take her eyes off the slippers, the fine etching in the polished metal, the way they shone like new-kindled flames in the morning sun. "You could have traded them away. They could would have fetched a fat lot of hedj here in Memphis—even in Tanis or Gebal. You could have traded them in Babylon."

"I could have traded them," Archidike said, "but I didn't. They're yours; they belong to you. I've already taken enough of what's yours by right. I wanted to see these slippers returned to you. It's the smallest good I can do you."

"Archi—" Rhodopis looked up, but the other woman had already turned away. Archidike swung the empty basket by its straps as she descended the stairs. In moments, she had vanished without a backward glance.

17

OUT OF THE DARKNESS

RHODOPIS LINGERED ON THE ROOFTOP FOR HOURS, CROUCHED IN the narrow band of shade cast by the mudbrick pigeon cote. She turned the bottle of hemlock over and over in her hands, examining its smooth, deep-green sides as if she might find the answers to her many questions written on the glass. Rhodopis was no poisoner, nor even an herb-woman; she had no idea how to deliver the deadly dose to Psamtik, nor how much to use. How many drops would kill a strong, healthy man of Psamtik's size and constitution? If she hadn't been so startled to see Archidike, she might have thought to ask—though Archidike was unlikely to know the answer.

She fretted, too, over how she might survive the usurper's death—for Rhodopis could already predict how the next handful of hours or days would spool out. As soon as it became clear that Psamtik had been poisoned, Rhodopis would be the primary suspect—the only suspect, in truth, for, since her arrival in the Pharaoh's quarters, no one had been closer to Psamtik than she; no one else had been so consistently in his company. She considered finding an ally in the kitchens, enlisting their help to slip the hemlock into Psamtik's food. But it would take days—weeks, perhaps—to befriend a kitchen servant so thoroughly that Rhodopis could safely bring them into the work. Besides, involving others would only place them in danger. Rhodopis had no desire to condemn any other person to a traitor's death.

In time, she understood that there could be no real hope of survival. Once Psamtik was dead, his loyal adherents would move swiftly, whether or not Cambyses broke free of the Delta and continued toward Memphis. They would seize Rhodopis and put her to death; the best she could hope for was a quick, clean ending.

Once that grim realization took hold, a curious peace settled over her mind. Rhodopis had nearly reached the end of her work, the end of fear and pain. But she would see Psamtik fall before death claimed her; the vengeance she had hungered for—the justice the gods owed, for all she had suffered—was in her hands now. All that remained was to add her heart's venom to Psamtik's wine, to watch as he drank down her secret power, drop after poisonous drop. So long as she had the satisfaction of watching him fall, she would go to whatever fate the gods intended, unprotesting and fulfilled.

Rhodopis returned to the king's quarters mere minutes before Psamtik appeared. His face was dark with anger, eyes narrow and glowing with the heat of his fury.

Rhodopis hurried to meet him as he stormed into the sitting room. "You've returned, my king, from your audience with the generals and commanders."

"Of course I have, you witless slit."

"Is there news from the north? I beg you to tell me, my king."

Psamtik threw himself down on the nearest couch and cast Rhodopis withering stare, laden with disgust. "I suppose you're eager to hear that this Persian upstart has dealt me a serious blow, are you?"

Her heart pounded with sudden intensity. Rhodopis laid a hand on her waist-sash, feeling the reassuring bottle behind the knot. "Why would I want that, my king? I'm your servant, your—"

"Spare me the platitudes and send for wine. I'm in no mood to listen to your bleating protests. Do you think I don't know what you are?"

She swallowed hard, waiting. His words were an eerie echo of those Archidike had spoken on the rooftop hours before. Had Psamtik learned somehow that Rhodopis was Cambyses' ally—his spy? Would she lose the chance to take everything from him now—now of all times, when she stood so close to victory?

"You're a *Greek*," Psamtik spat. "You pray to your corrupt gods for my destruction, like all the rest of your kind."

Relief shuddered through her. Rhodopis clasped her hands. "Not I, my king! I carry your son and heir. I pray only for your health and prosperity, for the sake of my child. How can I—"

"Silence," Psamtik roared. "I told you to send for wine. Now do it, and let me hear nothing more." He pressed his fingers to his eyelids, sighing heavily. "I have much to think over, after hearing what my generals had to say."

Rhodopis did as Psamtik commanded, keeping herself well out of his line of sight until the wine arrived. She took a tray inlaid with silver and ivory from the kitchen servant who appeared at Psamtik's door. The wine jug that balanced atop the tray was heavy, and rocked as she moved; Rhodopis was obliged to step quickly to keep it and the golden cup beside it from crashing to the floor. She set the tray on Psamtik's low, ebony-wood meal table, then filled his cup with all the grace and style of a well-trained hetaera.

When she proffered the wine, Psamtik snatched it from her hand so quickly that some escaped the rim of the cup and splashed on the tile floor.

"You've overfilled it," he snapped.

Rhodopis dropped to her knees, dabbing up the spill with the hem of her tunic. "I'm sorry to displease you, my king." She watched the wine cup from the corner of her eye as Psamtik took a long draft, then returned it to the tray. It was still half full.

Psamtik rose from the couch and began to pace, stalking across the sitting room to the garden window, then back again. Rhodopis scrambled to her feet and stood beside the table, hands folded before the knot of her sash, head bowed in a show of meek obedience. Psamtik's restless circuit took him to the window four times before he began to speak—to mutter, in truth, for his words hardly carried, so that whenever he returned to the far end of the room, Rhodopis had to strain to hear him. She couldn't have guessed whether he was speaking to her, or merely trying to sort his troubled thoughts aloud.

"Not a single one of my men had a good plan. Not one! Nothing but excuses and blind speculation. What can I do with speculation? Nothing! I need information, intelligence I can trust—"

Psamtik turned his back and paced toward the window again, voice fading below the heavy tread of his feet. Rhodopis slipped her hand behind the sash, wondering whether she would have enough time to dribble the poison into his cup before he wheeled around and came back again. She burrowed her fingers past the folds of her stained kerchief and picked at the tight rind of wax, the bottle's seal.

"No one knows whether it's nine ships or a dozen," Psamtik said, "or a hundred! It could be a thousand, for all anyone can say."

Rhodopis pulled her hand out from behind the sash and returned to her previous posture, willing herself to remain as still as a marble statue. Psamtik came closer. She could almost feel his anger preceding him, formless and invisible yet still somehow palpable, like the clouds of humidity that rolled off the river with every morning's first light.

"And are they Greek?" Psamtik thundered. "Are they Persian? Who exactly is invading—which rat-born scum thinks to take Egypt for himself as if my kingdom is a fruit on the vine for any passer-by to pluck? The reports from the north are all nonsense, all contradictory. I've half a mind to travel to the Delta myself and—"

He turned again and marched back to the window.

Rhodopis knew she mustn't hesitate any longer. She pried at the bottle's stopper again, almost crying out when the nail of her forefinger bent under the pressure. She bit her lip and dug furiously at the wax; a moment later, the stopper came free.

She glanced toward the garden window. Psamtik had paused there, muttering his dark curses out toward the open sky—toward the very gods who had made him stop, just for a moment so that Rhodopis could act. She drew the bottle out from behind her sash and held it over Psamtik's wine cup. Her hand shook with a terrible, coursing, forge-hot energy—half excitement, half fear. For a moment, she considered upending the entire bottle into the cup but discarded that idea with the next frantic heartbeat. If Psamtik spilled his wine, or simply left it untouched, she would have no poison left. Instead, she allowed only a few drops of the thick, pale-green liquid to fall past the lip of the bottle. A pungent, unpleasant odor arose from the poison; the droplets spread and coiled over the surface of the wine like grease polluting water. Surely Psamtik would notice that his drink had been compromised. But there was no time to fret. He would move again soon; Rhodopis didn't doubt it. She straightened, stuffed the vial back into her sash, and pressed a shred of wax over the bottle's mouth. Then she returned to her previous position just as Psamtik took up his restless circuit again.

"—would have sailed north myself, but that blasted fool

Ankhef said we couldn't risk the Memphis fleet. In case the Delta garrisons fail to stop these invaders, he said, and they come for the capital. Ankhef seemed to think that was likely, too! He probably does know more about the garrisons than I do, but why? Why should a Pharaoh be kept in the dark about his own forces? When I learn which fool I employ is responsible for that doltish decision, I'll make him pay—him and all his family."

Psamtik halted again beside his couch. He glowered down at the wine cup, and Rhodopis' mouth went dry. Had he noticed the difference in his cup already? Had he seen the slick of hemlock floating on the wine's dark surface, smelled its noxious scent? He would strike her down—call for his soldiers to haul her away to the same bleak end they had arranged for Khedeb-Netjer-Bona.

But then Psamtik nodded lightly, as if in answer to a voice only he could hear. He held out his hand. "Bring me my wine."

Rhodopis sprang to obey him. When her fingers closed around the golden cup, she swallowed hard—but a quick glance at the contents reassured her. The oily slick of hemlock had dissolved as the poison sank into the wine. The tell-tale odor had vanished, too, leaving only the sweetness of honey and the musky bite of the grapes.

Psamtik took the cup roughly from her hand and drained it. A red trickle ran from the corner of his mouth; he wiped it on the edge of his sleeve, then handed the cup back to Rhodopis.

"Only the gods can say where the invaders are now. Ankhef didn't seem to feel much hope that the Delta garrisons could rebuff them. There wasn't enough time to alert all the garrisons, for one thing—though how these ships managed to arrive at the mouth of the river without being seen first is a mystery to me. Someone in my council actually suggested *sorcery* as an explanation for their speed and invisibility. Sorcery! No doubt, it comes down to men idling at their posts.

Idling or sleeping—soldiers whom I pay to keep their eyes open. I'll have every last one of them whipped in a public square, and they can count themselves lucky for it. Whipping is the least any man deserves for dozing at his post and allowing my enemies to sail an *entire fleet* into my river!"

Psamtik paused in his ranting. He pressed a hand against his stomach, momentarily troubled by some pain or disruption. But then he tossed his head impatiently and went on. "All the reports agree that those ships move fast, though—faster than any of ours can sail. If even the most hopeful estimation is correct, then the invaders have already made it to Djanet. And after hearing what General Ankhef and his commanders had to say, I see little hope that our ill-prepared Delta garrisons could stop them. They've certainly taken Djanet by now."

Psamtik looked at Rhodopis expectantly. She realized with a start that he hadn't been merely talking to himself; he expected some response from her. Shuddering with anxiety over Psamtik's wine, she swayed from one foot to the other, not knowing what to say. As Psamtik's eyes narrowed in annoyance, she blurted without thinking, "Djanet? Where is that city, my king? I don't know it."

Rage darkened Psamtik's face. She could see the line of his jaw harden as he clenched his teeth. "That's because you only know it by its Greek name: Tanis."

His voice was dangerously quiet, a whisper, a purr. Rhodopis edged backward, trying to put some distance between herself and the king, but Psamtik loomed over her, right fist raised to deliver the first blow.

"Kmet is not a territory of Greece," he hissed. "I am not owned by your Grecian kings, not a slave to their whims." He grabbed the collar of Rhodopis' tunic, hauling her closer. "It's you who are mine to do with as I please, not the other way round."

His fist connected hard with the side of her face; light

flashed behind her tightly closed eyelids as a terrible, swelling pressure bloomed across her cheekbone. It would turn to throbbing pain soon enough, Rhodopis knew. The force of his blow tore Rhodopis from Psamtik's grip—and tore the neck of her tunic, too. She staggered back, crossing her arms over her abdomen.

"My king!" she cried. "Think of the child!"

"The child! I care nothing for the whelp you carry." Psamtik advanced on her, raising his fist again. "I'll have no half-Greek son, no heir beholden to the Grecian dogs who seek to tame me. You must think I'm a fool, to—"

He stumbled. One moment, Psamtik towered over Rhodopis, an obelisk of menace and hate. The next, he had dropped to one knee, gasping.

Rhodopis straightened slowly. She watched Psamtik with curious detachment as he panted and pressed his hands weakly against the ground, trying to push himself up from that animalistic crouch.

She crept toward him, one cautious step after another. "My king—are you well?"

Psamtik looked up. His expression was eerily calm... knowing. "You treacherous bitch."

"I... I don't know what you mean. Shall I send for a physician, my king?"

"No," Psamtik said shortly. "I'm well enough. I'm not a weak old man like my father was. You can't bring me down as easily as that." Beads of sweat gathered on his forehead as he turned to read the sun's position through the garden window. "I'm going to the throne room now, to announce my plan to my subjects. There are more duties I must see to, plans..." His voice trailed off, but Psamtik stood with a grunt—unsteady, but tall and poised as ever. He wiped the sweat away and smiled coldly at Rhodopis. "Go open my chamber door. Now."

Rhodopis did as Psamtik commanded. Her heart seized

when she saw the contingent of soldiers waiting on the other side—twenty, at least.

They didn't know what I would do today, she told herself, soothing away this newly sprung fear. *They've only come to escort the king back to the hall.*

Psamtik crossed the sitting room slowly, taking each step with exaggerated care. When he reached the doorway, his men saluted, but Rhodopis could see how each man's brow creased with worry.

"Are you well, my king?" asked the leader of the unit.

"Perfectly well. I'll go to the throne room now, as arranged, but two of you are to remain behind. See to it that this Greek trash doesn't leave my quarters. When I've finished making my will known to the people of Kmet, I will dispose of her, and gladly."

The door slammed shut a finger's breadth from Rhodopis' face. She felt the vibration shudder through the swollen, tender skin of her cheek; the sensation only seemed to fill her with an urgent energy. She knew at once that she most certainly *would* leave the Pharaoh's quarters. Not to save herself—Rhodopis was already resigned to her death—but because she was determined to watch as Psamtik drew his final breath. She would witness his fall before she, too, was forced down into the underworld by his followers. That lone moment of victory was her due. It was all she lived for now, the very force that kept her heart beating within her fragile chest. The poison had proved fast-acting, taking hold more quickly than Rhodopis had expected. If Psamtik succumbed in the throne room—without Rhodopis there to witness it—she would only be robbed of her triumph.

There was no use trying to leave through the chamber doors; that much was plain. Rhodopis turned away and hurried through the sitting room. As she passed Psamtik's favorite couch, she took the woven silk blanket that lay across its foot—

the same one she had wrapped herself in the night before—and draped it over one arm. She went straight out into the garden, blinking in the glare of the low afternoon sun. There she paused, turning in a cautious circle, searching for Psamtik's men.

The usual handful of guards patrolled along the top of the garden wall, but they seemed to take little notice of Rhodopis. No doubt, the command he had given his door-guards only moments before hadn't yet made its way to the soldiers on the wall above. But Rhodopis knew it was only a matter of time—minutes, perhaps—before those guards, too, learned of Psamtik's orders. She must move quickly if she hoped to reach the throne room before the hemlock finished its work.

Rhodopis hesitated no longer. She found the path to the two great stone urns, the monuments that marked the boundary between the harem garden and the Pharaoh's. She still disliked the sight of those massive vases—the memory of Psamtik's first and most terrible assault was never far away when she stood in their shadow, or even when she caught sight of the upper edges of the dark stone edifices through the sycamore trees. But the harem garden was the only route open to her now. She must press on past the painful memories or lose this chance forever.

How quickly would Psamtik's command spread to the guards on the wall? She walked as briskly as she dared past untrimmed flower beds and patches of weeds—the garden had lain neglected in recent weeks as chaos had spread throughout Psamtik's palace. Her legs ached with the need to run, but Rhodopis knew a sprint down the path would only draw the guards' attention and put an end to her plans.

She felt as if she walked for hours—for years, and all the while her left cheek grew more painful, ever hotter to the touch. Every beat of that throbbing ache drove her on, flooding her gut with a terrible hunger to watch as Psamtik suffered, as he toppled from his throne just as Amasis had done. By the time she spotted the two urns flanking the path ahead, she was so eager to reach the throne room and feel that last rush of victory that no memories rose from the weeds to haunt her. Rhodopis breezed between the urns unimpeded and plunged on into the harem's vast garden without so much as a shout from the guards atop the wall.

Her feet remembered the route from the garden's far end to the huge, red-roofed harem house; Rhodopis dodged and turned among the beds and ponds, following pavers and gravel paths so well known to her that she might have trod them the day before. Every slender tree, every stone planter spilling over with flowering vines, seemed to greet her like an old friend, encouraging in their familiarity.

As she drew closer to the quarters, she could see small groups of women seated on the stone benches of the most spacious courtyard, or standing together in the ragged shade of palms, spinning their flax in a distracted and desultory manner. Some of the children played on a sunlit patch of grass—even in her driven state, Rhodopis had the presence of mind to send up a prayer of gratitude for their continued safety. But she bustled past the children without another glance in their direction and hurried on to the courtyard.

Several of the women looked up in surprise.

"Rhodopis," Sobek-Neferu said in surprise.

Nebetiah called out, "Wait a moment. What are you doing here?"

The broken spinning circle erupted into chatter.

"We haven't seen you for months."

"Where did you go?"

"Stop—tell us what's going on in the city!"

"Is there news of Khedeb-Netjer-Bona?"

"We heard something about ships and an invading army."

"Yes; what do you know? What can you tell us? Is Memphis safe? Our families—"

"Rhodopis, wait! Please!"

But she didn't stop—she couldn't. Only the gods knew how swiftly the hemlock would work. Rhodopis shook her head in brusque apology, then pressed on into the harem quarters.

The sweetness of exotic perfumes and the rich spice of bath oils wrapped around her. At once, her head began to swim. The first days in Amasis' harem sprang up in her mind, vivid and intense memories that bewildered her. She recalled her isolation in the midst of the women, the loneliness she had endured —but she remembered, too, a smooth peace, a security she hadn't recognized at the time. Wondering at the curious warmth that filled her heart, Rhodopis thought she might have been happy in the harem—those first few weeks, at any rate— truly untroubled for the first time since leaving her family in Tanis.

But there was no time to linger, no time to mull over the unexpected nostalgia. The green arch was just ahead, the separation between the harem's interior corridors and those of the palace at large. There would be guards on the other side of that arch. She must be quick and sharp to evade them.

Rhodopis shook out the silk wrap and wound it around her head and shoulders. It covered her short, red-gold curls and, she hoped, obscured enough of her face that she would not be immediately recognizable to Psamtik's men. She forged ahead, so conscious of her servant's tunic that her whole body itched. But there was nothing to be done about her lowly garb. She must hope the silk wrap was enough to distract the guards and prevent them from looking too closely.

When she stepped beyond the green archway, a man's voice called out behind her. "Halt, my lady!"

Rhodopis stopped in her tracks and turned smoothly to face the guards. There were three of them: great, ugly hulks who carried not only swords at their belts but heavy wooden clubs, too.

"My name is Shamiram." She affected the same Persian accent she had used to fool Khedeb-Netjer-Bona's guardsman during the fight between Amasis' and Psamtik's factions. "I am the daughter of Cambyses, king of Persia. My king Psamtik, may the gods defend him, has summoned me to the throne room. I must go at once."

The guards glanced at once another, shifting their weight uncertainly on their feet.

One of them shrugged. "It makes sense. With Persian ships in the Delta—"

"They aren't Persian, you half-wit," another guardsman said. "They're Greek."

"The ships are Persian, all right. And I've heard talk of this Cambyses fellow, too. It's he who has invaded."

"*Tried* to invade," the first guard snapped. "We'll throw him back into the sea. No doubt he's been routed already, and is running back to his desert rat-hole with his tail between his legs."

Rhodopis bowed. "I beg your pardon, my good men. As the Pharaoh has called me to the throne room, I must—"

"You're Persian," said the third man. "So tell us: is it Cambyses who's come? Your father?"

"You shouldn't speak to the Pharaoh's women in such a familiar way," the first fellow said.

"Oh, come off it, Si-Hor. There's no general lurking behind a pillar, waiting to hand you a commendation for perfection."

"And anyway," the third man added wryly, "this pretty little mouthful won't be the Pharaoh's woman for long—not if Cambyses truly has come."

Rhodopis pulled the silk wrap more tightly around her shoulders.

"You've frightened her," Si-Hor said. "I always knew you

were a boor." He turned to Rhodopis and jerked his head toward the palace's heart. "Get along with you, then, Lady Shamiram. We'd accompany you, but we were told off 'specially not to leave this corridor. You do know the way, don't you?"

"Yes." Rhodopis bowed again. "I thank you, my good men."

"Good luck to you, my lady," Si-Hor called as she hurried away.

She recalled the route from the harem to the interconnected throne and audience rooms as easily and naturally as she had remembered the garden paths. Soon she found the plain, narrow, unmarked door that opened, Rhodopis knew, into a specific humble chamber, hung with long wool curtains that stretched from the stone floor to the impossibly high ceiling, separating the waiting room from the vast halls where the Pharaoh conducted the business of state and ceremony. The curtained chamber was empty, its lamps unlit. But through the dense blackness, she could hear the clamor of many voices—the ambassadors, nobles, and generals assembled in the throne room, waiting for Psamtik to speak.

Rhodopis pressed her back against the chamber door, listening to the cacophony. There was no mistaking the current of tension running along that river of sound. Psamtik's subjects —even his military leaders—were discouraged and frightened. Surely the usurper-king knew it. Rhodopis imagined fear gnawing at Psamtik, too—boring bite by bite into his heart, a worm devouring a corrupt and rotten fruit. The image made her smile.

After a few moments, the darkness thinned as Rhodopis' eyes adjusted to the chamber. She could see a faint line of pale-gray light running vertically from floor to ceiling, some twenty paces ahead. *That must be the curtain I want,* she realized, *the one that leads to the throne room.* She crept toward it with hands outstretched, shuffling her feet along the carpets, wary lest she should collide with a lamp-stand or a table and alert Psamtik's guards to her presence.

Her fingers brushed the rough texture of wool. She found the edge of the curtain, draped against the cool, smooth massiveness of a pillar. Rhodopis pulled the heavy curtain aside—just enough to edge her slender body into the throne room—and blinked rapidly, eyes filling with sudden tears as the light from dozens of lamps replaced the darkness. She stepped out of the waiting-chamber and let the curtain swing shut behind her.

She found herself behind the throne-room dais; the brickwork steps rose above her, inlaid with gold, adorned by small figures of lapis, turquoise, and malachite—a green so deep it was almost black. The Horus Throne was perched at the summit of the dais, and she could see Psamtik's rounded blue crown—the Khepresh, symbol of war—rising above the chair's gilded backrest. He had reached the throne room, then; he still lived. Rhodopis was not too late.

A row of pillars ran down each side of the vast hall, banded in bright colors, painted with the angular images of lotus blossoms and figures of long-dead kings. Tugging the silken shawl closer around her face, Rhodopis headed for the nearest pillar. Lamps burned on tripods between each one, but there was enough space behind both pillars and lamps for servants to pass, pressed close against the outer walls. Rhodopis slid quietly down the length of the throne room, making use of that narrow passage, sheltered from Psamtik's view by the cover of shadows.

At least a hundred people had gathered in the hall— perhaps more. They talked ceaselessly, and as rumor and desperation spread through the crowd, their clamoring grew louder. When she had gone some distance from the dais, Rhodopis left the servants' area and slipped out among Psamtik's subjects. The stench of sweat rose from the crowd, choking and sharp. Amid the fearful murmurs and tense gestures of anxiety, Rhodopis moved like the dancer she was, confident and poised, ready for whatever the gods cared to bring.

Psamtik's steward rapped his staff against the dais steps. Silence fell as the crowd looked up to the Horus Throne.

Psamtik sat upright on his throne, yet Rhodopis could read the strain in his tight shoulders, and his face was grayed by the effort of maintaining his illusion, his image of confidence and power. He flinched; one hand twitched where it lay on the arm of his throne as if he longed to clutch at his stomach. But he remained steady.

When he spoke, Psamtik's voice cracked with strain, as if it was all he could do to make himself heard. "You have heard by now that strange ships have sailed into the mouth of the river and menaced our Delta outposts. Those reports are true. Our enemies have attempted to invade Kmet."

The crowd issued a collective groan.

"We await more news from Djanet and other northern cities, but I... I will..."

Psamtik paused, shuddering, and seemed to shrink as the poison assailed him from within. Rhodopis held her breath, clenching her fists as she waited for the beast who called himself king to fall. For every pain that wracked Psamtik, making his mouth twitch and his hands jump as they held the crook and flail, a corresponding rush of power coursed through Rhodopis' blood.

Archidike said I was kind and good. It was almost enough to make Rhodopis laugh aloud. She didn't feel kindly now; there wasn't the least shred of goodness in her, not the smallest down-feather bit of it clinging to her spirit. Neither did she feel any shame at the realization. She was powerful—indeed, the gods had made her the very embodiment of power and irascible strength when they had delivered the bottle of poison into her hands. It was she, in the end, who controlled her life, her fate. She marveled at her own transformation as she watched Psamtik struggling to speak, fighting to maintain his pretense of superiority. She reveled in the hot, thick joy that thrummed along her veins and burned in the place where he had struck her—in all the places where he had ever dared to touch her.

He would fall soon—now. Or if not this moment, then the next. Her fists squeezed harder until her nails bit into her palms, and she willed Psamtik to fall, to slump, to break down weeping with pain and helplessness before the eyes of his court. She had all but won. All that remained was for Rhodopis to witness her tormentor's end.

But Psamtik's display of weakness lasted no longer than a few ragged heartbeats. The next moment, he drew himself up and continued, his voice somehow stronger than before. "I have taken the advice of General Ankhef; the Memphis fleet will launch before moonrise and form a blockade across the river to the north of the city. If these Greek and Persian abominations should chance to slip past the Delta garrisons—which is unlikely, for the gods are on Kmet's side—we will sink them into the Iteru's depths before they can take our capital. Send out your scribes; tell everyone. There is nothing to fear. This is not an invasion; it is a folly on the part of our enemies. And soon all the world will remember why Kmet is never to be crossed."

Psamtik flicked the lapis-beaded flail, a curt dismissal. The crowd responded to his speech with a cheer that sounded weaker than watered beer. And when Psamtik stood, though his movements were slow and careful, he seemed as steady on his feet as he had ever been.

Rhodopis watched him descend the dais with narrowed eyes. The poison had had some effect ... but he seemed to be recovering.

More. He must drink more hemlock if he's to fall and stay down.

Rhodopis was out now, out of Psamtik's grasp, free from his abuse, his dreadful proximity. She could slip away with the scribes and messengers, pass the palace gate and lose herself in the city. She could find her way to the Temple of Horus and shelter with Amtes until the fighting was done.

But what if Cambyses fell? The Egyptian ships were inferior —Rhodopis knew it was true—but what if Psamtik's blockade did manage to sink Polycrates' fleet, after all? She had never learned much about warfare, but still, Rhodopis knew it might take very little to turn the tide of Cambyses' power. Polycrates' ships were as swift as arrows, but he had only a handful to his name. A few lucky strikes by the panicked Egyptians—or the casual whim of an impulsive god—might be sufficient to send Cambyses and his army to the bottom of the Nile, just as Psamtik had promised.

Rhodopis could flee the palace now... or she could return to Psamtik's quarters and see her work through to its sweet and bitter end. She would die—hadn't Psamtik already sworn as much?—but he would die first, preceding her into the underworld.

She would follow him, hounding him, chasing him even through death. His spirit would never rest. Rhodopis would pursue him, lashing with her vengeance, until eternity itself was exhausted, and the gods made the world anew.

18

A BITTER KISS

RHODOPIS RETURNED TO PSAMTIK'S CHAMBERS THE SAME WAY SHE had left them. The guards at the harem archway did not attempt to stop her; if they questioned her as she passed, Rhodopis was deaf to their words. Nor did she hear the women as they cried out for news of the invaders or demanded an explanation for her presence. The world held no sound for Rhodopis, save the determined tread of her feet and the steady beat of her pulse in her ears.

In the Pharaoh's sitting room, she pulled the silken wrap from her head and shoulders and dropped it on the floor beside Psamtik's couch. The sun had set, stealing the light of day from the garden. No servants had yet arrived to light the chamber lamps; color faded slowly from Psamtik's apartments as purple dusk coiled itself ever tighter around the palace.

Rhodopis stood waiting, facing the double doors, calmly alert for any word from the gods—a whisper of assurance, a promise of death, the command that would spell the final word of Rhodopis' life and condemn her to her fate. She hadn't the least idea how she would deliver the fatal dose of hemlock to the usurper-king. Although the lamps did not burn, some mousy palace servant had cleared away the tray and the wine jug while Rhodopis had been in the throne room. The cup that had held the first few drops of hemlock had disappeared, too.

It made no difference. Psamtik would never take food or drink from Rhodopis' hands again; of that, she was certain. Either the gods would provide one last chance to bring Psamtik to his knees—however brief that chance may be—or they would not. Her only choice now was to remain watchful, and act swiftly when the opportunity arose... if it came at all.

Rhodopis neither trembled nor wept. She knew her final moments were at hand; the sun had set on her last day among the living. When Psamtik returned, he would have her dragged away by his guards. But she felt no chill fear, no pangs of regret. She was ready now for the conclusion of her story, ready to dance the final steps as the music swelled to its last triumphant crescendo.

As the last trace sunset's amber glow vanished from the sky, Rhodopis heard the stamp and snap of the door guards coming to attention. She had stood in silent expectation for several minutes; it had taken Psamtik a long time to return to his chambers. Had some business occupied him, she wondered—or had his show of mustered strength in the throne room been a ruse? Perhaps the poison was still doing its insidious work, after all.

But Rhodopis had no more time to wonder, no time to hope. The doors opened, groaning amid the shadows of dusk.

"My king, shall I send for a physician?" one of the soldiers asked.

Psamtik made no reply. Rhodopis could just see him, a hunched figure moving slowly at the dark threshold.

The guard said again, "My king? Are you well?"

Psamtik paused. The soldier's voice seemed to reach him faintly, like a distant call penetrating a thick river fog. Psamtik drew himself up, quivering with the effort. He stood shuddering for a moment, unspeaking. Then he took hold of his flagging strength and shook his head. "No." The word was clear and steady. "I am quite well; only preoccupied. If I need anything, I will send for you."

Psamtik pushed the door shut. The moment it had closed, cutting off the golden glow of the corridor's oil lamps, he sagged against its scarab-carved timbers. Rhodopis could scarcely make out the shape of his body in the dimness of evening, but she heard him groan deep in his chest as he struggled to marshal his flagging strength. He tried to push himself upright and away from the door, but fell back again. In the silence of his vast quarters, his gasping breath sounded loud as a storm wind.

Rhodopis waited, unspeaking and unafraid. Psamtik tried once to move; this time his legs held him. He stumbled down the length of the sitting room, hands outstretched as if he feared he might collide with unseen obstacles—tables or stools, or the vengeful spirit of his dead father. Rhodopis did not step out of his way, nor did she shrink back timidly. If he touched her in his dazed progress through the dark, let him feel her strength, the warmth of the lifeblood that still flowed through her veins—the blood that would go on flowing for as long as her work remained unfinished. Let him know in an instant, at the moment of contact, that Rhodopis lived on even as his life was strangled out of him, breath by burning breath.

But Psamtik didn't touch her. Nor did he seem to notice Rhodopis as he crept toward his bedchamber. He passed within a hand's breadth of her shoulder; even in the twilight, she could see the glaze of terror veiling his eyes as he fought for every breath, as he struggled against the realization that his great strength could wither in the span of a few short hours.

Psamtik staggered on into his bedchamber. The door hung

open on its hinges; there was nothing to impede the sounds that came from his bed, no barrier between Rhodopis and his suffering. She heard the crackle of dried reeds and camel's hair as Psamtik fell onto the bed—then the whisper of linens as he tossed amid his blankets. Now and then he grunted in pain, a short, sharp, beastly sound. He was so preoccupied with his pain—the agonizing path the hemlock traced through his body —that he had apparently forgotten Rhodopis, forgotten to send for his guards and condemn her to a traitor's death.

Quietly, Rhodopis lowered herself to the couch. Night's mild chill had begun to creep in, but she left the silk wrap where it lay. The nip of cold kept her awake, kept her thoughts sharp. She sat in silence, listening as Psamtik rolled and panted and moaned on the mattress. Occasionally, his restless thoughts drove him from the small comfort of his bed, and he rose—slowly, accompanied by ample cursing—to pace around his bedchamber with shuffling steps. The chamber lamps remained unlit; the dense blackness of the room seemed to isolate Psamtik's suffering, to set him apart like a stark full moon in a black sky. Even the loud chorus of night-time insects seemed to fade below the usurper-king's desperate cursing, the broken rhythm of his stumbling feet, and his occasional bouts of terrified weeping. Rhodopis was cognizant of nothing save for Psamtik's pain.

At least an hour passed in that manner—Rhodopis, the detached observer, quiet and content in the dark sitting room; Psamtik searching hopelessly for the ruthless potency that had so recently been his to command.

As the music of his slow decline played its strange and sweet refrains, Rhodopis shuddered with the urge to confront Psamtik, to talk to him—to taunt him, in truth. She imagined herself stepping into his path, materializing out of the night like a foreboding omen. She could do it, she knew. She could stop Psamtik's desperate wandering, halt him with a hand against his cold heart and say, *It's I who have done this to you. It's I who will win in the end. You never were the king of Egypt, and you won't be, now. You'll die a usurper and a traitor. The gods of Kmet will spurn you. That is the fate you deserve.*

Rhodopis trembled, but not from the cold. The temptation to toy with Psamtik in his final hours overwhelmed and wracked her, sending shivers of pure, unrestrained energy racing up her legs and spine. But it would be foolish to place herself in Psamtik's way now, foolish to remind him that she still lived. He had been blind to her presence earlier that night, but that did not mean his eyes would remain clouded forever. Even as the hemlock wore him away, he might recover enough of his wits to send for his guards and have Rhodopis dragged away.

Besides, Rhodopis told herself, *I shouldn't be so hard and bitter. Archidike was that way—heart turned to stone by life's cruelties. I can't allow myself to become what Archidike became.*

But why couldn't she? Why *shouldn't* she? Even as she cautioned herself to remain silent and invisible to Psamtik, she ached with the need to have her revenge, to savor it—to hurt Psamtik as terribly as he had wounded her. That desire was neither prudent nor wise, and Rhodopis knew it. All the same, it filled her with hunger stronger than any she had known before.

When moonlight had crept across the window sill, spilling a great rectangle of silver onto the sitting-room floor, Rhodopis heard the drumming of many feet and a murmur of voices in the corridor outside. Someone rapped a staff on the floor; she held still, waiting for Psamtik to emerge from the lightless bedroom, but he only went on shuffling and muttering. The knock hadn't been enough to penetrate the haze of hemlock and draw him from his misery.

Rhodopis stood and went to the door herself. It was a grave affront, for a person of such low standing to see to the Pharaoh's business, but Rhodopis was beyond caring. She wouldn't live long, and while she still drew breath, she held the power of life and death over Psamtik. She was the mightiest person in the king's quarters. Why should Rhodopis fear to answer the door?

When she pulled one door open, she found General Ankhef in the corridor, blinking in surprise even as he smoothed his features, so his bluff, square face would betray no distaste.

"My... er... my lady," Ankhef said, "I have urgent news for the Pharaoh."

Rhodopis shrugged. "You may tell me the news."

Ankhef glanced past her into the king's quarters, but she doubted whether he could see anything in the unlit chamber. "The king told me to alert him at once if there was any word from the north."

Rhodopis was about to bid the man again to tell her what he knew, but she heard a gasp in the sitting room behind her, followed by the thump of Psamtik colliding with a table in the darkness. Rhodopis moved away from the door, retreating into indigo shadows as Psamtik stumbled closer.

He was short of breath as he gripped the door's edge. "What is it?" Psamtik sounded surprisingly lucid. He had mustered the strength to shake off the effects of the hemlock—for the time being. "What news, Ankhef? Speak!"

Ankhef saluted, thumping a brick-hard fist against his chest. "The combined forces of our northern garrisons have turned the invading fleet back. Djanet is safe, my king—for the moment."

"What do you mean, 'for the moment'?"

"It's too early to know for certain whether the maneuver was decisive, my king. The invading fleet may have already made another attempt to push past Djanet and the Delta into the Iteru's lower reaches. Until we receive word that the invaders have left our territory entirely, and returned to the sea —or until we have confirmed that their ships have been destroyed—it's wisest, my king, to assume they are still bent on attack. And still capable of carrying out any manner of assault."

Despite Ankhef's sensible warning, the news breathed a new and tenacious life into Psamtik. He stood up straighter, relinquishing his grip on the door's edge. Lit by the corridor lamps, Psamtik looked as strong and capable as he had ever been. Ankhef's report seemed to suck the poison from Psamtik's blood. As the usurper folded his arms across his chest in the old familiar gesture of confidence, Rhodopis clenched her fists, biting back a cry of frustration.

"Very good, General. You may go."

"With apologies, my king," Ankhef said, bowing hastily, "I think it wisest not to wait for more news, but to plan our next maneuvers now. If this latest report is accurate and the invading fleet is on the run, it would be best to give chase, allowing our enemies no time to rally."

Psamtik nodded. "You're right, of course. I will meet you in the small audience chamber. I'll need time to prepare."

"Yes, my king." Ankhef saluted again and led his men away.

Psamtik shut the chamber door himself. This time, he didn't hunch against the frame gasping for breath the moment his guards couldn't see. As he found his way back through the dark sitting room to his bedchamber, Psamtik looked as steady and fit as he ever had. The only indications of impediment were the hand pressed against his stomach and the slight drag of his feet, slowing his usually brisk gait.

Rhodopis hesitated in her shadowy corner. She had suspected all along that Cambyses might never arrive in Memphis. Fate was too fickle; one could never rely on the whims of gods. It was well, after all, that she had insisted upon nearness to Psamtik—well that she'd had the foresight to procure the poison. She pressed a hand against the knot of her sash and felt the small vial behind it, ready and waiting.

It's come down to me, after all.

And now was the time—no mistake about that. If she didn't strike the final blow against Psamtik now, while he still remained in the Pharaoh's quarters, he and his generals would surely put paid to Cambyses' invasion.

Rhodopis breathed deeply, filling her lungs until her whole body seemed to expand, to stretch with the power inside her. The fear that chittered in farthest reaches of her mind stilled; in the silence that remained, she imagined she heard Aesop's voice. He spoke a single, reassuring word.

Now.

Rhodopis didn't remember crossing the long, dark sitting room. It seemed as if she found herself standing on the threshold of Psamtik's bedchamber in the blink of an eye, transported by some sly act of sorcery.

Psamtik lit the wick of his largest lamp, a clay figure shaped like a long-necked bird perched atop a golden tripod. The flame rose from the tip of the clay bird's beak, casting a wide orb of amber across the chamber.

Rhodopis blinked in the sudden light. Psamtik turned from the lamp; when he saw Rhodopis standing silently on the threshold, he gave a start and dropped the flint and lighting-stick to the floor. The implements clanged on the stone tiles, but Rhodopis never flinched.

"You," Psamtik spat.

He turned to one of his clothing chests, but the movement was too quick; he recoiled, squeezing his eyes shut and stifling a cry through clenched teeth. He lifted the trunk's lid more slowly and took out a red silk robe.

"I'll deal with you as you deserve when I've finished this business with Ankhef and the other generals. You thought you could destroy me—for the sake of your dung-heap homeland, no doubt—but you see how I've prevailed. You see how strong I am."

Psamtik cast off his old robe, which was wrinkled from his hours of suffering in bed. He began to dress in the new red silk, though his hands shook so badly that he fumbled the knots, whispering curses under his breath.

"Shall I fetch Ranefer to dress you, my king?" Rhodopis asked peaceably.

"To Ammit's gullet with that rubbish. Do you think I'm utterly witless? If I send you out into the corridor to wake Ranefer, you'll only run. But you can't run now, Rhodopis. You won't leave these quarters alive."

She smiled, unmoved by his taunts. She was already prepared to die—had been prepared for days. Psamtik could no longer cause her to feel any fear, and so he held no power over her mind or spirit—not anymore.

She caught his stare and held it. "At least let me send for refreshment," she said coolly. "You spent hours in agony, muttering to yourself... pacing... suffering. Before you speak to Ankhef, you should have food. Wine."

Psamtik strode toward her like a bull charging at a rival, thundering and roaring. He caught her by her jaw, fingers biting hard into the soft flesh of her cheeks as he held her head in place so she couldn't look away from his fury.

It was an unnecessary gesture; Rhodopis had no intention of breaking his stare, nor of blinking before Psamtik did.

"You will never have the chance to poison me again, you treacherous creature, you low worm... you *woman*. You think you've conquered me, but it's I who have had power over you from the start, from the night I first took you. I hold that power still, and if I hadn't urgent business in the audience hall, I would kill you now with my own hands. Don't think I'll give you a chance to escape. When I leave my chambers, you'll come with me; you'll go straight into the custody of my door guards.

They will keep you—bound hand and foot, if necessary—until I return to watch you die. And I will relish the sight, Rhodopis, believe me."

He let go of her jaw with a casual, tossing motion that set Rhodopis stumbling across the floor, but she recovered her balance quickly. She turned to stare at him again.

When Psamtik noted her easy, confident smile, his eyes narrowed to dark slits. "Perhaps I'll enjoy your body one last time before I cut your throat. Yes—I think I will. It'll be like the first time again, though I won't go as easy on you."

"Cambyses won't go easy on you when he reaches Memphis."

Psamtik jerked a knot into his sash, then looked at Rhodopis with a hard, hate-filled expression.

"You fool," Rhodopis said softly. "Don't you understand? Haven't you guessed why I returned from Persia?"

"It makes no difference now. The Persian dog's fleet has turned back, and I'll see that he's chased into the sea—and sunk beneath the waves." Psamtik crossed to another cedar chest, lifted its lid, and busied himself with the contents, searching for some article of clothing or a choice golden bauble. He didn't bother to look at Rhodopis again as he spoke. "Persia will be dealt with first, but once Ankhef and his men have dispatched my orders, you'll draw your final breath. It'll be a traitor's death for you, Rhodopis. Don't expect mercy."

As Psamtik ranted, Rhodopis slipped her hand into her sash. She found the smooth neck of the vial and plucked out the tiny plug of wax that had stopped the opening.

"But you'll need the luck of the gods to beat Cambyses," she said. "I know him far better than you do."

"I need nothing but my wits, my power. I—"

"A kiss for luck."

Rhodopis spoke no more. While Psamtik's back was still turned, she tipped the last of the hemlock into her mouth. Its bitter taste filled her mouth and burned in her nostrils like the fumes of a potent wine. Instinct screamed at her to spit the substance on the floor, but she resisted. In two quick steps, she was on Psamtik, seizing him by the arm, grasping hard. As his flesh yielded to her fierce grip, wild triumph swelled in her chest. Rhodopis wrenched at him with all her strength, spinning him about on his feet to face her—his fate, his death, his damnation.

Psamtik's eyes went wide with surprise and fear. The earlier effects of the poison seemed to flood back into his body until he shook like a priestess's rattle. When Rhodopis pushed him, he stumbled backward, unable to stop himself, unable to resist.

Psamtik's back hit the wall of his chamber with a loud smack. The gods and kings painted there towered above him; their thin, cold eyes stared down, unfeeling, as Rhodopis shoved herself against Psamtik's body, pinning him against the wall. He struggled, but every movement was feebler than the last. He had no more strength than a child.

Rhodopis lifted onto her toes and pressed her mouth against Psamtik's. His lips tightened; the muscles of his jaw clenched as he resisted. His fists batted at her, light as the paws of a kitten playing with a silken braid. He had put on a show of readiness for Ankhef, but that display had sapped the last reserve of Psamtik's strength. Rhodopis could feel his body tense with pain each time he swung at her. The prior dose of hemlock was still doing its work. If she could only make him accept this final dose, her work would be finished. She could rest easy, knowing Psamtik was dead.

All at once, the memory of the sapling grove returned to her —the damp earth beneath her, her fingers clawing uselessly at Psamtik's chest as he forced his will and his body upon her. The repulsive nearness of him, his leering, triumphant face pressed against her own, wet with tears. She had had no choice, no power... but now it was Psamtik whose strength was gone. It was Psamtik who must take what Rhodopis forced upon him, he who must accept the will of the woman whom he'd thought a victim, cowed and subdued.

Rage at all he had taken from her, all he had done to her, surged in Rhodopis' heart. Rage, and an unshakable confidence in her strength. Swift and hard, powered by the force of her anger, she brought her knee up in a brutal strike to Psamtik's groin.

His body gave a tremendous jerk. Against his will, he cried out; Rhodopis forced her tongue between his lips, spat the poison into his mouth. His moan of despair filled her with fiery triumph; she felt her cheeks burn hot as embers.

Rhodopis pulled back, then clamped her hand over Psamtik's mouth, even as her own jaw fell open. The bitter taste of hemlock had filled her mouth with saliva; gagging, she let the dregs of the poison run down her chin and onto her tunic, for despite her commitment to this grim duty—despite acceptance of her inevitable death—she found herself suddenly frantic to live on. She prayed she had swallowed none of the poison, even as she pressed her hand harder against Psamtik's mewling lips. He was so weakened by the hemlock—and by the pain of her blow—that one hand across his mouth was enough to make him her captive, utterly helpless to her whims.

"Swallow it. Do as I say." Her voice rasped in her throat; she sprayed spittle from her lips with every word, covering Psamtik's fine red robe with droplets of poison.

Weakly, he shook his head. Tears welled in his eyes.

"Swallow."

With her other hand, Rhodopis pinched his nose shut.

Psamtik's eyes bulged; all the cold hatred vanished from them, and he pleaded with her silently, begging for his throne and his life. Rhodopis only bore down harder, grinding the back of his head against the wall, slavering like a lioness on the hunt as she stared into Psamtik's desperate eyes.

His throat moved convulsively. The pleading look vanished from his face; he stared blankly into the chamber as the realization of what he'd done struck him with full, brutal force.

Satisfied, Rhodopis released him and backed away.

Psamtik stumbled away from the wall. His expression was dull, stunned, like a beast whose throat has been freshly cut, clinging to its last heartbeat of life before the blood leaves its body in a hot, red rush. Some force seemed to take hold of him, commanding him to reach through the haze of death and see the one who had delivered him to his fate. He met Rhodopis' steady gaze, then opened his mouth as if to speak. But he could do nothing more than rasp out one long, strangled breath. Psamtik's legs buckled; he fell to the floor and lay unmoving.

Rhodopis bent double, spitting mouthful after mouthful of saliva onto the floor. She looked around desperately for a cup of wine, a skin of beer, an ewer of wash-water—anything she might use to rinse the hemlock from her tongue. She had swallowed none of it; she was certain of that. But might it have trickled down her throat, all the same—or seeped beneath her tongue?

For a moment, as she watched Psamtik's face contort with his labored breath, she told herself all would be well. She hadn't ingested the hemlock; the gods would spare her, after all. But as she straightened, her breath came short, burning in her lungs. An insidious numbness tingled along the soles of her feet, creeping slowly toward her ankles, moving higher with every beat of her heart.

I'm finished. Rhodopis ached with dull sorrow at the realization.

She staggered to Psamtik's bed and crawled atop the mattress, then pulled a linen sheet up to cover her chilled, shuddering body.

Weariness dragged at her mind and flesh, and a long, sharp pain stabbed deep into her middle. Even to keep her eyes open was an agony, an effort she couldn't bear. She allowed her lids to slide heavily closed. Psamtik's last rattling breaths were the only sound she could hear.

I'm finished… but so is Psamtik.

As darkness closed around her, Rhodopis smiled.

※ 19 ※

FAREWELL

First, she smelled the smoke. It worked its way into her dreams—troubled, fragmented dreams of chasing Aella through a darkly shadowed wood. Rhodopis pleaded with her sister to come back, not to leave her alone in the darkness, but Aella didn't listen. Rhodopis could only follow her, stumbling through the forest, chasing the far-off glint of the rose-gold slippers Aella wore until the burning rasp of thick smoke made her stop, leaning against a tree for support as she gasped for every burning breath.

After the smoke, Rhodopis grew aware of voices crying out in anger or pain—men fighting and dying. She tossed in her bed, moaning in weak resistance against the sound. Was she in the diplomats' wing again, playing slave to the false ambassador of Carthage? This was Psamtik's coup, then—the day Amasis fell. So she hadn't killed Psamtik, after all. He still lived; her work still lay ahead, dreadfully dangerous and yet undone. The thought made her too weary for words, too weary to wake. Much better to stay where she was, wrapped in the shelter of dreams, than to rise and face Psamtik—to know that he held the Horus

Throne and Egypt itself. To know he held Rhodopis' fate still, like a fragile egg ready to be crushed in his uncaring fist.

Someone spoke to her from a great distance—down the length of a corridor with a green archway. Sometimes the voice was Aesop's, comforting and low. Sometimes it sounded like Amtes, murmuring sympathy in the half-light of a ship's curtained cabin while she pulled a comb slowly through Rhodopis' hair. Now and then, the voice belonged to Phanes. It had been so long since she'd heard Phanes speak that at first Rhodopis didn't recognize the sound—only the feel of his presence, confident and wise.

But no matter whose voice Rhodopis heard, the words were always the same: *Come back.*

In dreams, she flew over Memphis, darting and twisting in the air like one of the little garden birds—or soaring like a messenger pigeon, straight and true to her course. Below, she saw the Nile black with boats: the swift, sleek vessels of Polycrates' fleet, flying banners of Ishtar's blue-and-gold; the Egyptian boats wallowing or yawing side to side, struggling to turn, to deflect the Persians as they charged toward the quay. She saw Egypt's fleet break and retreat, putting up their sails to escape upriver—and then the triumphal march of the Persian army through the streets of Memphis, the city's people cowering in the alleys, bewildered and meek.

Through the sounds of fighting, through her friends murmuring for her to return, Rhodopis could hear nothing else. Psamtik no longer labored for his breath on the floor of his bedchamber. Nor could she smell him, the stink of his sweat under the haze of smoke. He was gone—dead. Truly gone, never to trouble her again. In the realm of dreams, Rhodopis was certain of nothing, save that Psamtik was dead.

She longed to run through the forest again, to find Aella and hold her little sister close. But the trees had vanished around her, fading into shadow. There was nothing to see but blackness, so Rhodopis opened her eyes.

She closed them again an instant later, wincing as the pain of lamplight stabbed into her head.

"She's awake."

Someone took her hand. Rhodopis squeezed it, locking her fingers tight around solid flesh and bone. This was not the dream-world. This was real—real as the pain in her belly or the dry, burning sensation in her lungs.

"Gods be praised," another voice answered. "Help her sit up if she can. We must get her to drink this. It will help alleviate the effects of the hemlock."

Warmth came near to her face; she could sense the mass of something—someone—close beside her ear, though nothing touched her.

"Rhodopis." A woman's voice, rich and low. "Sit up, now. Come; it's time to wake."

"Let me help her." The hand she held opened; fingers disentangled from her own, and she could sense a reluctance in that parting. Someone shook her shoulder, gently.

"Come back, Doricha. It's time you woke."

She knew that voice, that presence. Rhodopis opened her eyes again, slowly, squinting through her lashes. "Aesop?" Her voice was a frog's croak. "Where am I?"

"You're in the Pharaoh's bed, where we found you. We thought it best not to move you until you'd recovered."

Three figures loomed over her, silhouetted against the lamps. Aesop was unmistakable, with his crooked shoulders and densely curled hair. She reached for his hand again and sighed in relief when she found it.

"Sit up," Aesop urged again. "Do it for me."

Rhodopis rolled weakly on the great bed, trying to find enough purchase to push herself to a sitting position. The Pharaoh's chamber whirled around her. The dizzy sensation lurched in her head and stomach; she retched and choked on bile, but struggled up to a half-sitting position. She rested her back against a heap of silk cushions.

Rhodopis blinked through sleep-crusted lashes. The faces of the other two figures materialized before her, slow as stones emerging at the bottom of a pond when disturbed silt settles into it muddy bed.

"Amtes," she said, wondering. "And Phanes. Are you really here? Am I here? Or have I—"

"Died?" Amtes tossed her head in amusement. "Not this time, but it was a near thing."

Phanes passed a horn cup to Aesop, who held its smooth rim to Rhodopis' mouth.

"Drink that," Phanes said. "By and by, it will reverse the effects of the hemlock. I don't know how much you ingested, but it couldn't have been a large quantity. Otherwise, you would be as dead as Psamtik."

She sniffed the amber liquid. It had an unpleasant, salty odor with a noxious sting. The smell reminded Rhodopis of the black dye with which Amtes had disguised her natural hair color.

"What is it?" Rhodopis asked.

"Medicine for what ails you," Phanes said sternly. "That's all you need to know right now."

Rhodopis gagged again, and Phanes seemed to take some pity on her. "It is partially derived from apples; I can tell you that much. You ate plenty of apples when you were in Persia, did you not?"

"Yes, but they never smelled like this."

Aesop stroked her forehead, brushing back the short curls. "Drink it, Doricha. You won't recover any other way."

Rhodopis pinched her nose shut so she wouldn't taste the foul brew, then closed her eyes tightly and nodded. Aesop tipped the cup slowly, allowing her to gulp down the medicine.

It was thick in her mouth, and even with her nose held shut, she could still taste a bitter, ammoniac graininess that reminded her of the back alleys of Tanis. When she had swallowed the foul stuff down, she fell back against the cushions, gasping and shuddering.

"Now that you've taken it all, I can tell you what's in it." Phanes sounded too amused for Rhodopis' liking.

"Please don't," she croaked. "I think I'd rather not know, after all—'less you want me to bring it all up again. Don't scowl at me, Aesop," she added desperately. "I'm in a bad way. You can't expect me to talk like a cultured Memphis lady when I'm all but laid out for my funeral."

Aesop chuckled. "I wasn't scowling."

Rhodopis shook her head weakly, trying to clear the fog from her thoughts. "Phanes... in Memphis. So Polycrates' fleet made it past Tanis, after all."

"Yes," Phanes answered gently. "We captured an Egyptian vessel outside of Tanis and forced them to send a false message to Psamtik. We hoped that he would let his guard down, even for a few hours. Cambyses had been prepared to contend with the northern garrisons, of course, but they gave us a harder fight than we'd expected. We thought if we could put Psamtik at ease, or even lure him away from the city on one of those hulking, useless Egyptian boats, we could take Memphis more easily. But as we sailed south from Tanis, we found none of the opposition we had expected. Cambyses and Polycrates were braced for it as we neared Memphis, but only a handful of ships came out to meet us, and they turned tail as soon as they understood how much faster we could move."

"I dreamed," Rhodopis said vaguely, "of hundreds of ships. Covering the surface of the Nile."

Aesop took her hand again. "No. Memphis fell quickly."

"Like a fat, ripe fig from a tree," Amtes added.

Phanes took the cup from Aesop, set it on a nearby table

among an array of vials and jars—his herbs and potions, Rhodopis supposed.

"Only a few commanders dared to bring their men out to face us," the physician said. "We didn't understand at first, but when we landed at the quay with hardly a skirmish and marched up the streets toward the palace, we learned the reason why. The palace was in disarray by the time we got here —total chaos." He winked. "It seemed someone had already killed the usurper and done the hard work for us."

"He is dead, then? Truly?"

"Truly," Aesop said. "You did it, Doricha. As soon as I realized Cambyses had come, I went to him while he was still marching his men through the streets. I told him I was your friend—that I had helped you lay the footing for his triumph. Cambyses allowed me to accompany him to the palace; that's how I got in, despite the chaos. And it was chaos. The palace was the last stronghold for all those who'd been loyal to Psamtik. They didn't give ground without a fight, even though their king was dead. They fought like demons, too. They were desperate, you see—desperate to hold onto Psamtik's dream."

"His dream of destruction," Rhodopis said. "If Cambyses hadn't won, Psamtik's followers would have carried on killing Greeks, for no reason other than their birth."

"You know I long to see Kmet return to its traditions," Amtes said, "but I have no desire to see innocent people killed. We can reform Kmet without behaving like rabid dogs."

"All the rabid dogs have been run off now," Aesop said. "Run off or killed. Memphis has fallen to Cambyses. As battles go, this one was short. Not bloodless, but over and done with quickly. Thanks to the gods for that."

"Thanks to Rhodopis for that." Phanes began sorting through his collection of herbs, packing vials and packets made of folded papyrus into a sturdy, lidded basket. "There's no telling how much strength Psamtik and his loyal men might have gained if you hadn't timed the killing just so, Rhodopis. We had expected to find some division between Psamtik's loyalists and those who had grown used to the old Pharaoh's ways. We hadn't expected so much unity. I despaired more than once; a time or two, I felt sure we'd be defeated here in the palace, after having come so far—after tasting so many victories. If Psamtik had remained alive and healthy for another ten days, he might have consolidated his power, united Egypt, and chased us all the way back to Babylon. He might have won sympathy from some foreign power, and brought more troops in from Carthage or Mitanni or gods-know-where. Babylon might have found itself invaded by way of retaliation. In short, your timing couldn't have been better, my dear."

Rhodopis smiled weakly. Could Cambyses truly have taken the Horus Throne? It seemed too much to hope for. Surely, Rhodopis thought, she was still dreaming.

"How did you find me?"

"We came down on Memphis so swiftly that Psamtik's people had no time to move his body," Phanes said. "But as we fought our way into the palace, we heard cries that the Pharaoh had already perished. The soldiers were shouting the news to each other, even as they tried to force us back through the gate. When we'd subdued the palace, Cambyses sent me to find Psamtik's body, to be sure he was truly dead. It was one of our captives, a General Ankhef, who told me where to look. He had entered the king's quarters to find Psamtik when we appeared from the north, but found the Pharaoh dead. Ankhef pulled the body away, trying to hide the truth of what had happened from his men. No one could be spared to handle the body properly —not even servants. It was panic in the palace, by all accounts —in the city, too. Ankhef told me I'd find Psamtik's corpse covered by a silk blanket in his sitting room, laid out on his couch. I did find him there, just as Ankhef had promised.

"But when I had my men inspect the king's chambers—

searching for enemies in hiding, you see—they found you lying still as death in the Pharaoh's bed. I could tell at once that you'd taken hemlock, but you were still breathing. I set to work straight away, to bring you back from death."

"He pulled you right out of death's hands," Amtes said. Awestruck, she watched Phanes as he bundled away the last of his herbs. "He has promised to teach me everything he knows, once the dust settles here in Memphis."

"Yes," Phanes said fondly. "This young priestess of Horus has the right temperament for the work. There aren't many female physicians—or any, as far as I know—but now and then the gods place something new upon the earth. I found her out in the garden, calling your name, and brought her in to help tend you. She had come to deliver another vial of hemlock poison."

Amtes laughed, dabbing sweat from Rhodopis' brow with a soft linen cloth. "I thought you could use another dose. One can never be too cautious when one must kill a Pharaoh. But my timing was bad; I was caught in the fighting, and had to hide in the garden, praying no one found me."

"Psamtik was no Pharaoh," Rhodopis said. "He was a thief, a murderer. He was a beast."

"But he's gone now," Aesop said. "He can never hurt you again."

She sighed, sinking deeper into the great bed, and closed her eyes. Tears of relief burned behind her lids, then broke to run in twin streams down her temples. She could hear them falling, pattering softly against the silk of her cushions.

After a moment of contented silence, Rhodopis said, "King Cambyses—he survived the battle?"

"Yes," Phanes said. "He's hale as ever, thank the gods."

"I suppose he's the Pharaoh now."

"The last thing Kmet needs is a foreign king on the Horus Throne," Amtes said darkly. "Amasis was bad enough."

"Cambyses won't try to turn Kmet into Persia," Phanes said. "I give you my word on that. I would never have supported his cause if I'd had any reason to believe he would harm Kmet, rather than heal it. You do trust me, don't you?"

Amtes nodded in answer, though with a sulky air.

"In time, you'll see. Cambyses is a wise, thoughtful ruler. This land is his now, but he will be a good steward; he will care for the Kmetu people—and the Greeks who have made Egypt their home—with the greatest respect. I long to see Kmet return to the old ways, too, Amtes—we all do. I wouldn't have risked my life bringing Cambyses to the Horus Throne if I'd thought there was the least danger that Kmet would be further corrupted by his rule."

"I suppose I must trust you," Amtes said, "since I'm to be your apprentice now."

"I feel as if I can't quite trust you," Rhodopis said, offering another shaky smile. "After such a long, terrible struggle—and so much danger—can it truly be over?"

"It is," Aesop said. "We owe this victory to you."

"I want to see for myself." Rhodopis raised herself again, sitting amid the pile of cushions. This time, it was almost easy to lift herself from the bed, though her arms still trembled. "I want to go up to the rooftop and see the fleet for myself. I won't quite believe it's over until I've spotted Polycrates' *Omen* down there in the river."

Aesop snorted. "The roof? Put it out of your head. You aren't strong enough."

"I think she's well enough to try it," Phanes said. "She's responding marvelously to the antidote. Look, Amtes—can you see how her color has improved already? Fresh air will be good for her. Just make her go slowly, and be sure she doesn't topple off the stairs. She will still feel rather weak for a few more days."

"If you want her to go up to the rooftop," Aesop said tartly, "you had better come along. If she collapses, I won't know what to do."

"Amtes will go with you." Phanes tied the lid of his basket shut and slung it over his shoulder. "I've business in the harem."

"Muyet and your boys." Rhodopis grinned at the physician. "They'll be so glad to see you."

"As will I." His eyes filled with tears; he blinked them away, but his voice cracked as he spoke. "When I received word from you, Rhodopis, that my wife and sons still lived, I couldn't quite believe it was true. And yet, the news made me work all the harder for this victory—this moment. I can't wait any longer to hold Muyet in my arms. Nor can I wait any longer to see how my boys have grown." Phanes bent over the bed, brushing Rhodopis' forehead with a kiss. "Thank you—you sweet, wondrous child."

"She's no child," Aesop said quietly. "She has survived more than most soldiers ever could, and has accomplished more than most kings."

With a sudden, brusque change of mood, Aesop tugged away the linen sheet and offered his arm to Rhodopis. "Come along, then, if you honestly are fool enough to climb to the rooftop. You can lean on me the whole way."

"Wait—I found these in the sitting room, while you were still unconscious." Amtes stooped beside the bed and came up holding the rose-gold slippers. She tied them to Rhodopis' feet, then helped Aesop maneuver Rhodopis from the bed.

Their progress through the bedchamber and out into the garden was slow, but Phanes had been correct: despite a tingling in her feet that rendered every step clumsy, Rhodopis could feel her strength returning, little by little. The late-morning sun had nearly reached its apex; the warmth was like a balm, fortifying and sweet. Birds trilled among the flower beds, heedless of the bloodshed that had engulfed the palace.

The perfume of lotus and jasmine hung in the air; the scents were sweeter than they'd ever been before, bringing tears of gratitude to Rhodopis' eyes.

She still couldn't make herself believe that her duty was truly finished. Not until she saw Polycrates' ships would she allow herself to rest.

Aesop maneuvered Rhodopis near the wall as they slowly ascended the staircase. He remained between her and the long drop to the garden below, while Amtes trailed behind with one protective hand on Rhodopis' back. They reached the rooftop safely, and Rhodopis looked about, taking in the familiar pigeon cote, the low brick wall at the roof's edge, the vast blue stretch of the river beyond. She could not yet see the quay from her vantage, but the Nile was devoid of ships. Not even fisherman's boats moved along its surface. Memphis had indeed been subdued. Perhaps she could trust in her friends' claims of victory, after all.

But something—an unseen harbinger of sorrow—struck Rhodopis with a sudden wave of fear, a sharp pain of foreboding. There was a heaviness in the air, a dragging weight of loss. Rhodopis didn't understand the sensation that overwhelmed her. Nor could she have explained why her eyes filled suddenly with desperate tears.

Then, above the disordered clamor rising from the city, Rhodopis heard a ragged moan. She turned toward the pigeon cote, pulling Aesop with her. Just on the other side of the cote's long band of shadow, a lone form lay flat on the sun-scorched rooftop, half covered by a dark woolen cape.

Rhodopis wailed in agony, a cry of denial the gods wouldn't bother to hear. In one painful heartbeat, she recognized the woman's shape, the sharp line of her cheekbone and the long black curls splayed around her head. Rhodopis tore herself away from Aesop and Amtes, staggering across the roof until she fell to her knees beside Archidike.

Archidike lay sprawled on her back, eyes closed tightly against the sun's glare. Flies crawled over her skin, but she made no move to twitch them away; more buzzed in the air around her, drawn by the stench of blood. Her chest stirred little with her shallow breaths. When Rhodopis' shadow fell across her face, Archidike moaned again.

"Gods have mercy," Rhodopis whispered. "Archi, what happened?"

"Rho... is it you?"

Her voice was so faint, so painfully dry, that Rhodopis could scarcely hear it. She took Archidike's hand. Her fingers were stiff and cold.

"Yes, darling, yes. It's me."

Amtes and Aesop had rushed to the sad scene, too; Amtes pulled the wool cape aside, then covered her mouth at sight of Archidike's abdomen. A deep wound had pierced her belly just below the ribs, soaking her simple tunic and pooling around her body in a half-congealed slick.

"Oh, gods," Rhodopis murmured. "No, Archi, don't die. Not like this."

Regret flooded into Rhodopis' heart, rising high and fast enough to drown her. She cursed herself for the bitterness that was all she had given Archidike at their last meeting. Now she knew with agonizing clarity that Archidike had always been her friend—yes, and she had loved Archidike, too, despite her hardness, her cold exterior. How could Archidike have been anything other than she was? Now that Rhodopis knew the truth of her friend's life—the cruelty of Archidike's mother, the way she had fought to rise above her lot in life—she understood Archidike, forgave her everything.

If I had my life to live again, she prayed with futile passion, *I would do it all differently. I would have shared with you everything, right from the start, Archi. It would have gone just as you'd wanted —the two of us against the world.*

"Rho. You came back." Archidike drew a ragged breath; specks of blood dotted her lip. "You're here."

"Yes, dear one, I'm here. But why are you here? *Why, Archi?*"

"I had more hemlock for you. Brought it... so you could do... what needs doing."

Rhodopis had no more strength to hold her head up; she sagged forward, watching helplessly as her tears fell on Archidike's chest.

"It's done," she said. "Done, Archi, thanks to you. I couldn't have seen it through if you hadn't helped me. If you hadn't brought me the hemlock."

"I couldn't find you this morning." A faint whisper was all Archidike could muster. "I thought you'd be here, on the roof, where I found you last."

Mute with remorse, Rhodopis shook her head.

"But you weren't here. You weren't."

"No, dear. I wasn't. And I'm sorry for it."

"I waited where I saw you last, but then someone..." Archidike coughed weakly. "Someone started shouting that the king was dead."

Cold realization struck Rhodopis like a fist—as Psamtik's fists had so often done, hard and merciless. "Someone found you here. Is that it? Found you and thought you'd killed Psamtik."

Archidike's head moved slightly—a nod. "Wish I had killed him. For what he did to you."

Rhodopis squeezed Archidike's hand harder, as if by force of will she might reach across the abyss between life and death, and pull Archidike back. But the blue fire was already fading from Archidike's eyes. She had set one foot in the underworld already.

"Oh, I'm sorry, Archi—I'm so sorry for everything. Can you ever forgive me?"

"I'm the one who needs forgiving." Archidike's lips trembled as she tried to smile. "Duckling."

Rhodopis pressed her friend's cold hand against her cheek. Then she kissed Archidike's fingers, again and again. "Of course I forgive you. Don't be foolish—of course I do."

Archidike's face crumpled with pain—but whether it was the terrible wound that pained her or her memories, Rhodopis couldn't have said.

"But I took... everything. From you."

"It doesn't matter. Not anymore." Rhodopis laid Archidike's hand carefully on her chest, then untied the rose-gold slippers with trembling fingers. She crawled to Archidike's feet, careful to avoid the pool of blood. Flies rose lazily into the air as Rhodopis brushed them from Archidike's body.

Amtes—tears streaking her face—had to help Rhodopis remove Archidike's old sandals, but once they were cast aside, Rhodopis waved Amtes away, too. She alone secured the priceless slippers on her friend's feet, then returned to her side and once more took Archidike's hand.

"You can have it all, Archi. All of it, even my slippers. It'll be just like you wanted—the two of us sharing everything, living together, all set up for life. The best hetaerae in the city—and the richest, too."

"Do you really forgive me?" Archidike had gone pale around her mouth, and paler still. Her eyelids fluttered as her head rolled from side to side; she seemed to see nothing now.

For an answer, Rhodopis bent and kissed her mouth, tasting the blood that had gathered on her lip. Archidike smiled for one brief moment. Then the smile slid from her face. She went limp in death's cold hands.

"No! No, Archidike!" Rhodopis patted her cheek, shook her shoulders, but Archidike did not respond.

Amtes sniffed loudly, then gently closed Archidike's half-open eyes.

"Isn't there anything you can do?" Rhodopis cried.

Amtes sighed, wiping away her tears with the back of her hand. "Not even Phanes can help her now. She's gone, Rhodopis."

Rhodopis threw back her head, wordlessly wailing her grief. The terrible cry startled the pigeons in the cote; they flew around and around their small enclosure, wings clattering like the drums of an army. Her grief was loud and sharp enough for the gods to hear, but they paid no heed. Rhodopis had already done what the gods had required; they had no more use for her now, no interest in easing her sorrow.

Aesop was crouched beside her now, holding her, rocking her. "You must be calm," he said. "You mustn't carry on this way, Doricha. It's dangerous, in your state. Hush, now. Hush."

But Rhodopis could neither quiet herself nor control her grief. She tried to stand, staggering halfway to her feet before a wave of dizziness dropped her. She fell hard on her side and rolled against Archidike's too-still body, heedless of the flies and the blood, clutching her dead friend and sobbing all the harder.

"In the name of every merciful god," Aesop shouted, "Amtes, run and find Phanes! She's too fragile for this; she'll die of grief if you don't hurry."

Rhodopis never heard the pounding of Amtes' feet as she ran for the physician. She heard nothing but her hoarse cries of pain and the hollow beat of her aching heart.

REWARD

WHEN RHODOPIS NEXT SET FOOT IN THE GREAT THRONE ROOM OF the Memphis palace—some five days after Cambyses' arrival—she found the massive chamber draped in blue and gold. Cambyses' men had removed the silk banners from the masts of their ships; now those banners hung in the gaps between Egyptian pillars, rippling slowly whenever a passing servant chanced to brush against the fabric or when gentle currents of myrrh-scented air stirred along the length of the hall. The striding lion of Babylon roared silently from every lapis-blue flag; the light of oil lamps snared among golden threads, playing and glittering through the lions' manes, accentuating the sharpness of their exposed teeth.

Rhodopis craned her neck, watching the lions dance slowly against their blue fields as she walked toward the Horus Throne on its dais—toward the man who now occupied that gilded seat. Phanes and Aesop, accompanying her to either side, remained just as silent as she, but from all around the throne room came the sounds of work, a steady bustle—servants hurrying to and fro, scribes scratching out their messages and whispering in one another's ears, noblemen rehearsing the words of the fealty oaths they would soon swear to Cambyses, the conqueror.

All trace of Psamtik's reign had vanished. Those men who would not renounce their loyalty to the usurper had been sent back to Babylon in chains, to toil in slavery to their new king. But Aesop, who had already pledged himself to Cambyses' service, had reassured Rhodopis that only a few men had chosen to cling to Psamtik's mad dream. The rest had found themselves convinced by Cambyses' first few days upon the Horus Throne. The Persian may have conquered Egypt, Aesop had said, but from the first hour of Cambyses' reign, he had taken great pains to reassure his new subjects that he would keep his Persian ways to himself. He had declared to a crowded throne room that it would please him to see the old, true traditions of Kmet restored to their rightful place once more, every bit as much as it would please his Kmetu subjects.

And whenever duty required him to remain in Babylon, Cambyses had vowed to leave his new kingdom in capable hands: those of his two new brides, Tjenmutetj and Ta-Sheren-Iset, daughters of Pharaoh Amasis and his murdered chief wife.

Rhodopis could see both young women now as she neared the dais. They sat proud and easy upon their twin thrones, one to either side of Cambyses, and Rhodopis was pleased to see that it was they, not the Persian, who held the crook and flail—one each, laid across their laps. Rhodopis caught the gaze of Tjenmutetj, the elder of the two. She lowered her head respectfully, but not before she saw the spark of gratitude flare in Tjenmutetj's eyes.

The conquering king had chosen Egypt's simple cloth Nemes crown—the one of which peace-loving Amasis had been so fond—rather than a wartime head-dress. He wore Egyptian clothing, too: a long kilt of white linen, folded at the front into hundreds of intricate pleats. He was bare above, save for the golden falcon spreading its wings across his muscular chest, and he had lined his eyes with kohl after the Kmetu fashion. Rhodopis noted, however—not without a tiny smile of amusement—that Cambyses had allowed no one to remove the hair from his chest and stomach. Nor had he shaved his ample beard, as any Kmetu man would have done. It seemed he was willing to yield only so much to Egyptian custom.

"There she is," Cambyses said. "Our secret weapon—our savior. You are a welcome sight, Rhodopis."

She bowed low before the dais, then stood waiting in humble silence.

"Phanes told me you were ill—poisoned."

"Yes, my king. It was my fault entirely."

"Phanes told me, too, how you came to be poisoned. You say it was your fault, yet without your bravery—your willingness to sacrifice yourself for our cause—the battle would have gone differently. I may not be sitting on this throne now if it weren't for you."

Rhodopis could think of no reply, so she held her tongue. Had she acted, in the end, for Cambyses' cause—for Phanes' cause? Back in Babylon, she had felt devoted to their secret work. Later, too, when she had masqueraded as Eulalia among the Memphis elite. But when the gods had opened the way for her to strike Psamtik down, Rhodopis had acted only for herself. It was vengeance that had driven her, not loyalty to Cambyses.

Tjenmutetj spoke. "We are grateful to you, Lady Rhodopis—my sister and I. The usurper Psamtik took us to the Temple of Horus by force and made us swear vows of marriage before the god. But he never came to us afterward." Her face darkened. "I mean to say, he never... consummated..." She trailed off.

Ta-Sheren-Iset took up where her sister had faltered. "We have spoken with the priestess Amtes. She has told us how you intervened with Psamtik to save us from that fate. We are grateful to you." She was remarkably well-spoken for one so young; she and her sister would make fine leaders, pillars of strength to guide Egypt into its new future.

As Khedeb-Netjer-Bona's daughters smiled down at her, waiting for her to speak, a lump rose in Rhodopis' throat. It grew larger and tighter by the moment; she swallowed hard. "I'm only sorry, my ladies, that I couldn't help your mother. Khedeb-Netjer-Bona was a... formidable woman. I respected her." *Even when I feared her.*

"We will carry on in remembrance of her," Tjenmutetj said.

Ta-Sheren-Iset added, "We have married this king of our own free will. He asked us to join in marriage with him, and rule Kmet in his name whenever he is gone."

"It made for a welcome change, to be asked rather than forced," Tjenmutetj said with a hint of a chuckle.

Cambyses' thick, dark beard did not quite hide his smile.

"I wish you much happiness and prosperity, my ladies," Rhodopis said. "King Cambyses is a good husband—kind and generous."

"You have first-hand knowledge of that," Cambyses said. "You are still my wife, after all."

Rhodopis' face burned so hot, she almost flinched—but there was no flame from which to shrink away. She hadn't thought of herself as one of Cambyses' wives since confessing her duplicity to him in that dusty Babylon courtyard.

"We would be most glad to have you here, in the harem once again," Tjenmutetj said. "You would be given the finest quarters and all the respect due to a wife of our king. And," she added hastily, "all the respect you are due thanks to your bravery and service. But if you wish to go back to Babylon when Cambyses returns, we shall not prevent you. You have done so much in the name of the husband we now share, Rhodopis. Because of you—and Cambyses, of course—Kmet will flourish as it hasn't done for fifty years or more. You deserve to be close to Cambyses if that is your wish."

Rhodopis smiled tremulously, but she hung her head. The very thought of remaining in Memphis filled her with a cold, sinking sensation—as did the possibility of returning to Babylon. She had loved Babylon—its beauty, the wonders of the palace, the brilliance of Persian life. Most of all, she had loved the women she'd met in Cambyses' harem. But now Rhodopis knew she could never live happily among the powerful and wealthy. Days of rest—and treatment administered by Phanes —had dulled the sharp edge of her grief. But she could still feel the coldness of Archidike's hand in her own, could still taste her friend's blood on her lips. It was the fight for riches and freedom—for the right to stand among the highest of the high —that had torn Rhodopis and Archidike apart. She would never find contentment with such a life; Rhodopis was sure of it.

"Why do you not speak?" Cambyses said. "What Tjenmutetj told you is true: you have only to make your wishes known, and I will see to it that they are granted." He paused, and looked from one of his chief wives to the other. "*We* will see to it. Wherever you desire to live, Rhodopis—you need only tell us. We owe you much."

"My king..." Rhodopis faltered. A flock of frightened birds seemed to wheel and flap inside her chest, their wings buffeting her heart. "My king, what I wish most is to... to leave."

"Babylon, then." A faint note of disappointment colored Tjenmutetj's words. "I can't fault you; I have heard much about Babylon from Shamiram and Ninsina, the king's daughters. It sounds like a wonderful place. I hope to see it myself, someday."

Rhodopis shook her head, willing herself to speak. Why couldn't she be rid of the cursed lump in her throat? Was it a holdover from her illness, a lingering symptom of the hemlock?

"No, my lady," she finally managed. "I want to go someplace quiet. Someplace far away—far from any court and any king."

Her face heated again; she glanced at Cambyses in sudden panic, then bowed so low her short curls almost brushed the floor. "Forgive me, King Cambyses. I meant no disrespect."

Cambyses laughed so loudly that the murmuring of scribes within the throne room halted for a moment. His booming chuckle seemed to stir the long blue banners.

"Stand up straight, my girl—my wife."

Cambyses rose from the Horus Throne and descended the steps of the dais. Rhodopis tried to bow again, but he caught her by the hands and gently guided her upright.

"It's only natural, what you request—what you desire." Cambyses brushed her cheek with his fingers. "I won't restrain you, Rhodopis. Nor will I command you to accept a future you do not choose—a life that is not your own." His smile was rueful now, his eyes rather sad. "But I will miss you. Wit and courage to rival yours aren't easily found—not in women or men."

"Thank you, my king."

"But you must let us give you some reward," Ta-Sheren-Iset said. "It isn't just, to send you away without showing our gratitude."

"My lady, the only reward I want now is peace. A simple, quiet life far from any throne."

"Then you shall have it," Cambyses said. "But I will give you one gift more: a divorce."

Rhodopis giggled. She couldn't help herself; it was too absurd, to call divorce a gift.

Cambyses grinned as he watched the flush of surprise color her cheeks. "Truly. I'll do it right now, in fact, as easily as I married you. Rhodopis of Thrace, you are my wife no longer. You are free now to wed another man—if that is your wish. Or to take a lover, or a dozen, or a hundred, if that is your wish. You are free to resume your life as a hetaera, if it pleases you, or to pursue any other interest. Only remember this: if you should find yourself wanting—for anything, whatever the need or desire—you have only to call on me, or on these good ladies of Kmet. We will see to it that you don't go wanting for long."

Rhodopis nodded again.

Cambyses jerked his chin toward Rhodopis' companions. "Phanes and Aesop, you will take care of all necessary arrangements. See Lady Rhodopis safely to her destination—wherever that may be. Until she is happily settled into her new life, that is to be your first, last, and only duty."

Mute with gratitude, Rhodopis bent her neck and kissed the backs of Cambyses' hands.

Then she turned her back on the Horus Throne, on the king of Persia and his two Egyptian brides. She cast not so much as a fleeting glance at the great lion banners as she strode from the throne room; they faded in the periphery of her vision, receding until they seemed as distant as her memories of Thrace.

When the hall's massive double doors opened for her, Rhodopis stepped through, facing toward the new life that was hers alone to build.

She never looked back.

EPILOGUE

WHEN THE AFTERNOON BREEZE MOVED AMONG THE GRAPE VINES, it carried the scent of the sea, bracing and sharp. The odors of salt and seaweed mingled with the musky sweetness of ripe fruit. Rhodopis laid her long, shallow harvesting basket on the bare earth between vines and reached back into the twisted, woody growth. She found a heavy mass of grapes by feel alone and worked her small knife carefully, severing the stem. The cluster of orbs, dark as sapphires, fell into her outstretched hand.

She withdrew the grapes from the tangle of vines and examined them. The bunch was large, each perfect fruit plump and taut with juice. A dusty-white bloom covered their skins, and the alluring sweetness of their scent suddenly filled the air. She couldn't resist tasting one—it burst with a complex flavor on her tongue. Tuia, the mistress of winemaking, would be pleased with the crop, or so Rhodopis hoped.

Though Rhodopis now owned the seaside vineyard and the small but beautiful house overlooking it—gifts from Cambyses —she knew little, as yet, about making wine. Tuia, who boasted more than two decades' experience at her craft, had assured

Rhodopis that she would teach her everything a winemaker needed to know. Every day brought new wonders, a growing sense of satisfaction as Rhodopis worked at Tuia's side, learning the secrets of fruit and yeast—the humble, transformative magic of fermentation.

She plucked another grape from its stem, then another, delighting in their sweetness. Bees and wasps, drawn by the juice of split grapes, hummed among the wide, soft leaves. Beyond their pleasant drone, Rhodopis could hear the endless murmur of waves as they rolled placidly onto the beach and retreated again. She had fallen in love with that gentle, constant music the moment she'd first arrived at her new estate three months ago.

Rhodopis picked another grape from the bunch but paused with it partway to her lips. She rolled the grape slowly in her fingers. Below the pale flush of bloom was the fruit's natural darkness. As she examined the deep color, a memory surfaced with a sudden, bright flash. She was a child again, trembling in Iadmon's andron, toting a heavy pitcher of wine in her thin arms. She could almost hear Xanthes' laughter, his coarse jokes —she could all but feel his possessive stare, his hands pawing at her body.

Rhodopis tossed the grape into her mouth and bit down hard; the fruit gave an explosive pop as she crushed it. Even the seed cracked between her teeth. She swallowed the pulp and spat the fragments of seed into the soil. It would never grow now, broken as it was. But Rhodopis was flourishing there among the vines.

During her last handful of days in the Memphis palace, Rhodopis had carefully considered where she might go next— what life she ought to construct from the strange pieces Psamtik had left her with, the bits and bobs that had come from Iadmon's meddling, from Xanthes and Vélona, from Khedeb-Netjer-Bona and old King Amasis. From Archidike. At first, she had entertained thoughts of returning to Thrace. Where else would she go, after all? But Rhodopis had quickly discarded the idea. Thrace was the land of her birth, but it wasn't her home—not anymore. She had lived too long in Egypt; the Nile had cut a track through her spirit and flooded her with its essence, as it did every season when the rains fell far to the south.

Babylon tempted her with its beauty, but it would have been quite impossible to live happily there. Beyond the city, there nothing but desert—and within the walls of Babylon, Rhodopis would never be free from the influence of powerful men.

Instead, she had asked Cambyses for a small estate at the northern edge of the Delta. There she hoped to learn a new trade—anything business a woman could manage on her own, for Rhodopis craved solitude now, the peace of her thoughts and the comfort of what pleasant memories she possessed. She had asked for land at the edge of the sea, where she might watch the northern horizon, remembering Thrace and those she loved who still dwelt there.

When she had arrived at the vineyard, Rhodopis had hired a scribe with a fine, steady hand and dictated a letter to her family. She had sent her love, of course, boundless and soaring. She had spared the details of her life as a hetaera, but had reassured them all—her mother in particular—that she had found a new life now, a new occupation, and bore them no ill will. Rhodopis told her family nothing of the part she had played in the fall of the old Egyptian regime. She made no mention of Cambyses—neither her critical role in his capture of the Horus Throne nor any admission that she had ever been his wife. It was enough that her family should know she had ended up safe, well, and happy. She was content to leave them ignorant of the rest.

When the letter was finished, Rhodopis had signed it with her old name, then given it to a Greek merchant—one of Polycrates' men—to carry to Thrace, along with enough silver to keep her family living in comfort and high style for the remainder of their lives. If she never chanced to see them again, she would at least sleep well at night knowing they wanted for nothing. As for the merchant entrusted with the gift—Polycrates was now a thoroughly wealthy fellow; his association with Cambyses had paid off handsomely, making him richer and more untouchable than any pirate had a right to dream of. Polycrates owed Rhodopis a great debt of gratitude, and for that reason alone, she trusted his man to do right by her.

She had also trusted the merchant with a second cargo: a large offering of silver and a small forest of iron spikes, said to be lucky and loved by the gods. The offering was to be delivered to the holy sanctuary at Delphi. Rhodopis had never seen Delphi herself, of course—nor did she expect she ever would. But though their individual wills were often inscrutable, and their collective actions sometimes seemed whimsical, she knew she owed much to the gods. It was they who had opened the way to her, they who had laid the path to her vengeance, piece by piece. A gift of silver and iron seemed the least Rhodopis could do to express her endless thanks.

In truth, Rhodopis didn't even know exactly where Delphi was. All she knew was that it lay somewhere to the north—the direction from which her fortune had always flowed. She stood still among the grape vines, staring north over the leaves, north across the endless green expanse of the restless sea, while bees wreathed her red-gold hair in lazy circles, drunk on the sweetness of sunshine.

"Rhodopis!" Tuia's cracked, earthy voice reached across the vineyard and shook Rhodopis from her reverie. "Rhodopis, where are you?"

Rhodopis laid the bunch of grapes into her basket and quickly cut another. She was the owner of this land now, but Tuia was the undisputed mistress of the vineyard and everything it produced; the old winemaker would remain the lady of the estate until she pronounced Rhodopis ready to take over the business for herself. That day was still far off. For now, Tuia would scold her if she found Rhodopis' harvesting basket so dreadfully empty.

She dropped two more heavy clusters of grapes into the basket, then straightened, peering back over the tops of the vines toward her house. "I'm here, Tuia. I'm cutting grapes. What is it?"

"You have a visitor. Shall I send him to you, or will you see him inside the house?"

Rhodopis couldn't imagine who might have come—unless it was a messenger carrying a letter from Memphis. Or… from Thrace. Had her family sent some reply? Her heart began to pound. All at once, she knew she would rather read the letter here, in the peace of the vineyard under the blessing of the bright sun, than anywhere else—even in the comfort of her own home.

"Send him to me, Tuia. I'll have more grapes for you soon."

Rhodopis slipped the small harvesting knife into its leather sheath and let it fall into the basket among the grapes. She stood waiting as the messenger approached. She could hear him coming through the rows of vines, the leaves rustling to mark his progress. The bees went on droning, as undisturbed by this newcomer as they were by Rhodopis. But with the next beat of her heart, she heard the bees' sweet song no longer. Her ears, her mind, her heart focused only on the approaching man's gait. She knew it was a man, indeed—for she recognized the distinctive sound of his footfalls, the slight drag caused by the bend of his spine.

By the time the grape leaves parted to reveal his face, tears stood in Rhodopis' eyes. She pressed her fingers to her lips.

"Hello, Doricha," Aesop said.

She shook her head, fighting to speak, but the rising tide of joy in her chest drowned out all her words.

"It's good to see you again. You look well, and this land is..." Aesop whistled as he gazed down the row of vines to the sea. "Beautiful."

Rhodopis found her words at last. They bubbled from her, mingling with startled laughter. "What are you doing here, so far from Memphis?"

"It's not so far. I sailed three days to find you. You've certainly gone on longer journeys yourself."

She embraced him, pressing her face against his shoulder. "You still smell like papyrus and ink."

"That's no surprising news. Papyrus and ink are my whole life now. I've served as chief scribe in the palace these past three months, you know."

"Have you? You've risen high, for a former slave."

"As have you."

Rhodopis shook her head, folding her arms beneath her breasts. "I'm no one of any import now—just a winemaker's apprentice. I wouldn't have it any other way."

"A winemaker's apprentice who owns her own vineyard." Aesop tilted his head, a wry expression. "A winemaker's apprentice who sent a king's sum of silver to Thrace, and who lined the mountain trail to Delphi with beautiful rods of iron. We've heard all about it, back at the palace."

"Have you?" She blinked, truly surprised by the news.

"Of course. The two chief wives still speak fondly of you, and Cambyses has maintained an interest in your doings."

"He's been ever so good to me—provided me with all the silver I could have wished for."

"Yet I know Cambyses wishes you would allow him to do still more."

Rhodopis tossed her head; the bees stopped circling and retreated to the vines. "I need nothing more than this. I'm happy, Aesop—truly happy. I never thought I'd find happiness again, after... after Archidike. I still think about her all the time —what might have been, if she had survived, and we'd been able to reconcile. If we could be friends again."

"I know," Aesop said softly. "You poor, sweet thing. It may comfort you to know that Amtes saw to Archidike's burial herself. She doesn't rest in a royal tomb, by any means, but she was committed to the gods with love and respect. Amtes saw to it that she was laid to rest in the slippers—those pretty shoes you gave her, at the last."

Rhodopis hung her head. "I'm glad to hear it. Thank you for telling me."

Aesop brightened a little. "Amtes sends her greetings. She too has found favor with the royal family; the chief wives consult her daily and pay her well. She has been helping them restore Egypt to the way it ought to be—the way it was before Amasis turned the place on its ear. Phanes sends his best wishes, too—he and his wife and his fine young sons have all taken places of honor in Cambyses' court. They have bright futures ahead of them, and Cambyses is very fond of them all."

"And how does the king fare?"

"I must say, for a man without a drop of Egyptian blood in his veins, Cambyses makes an excellent Pharaoh. Were it not for all that hair, one would never guess he wasn't born Kmetu. He's a sensible and ambitious man, but not a vain one. He doesn't require his subjects to worship him—he only wants his kingdom to be productive and secure. He knows he'll get the most out of Egypt if he allows Egyptians to be themselves. Of course, the wounds Psamtik left—and Amasis before him— won't heal overnight. It will take months before true peace exists between Greeks and Egyptians—perhaps years. But Cambyses is committed to the cause. He doesn't intend to leave Egypt until he can be certain it's secure. Even then, he'll have the chief wives to maintain peace and rule in his stead. They are blossoming in their role—born to rule, as their mother was before them."

Rhodopis picked up her basket and headed back toward her house. Tuia would scold her for having gathered only a few bunches of grapes, but there would be plenty of time tomorrow to resume the harvest. For now, Rhodopis wanted to hear more news of Memphis. She wanted to hear Aesop's voice and draw comfort from his unexpected presence. He walked beside her, reaching out now and then brush the grape leaves with his hands, or to sample a bit of fruit from the vines.

"Tell me about the city," Rhodopis said. "What is Memphis like now that Cambyses holds the throne?"

"Oh—the same as it ever was, I suppose."

"Are there still hetaerae in Memphis?"

"Yes; I doubt that will change, no matter how thoroughly Amtes and Phanes resurrect the Egypt that once was. Hetaerae have become a part of Memphian life—a thread in the weave." He paused, casting a searching gaze over Rhodopis. "Do you ever miss that life, Doricha?"

She blushed to hear him say the old name. "I don't miss the work; that's sure enough. But the company was good. The conversation, the parties, the music."

"Life gets rather dull out here in the countryside, I suppose."

"I wouldn't call it dull. I'd call it quiet. Peaceful. But sometimes I do long for a good supper party filled with clever guests and lit by golden lamps. When it comes down to choices, though, I'll take the sound of the sea over harps and flutes, and moonlight on the vineyard over the most beautiful estate in the city."

"You make it sound positively bearable, living here." A thread of speculation wound itself around his words.

"I've never been happier in my life, Aesop, and that's the

plain truth. This place doesn't shine like the city, but the gold and silver of Memphis never brought me any real joy."

He smiled to himself as they walked on in silence.

Rhodopis led him out of the vineyard rows. They started up the short slope toward her house. The sun was lowering gently to the west; great stripes of violet-blue shadow stretched from the house and the brewing shed beside it, over the golden hillside. Somewhere in the distance, from one of the nearby farms, a cow called lazily. Young children played in an unseen irrigation ditch; Rhodopis could hear their laughter and the splashing of water carrying across the fields. Small sounds, and far away, but distinctly joyful.

As they trod up the hill, Rhodopis said, "How have the people of the city taken to their new king?"

"For the most part, they like Cambyses well. And why not? He doesn't wish to turn them all to Persians. He has taken the people's interests entirely to his heart; he has even begun rebuilding old, damaged structures—those that were burned or defaced during the riots."

"Has he? That's fine news—good old Cambyses! From the moment Phanes first told me of his secret plan, I knew Cambyses would make a grand Pharaoh. He knows how to rule a kingdom, and no mistake." She gave Aesop a mischievous grin. "D'you think he'll rebuild that old beer shop?"

"He has already begun—or his men have started the work, at any rate."

"Will you go back and live above it?" she teased.

But Aesop neither laughed nor smiled. He halted halfway up the slope, turning to Rhodopis with a sober expression. "I had thought I might leave Memphis altogether."

She blinked at him in surprise. "So soon after becoming chief scribe? Doesn't the work suit you? Where will you go, Aesop?"

"I'd thought I might come here... to the Delta."

Though Aesop fell silent, shuffling his feet in an uncharacteristic show of hesitancy, Rhodopis sensed he was searching for something more to say. She waited, brows raised in startled expectation.

"I had thought," Aesop said, "I might live with you here—at your estate. If you'll have me, of course."

A glad laugh burst from her chest, fairly stealing her breath away.

"But it's your choice, of course," Aesop added hastily. "If you'd rather live alone... if you don't prefer me—"

"Won't you miss the city life?"

He met her eyes then and held her in place with a long, warm look. "Not as much as I miss you."

Rhodopis shifted the basket of grapes to the crook of her elbow. She took Aesop's hand and continued up the hill.

"I hope you'll stay here with me for a good, long while, Aesop, and that's the truth. I've missed you, too—more than I can say."

On the slope behind them, the sun lay golden on the dry grass. The bees settled and sang among the vines, content with the sweetness of a peaceful afternoon.

I've carried the seed of the idea for this novel—or series of novels, depending on how you read the story—for more than five years. It surprises me now, looking back on all the time that has passed between my first tickle of inspiration and the completion of *White Lotus*. It doesn't seem so long ago that I first heard the story of the original Cinderella, and it's hard to believe Rhodopis and her companions have lived in my thoughts for so long before I finally got around to telling their story.

In the spring of 2012, I worked for a pet insurance company—as enjoyable a "day job" as any writer can ever hope to have, for not only did most of my co-workers bring their dogs and cats to the office, but we were also allowed to listen to whatever we chose while we reviewed medical records and combed through claims. I've been a podcast addict since podcasts first appeared, so naturally, most days I put in my earbuds and treated myself to any interesting podcast I could find.

It probably won't surprise you to learn that I love history podcasts more than almost any other genre (though I will confess a weakness for "true" ghost stories and tales of the paranormal.) On this day, in the springtime of 2012, I happened to be combing through archived episodes of *The History Chicks*, searching for any subject that would pique my interest. That was when I found one of their earliest episodes—number 3, in fact, titled "Cinderella." But the show's description mentioned ancient Egypt—not a setting I had come to associate with Cinderella. I gave a listen and was instantly hooked by the biography of Rhodopis, a mysterious figure from ancient times who bridges fable and verified history.

The mythos that surrounded Rhodopis—possibly making her a legend in her own time—is the earliest recorded iteration of the Cinderella story. Other cultures throughout human history have told their own versions of Rhodopis' story, a rags-to-riches tale that always involves the loss and recovery of a single pretty slipper. It's possible that some other legend predates the Egyptian tale of Rhodopis, a down-on-her-luck dancing girl whose lost shoe elevates her to glorious heights. But so far, historians haven't identified an earlier version of the tale.

But I found special familiarity in the story of Rhodopis, beyond her obvious connection to Cinderella. As I listened to the *History Chicks* episode, I realized that more modern story-tellers had drawn on the ancient Egyptian fable for inspiration. I could now clearly see that one of my all-time favorite books, *Maia* by Richard Adams, had also been heavily inspired by Rhodopis.

That settled it. I knew I had to write a novel about the life of Rhodopis, and in so doing, offer a salute to *Maia*. But it took about another year of pondering and combing through podcasts and history books before I found my own unique take on the source material.

In gleaning more shows for history's most exciting tidbits, I found the excellent *Ancient World* podcast, a tremendously exciting and enjoyable show which I can enthusiastically recommend to fans of ancient history. (Side note: The *Podcast History of Our World* is another show ancient-history fans can't miss.) In June of 2013, *Ancient World* presented the tale of the last native dynasty to ever hold Egypt—the twenty-sixth—and its fall to Persian rule. The tale of Pharaoh Ahmose's downfall (he's called Amasis in this book, of course), the defeat of his son Psamtik, and the considerable scheming and intrigue that took place within the Egyptian court were too juicy to pass up.

A woman had been involved in the spectacular back-stabbing that paved Cambyses' path to the Horus Throne—Nitetis, daughter of Pharaoh Ahmose. I wondered whether I could dust off my ideas about Rhodopis and insert her into the story of Ahmose's demise and Cambyses' capture of Egypt—and to my delight, I learned that Rhodopis had lived during the 6th century BCE—exactly the right period to have participated in Cambyses' victory.

Once I knew I could combine both stories into one, the particulars of the story came together quickly, but other obligations forced me to leave *White Lotus* on the back burner for many years. The action-packed plot never loosed its hold on my imagination, though—nor did the characters, each of whom I could see so vividly in my mind. In 2014, I left my day job behind and began writing full-time, but I had promised to complete a whole string of other projects, and *White Lotus* came no closer to the top of my queue. Next came my partnership with Lake Union Publishing, and more obligations to fulfill. I was thrilled when my schedule finally opened up in the fall of 2016, and I had the opportunity to write the story that had haunted me for years.

I should have known from past experience that the story would grow, expanding from one book to three. The same thing has happened to me twice before, with my *She-King* series and *The Book of Coming Forth by Day*. But far more than my previous series, *White Lotus* has always felt like a single book to me—one

I broke into three parts out of necessity, not through any businesswoman's design. As I write this note, I am working on compiling all three manuscripts into one large file to send to my printer. I don't think I'll feel that *White Lotus* is truly finished until I hold a bound copy in my hands, containing all six parts of the story—from *Slave* to *Assassin*.

Enough about my feelings regarding this book, this long-term resident of my imagination. Here's the known history behind Rhodopis and the fall of the twenty-sixth dynasty.

Strabo, the ancient Greek historian, gives us the earliest known source of Rhodopis' tale. He recorded the story in the first century BCE, when the legend was already about five hundred years old. In Strabo's account, a hetaera called Rhodopis is bathing in the river when a bird of prey steals one of her beautiful golden sandals from the riverbank. The bird flies away with its prize in its talons—and straight to the Pharaoh, in whose lap he drops the sandal. The Pharaoh, overcome with admiration for this beautiful object—and moved by the strange event—sends his men out to find the owner of the slipper. Once the king's men find Rhodopis, the Pharaoh makes her his wife.

Later writers also recounted the same story, albeit with subtle variations. Aelian, in his *Miscellaneous History*, actually gives the Pharaoh a name: Psammetichus, or Psamtik, plausibly dating Rhodopis' life to sometime during the reign of Psamtik and/or his father, Ahmose II—at the end of Egypt's twenty-sixth dynasty.

That's the legendary Rhodopis. But was she a real woman? If so, how closely did her life resemble the whimsical charm of her legend?

Five centuries before Strabo, Herodotus wrote of a certain popular courtesan in his book *Histories*. Her name was Rhodopis, a Greek moniker meaning "rosy cheeks," though whether she took her name from an existing legend of the hetaera who lost her shoe, or whether the legendary Rhodopis was named after the real woman, we can never know for certain. The Rhodopis of Herodotus' account came originally from Thrace and was slave to Iadmon, a wealthy man from Samos. Iadmon also owned the renowned storyteller Aesop— yes, he of the tortoise and the hare. Iadmon took his household, Rhodopis included, to Egypt during the reign of Pharaoh Ahmose II (Amasis), and while in Egypt, Rhodopis was freed from bondage—for a large sum of money—by Charaxus, the brother of the famous poet Sappho. Charaxus had fallen in love with Rhodopis, and evidently decided he couldn't live without her.

Little else is known about Rhodopis—either the hetaera of legend of the real Thracian woman. But as you can see, there's drama enough already to concoct an interesting story.

Herodotus also wrote about another hetaera called Archidike, who had also lived in Egypt near the time of Amasis' reign. Archidike was said to be "notorious," and was described as both arrogant and avaricious, charging outrageous prices for her company. Archidike ended up in court at least once; she was apparently tough as nails and determined to make the most of a hetaera's life.

Ahmose II, also called Amasis, ruled Egypt from 570 BCE until 526, and his reign was not the smoothest in Egypt's history. He rose from humble beginnings as a minor general, taking the throne during a revolt against the previous Pharaoh. His tenure on the Horus Thrones was marked by a few blunders—among them, the banishing of a physician called Udjahoresnet to the kingdom of Persia. Exiled Udjahoresnet became good friends with Cambyses II, King of Persia, and together they plotted the downfall of Amasis and the capture of the Horus Throne.

Knowing that no Egyptian king had ever given one of his daughters in marriage to a foreign prince—Egypt had a strict policy of *receiving* foreign brides, not making them—Udjahoresnet advised Cambyses to send two of his own daughters to wed Amasis. Cambyses did, and once the women were settled at the Egyptian court, he requested one of the Pharaoh's daughters for his own wife. Fair's fair, after all.

It's believed that Udjahoresnet and Cambyses expected Amasis to refuse the request, an insult they could use to justify invading Egypt. But Amasis surprised them by sending a woman to marry Cambyses: Nitetis, whom Amasis claimed was his daughter.

Unfortunately for Amasis, Nitetis soon confessed the truth to Cambyses. She was not the daughter of Amasis, but the daughter of the previous Pharaoh, the one whom Amasis had overthrown during his revolt, years before. Obviously, Nitetis had no reason to love Amasis, so she quickly joined in the plot to overthrow him and usher in the Persian conquest of Egypt. You can see where I found all the inspiration for my take on Rhodopis' life story.

Phanes was a real man, too—a councilor of Pharaoh Amasis. Phanes left the royal court over some disagreement that Herodotus never specified, though he did indicate that the matter was "personal" in nature. Amasis sent a eunuch after Phanes to fetch him back to the court, but Phanes "bested" the man (presumably killing him) and fled to Persia, where he joined in Cambyses' plot to overthrow Egypt. Apparently, Amasis really knew how to tick a guy off; it seems nearly everyone who left him ran straight to Cambyses. In this book, obviously, I combined Udjahoresnet and Phanes into one character, the exiled councilor whose wise advice helps ensure Cambyses' victory.

When his plans seemed secure, Cambyses set out to invade Egypt, but Amasis died before the Persian fleet arrived, leaving his no doubt bewildered son Psamtik III to rule in his stead. Psamtik's reign was very short, and I doubt very much whether he was as evil as I made him out to be. In fact, I feel rather sorry for the Psamtik of history. He probably dreamed of ascending to the throne one day, as all Pharaoh's sons must have done. What a cruel twist of fate, that he only obtained the Horus Throne once the Persian invasion was already underway, and ruled (in a panic, I am sure) less than a year.

The fall of Egypt and the capture of Memphis did not happen as quickly as I indicated in my fictional take on the story. Several large battles occurred between the Egyptian and Persian forces, including the Battle of Pleusium, which ended with the Egyptian forces falling back on Memphis. Cambyses put the city under siege, which ended with the brutal execution of at least two thousand Egyptians. It was not the quick, relatively bloodless encounter I made it out to be; I shortened the whole affair because this story had already swelled from one book to three. It didn't need to grow any larger.

I am glad and relieved to finally have *White Lotus* finished, the tale told and my work among the last native dynasty of Egypt complete. I can finally bid farewell to Rhodopis and her friends, passing them along to you, Reader, with the hope that they will continue to live in your imagination. I'm a touch sad to see them go; they've been with me for so long. They've left a curious emptiness in my mind and my heart, but I have no doubt that another idea with take root there soon, and sprout into my next book—or my next series, as fate may dictate.

Libbie Hawker
Friday Harbor, Washington
November 2017

ABOUT THE AUTHOR

Libbie Hawker writes historical and literary fiction featuring complex characters and rich details of time and place. She is the author of more than twenty novels, including the Washington Post bestseller The Ragged Edge of Night, written under her pen name, Olivia Hawker. She lives in the San Juan Islands of Washington State with her husband and several naughty cats.

When she's not writing, Libbie enjoys spinning wool, knitting sweaters, and gardening at Longlight, her one-acre microfarm.